HAVANA HEAT

A NOVEL

HAVANA HEAT

A NOVEL

DARRYL BROCK

NEW YORK, NEW YORK • KINGSTON, NEW YORK

NotAR

G.H ⁴/₀₉

Total/*SPORTS ILLUSTRATED* is a trademark of Time Inc.
Used under license.

For information about permission to reproduce selections from this book,
please write to:
Total/*SPORTS ILLUSTRATED*
100 Enterprise Drive
Kingston, NY 12401

Cover design: Todd Radom
Interior design: Joseph Rutt

ISBN: 1-892129-23-X
Library of Congress Catalog Card Number: 00-100099

Printed in the United States of America

To the memory of my grandfather, Stanley,
who saw them play.

To my father, Charles,
and those formative backyard contests.

To my son, Greg,
and the B & B League.

To the wiffle champs, Graham and Will,
the little guys, Thomas and James,
and all the games to come.

A C K N O W L E D G M E N T S

The kernel of this story came to me obliquely, years ago, from John
Thorn, who now happens to be its editor. I am indebted to John and to
Laurie Harper of Sebastian Agency for their friendly guidance and outstanding professional skills, to Todd Radom for his design work and to
all of the following:

Katharine B. Kelley, the sage of Baldwin City and a charming
lemonade date, for her help with Luther Taylor's Kansas roots; Scotty
McCaulley, whose field work first brought the Midwest home to me.

Delia Todd, my deaf friend and tireless researcher, who introduced
me to many fascinations of Deaf Culture, including an American Sign
Language class; Joan M. Forney, Ed.S., Superintendent of the Illinois
School for the Deaf; Dr. Robert F. Panara, author of Great Deaf
Americans; Randy Fisher, chairman of the William "Dummy" Hoy for
the Hall of Fame Committee.

Jorge "El Jiribilla" Abich, my Cuban hiking amigo, for opening his
past as well as translating obscure Spanish passages, as did Keiko Hess
and Ron Tasto; Peter "Havana Pete" Bjarkman and Mark Rucker, ace
travel compañeros, for sharing their expertise on Cuban baseball.

The Spanish War: An American Epic—1898 by G.J.A. O'Toole and Cuba
or The Pursuit of Freedom by Hugh Thomas, for background information

on the struggle for independence and the role of black Cubans.

The National Baseball Hall of Fame Library and a number of SABR researchers, including Dr. Richard S. Cohen, Ed Hartig, Fr. John E. Hissrich ("The Baseball Padre"), Bill Kirwin, Len Levin, Jerry Malloy, Andy McCue, Steve Riess, Troy Soos and Lyle Spatz.

Heart-nourishing personal support came from Peter S. Beagle, who knows every tricky hop in the writing game; the Dolas family, who believed from the first; Joshua Karton, who came through hugely in the clutch; and Steve Fields, friend and confidant extraordinaire.

Most of all, as ever, I am indebted to my wife, Lura, for her boundless love and patient understanding.

Hear me a little; for I have only been
Silent so long. . . .
William Shakespeare,
Much Ado About Nothing

P R O L O G U E

Olathe, Kansas

April 1958

He sat at the head table, thinking that when he was a student here no cafeteria tables or hard-soled shoes were allowed on the hardwood. But that was years ago, when the floor was new and shiny. Now he'd come full circle, and at 83 he knew he was in considerably worse shape than the venerable building. His alma mater, the Kansas School for the Deaf, had designated a scholarship in his name: the Luther Haden Taylor Award, to be given each year to the outstanding scholar-athlete.

And so he'd come back.

A fine thing to be honored, of course, but he'd appreciate it more if the old gym weren't so damned drafty. He was cold a lot of the time now. Old man's bone-chill. The speaker, some hearing legislator from the area, was going on about his glory years with the Giants. Earlier they'd shown a movie and he'd seen himself as he looked nearly sixty years ago, parading around the diamond before the Series. But the film was jerky, the figures comical-looking. It hadn't been like that.

What . . . ? He hadn't paid heed to the student signer. The politician was looking at him, eyebrows arched, arm stretched toward the things on display: his silver lifetime National League pass; his Championship medal with its crossed bats and 22 diamonds; the ball from when he'd licked Three–Finger

Brown and dumped the Cubs out of a flag race; his old spikes and glove. That was where he'd stopped paying attention: when the politician held up his glove like some prehistoric relic.

The signer was pointing at a wooden figure at the far end of the display. They wanted to know what it was. Well, it was too complicated to try to tell them—but that little carving had as much business here as anything else. Maybe more. He grinned at the politician, who regarded him blankly, then went on. Seemed like he'd been talking an hour.

All the fresh-scrubbed faces. . . . The boys up front were too young for him to have coached, but others seated behind them, old enough to be their fathers, had come back to pay their respects, plus a bunch from the deaf campus in Illinois, where he lived now. So many faces. Tomorrow a lot of the boys would be out on the green diamonds, getting ready for the new '58 season. Nobody loved sports more than deaf kids; it was one place where they could compete on more or less equal terms.

Over to one side, his face shadowed in the dimness beyond the platform lights, sat a boy with strong, lean features. Curly dark hair, intelligent eyes. The shadows lent his skin a dusky caramel tone.

Your imagination's going extra innings, he told himself, but his eyes lowered reflexively to the copy of Time Magazine beside his plate that he'd been carrying for days. It was folded open to an article on Cuba. A battle map bristled with arrows and star-shaped explosions, most of them in Oriente Province, stronghold of the surging rebels. CASTRO'S HOT CORNER was the caption. Funny how baseball lingo was everywhere now. In his youth it had been disreputable slang, unfit for formal expression.

He stared at a photo of Fidel Castro, smoking a cigar and looking chesty (or cocky, as they called it now) like a sure-fire worldbeater. Rumor had it that the bearded leader was once a promising hurler. If he'd been better at it, maybe he'd be toiling in the I-League now, even the majors, and there'd be no revolution in Cuba.

Whatever else those red-inked bursts signified, they surely meant people were dying.

Was the boy all right?

Which was silly.

By now the "boy" could be a grandfather.

His fingers drifted leftward to the margin, where Matanzas would be. A sunlit image played in his mind: royal palms rising gracefully from a green valley floor, the balmy air laced with tropical smells, the light radiant and warm, very warm. . . .

He felt his elbow nudged and looked up. The students were clapping, deaf-style, hands waving, fingers fluttering like aspen leaves. To his relief, the signer repeated the politician's last phrase, something about his still being active in baseball even at his ripe age. But it wasn't true. He'd had to quit umpiring after collapsing with chest pains during a college contest four years ago. That had been his last involvement. Now the speaker was saying that he still scouted for the big leagues. The truth was that he scarcely got outside any more. Lately he'd been reduced to watching the boys practice from his cottage window on the Jacksonville campus where he lived. He missed the game even more than he'd imagined he would.

Damn, it was colder than a brass monkey.

He glanced at the boy in the shadows.

Cuba . . . so long ago. Coming across the news article had sent him rummaging through his souvenirs for the wooden figure. Ever since, the images had been flowing in his brain. Now he scarcely had to focus for them to come.

Dusty ballfields. Frenzied crowds. Behind him, in center, Donlin waving his cap and prancing with those jaunty little bird steps. Mathewson studying him from the bench with steely blue eyes, missing nothing. McGraw kicking dirt in the coacher's box, bulldog jaw jutting out, mouth open and yapping as usual.

He shifted his feet on the wheelchair's rest and imagined the packed slope of a mound beneath them. Digging his spikes against the slab, spinning into his motion, ball high overhead then up from the ground, arm whipping toward the batsman. . . .

The images came.

He tried to slow them, to find a beginning, which wasn't overly hard, considering he was back here, scarcely twenty miles from where he grew up. It had begun, like now, when he came home.

PART ONE

THE SIGN

Keep your splendid silent sun,
Keep your woods O Nature, and the quiet places by the
    woods,
Keep your fields of clover and timothy, and your corn-fields
    and orchards,
Keep the blossoming buckwheat fields where the Ninth-
    month bees hum;
Give me faces and streets—give me these phantoms
    incessant and endless along the trottoirs!
Give me interminable eyes—give me women—give me
    comrades and lovers by the thousand!
Let me see new ones every day—let me hold new ones by
    the hand every day!
Give me such shows—give me the streets of Manhattan!
                            —Walt Whitman, *Leaves of Grass*

O N E

Baldwin, Kansas
October 1911

IF MONTE CROMER HADN'T shown me that picture, it's likely none
of this would have happened. Monte wanted to get his piece in that
day's *Baldwin Ledger*, so I agreed to meet him at Warner's Cafe, where
I liked the hotcakes and eggs, the close, smoke-choked atmosphere,
even the reek of grease—all reminders of when Pa used to bring me in
as a little boy. Except for Big Edna, the giant waitress whose arms out-
bulged mine, it was a man's place in the early mornings. Which partly
explained why Della looked so peeved when I went skipping out
before breakfast. In our 18 years of marriage she'd had precious little
success keeping me at home.

Around us, farmers and grain-elevator men sporting blue-striped
engineer's caps were pushing back their chairs and streaming out into
the crisp daylight. Monte was interviewing me, same as he did every
year when I got home from playing ball, even though I was no longer
a big leaguer. This season I'd started with Buffalo in the Eastern League
and been traded to Montreal halfway through. It was the top minor-
league level, the high bushes.

Monte's technique was to talk real loud (I could tell from the veins
in his neck standing out) and real slow, as if I hadn't the brains of a rock-

pile. It's a common experience for deaf folks. The good part was, I didn't have to strain to read his lips. I could have done it from 50 feet away.

"Dummy," he was saying, "check out these figures."

In earlier years I might have taken offense. Folks in Baldwin generally called me Luther. But I knew Monte was just trying to put himself inside the sporting circle by using a tag I'd carried for 16 years. In baseball, a small man was "Shorty," a southpaw "Lefty," a German "Dutch" and so on for practically everybody—a good deal of it too rough to repeat. Every deaf player I'd ever known of was called "Dummy." Once I'd talked it over with Bill Hoy, the old Reds outfielder and first "Dummy" to make it to the tip-top level of ball. We agreed that the moniker did us no real harm, just made us try harder.

I drank my coffee and studied Monte's list of my accomplishments. In 1904, my biggest year, I'd notched 21 victories for New York; 15 the next year; 17 after that. One hundred fifteen victories in nine seasons. Twenty-one shutouts and 160 complete games; career ERA of 2.75. Monte's figures were accurate. No surprise, since he used the same ones every year. With my pencil I scratched out the victory total and wrote in a new one: 220.

It looked good.

Monte squinched up his forehead. "What's that?"

"How many I'll have before I'm done," I scrawled in the margin, then added, "My arm's back."

He smiled indulgently. I was going on 37, and three seasons had passed since my last National League appearance. It didn't take a mind-reader to guess his thoughts. He jabbed a finger at his next item: *O'Day kicking you out—still your favorite yarn?*

Well, it never had been, really, but after I told it to Monte it became *his* favorite. Clowning's always come easy for me, so whenever umpires got my goat I'd naturally start cutting up—imitating them behind their backs, pinching my nose or twirling a finger beside my head to show what I thought of their calls—which generally set crowds to laughing. Old prune-faced Hank O'Day, the ump who cost us the '08 pennant, got to where he'd toss me just for blinking funny at him.

Naturally I expressed myself in Sign, too, my fingers talking a blue streak. One afternoon I noticed O'Day studying me close. Suddenly, to my amazement, he spelled out on his fingers, YOU GO CLUBHOUSE, PAY $25. A deaf relative, it turned out, had taught him in the off-season. Later he said he hadn't picked up *everything* I'd called him, but enough to toss me three times over.

I knew Monte would print it again no matter what, along with how I'd wanted to be a boxer but my parents nixed the idea. How as a catcher I'd led the Olathe Deaf School to an undefeated record, started pitching, climbed up the bush leagues, and gone to the Giants the same year as Christy Mathewson. There I'd hurled alongside the great Matty under manager John J. McGraw, baseball's "Little Napoleon."

Why did we even bother doing this?

"Good to be home?" he asked.

I nodded. In frigid Montreal I'd hungered for the prairie autumn. Now I was savoring familiar pleasures: the maples burnished golds and reds, the acrid odor of burning cornhusks, the sight of Sim's little girls gathering pawpaws and black walnuts and persimmons just like I used to do. And being home with Della, too, although certain things between us were already starting to come up again.

I tapped Monte's hand and pointed to what I'd written: *My arm's back* He tried to laugh it off, but I held his gaze until finally, with a regretful look, he brought forth *The Sporting News* and opened it to the Eastern League final stats. He'd underlined my tallies: *Taylor 8–10 4.53.*

Hardly a grand showing.

No doubt Monte expected the sheepish grin I'd given him the last couple of years when I was barely surviving on a rag of an arm. But now was different. Two months ago, for the first time since '08, when I'd strained a cord near my shoulder and hurt it worse trying to work again too soon, the strength in my pitching wing had miraculously reappeared. In a glorious rush I'd won my last five starts at Montreal, pitching all the way each time. My hummer moved like a snake and my dropball, thrown with mustard again, plummeted like a rock off a ledge.

I wrote it all down for him and slid my pad over with a flourish. He read it, then gave me a look in which I saw pity and condescension. He took me for another washed up ball-player trying to hang on past his time. My hackles rose. If there's something I've never been able to stomach, it's being felt sorry for. People could call me Dummy all they wanted, and it was true I could only speak a few simple words. But I'd been valedictorian of my class in school, and every year I plowed through more books than a lot of folks do in their whole lives. I kept my brain in good order, even if I didn't go around making a display of it. Monte was ten years younger than me but pudgy and soft, never much at athletics. It occurred to me that some part of him might enjoy seeing me brought down.

I slapped the tabletop, bouncing forks and spoons. Monte blinked. "You come see for yourself," I told him, framing each word deliberately with my lips and hands. "I'll work out with Sim and when I'm ready I'll call for you. Just a few days. I'm coming all the way back. *That's this year's story!*"

"Okay, Dummy." He raised his hands placatingly, and when he was sure I was calm, pointed to the next question on his list: *Who's big league material in the Eastern League?* I tapped my chest.

"Besides you."

I shrugged and spread my hands. The Senators had been looking at Gandil, our first baseman, a roughneck, hard-edged kid who'd already played a little up in Chicago. He'd done some prizefighting, and up in Montreal we'd strap on the gloves and go at it pretty good. In the gym one day a gambler offered him $25 to throw off a game. Gandil gave me a long look. I told him the thing to do was go to the owner and report it, which I believe he did. A promising kid with real good fielder's hands. But the truth was, I was the best prospect, and I saw no reason to boost anybody else.

"Okay." Monte frowned slightly. "One more question."

And then he spread out that picture.

It was from one of the Topeka dailies, a full-page shot of the upcoming Series opponents: New York's Giants and Philadelphia's Athletics.

"Seeing as how your arm's back," he wrote, glancing up at me with a cheesy smile, "I guess Muggsy could use you now. What's your prediction how it'll come out?"

As I stared at the picture, time seemed to stop.

Then it seemed to jump backward.

Since the end of my own season I hadn't paid much attention to the majors. Oh, I knew McGraw had taken the flag, but I hadn't given it any thought.

That photo hit me like a sock to the belly.

The dark shapes were segmented by white stockings, belts, cap visors. Six years before, for the 1905 Series, McGraw had switched our regular pinstripe uniforms for coal-black togs. Coming on the field, we'd looked like angels of death—and played like it, too, taking the championship four games of five. Now, facing them again, McGraw, superstitious as any man alive, was going back to what had worked before. Faces were smudgy but I picked out Matty and Ames and Wiltse, my old pitching mates. Suddenly I missed them so much I felt an ache in my innards, and I guess some sort of noise escaped me. Looking embarrassed, Monte reached out and folded up the sheet.

"I'll come see you throw, Dummy," he wrote. "Let me know when." He stood up and I did likewise, putting on the best face I could. As Ma used to say, "Smile and folks'll never *know,* whatever they might suspect."

That newspaper picture stayed in my mind. I couldn't shake the gnawing feeling that there was something in what Monte had put jokingly: If my arm was back, then maybe McGraw *did* need me.

The rest of the day was blurry. I put in the hours I'd promised my brother Sim at the family grocery on 6th Street. Our folks had farmed outside Oskaloosa until the early '90s, when overproduction brought corn down to ten cents a bushel, and railroad rate-gougers and sticky-fingered Eastern bankers finished the job of ruining small farmers all over the grain belt. With what he had left, Pa bought the little store.

The sign out front read "TAYLOR MERCANTILE" and we called it the family's, but now it really belonged to Sim (short for Simpson) and his wife, Hattie Mae, who made a show of divvying up profits according to the time we each put in—never much in my case. Anyway, I didn't need the money and tossed my share back into the operation. Sometimes when I was off playing ball, Della helped Hattie Mae arrange stock and take inventory. She wasn't comfortable around hearing people and didn't like working the counter. Today I didn't either. I busied myself out in the back, unloading pallets of corn meal and sorghum. When I finished, I went inside and set about rearranging the whole storage room, sweating as I hefted barrels and gunny sacks and cartons of dry goods.

Sim came back and eyed my changes. "Still nobody to spar with?" he joked. His signing was quick and precise, almost delicate for a man of his bulk, with family quirks that would have stymied an outsider, even a deaf one. Three of us six Taylor kids had been born without hearing. I was the youngest except for Ben, who died in the same variola plague that carried off our folks, so I'd grown up in the best possible learning situation, reading lips from the outset plus everybody around me using Sign—despite certain teachers at the deaf school who tried to get us to spell out everything in English on our fingers, which would have taken ten times as long.

In the past decade, our deaf sister Fanny had moved to California, and the others had married and scattered. Only Sim and I were still in Baldwin, using the old family language. Sim wasn't deaf but he was closest to me in age and we'd always stuck together. Nobody knew me better than Sim. Not even Della.

"They're all scared," I told him, which might even have been the case. For twenty years I'd kept fit by boxing. My regular sparring partner was out of town and nobody else was close to my ability. It had always been like that. On my first Baldwin ball team a kid had refused to play second base when I pitched—I threw too hard on pickoffs.

Sim held out a plug but I shook my head. Once in a blue moon I'd take a chaw, but I'd seen too many players get to where they couldn't do a damn thing without the stuff. "You oughta give it up," I told him.

"Something eating at you?" He eyed me shrewdly, probably wondering why I was avoiding the counter. Normally I'd keep my pad handy next to the register and catch up on everybody's doings while adding up their totals and clowning with the kids. Sim said business always picked up when folks knew I was there.

I considered what to tell him. He wouldn't likely be fooled by my pretending nothing was wrong. And yet I didn't feel like going into it— whatever exactly it was.

"Would you catch me?" It seemed to come out on my fingers before I'd even had the thought.

His eyes probed mine, face not showing much, as usual. I knew he was wondering why I wanted to limber up with winter coming on, something I never did. To his credit, he didn't ask. "Still got B's mask?" he signed. "And leg guards?"

If it had been anyone else I'd have smiled at the notion of such a big solid man needing protective gear to have a catch with me. As a boy Sim had been one hell of a player, fleet, sure-handed, good with the bat—until the day a wild pitch hit him so hard that the ball stuck fast in his mouth, blood and shards of teeth flowing out around it. It was the worst thing I'd ever seen. Thank God I hadn't thrown that ball. Sim wasn't the same afterward, and eventually gave up playing. Roger Bresnahan, my old Giants batterymate—he was known as the twitchiest Nervous Nellie in the game—had been ridiculed when he invented shin guards, but he got the last laugh when they came into general use. He'd given me some of his old equipment. Once I got to throwing hard, Sim would want it. Especially the mask.

"I'll bring it all tomorrow."

That evening after we closed, I sat in the square across from City Hall and watched the swallows swoop and dart in the gathering dusk. The air was mild and perfumed with fresh-mown alfalfa. I tried to tell myself how good it was to be back after the long summer in Canada and the East. But the image of the players in those dark uniforms would not go away.

Sim's older girl, Marcy, came along with two friends who tried to talk to me. I pointed to my ear, shook my head and wagged my finger no. When Marcy told them I couldn't hear, they backed off a bit, their eyes large. It's the sort of thing that makes some deaf people feel bad, like they were monsters or something. Not me. Usually I see it as sort of humorous. I twisted my face into funny shapes and set about plucking pennies from their noses and ears. Then I worked the handle of the city well pump for them while they bent to drink. Marcy looked proud to have such a sockdolager uncle.

As a boy I'd never needed a timepiece downtown, knowing the hour from the shadow cast by the City Hall tower. Now I realized it was nearly seven. Della would have dinner ready. I headed for Schnebley's Rexall, at 8th and Main, where the street had been bricked recently—old Indian Charley was still the local champion, eight brick-feeders barely able to keep up with him once he reached top speed—and where I parked my auto to cut down on the dust.

At the age of 15 I'd tried to drive a neighbor's car and wrecked it. Our family was dirt poor, so I'd tried to make the repairs myself and botched the job. The story got out and I'd been humiliated. After we took the flag in '05 and I was flush with my Series share of $1,142 (and a new contract for the princely salary of $2,700), I celebrated by buying a spanking new Chalmers, easily the fanciest road machine in Baldwin then. Folks dubbed it "Luther Taylor's Speechless Carriage." Driving Della through the streets that first time, rolling in glory past all the envious stares, had been sweet beyond compare.

But now the Chalmers seemed just another reminder of that World Series, and I imagined black uniforms in the gleaming onyx surfaces. I spun the crank, careful to avoid kickback. No good taking risks. Once I was back in the big-time, maybe I'd pick up one of the slick new self-starting models, a sleek Reo, maybe, or a big Everitt Four–36, with chrome nickel steel throughout and a honeycomb radiator.

I steered through the streets, past whitewashed houses set back on lawns with long screened porches and attic gables topped by pigeon roosts. All so familiar. So different from the cold stone of Montreal. I sounded the klaxon and a cluster of orange-sweatered Baker University students waved. I could barely feel the horn's vibration myself, but I loved to see the fun folks got out of hearing it.

The old School for the Deaf still stood at 9th and Indiana. The joke went that when the new deaf-and-dumb campus had opened in Olathe, the deaf ones went and the dumb ones stayed behind. I thought it was pretty funny, but it got Sim's hackles up to hear anybody say it.

Della and I lived north of town, just beyond an area called Palmyra, originally a repair station on the Santa Fe Trail. When I came to where the Trail crossed the road I slowed down. A twister had plowed through while I was away, and the old wagon ruts were bare and exposed like bleached bones. I had an urge to get out and look for arrowheads; after a storm is a good time to find them. Where the Perkins farmhouse had stood, a half-mile farther up the road, nothing was left but a stone foundation and twisted pipe. The house had vanished, literally, into air, leaving the family huddled in the basement with sky above them. Sim had gotten a long look at the twister and said it looked like a runaway fire hose, whipping this way and that, bruise-purple and glowing pale on the inside. It pulled plumbing straight up though the roofs of several houses but left walls standing. Sucked the Millwrights cattle pond dry without touching a head of livestock. Carried a boy three miles in the direction of Kansas City and set him down without a scratch. Reverend Holcombe claimed that the vortex, passing a few hundred yards from their house, had cured his wife's lumbago, but when he sermonized about it being the Almighty's work, congregation members who'd been rougher treated thought he was being high-hat and didn't take kindly to it.

I drove past stubbled fields of corn, sorghum, sugar beets and soybeans, mostly all harvested by now, and squares of wheat and bluestem grasses, gold-tinted in the last rays of the sun. They say that 50 years ago the natural prairie grass still stood as tall as a man on horseback. In the distance were lines of elms and sycamores. A late-working cornhusking rig sent up lazy dust plumes, the driver waving from behind his horse team. A new Chicago Aermotor windmill was working near storage pavilions crammed with field corn destined for hogs, and grain silos stood like great pointing fingers. One bore the inscription, *Matthew 6:19–20*, in faded paint. As a child I'd looked it up:

Lay not up for yourselves treasures upon earth,
where moth and rust doth corrupt,
and where thieves break through and steal;
But lay up for yourselves treasures in heaven. . . .

It struck me as odd advice to find on a repository of worldly treasure. Didn't the owner want his grain?

I turned into the driveway of fine blue shale I'd put in last year, and pulled up at a white frame house with green storm shutters. Sim helped me build it after the '06 season, when Della and I bought this plot near a creek in a cottonwood dale. Two cleared acres offered space for chickens and hogs and all the produce she cared to grow. At first I'd worried about leaving her alone out there. But Della, who'd spent her childhood in the Carolina mountains, flatly refused to live closer to town. Fortunately, the neighboring Bartletts, half a mile away, had taken to her like she was kin. I'd rigged a flag she could hoist from inside the house if she needed help.

I pushed a rod beside the door, setting ball bearings to knocking against each other in the kitchen (which is how we tell someone's at the door) so as not to startle her. It wasn't necessary. She'd felt my tread on the porch boards—it was uncanny how Della could do that—and was already on her way to the door. I searched her face for trouble. I was late, and we both knew it. Brushing a wisp of blonde hair off her forehead, hands streaked with flour, she waved for me to wash up. Mouth-watering smells came from the kitchen.

The years had thickened Della. She was hardly the willowy girl of 16 I'd started courting back when we were still in school at Olathe, when I'd been the sports hero and she the campus beauty. Sometimes it shocked me to see the deepening lines on her face. I tried to get her not to work so hard on our place, but it was what she loved. When we met she'd been perfect, a flaxen-haired doll with porcelain skin. I'd aged too, of course, but not so much on the outside. Maybe playing ball—a boy's game, most thought—kept me looking younger.

On my way to the wash room I stuck my head in the kitchen, where a pork tenderloin with poached apples simmered on the stove. Last night it was chicken with butter crumb dumplings. The night before, catfish grilled in corn husks; before *that*, bobwhite quail and candied yams. Whenever I came home it was the same. Della made me feel like a returning hero, as if she was still that star-struck girl sitting in the stands. Maybe she wanted to go back to those days too, same as I did sometimes. But the truth was that things were more complicated for us now.

She informed me, her signing graceful as always, that I could possibly be of some use by fetching up a jar of corn relish.

In the dim coolness of the storm cellar I rummaged through emergency stores: bottled water, tinned meat, bedding—and a loaded shotgun Della insisted on keeping for unwanted visitors. Once as a girl she'd huddled with her folks in a dirt cellar while marauding Indians torched their farmhouse. Troops arrived in time to save them, just like in the five-cent flickers. I tried to tell her that the Sioux hadn't raided hereabouts in more than thirty years, but it made no great impression. Della knew how to load and fire, she had a steady aim, and she wasn't about to let anybody mess with her property. Myself, I wouldn't want to cross her.

I hunted through the shelves of preserves she'd put up in recent months: mulberry jam, apple and plum butter, lingonberry sauce, Dutch honey, rhubarb, pickled asparagus. To reach the relish I had to stand on an old butter churn, and when I stepped down it kicked out sideways. Beneath it I saw the thick scrapbook Della had put together on my baseball career. I was touched to think she stored it down there, safe from calamity.

Then I made the mistake of opening it.

As if guided by fate, the pages spread to reveal the picture Monte had shown me that morning. Except that this one had been taken six years ago. Spread across the page were the Giants of 1905 in our black outfits. "SERIES TO OPEN TODAY!" said the headline. Below, Della had drawn stars around a paragraph:

Luther Taylor, better known as the Dummy, has done splendid work for the New York club for years. To many batsmen he is a riddle. As good an authority as Kid Gleason is quoted as saying he would rather face Mathewson than he would Taylor.

She'd underlined another, by Bozeman Bulger of the *Evening World:* "If anybody should ask who is the real bon-bon of the Giants, tell him his name is Taylor and you'll win."

And a poem by William F. Kirk in the *American:*

There's nobody else like you,
You're a pitcher tried and true.
When you do that corskscrew turn
And your speed begins to burn,
You create profound concern,
Dummy Taylor.

Yesterday you made 'em stare
When your foemen fanned the air.

Air was mostly what they struck—
Now and then they raked the muck—
And 'twas not a case of luck,
Dummy Taylor.

As a talker you'll never shine,
But full many a friend of mine
Could secure the world's regard,
If he didn't talk so hard,
And performed like you, old pard,
Dummy Taylor.

I stood there staring at the page, overcome by the feeling that I should be . . . where? I didn't know. But not there. Not in a hole in the middle of the damned Kansas prairie. Something changed in the light behind me. I turned to see Della fingering the gas lamp key and frowning down at me. I closed the scrapbook.

"L-U," she signed; it was my family nickname. "What are you doing?"

I gave her a cheerful thumbs-up and brandished the relish, but I knew she wasn't fooled. She waited on the steps and together we went up to eat.

"The Bartletts are looking to sell ten acres," she signed, after passing me the acorn squash.

"What for?" It struck me as curious that the prospect of having new neighbors so close didn't upset her.

"They need the cash."

"I see."

Later, watching me tackle her cinnamon cream pie, she signed, "It's the piece right next to us they want to sell."

"Oh." I could see that she expected more of a response. "Any buyers?"

"I wondered if *we* might be for it, Lu." Her left hand touched my arm. "They'd give us first chance."

I put my fork down, aware of a tightness in my belly beyond the food I'd packed in. "Where would we get that kind of dough?"

"I could use my inheritance."

Della's aunt had left her a small amount, but it wouldn't begin to cover the purchase price. "We don't need more land," I told her. "We've got plenty here to keep us busy."

She rose and began clearing the dishes.

I didn't sleep much that night. In the gray light of morning Della moved over close and fondled me until I grew hard, then took me into her. It seemed so easy and natural—hardly the case during a lot of our time together. The notion of raising kids terrified Della. Her favorite aunt—the one who'd left her a legacy—had been born deaf, like us, and had lost her baby when it choked in its crib. Later, unable to forgive herself for not hearing its cries, she'd taken her own life. As a consequence of that, plus the fact of several states considering legislation to bar deaf couples from having kids (no such laws were enacted but it caused a lot of talk and you can imagine how the subject made us feel), Della had sworn off ever becoming a mother. For a long time she wouldn't even stay alone with Sim and Hattie's daughters.

In her thirties her resolve had weakened. Knowing I wanted a big family like the one I'd grown up in and heeding my promises of hiring all the help she'd want, she'd decided to try. That was three years ago. Nothing had happened. Now it looked like kids weren't in the cards for us—a sadness that grew heavier with time.

The next day was Sunday. At Della's urging we drove up to Lawrence for a deaf church service. "That's the property there," she signed as we left our gate.

Like most of what surrounded us, apart from the creek and cotton-woods, it was flat and fallow, good land for grain. But it would need hundreds of man-hours to sow and water and harvest. To me it looked like a trap.

"No," I told her.

Her hands stayed in her lap the rest of the drive.

On the way home I picked up a paper to see what had happened in New York, where the Series had opened the previous day, October 14, later than usual. They'd stretched the regular schedule to allow Mr. Charles Ebbets, owner of the "impoverished" Brooklyn club, to take in a big Columbus Day crowd. I had trouble doping that one out. Ebbets was commencing to build a gigantic new ballpark. It seemed to me a man who could afford *that* didn't need charity from the schedule-setters. But then, owners are a breed unto themselves and stick together like thieves—which is what a lot of ballplayers think they are.

Mathewson had opened against Bender, Connie Mack's Chippewa ace. While Matty hadn't matched his shutout opener of 1905, he held the Athletics to six hits and managed a 2–1 victory, despite Bender notching 11 strikeouts and yielding only 5 hits.

Same old Matty.

That night Della watched me pack a canvas bag with the stuff Sim wanted, along with my glove, spikes and several new white balls.

"Coaching the town boys?" she asked.

I signed no, but didn't elaborate.

Looking oddly wary, she tapped me on the shoulder and pointed to the bag. "Then what's that for?"

"Just a catch with Sim."

"I see." Her lifted eyebrows made it clear that she didn't. Normal for us this time of year would be to pack for a hunting trip. "He wants this?"

I nodded. "Me, too."

I could see that it perplexed her. In the beginning baseball had been all promise and glory for us. The game was still our meal ticket, but the glory had long since passed. The long seasons of being alone had taken their toll. I'd crowed to her about my arm coming back, of course, but I didn't think she believed it—or even wanted to. Sometimes I suspected she secretly liked it that my career was petering out. It meant I'd be home like other husbands. She stopped watching me and busied herself sewing.

I didn't try to explain. What would I tell her? That I needed to prove my ability to a small-time reporter?

Or maybe to myself?

———— • ◆ • ————

SUNDAY BALL WAS not allowed in the East, so there was no Series news that Monday. I tried to put it out of my mind as I spelled Sim in the store. That evening we walked together over to the high school diamond, where we began tossing the ball leisurely. Its graceful arc between us, the white passage in the lengthening shadows, reminded me of when we were boys begging Pa to throw us high balls beside the barn at nightfall.

Gradually I increased the distance till I stood on the mound. Sim reached for the bag of catcher's gear, but I waved him back, assuring him I wouldn't pull anything tricky. I threw from a slow windup, feeling the long muscles of my back stretch pleasurably. The evening shadows seemed to stand still. My throws, straight as string, hardly caused Sim's mitt to move. It all felt so good that I put a little more vinegar on the ball. Sim burned it back from his squatting position, which I took to mean he wanted another one. I gave it to him with lots of pepper. The ball slammed in and then he was on his feet dancing around and throwing the mitt at me.

"Goddamnit, Luther!" he said, rubbing his hand and glaring.

"Sorry," I signed. Nothing seemed to be broken, but his palm was swelling and purpling. I hadn't realized how hard I'd thrown. The worn-down padding in Bresnahan's mitt hadn't done much good. "I'll get some beefsteak for it."

"I'm too old for this nonsense." He pointed to his knees to indicate pain there, too, and after I'd rubbed my arm down and pulled on a wool shirt to keep in the heat, he reached for my liniment, a blend of Vaseline and Tabasco that players called "go-fast." Sim smeared it on his knees, got a funny look on his face, and began kicking his legs like a scared colt. I couldn't keep the grin off my face.

With a resentful look he said, "You really got your mind set on doing this, Lu?"

I spread my hands. "Well, sure, but. . . ."

"Maybe I can find somebody else to be your backstop."

We picked up the gear and started walking back. After a few paces he threw his arm around me. "Tell you what, though," he signed with his uninjured hand. "If I was McGraw, *I'd* sure as hell hire you back!"

———— •◆• ————

I AGITATED THE ball bearings and then trod heavily so I wouldn't startle Della, but she was nowhere in sight. Finally I found her in the upstairs bedroom, staring out the window at the Bartletts' property. When I touched her shoulder, she jumped.

"What are you doing?" I signed.

"Nothing," she replied.

———— •◆• ————

TUESDAY NOON I dashed out of the store and over to the tiny news stand on 5th between Macon's Harness & Surcingle and Doc Utter's

Dental Parlor; the latter's window sign read *Digger of Teeth,* which struck me as singularly poor advertising. I stood on the board walk and scanned the sporting page. Game Two had taken place in Philly—the teams shuttled between the cities after every contest—and matched two southpaws. McGraw went with Rube Marquard, who I remembered as a smug-faced 18-year-old pup just up from Indianapolis at the end of the '08 season. Signed for a ridiculous amount, Marquard was tagged the "$11,000 lemon" until this season, when he'd blossomed and won a record 19 consecutive games and 24 altogether. Opposing him was Eddie Plank, the savvy crossfiring veteran, who had 23 wins himself. They'd gone into the bottom of the sixth tied 1–1, whereupon Marquard served up a fat one that Frank Baker, the A's third baseman, poled into the bleachers for a game-winning homer that knotted the Series.

An item at the bottom of the page noted that Mathewson, in a column for one of the New York dailies, had ragged on Marquard for throwing the fatal pitch. I read it again, carefully. That was not the Matty I knew. Oh, he could be critical, but only if he thought you mucked a play in the pinch because you didn't concentrate. Then he'd stare a hole through you, and if he was truly riled he might say something, but only to you or another veteran—nobody else. And NEVER to the whole world in a metropolitan sporting page!

I was starting to get an uneasy feeling about my old club.

———— • ◆ • ————

THE HIGH SCHOOL CATCHER was tied up with farm chores but he'd soon be free. Sim volunteered to handle me in the meantime if I held back. I promised I would. He put extra padding in the mitt and brought out a milking stool to sit on. It made a ludicrous picture and of course I ribbed him some—but also let him know I was grateful. It felt awfully good to work out before heading home on those mild evenings. When we took breaks we sat facing each other on a long bench, our hands moving easily in the old talk. People who feel sorry for deaf folks don't have it quite right. Sign is a rich language, and while it's true that deafness causes problems, it also makes for a special kind of closeness. For one thing, you have to pay *closer attention* to others when you can't hear their words. You come to know them in ways that are direct and intimate. And you're probably less likely to be fooled.

All our lives Sim and I had been like that.

———•◆•———

BACK IN NEW YORK for Game Three, Matty pitched on two days rest against Jack Coombs, another of Mr. Mack's star flingers. The Giants took a 1–0 lead into the ninth, then, like Marquard the day before, Matty threw a ball that Baker slammed over the fence. Aided by two errors, the A's won in extra innings. Now the Giants trailed in the Series and had to face Bender today on his home diamond. Already the scribes had dubbed Baker "Home Run," and Marquard had retaliated with some knocks in *his* New York column about Mathewson's choice of pitches.

I threw the paper down in disgust.

Which turned out to be a simpler reaction than I had the next day, when I discovered that they'd been all set to play Game Four in Philadelphia when heavy rains washed out the contest.

Heavy rains. . . .

My mind drifted back to the fall of 1905. I'd been scheduled to pitch the third game. *Mathewson . . . McGinnity . . . Taylor. . . .* That was the rotation. But my turn never came. After Matty's shutout, McGinnity lost to Bender, 3–0. Rain postponed the next game. On the next day—

my day—McGraw decided that Matty was rested enough and started him. Matty won again, 9–0. Then McGinnity beat Plank, 1–0. McGraw passed me over again, and Matty took the final honors, 2–0. Five straight shutouts, four of them by us.

The greatest pitching that ever could be.

And I'd been left out.

To his credit, McGraw tried to soften things, telling me to be ready in case Matty ran out of fuel. In a special pre-game exhibition, he had me toss balls with Jim Corbett, the ex-heavyweight champ, who fancied himself a ballplayer just as I fancied myself a pugilist. We clowned some and the big crowd laughed and cheered.

But Matty had needed no help.

It all hurt more now than it did then. I'd bought the Chalmers and figured, like everybody else, that we'd be in the Series for seasons to come. But the next year Matty was weakened by diphtheria, and Donlin, leading the league with a .340 average, broke an ankle, and we finished ten games behind the Cubs. In '07 Donlin left for vaudeville, McGinnity and others faded, and we dropped to fourth. In '08 Merkle's so-called bonehead play cost us the pennant—actually it was the work of O'Day and league president Pulliam, both deep-dyed McGraw-haters, that chiseled us out of the flag and gave it to those god-dammned Cubs.

That winter I'd gotten my release.

Heavy rains....

———— • ◆ • ————

"HAVE YOU THOUGHT any more about that land?"

My fists tightened on the pipe wrench I was using to try to fix the leaky sink trap in the kitchen. I'd just skinned my knuckles and my mood wasn't the best. For a second I considered slamming the wrench against the resisting pipe, then put it down and finger-spelled slowly, as if to a dense child, "I . . . DON'T . . . WANT . . . IT!"

She turned away with pursed lips. The subject didn't come up again.

———— • ◆ • ————

IT STORMED THE next day in Philly. And the next.

In Baldwin I threw to Sim, feeling stronger each time. Wanting to cut loose, I brought an old mattress down, propped it against the backstop, then walloped the dust out of it with fastballs. Sim thought it looked like I was getting ready to pitch in competition. He wondered why.

I didn't have an answer.

Next morning I read that rain had put off the Series for the third straight day. Then around noon, as if blown from the eastern seaboard and over the Alleghenies and down the Ohio and out across the prairies, the first fingers of wind-lashed storms clutched at Baldwin.

A soggy day passed. Another. Water fell without letup. Consumed by jitters, I tended the store, cleaned and sharpened my tools at home, caught up on the latest monopolies and scandals in the back issues of *McClure's* that Della had saved. As the wetness went on, I got wound up tighter and tighter. The rain that drummed on the store's metal roof seemed to pound relentlessly in my head.

As if seeking shelter, my thoughts fixed on the two years we'd clinched pennants, when everybody was loose after the pressure of the race, and McGraw would put himself into the lineup. Old-timers came around and McGraw even let one of them, "Orator" O'Rourke, catch a game, though the man was in his fifties. I knew it was silly, but I kept picturing everybody I'd played with in the bigs—and a number before me—gathered around McGraw at that very moment.

I ought to be there too.

As the rain pounded on, my imagination took a further step and came up with the feverish notion that McGraw had summoned the rest—but was snubbing me. He'd left me out in '05. He was doing it again in '11.

I visited the *Ledger* office to look through back issues of *The Sporting News*. What I found didn't improve my outlook. Sure enough, in the final games this year, with the pennant safely won, McGraw had fooled around with his lineup: this time not with some old broke-down backstop (to be fair about it, O'Rourke actually caught a hell of a game) but the team mascot, some halfwit by the name of Victory Faust. McGraw let him pitch in two games. I read it again, my eyes bulging.

He'd actually pitched the MASCOT!

———— •◆• ————

"WHAT'S BOTHERING YOU?" Della's outspread hands held the question before settling on her hips. "I've never seen you like this."

I looked at her uncertainly.

"It has to be more than the rain and not being able to toss the ball with Sim."

I tried to give it a casual wave-off, but she knew me too well.

"Hattie told me she saw you parked out by the railroad tracks between the freight elevators and the molasses mill, all alone, just staring into the rain."

She pretty much had it right. Except that I was also clutching in my hand a gold medal the size of a quarter-dollar, with crossed bats circled by 22 tiny diamonds and the words, *World's Champions 1905*.

Della stepped close and took my hands and squeezed, as if trying to force the fingers to talk. Her eyes searched mine. "What is it, Lu?"

I poured it all out then, telling her about missing my Series turn, about knowing beyond any doubt that my arm was back strong as ever, about McGraw. . . .

When I was finished she just stood there staring at me. Usually I could guess what she was feeling. I'd like to think it was sympathy, although the odds were about as good for disgust.

Finally she signed, "Maybe you should go back there and get it out of your system." Her eyes held mine. "Go *now*, I mean."

So many feelings were working in me that I couldn't have begun to sort them out. "Would you come, Del?"

"Would you want me to?" Something was going on behind those brown eyes but I had no idea what.

I nodded.

Her lips tightened. It was not a trip she would willingly make. Cities frightened her. My first season in New York we'd tried living there, and she'd scarcely left our rooms. A miserable experience. The next spring she'd set off with me for training camp in Savannah, but then refused to go on after we visited her folks in North Carolina. It wouldn't be right to try to drag her along now. But how could I justify going by myself? It would cost a fair amount, and for what?

I tried to assure her it was just a passing thing.

———— • ◆ • ————

AFTER A SOLID WEEK of downpour in the East and five days' worth in Baldwin, the papers said that the Atlantic weather front was finally breaking up. On Monday, the field in Philly would be drained and readied for play. On Tuesday, the Series would resume.

This was Sunday.

In spite of myself I began calculating how fast I could get there. On the front page, as if to tempt me, was a story of the nation's recent first cross-country flight, from New York to Pasadena. For a few wild seconds I considered finding an aeroplane to fly me to Philly. A Kansan named Clyde Cessna had been going around giving aerial demonstrations in his Comet monoplane. Maybe I could find him and get a lift back East. Which shows how addled I was, given that I'm afraid of heights and I get jittery just climbing above the bottom steps of a ladder.

Then it came to mind how last season the Cubs had traveled nearly 200 miles, from Columbus to Pittsburgh, by express train in the record time of under four hours. If they could do that, I surely ought to be able to cover the 1,300 miles or so to Philly in time for Game Four.

If I left today.

———— • ◆ • ————

"YOU'LL BE WRETCHED all winter otherwise." Della looked resigned. "I reckon you need to go."

I hugged her.

"Lu?" she signed hesitantly.

"What?"

"It's not another woman. . . ."

I froze, thunderstruck. There'd been a time—just once, but it lasted a while—when I'd given in to temptations offered ballplayers full measure in big cities. I'd dallied with a flock of dance-hall girls and then narrowed the field to carry on a lengthy fling with one. Della found out and it nearly finished us. I'd promised her that there wouldn't be any more of it. And there hadn't.

"It's baseball, Del, nothing else."

I think my shocked reaction reassured her more than anything I could express. She was expert at reading me.

"You'll be gone a week?"

"No more, I promise."

I set about packing in customary style, tossing clothes into my valise. Della patiently folded and arranged them.

An hour later I was aboard a Santa Fe express bound for St. Louis. As the miles clicked by, the rain slackened and finally stopped. Tracers of sunlight pierced the overhanging clouds. My mood brightened with the day.

I was heading back to the Big Time.

T W O

SHARING MY CAR was a family of six from Topeka and a stripe-suited drummer boosting agricultural implements who ignored me once he found he couldn't sell me anything. The others grinned like monkeys each time our eyes happened to meet. It was nervousness, that was all; they didn't know how to act toward me. A lot of deaf people are bothered by that sort of thing. Made to seem stupid, they feel shut off from the "normal" world, and so aren't much interested in socializing with hearing folks.

Not me. I'd been raised to mix with everybody, and that's generally what I did. In this case I pulled a few sleight-of-hand coin stunts to loosen up the kids, then together we commenced sketching their comic-strip favorites: Willie Fibb; Buster Brown; Uncle Crabapple. Soon my pad was going back and forth, lickety-split. When they found I was headed for the World Series, the youngest boy lit up like a lamp. He'd been staring at my fingers; now he asked why they were gnarled and lumpy. I explained that I'd started as a catcher before switching to pitcher, so of course he asked where I'd played. What could I do but tell? Well, that tore it. Suddenly I was a gold-plated hero, and all of them, even the drummer, were asking no end of questions. A familiar pattern. Sometimes I felt like an ambassador to the country of the hearing.

———— • ◆ • ————

I ARRIVED WITHOUT much time to spare. Philadelphia's North Station sat only six blocks from Shibe Park, the Athletics new north-end ballfield, but instead of going there I headed downtown to the Continental Hotel, where we'd stayed in '05, thinking to catch the Giants there. I was wrong on two counts. McGraw *had* used it again out of superstition, but after losing Game Two he'd switched to the Majestic on North Broad. So I went there, only to learn that Shibe had its own dressing rooms. Visiting players no longer had to suit up in their hotel rooms and parade through the streets, often the targets for insults and flying objects. The Giants had left an hour before.

As I tipped the Majestic doorman to hold my valise I had the shocking thought that for the first time in two decades I might have to pay to see a game. I wrote, "Know where I can get a ticket in a hurry?"

He grinned at my greenness and showed me that morning's headline: SCANDALOUS TICKET SPECULATORS. It seemed that New York agents had connived to purchase nearly 5,000 tickets for the Series opener last week—tickets denied to the public and scalped at lofty prices.

Swell, I thought.

———— • ◆ • ————

NEAR THE BALLGROUNDS, massed fans slowed the Broad Street trolley to a crawl. I jumped off and forged up Lehigh Avenue, where I caught my first glimpse of Shibe Park. Framed of steel and concrete, it had opened two years before at a cost of $300,000. I'd expected something factory-like, but what rose before me seemed more a cathedral: massive walls of brick with arched windows and ornamental columns that supported a copper-trimmed mansard roof of green slate topped by a flag-decked cupola.

Feeling oddly humbled by at sight of it, I was reminded of the time Dad took Sim, Ben and me to Sportsman's Park in St. Louis. We stood behind the outfield ropes where I kept my eyes glued on my slugging hero of those days, Tip O'Neill, who nabbed a long ball on the dead run not ten feet from us; I could still picture O'Neill's straining face, one leathery cheek bulged with tobacco. Comiskey's Browns had seemed like gods to me, their old wooden ballpark a vast palace. Now, standing in the shadow of Shibe, I felt a flash of that old wonder.

Ticket booths were open, but the lines for them took up a whole block. I took a peek at my prized watch and, wary of thieves, shoved it quickly back in its pocket. Nearly three o'clock. Starting time. Cursing the fates, I paid a scalper $7.50 for something called an Upper Pavilion Loge and started to make my way up a long curving ramp toward the players dressing rooms. A uniformed guard blocked me. He didn't care who I was or who I'd played for: I had to take the central stairway along with everybody else.

Entering the huge double-decked stand, I felt another flicker of wonder. The field below formed a fine panorama, the grass and red infield dirt in perfect shape. The papers said that gasoline had been burned over the sod to dry it out. How was it done without frying the grass? Bleachers curved toward the field from both ends of the giant grandstand. Fans not only jammed them, but stood six-deep before a low temporary fence around the outfield, clung like bugs to the regular wall beyond it, and clustered like crows on the porches, balconies and rooftops behind right field.

From my high-tiered perch I watched the squads line up before their benches: Giants in black, Athletics in white. All tiny as ants. I couldn't begin to make out their faces. Was this the future? In Brooklyn, Detroit and Chicago, monster ballyards were either finished or going up. For my money, it was the worst possible way to experience the game.

At least I could pick out McGraw's squat figure as he marched to the third-base coacher's box and Charley Bender's graceful stride as he took the mound. Beside home plate a man lifted a megaphone to his mouth.

Play ball!

On the second pitch the pint-sized New York leadoff man, Josh Devore, drove a ball up the middle that Bender couldn't stop. The next Giant batsman slammed a triple into the right-center gap for a run, and soon scored himself on a sacrifice fly. Three hitters. Two tallies. Around me, the Philly rooters had stopped bouncing up and down.

Bender got the side out. Mathewson came out for his turn. Seeing the familiar motions—tug at the cap, arms high over his head, pump motion with hands apart, easy release—I suddenly couldn't stand sitting up there any longer. *This isn't baseball!* I went down to the lower level and, using my pad, said as much to an usher.

He gave me a fishy look. "You say you can't be up there on account you're deef?"

"No," I wrote, and patted my chest. "On account of my heart."

His look didn't change. I slipped him three dollars. The look softened. "Well . . . "

I gave him two dollars more. I'd just forked over the equal of a week's pay for most working stiffs.

"Follow me." He showed me to an empty seat ten rows behind the Giants bench. Much better. Now I was close enough to pick out faces, although there weren't that many I knew. On the Athletics, only Bender, Plank and one or two others remained of their '05 club. As for the Giants on the field, Mathewson was the only carry-over. Ames, Wiltse and Devlin were in the dugout, I knew, but Matty alone was still a front-liner. Some of the younger players had come up as rookies during my last years. Now they were the regulars. Among them was Buck

Herzog, for whom I had a singular lack of affection. I looked around
the vast new stadium, thinking that just about everything had changed.

McGraw stepped onto the lip of the dugout. I stood and flapped my
arms at him. He didn't see me, so I made a noise guaranteed to get his
attention. Donlin once likened it to a crazed jackass's shriek—piercing
(whatever that is) and unsettling—and McGraw used to take delight in
ordering me to set it on opposing flingers in the pinch. Now I threw it
full force at him. Derbied heads swiveled and faces looked up at me in
alarm.

McGraw spotted me at once—not a difficult thing; I was standing
with my fists clenched over my head—and recognition showed in his
pug face. But not the welcoming smile I'd hoped for. He dipped his
head in a curt nod and turned away. I knew I'd violated a cardinal rule:
never bother him during a game; but these were special circumstances.

It's Dummy Taylor! I wanted to shout. *I'm back!*

A boy thrust a scorecard and pencil at me and I scribbled automati-
cally. He peered at the autograph, then showed it off to his friends,
who pestered me to sign for them. I perked up a bit. *Somebody* was glad
to see me. What had I expected, I asked myself. McGraw to invite me
down to sit with him on the bench?

I guess maybe I had.

Mathewson's speed wasn't quite up to what I expected, nor his
shoots quite so dazzling as I remembered. He got through the first
inning, but in the second gave up a double and misplayed a bunt; only
sharp fielding behind him and a busted squeeze kept the A's off the
board. But two innings later they swatted three more doubles and
scored as many runs. I'd rarely seen Matty knocked around the lot like
that. In the next frame, a sharp single and another double boosted their
lead to 4–2. Bender, meantime, had hit his stride and was firing fastballs
like buckshot.

Salting the Giants wounds was the fact that when they did get runners on base, they were nailed trying to steal. This puzzled me.
McGraw's youngsters were jack-rabbits, and stealing was their game;
this season they'd smashed the National League stolen base record. So
how come Jack Lapp of the Athletics, not exactly steel-armed as catchers went, was knocking them down like shooting-gallery ducks? Lapp
seemed to know just when we'd try to run, the same way that the A's
batsmen seemed to know what Matty would throw.

Hmmmm. . . .

Sign-stealing is an art as old as signs themselves. I knew a lot about
the subject, being the first pitcher to have my catchers use finger signs.
Back in the eighties, the deaf hurler Eddie Dundon—I'll have more to
say about Mr. Dundon in a bit—was using his hands to call balls and
strikes whenever he umped games, and later on Dummy Hoy played a
big part in getting umpires to signal all their calls. Out of necessity, us
deaf players paid attention to gestures and movements others might
miss. And my eyes were sharp. I could read an auto license two blocks
away. McGraw always considered me one of his best sign-watchers;
whenever he got suspicious he'd tell me to be on the lookout. Now I
began studying hard.

It didn't take long to see that the A's hitters were acting funny. Not
looking at Davis, their captain, in the first-base coacher's box, so much
as *listening*, their heads cocked slightly toward him. I borrowed a set of
binocular glasses from a neighbor. Sure enough, Davis was yelling,
"All right!" before pitches. But not *every* pitch. I watched the pattern
and soon had it doped out: Whenever he yelled, Matty threw a fastball.
The puzzling part was that Davis didn't seem to be paying attention to
Matty, but looking more toward his own dugout.

Was Connie Mack, the A's manager, reading our signs?

Mr. Mack knew every trick in the book, of course, since he'd written a good share of it during his 30 years in baseball. He was slippery, too, not above conniving despite those church-going vested suits of his. Last season he'd been caught red-handed stationing an injured Athletic atop a building beyond the fence. Sighting through a scope at the opposing catcher's fingers, the player had twisted a weather vane to tip pitches to his mates.

I scanned for glints of lenses, mirrors and the like, but found none. McGraw, a master sign-manipulator himself, was staring hard at Davis, so I knew he'd picked up the same pattern. Before long he called "Chief" Meyers, his Indian catcher, over to him, and thereafter Matty stopped looking in before throwing. I knew what had happened: Meyers had been ordered to forget signs and just catch whatever Matty threw.

Yet somehow they were still reading the pitches!

McGraw's snakebit expression told me that he was as stymied as I was. Lacking anything more promising, my eyes drifted to the Athletics mascot, a hunchback midget, perched at the edge of their dugout. (Most teams have mascots; ours used to be a little colored boy whose head we rubbed for luck.) Something about him bothered me. I borrowed the glasses again. The hunchback was staring at Matty, eyes wide and fixed, still as a garden statue—except that sometimes before pitches he'd suddenly cross his arms. It took me a minute or two to make sure of the system: on breaking balls he crossed his arms and Davis kept mum. If he left them hanging down, Davis yelled. Either way, the hitter knew what was coming.

Since we weren't using any signs, the mascot had to be reading something off Matty. I walked down behind the Philadelphia dugout and stooped beneath the rail close above the hunchback, trying to see from his angle. But I couldn't get low enough. He might be seeing a subtle flash of fingers gripping the ball. A quiver of the glove. A telltale flex of knee or shoulder. Whatever the tipoff, I couldn't spot it. Hard to fathom—this was Mathewson, after all—but nothing else made sense.

I wrote a note, folded it with *URGENT!* on the outside, and convinced a cop stationed by the railing to deliver it to McGraw, who read it and stared long and hard at the hunchback. After Matty's next pitch, he marched out to Bill Klem at home plate. The two were long-standing enemies (what umpire wasn't McGraw's foe?), and once McGraw had gone so far as to try to get him fired. More typical, though, was the time Klem came to the mound to stop McGraw and me from stalling; as soon as he turned back toward home, McGraw tossed water on his shoes from a tin cup and handed it to me. I was the one who got tossed, which was okay with McGraw, who was about to lift me anyway. He always paid our fines.

Everybody knew that to get Klem's goat, all you had to do was call him "Catfish." He was sensitive about his big lips, which did sort of resemble a fish's. My old roommate Mike Donlin taught me how to pronounce the word, and one day after Klem had called me out on strikes when I was batting, I said *Catfish!* big as life as I stalked away. Klem jerked around like his pants was on fire, glared suspiciously at me, then at the pitcher, then at McGraw in the coacher's box. While he was doing that, I said it again, and he practically lifted off the ground as he thumbed the Giant hitter approaching the plate out of the game. It was probably my proudest moment in a fine career of umpire-baiting. McGraw, I knew, wasn't foolhardy enough to use the hated nickname now.

He said a lot else, though, and kneeling where I was, I could follow most of it. McGraw claimed that the hunchback should be banished from the field. Klem looked perturbed. McGraw kept up his argument, spicing it with some juicy cussing. Mr. Mack came out on the dugout lip—he wasn't in uniform, so he couldn't go on the field—and beckoned for Davis to find out what the fuss was about.

"That little bastard's jinxing us," McGraw exclaimed. "He's gotta go."

"He's always there," Davis said. "That's his spot."

"Then I want my jinxer out, too," McGraw said.

"Fine," said Davis. "Put him at the far edge of your dugout."

"In front," McGraw insisted. "Where he'll hex your boys like that fucking midget does mine."

Klem had had enough. "We're leaving things the way they are, gents," he announced. "Go play ball."

McGraw turned away with a scowl, Davis with a smile. I doubted that the matter was finished. Sure enough, after the very next pitch, McGraw stalked out to the mound and summoned his captain, second sacker Larry Doyle. The purpose became clear several pitches later, when Doyle called time to complain that the hunchback was spoiling his concentration. Klem, eyes narrowed, ordered him back to his position.

Matty got the third out. The teams traded places. Now standing in the first-base coacher's box was a gawky, gangly individual whose ebony uniform hung loosely on his stringbean frame. "Who's that?" I wrote to the man beside me. "Their mascot," he answered. "Faust."

Oh, yes. Victory Faust. The one McGraw let pitch. Now he was participating in the goddamn Series. I shook my head in disgust. Even before the first batsman stepped to the plate, Faust unleashed a bewildering series of signs, all of them nonsense. The A's began to imitate him, their mouths framing insults. Faust seemed oblivious to it all—until after Bender's first pitch, when he wheeled dramatically to point and bellow at the hunchback, spit flying from his lips, which I had no trouble reading: "DID YOU HEAR WHAT HE CALLED ME?"

Everybody seemed to freeze. Then Faust charged the hunchback, who, to my surprise, did not flee but actually moved toward his attacker, who was easily four times his size. Faust launched a kick designed to catapult the little fellow into the Upper Pavilion Loges. The hunchback sidestepped, seized the uplifted leg, and sank his teeth into Faust's thigh. Face contorted in a scream, Faust brought up his clenched fists to drive the midget's head between his shoulders, but then the A's were on him, followed by a swarm of Giants. A lot of chesty milling followed, with no punches thrown.

Klem tossed both mascots, of course, and the home fans were jubilant, thinking their little man had shown superior spunk. They were right. But the reality was that McGraw had gotten what he wanted. On his way back to the dugout he rewarded me with a grim wink.

Things, I reckoned, were looking up.

In the eighth, Matty got lifted for a pinch-hitter. He hadn't exactly shone. Seven of the ten hits off him had been doubles. Hooks Wiltse, a gaunt left-hander with haunted eyes and a cadaverous face ("long enough to eat oats out of a feedbag," Donlin used to say) came in to pitch. Hooks won his first twelve starts as a rookie in our first pennant year, 1904, and over the years we'd dueled in a friendly rivalry. Rooting for him now, I watched him comb the front slope of the mound with his spikes, then turn his back on the plate. He brought his glove up to his face, and I knew he was spitting a stream of licorice juice into its palm. Unlike Matty and me, Hooks had short fingers. With the slippery liquid he could get extra bend on his shoots and also darken the ball, making it harder for batsmen to pick up.

After breaking a finger back in May, Hooks had gone only 12–9 this season, a poor record for him. Today he turned in a nice piece of work in keeping the A's from doing any more damage. But it didn't much matter as Bender shut the Giants down the rest of the way. Now we trailed in the Series, 3–1, only one loss away from extinction.

I rushed down past open-mouthed, cushion-tossing fans to catch

McGraw before he disappeared into the clubhouse. Just as our eyes met, a news scribe stepped in my way.

"Dummy Taylor?"

I recognized him; in past seasons he'd covered the Phillies. He thrust a notepad at me. "Saw you down by the mascot," he'd scrawled. "Was he up to something?"

I made a mistake then. Flattered at being recognized, I wrote, "He was tipping our pitches—but I caught on to him."

McGraw arrived at the rail and the reporter swung around and asked him something. McGraw snarled an answer, and the scribe turned back to me. "He says you had no connection. Says he doped out the hunchback before you showed up."

I looked at McGraw. His small, pale eyes probed mine. His jaw was set in a lump and he looked ready for a scrap. It was brazen but typical for him to grab the credit. *If you knew it,* I thought, *then why the hell didn't you do something about it before the game was lost?* I shrugged at the reporter, thinking that it was no good getting myself into the manager's doghouse before I'd even started. McGraw hated to be shown up. Especially by his own players, present or past. Once, asked if he was married, a rookie actually blurted to a reporter, "You'd better ask Mr. McGraw."

Shoving the scribe aside, he said, "What's up, Dummy?" but gave me no chance to tell him. Switching to his fingers, he began spelling with aggressive punching motions. I was impressed by the deftness he still showed. Years ago I'd taught him the deaf alphabet and he'd proved a prize pupil, soon insisting that all the Giants learn. For a while we'd even used fingerspelling for on-field signals, McGraw spelling out S-T-E-A-L big as life, until brainy opponents like Evers and Leach caught on. Now he spelled: T-O-M-O-R-R-O-W W-E G-E-T T-H-E-M, and jabbed me in the chest. I took it to mean he thought that the Athletics' edge was gone.

Thanks to me, right?

"What brings you here?" he asked. "Business?"

Yes, I thought, *with you.* "I came from home."

"From Kansas?" He frowned. "What the hell for?"

"To see you."

Something in his face hardened. "I guess you'll be wanting tickets like the others."

The rudeness of it stopped me. Sure, he must have people coming at him from all sides, but did he really think I'd come so far for *that?*

"I just want to talk to you."

"About what?"

"M-Y A-R-M I-S B-A-C-K," I spelled, adding a pitching motion to leave no doubt.

"So?" His eyes were chips of blue glass. "You want a tryout in the middle of the goddamn World Series? After we lost a fucking game?"

I sighed. It was well known that McGraw was the world's sorest loser, but didn't the man feel any gratitude for what I'd done?

A crafty look replaced his stare. "If things go right tomorrow, maybe we could talk about it, okay? There'll be a seat at the Polo Grounds for you." A smile curved his lips. "A top-notch seat."

"We'll meet after the game?"

"Maybe." He turned toward the clubhouse.

I stood there uncertainly. In Baldwin I'd dreamed of wearing my old uniform again, of being welcomed in the dugout, on the train, in the hotels. Horsing around in the bullpen. Basking in the sunlight and the bright glances of pretty girls in the grandstand. But here, now, in the cluttered reality of Shibe Park, this seemed the best I could hope for.

———— • ◆ • ————

THE GIANTS LEFT the city by chartered express. No other trains were available that night, so I took a room at the Majestic and went out to see every flicker I could find. Deaf folks can follow along as well as anybody in movie halls. I hoped they'd never add sound. Norma Talmadge was silly in *Tale of Two Cities,* but Blanche Sweet, the star of *Fighting Blood,* reminded me of how Della used to look. Feeling guilty about wishing she still did, I mailed a note from the hotel letting her know I'd arrived okay.

Next morning I boarded the first cars to New York. Tubes had been installed beneath the East River, and trains now whisked through them straight into Manhattan. A revolutionary thing, crossing the Hudson without having to disembark in New Jersey and take the ferry.

I emerged in the spanking new Penn Station, open only a few months. High-arching girders and glass ceilings made the upper levels seem far distant from the locomotives rumbling in its depths. The Great Room, a passenger concourse two blocks long, was fashioned of Italian marble edged with columns six stories tall. Clusters of electric globes blazed everywhere. I stowed my valise in a locker in the men's waiting room, which seemed like a chapel with its ornate ceiling, iron chandeliers and rows of benches. Outside, on the busy sidewalk, neck craning back like the rawest country rube, I stared up at stone angels and eagles and brass-rimmed clocks on the station's facade.

I set out to see favorite spots. First the Battery, where gulls circled and ferries trailed foaming wakes. I stared at Miss Liberty with her beckoning torch. Now that every fourth American was a foreign-speaking immigrant, people were having second thoughts about her message. Myself, I didn't favor shutting anybody out—but in Baldwin there weren't very many strangers.

I sipped coffee and read the morning papers in Madison Square. The Metropolitan Building loomed overhead, and all around me the city's powerful vibrations sent a *thrum* up my butt and backbone—a sensation Della hated. She was strong for the wide prairie spaces, where you could see things coming miles off and have time to get ready for them. I appreciated that, but had come to love the compressed excitement of the city. It made me feel alive, like being on the mound in a close game, the crowd in a tizzy.

An aeroplane disaster took up the headlines. The poor aviator—"birdman," one paper called him—had lost control during an exhibition of spirals, tried to leap from his seat at the last second and been crushed in the wreckage. There were photographs. You might as well drink rat poison as climb into a flying machine.

J.P. Morgan had paid a visit to the Tax Commissioner to appeal an assessment, and in less than 30 minutes wickered them out of $4000. Double what I'd make in a whole year. It put me in mind of standing with my folks among thousands of depression-plagued Kansans to hear—see in my case—Mrs. Lease, the famous Populist orator, a tall, stately woman with thick dark hair. I remembered her silhouetted in a black dress and hat against a field of yellow corn, mincing no words as she lambasted silk-hatted easterners who'd never planted anything in their lives but were squeezing the lifeblood from our crops. "Raise less corn and more hell," she exhorted us. "Let 'em know the Kansas prairies are on fire!" Even Ma applauded when she finished: "I hold to the theory that if one man has not enough to eat three times a day and another man has $25,000,000, that last man has something that belongs to the first!"

A fitting judgement for Morgan and all his ilk.

In politics, Taft and TR were going for the Republican nomination. I'd seen 'em both show their stuff at the ballpark. Taft had the better arm. Jersey's Governor Wilson looked to be the Democrats' pick—odd not to have Bryan in the running; I'd gone for him in '96, the first time I could vote. There was nothing in the papers about Bob La Follette, of course, the only one standing up for Midwest workingmen and farmers.

As usual, the foreign scene was a mess. Sun Yat Sen's boys were trimming the Chinese army, the Mexicans were throwing a revolution, Turks and Bulgarians were battling, Italians and French were squabbling, and the Huns didn't much care for anybody. George Washington had it right: stick to our own business.

Keeping a cautious eye on horse and auto traffic, I worked my way uptown, marveling all the while at new construction. The Flatiron Building, that curious prow-shaped structure at 23rd Street that seemed to be towing Broadway in its wake, had been finished just about the time I arrived in New York. In my mind it was the city's hub, the emblem of the new century. But Penn Station, at 33rd, had already eclipsed it, and a greater rail station yet, to be called "Grand Central," was rising farther uptown. Where the old reservoir had stood at 41st, a new Public Library of white marble stood guarded by massive stone lions.

How long could this keep up?

In Times Square, *Pink Lady,* starring Hazel Dawn, was playing at the New Amsterdam. The Dolly Sisters headlined Ziegfeld's Follies at the Jardin de Paris. I gazed around fondly at all the clustered theaters: the Lyric; Belasco's; Hammerstein's Victoria; the Shuberts' Casino with its Arab turret and its slogan, THE WHIRL OF THE TOWN, atop the marquee. I'd spent many happy evenings in all of them. Not to mention a few in some of the parlor houses that dotted the area.

But that was the past.

My wild oats were planted.

Still, I couldn't help but notice that fashions for the fair sex had changed. Hair was shorter, dresses and skirts had risen a few daring inches almost up to the ankle, and there were none of the "peekaboo waists" so popular three years ago. A startling thing to glimpse a shapely midriff through gauzy fabric in broad daylight.

Now the ladies carried themselves with a businesslike air, as if not to be trifled with. The suffragettes' work, no doubt. The vote had come through for them in a dozen states, California the latest. Hattie Mae was involved in Kansas, which looked about to go over. I'd even heard that my old Broadway pal, Lil Russell, as ladylike as anyone could want, had joined up. When the Giants first put women at their ticket windows back in '06, you'd have thought the world was ending—but by next season they were taken for granted.

A new time was here, no doubt about it.

But no amount of pondering change could have prepared me for the Polo Grounds. Although still in its old Harlem location, in Coogan's Hollow beneath the well-known bluff that generations of boys had climbed up to watch games, it was hardly what I had known. Back in April, when fire gutted the old wooden structure, an army of workers had labored to rebuild it. It reopened at the end of June, fireproofed and enlarged, with a capacity to seat 40,000. I hadn't been able to fathom that number until now, when I finally laid eyes on the concrete-and-steel monster. Just then it looked like that many ball nuts were pouring off the El and down the long ramp behind right field to mob the ticket booths on Eighth Avenue.

At the press window the line was shorter. My "pass" was a handwritten note from McGraw indicating my seat, which turned out to be behind the Giants bench in almost the same spot I'd inhabited at Shibe. He must have figured I'd be at my jinx-busting best there.

Inside were more startling changes. The old crescent grandstand was now an enormous double-tiered horseshoe, every seat with a back and armrests. Bleachers extended all the way around the ground, even

closing off center field, where a single rope used to keep fans off the
field. The curved upper facade, which bore the coat of arms of all the
National League clubs, smacked of a gaudy carnival midway. It
seemed that in the three years I'd been away, the plain old girl I'd
known had come into one hell of a lot of money and dolled herself up
with painted gewgaws.

That was it: come into money. Baseball was piling up fortunes.
What I'd seen in Philly and now here left no doubt that the big-league
game was booming like never before. It was a monopoly, too, in its
way, like U.S. Steel and the other trusts. Lately there'd been talk of
ballplayers organizing for collective bargaining. Gompers of the AFL
was said to be interested in forming baseball locals.

All I wanted was my modest share.

If McGraw would just give me a look. . . .

The Giants went through their warmups in rah-rah style. Next to
the Athletics, who worked stolidly, they seemed like eager boys.
Which wasn't too far from it. I figured we'd be lucky to survive today.
Mr. Mack's club was solid at every spot, and Jack Coombs, 28–12 this
year, would be tough on the mound. McGraw was countering with
Marquard, who looked as sour as I remembered—maybe he was still
smarting over Baker's homer and Matty's public knock.

I felt a tap on my shoulder and looked up into the craggy face of
DeWolf Hopper, an actor who'd boosted his career with stage rendi-
tions of "Casey at the Bat." Beaming as he shook my hand, he made a
sweeping gesture, and I realized that my neighbors were hardly average fans. I nodded to comedian Will Rogers and tenor John
McCormack. Jim Corbett waved. Beyond him I glimpsed Donald
Warfield, Julia Sanderson and others. Bigtime performers and long-
time ball nuts. They flocked to the Polo Grounds when matinees didn't
conflict. A number of theaters must be dark this particular Wednesday.

The game opened with two scoreless innings. The mascots stayed in their dugouts, and I saw no hint of sign-stealing. In the third, Larry Doyle muffed a double-play feed and left two A's runners alive. Doyle was Donlin's successor as team captain. He was a good player with no scare to him, but I couldn't help thinking that my old mate Billy Gilbert would've made that play smooth as pie. Especially in the pinch.

Hell, we had a better club, simple as that.

A popup followed. Then Marquard got a pitch too far up and Rube Oldring promptly smacked it into the left-field seats. Just like that the score was 3–0. Marquard looked ready to eat his spikes. While the fans around me slumped in their seats I felt a hand grip my shoulder. No polite tap this time. A top-hatted, jockey-sized gent stood frowning over me. A lapel pin identified him as a member of the Lambs, a posh New York club to which many of those sitting nearby belonged. The little gent looked familiar. I tried to follow what he was saying, but his mouth was going too fast. When I didn't respond, he waved something in my face—a rudeness I seldom appreciated. I caught his wrist—the quickness of it made him blink—and I saw that it was a calling card fashioned after the king of clubs. Each season McGraw handed out personalized celebrity passes; one year it was penknives with peep-hole views of the Polo Grounds; now it must be playing cards. The little man's autographed picture filled the center of his.

Bouncing on his toes, chest puffed out like a pigeon's, he jabbed a finger at me, and it didn't take a genius to see that he was claiming my seat. I pointed to the empty one beside me. He shook his head and looked around for an usher. I sat where I was, neck reddening. The signature on the card had been easy to read: *George M. Cohan.*

For reasons I couldn't begin to fathom, McGraw had assigned me the seat reserved for Broadway's brightest star.

THREE

I'D MET HIM ONCE, at our victory banquet in 1904, the year I won 21 games. *Little Johnny Jones* had just opened with swell songs like "I'm A Yankee Doodle Dandy" and "Give My Regards to Broadway." Back then, the two of us were worldbeaters.

Cohan still was.

Known as one of Gotham's most rabid ball nuts, Cohan asked auditioning performers what positions they could play, fancied himself a pitcher—he couldn't throw a lick—and bet big on all our games. At that banquet he'd played up to Matty, McGinnity and me like some Stage Door Johnny. But now he showed no sign of recognition. I handed him McGraw's note and pointed again to the seat beside me. His face grew redder. Then he half turned and I realized he wasn't alone. A buxom woman swept grandly along the row toward us. Her voile dress, reflecting the sun in tracers, was draped with strands of pearls and an emerald pendant. Her skin was pale, eyes blue, hair burnished gold. Every eye in the vicinity followed her, even those of some players. In her time she'd reigned as the "American Beauty;" it looked to me like the years hadn't dimmed her glory.

We were staring at Lillian Russell.

"Dummy, darling!" she exclaimed, arms outstretched as if we were lovers. I want to get it down right here that we'd never been, though the notion might have crossed my mind. Ten years ago, Matty had dragged me with him to ump a celebrity game in Central Park. We were ambling along when Diamond Lil, heading for the same event, came barreling around a curve on a gilt-trimmed bicycle. She pumped the brakes, which worked so well that her pal, Marie Dressler, following on another wheel, plowed into her. I tried to catch the bars as Lil toppled, but instead provided a cushion for her. Matty said that at that moment I experienced what many men had dreamed of. Mostly I remember the wind knocked out of me.

After that we were chums. Lillian came to the ballpark to see me pitch and I caught all her shows. I could tell by Matty's sneaky glances at her that Lil had made an impression, which was kind of funny since when it came to women he was the original Puritan. Matty wouldn't talk to a teammate, or even a sportswriter, if he knew the man had a wife at home and was carrying on. Luckily, he never found out about me. Another curious thing was that unlike her sisters across the country, who swooned dead everywhere Matty showed up, Lillian scarcely seemed to know he was alive.

I was the one she liked, her "ballplayer beau."

This is probably where I should explain that certain women have been partial to me. Older ones in particular, which definitely included Lillian. It was my face, partly. Not that I was a matinee Apollo. No. "A mug only a mother could love," one scribe put it when I started out in the bush leagues, and added, "the ugliest"—which might have landed him on the floor if he hadn't finished with, "BUT the most colorful on the ball field." I didn't agree with that "ugliest" either. The man never laid eyes on Moose McCormick or Bad Bill Dahlen.

Anyhow, as homeliness goes, mine was a special brand. When I was little and we still had our farm, I was watering the horses one afternoon when a panicky mare kicked me square in the jaw. It left me with a slightly scarred and hiked upper lip and a pushed-in nose—the overall look being brave but bashful, as Della says—and seemed to make those women I mentioned want to indulge their motherly instincts. They'd touch my lip and say "Ouch," as if I was still that hurt little boy. Which is curious, since I'm not built along cuddly lines. I'm tight-strung and lanky: six-two, 175, "iron-fisted and square-jawed," as one wordsmith put it.

I've also got button eyes and a quick grin that Della calls "mischievous." I'm generally cheerful and have a nice "silent laugh," as Lil once said. I like a good time as much as the next man. And, probably because I don't talk, a surprising number of folks—not just women—confide things to me. Lillian, for example, learning I was born in Oskaloosa, confessed she was from Clinton, Iowa, and her real name was Helen Louise Leonard. She swore me to secrecy. They always do.

Now, as she gripped me in a hug designed to damage a feebler man, I noticed crow's feet edging her eyes. She'd put on weight, too, but if anybody could carry it, Lillian could. Smiling sweetly at Cohan, she told him to find another seat. Then, taking my arm possessively, she plumped herself down and dragged me with her. By then Cohan seemed to know who I was. He didn't look pleased about it. He huffed for a bit and finally summoned an usher, who set about checking ticket stubs until he found a trespasser several rows behind us and took that seat.

Following the game wasn't easy with Lillian chatting away beside me. Red Ames came in for Marquard and managed to muffle the A's, but we weren't scoring off Coombs. Like most veteran stagers, Lillian formed her words distinctly, so I had little trouble following her lips (a pleasurable task) as she explained the seating mixup. It seemed that in one of the early Series contests Cohan had bet on Philadelphia. Word of it reached McGraw, and the two got into a war of insults. Lillian felt positive McGraw was using me to get revenge.

So I'd come here to advance myself but instead become a pawn in McGraw's game. My resentment must have shown. Lillian got a tender look in her eyes and invited me to come that night to see her new show, *In Search of A Sinner*. I told her I would unless I could follow the team back to Philly—a prospect seeming more and more unlikely.

She gave me a close look. "You want to play here again, is that it?"

I nodded and told her about my arm.

"Well, then, you *should!*" she exclaimed, as if it was settled. "I'm coming back next year myself. We'll do it together!" Filling several pages of my pad with her elaborate whorls, she explained that Weber and Fields, who'd made her a star in the '80s, were reforming their famed Music Hall Revues and had offered Lillian $2,000 a week to join them.

So much dough. And with her old team. Exactly what I wanted for myself. Watching Coombs duck into his windup, I felt my nerves and tendons and muscles react. Lillian had spent her life singing. I'd spent mine throwing things: skipping rocks on creeks; hurling pebbles from the gravel drive of our farm till I'd damn near plucked it clean; getting to where I could hit anything I aimed at, so powerful and tireless and *good* at it that it naturally became my meal ticket.

I was aching to *throw!*

Bottom of the ninth now, trailing 3–1.

Losing the Series would be the worst possible setup for me with McGraw. I crossed my fingers on both hands and prayed for a miracle. The first Giant grounded out. I shut my eyes and squeezed my fingers tighter. I felt Lillian jerk beside me, and looked in time to see the ball bouncing over the grass and a black-suited runner cutting hard around first and sliding into second. The crowd rose like a single creature, its arms waving antennae-like, its stamping feet sending vibrations that came up through my shoes.

All of it died when the next hitter went down.

One out left. Two runs needed to tie the score.

A pinch hitter emerged from the dugout. I recognized him: Otis Crandall. He'd come up in '08 and replaced me as the thrower for late innings, when games were on the line. He'd done the job splendidly, winning twelve times while getting us out of many a tight spot. Damon Runyon of the *American* had called him "the physician of the pitching emergency," and so he became "Doc" Crandall, known otherwise as the Boy Wonder.

He was a dozen years younger than me.

As if all that weren't enough, Crandall could also hit. He'd knocked out four homers down the stretch in '08. Naturally, I'd been jealous as hell. For his outstanding rookie work Crandall got $100 in cash, a prize watchfob made from a $20 gold piece, and two suits of underwear.

I got fired.

Still, I rooted hard for him now. A stocky, humble Hoosier farmboy, Crandall wasn't really a bad sort. As he stepped in and waved the bat, Lillian and I rose with everybody else. Coombs delivered a hummer. Crandall swung and rocketed the ball between the fielders to the wall. Lillian grabbed me and we did a wild dance as the runner came home and Crandall pulled into second. We trailed only 3–2. Scarcely had we taken a breath when Devore, the next Giant, sent us into new gyrations by punching the ball cleanly over shortstop. Crandall, running hard, slid home with the tying run.

Pandemonium!

An inning later, with dusk beginning to lower over the Polo Grounds, Larry Doyle made up for his key error by doubling down the left-field line, his fourth hit of the day. Again we were on our feet, the grandstand quivering. A bunt moved Doyle to third. Merkle, the unlucky "goat" of '08, sent a fly to medium right. Doyle set himself to sprint as the ball settled into the fielder's glove. The throw came in, low and true, and Doyle hurled himself into a fallaway slide. Lapp twisted to make the tag, but Doyle was already past. Cussing a streak, the catcher picked himself up.

Lillian was tugging at me but I held her off. Klem had made no sign. Did Doyle miss the plate? I waited for the A's to react or Doyle to dash back and tag, but neither happened, and at length Klem left his post. I breathed again. We'd won it.

Time now to tackle McGraw.

Since his note had said nothing about entering the clubhouse, I figured I'd better get down to the field. To my surprise, Lillian insisted on going. She took my arm and we promenaded down grandly, people clearing before us as if we were royalty.

So many cops lined the diamond that the nuts didn't dare mob the field like I'd seen so often. There was no need for the Giants to dash for the dressing rooms out in right (which had caused Merkle's downfall in '08, the rookie failing to touch second on a run-scoring hit, veering instead toward the clubhouse to avoid being engulfed by lunatics) and most of them were still clustered around home plate. McGraw, however, had already reached the edge of the infield. I let loose with my jackass call, but it was swallowed by the hubbub.

Seeing my consternation, Lillian poked my arm to indicate she would handle things. She opened her mouth wide and for an instant her neck swelled. McGraw froze in his tracks. I didn't hear it, of course, and could only try to imagine. I'd read in the papers that she was a "silvery soprano" and that her trademark songs required no less than 56 high C's in a single week of performing. But whatever she called out to McGraw was not silvery. He wheeled around as if stung by a hornet, and then I was shocked to see her lips forming the name, "Muggsy!"

Now, if you're going to call McGraw that, you'd better be ready to back it up. I'd seen him flatten a reporter against a locker and cuss him nose to nose till the poor fellow nearly wet his knickers—just for calling him Muggsy. Except for the occasional new yannigan put up to it by veterans, no player ever dared say it.

So I was flabbergasted when McGraw came toward us, peaceable as a lamb. Lillian reached down her gloved hand like a queen and he bent over it in a fine, courtly way. Then she set to making pretty little frowns and scolding him. I got her general drift: Why was poor Mr. Taylor up in the stands instead of with the team, where he belonged? Why had he been so cruelly used against Mr. Cohan? Weren't such things beneath a gentleman? McGraw tried to say I needed to be there on account of the jinx, but Lillian wasn't buying. She told him I deserved better. Amazingly, he took it from her, even shuffling his feet once like a schoolboy. He must have been stuck on her at one time, I decided. Maybe still was. His eyes shifted to me, and I wanted to shrink. Lillian kept talking. Finally he nodded to each of us and marched off.

"Tonight," she told me with a triumphant smile. I looked at her quizzically and extended my pad. "He'll talk with you tonight," she wrote. "On the train."

———— • ◆ • ————

I'D WANTED IT so much: the swaying cars redolent of cigars, dim and cozy, barreling through the night. The only disappointment—but it was sizable—turned out to be the Giants themselves, most of whom paid me not the slightest attention. I soon concluded that my old mates, sparked by such free souls as Bugs Raymond and Turkey Mike Donlin, had been a hell of a lot looser than this bunch, who seemed about as lively as church deacons. Hadn't they just come from behind to take a must-win Series game? I eased over to where three of them—Meyers, Marquard and Herzog—were bending over gate tallies, apparently trying to dope out why, with the papers reporting crowds of 30,000 to 50,000, the official league figures (therefore player shares) were considerably lower. Meyers and Herzog were college men; perhaps that accounted for it. In my time, Matty had been about the only one, but now the game was seeing more of that fancy breed. Maybe that's what educated players did between games—counted their money.

Meyers turned and saw me. "John Meyers," he said, extending his hand.

"Luther Taylor," I wrote on my pad. Unlike my old crowd, none of these young Giants knew Sign or fingerspelling. "They called me Dummy."

Realizing I was deaf, he looked at me closer, then nodded in recognition. "Saw you pitch," he wrote. "You were damn good. Call me Chief if you want. Everybody does." He shot me a humorous glance. "Fuck 'em!"

I liked this Indian. I offered my hand to the others. Marquard shook half-heartedly. If he remembered me, he didn't show it. Herzog ignored my hand and sneeringly said something I missed except for "dummy."

"Pardon me?" I wrote.

He didn't take the pad but mouthed the words again so that I couldn't miss them: "I said you still look like your name—a goddamn dummy." He wasn't smiling. He had a long, pointy nose. Just then it was tilted up like he smelled something he didn't like. Herzog was a rough-looking type, and his stare seemed to say he'd like to show me just how rough. I remembered him as a fresh-mouthed busher when he joined us in '08. He insisted on being called "Buck"—his honker had earned him the moniker "dick-face"—and he promptly pissed everybody off by refusing to play in an off-day exhibition. McGraw sent him home for six weeks. When Herzog came back, we rode his ass even harder. Somebody nailed his spikes to the floor, and he made the mistake of accusing me. Before I could even begin to set him straight, Bowerman, the big catcher, considered the hardest man in the game at that time, knocked him flat for his trouble. It hadn't improved Herzog's attitude. Even McGraw, who admired his grit on the diamond—why not? the two were peas from the same pod—traded him away after the '09 season, only to snatch him back this year to replace the slowing Devlin.

Bowerman was no longer around, and the truth was that while I'd never been one of Herzog's main persecutors, it looked like he hadn't forgotten his rough treatment. Now he was the veteran and I was the outsider. I tried to think what to do. It would be a sweet chore to teach him a lesson in basic manners, but McGraw wouldn't appreciate me mixing with his star third-sacker on the eve of a crucial Series game.

"Glad to see you too, Buck," I began to scrawl.

Herzog must have had the printer's knack of reading upside down, because he tried to knock the pad from my grasp—but I moved faster and he missed. I gave him my silly clown's grin, and things might have gone farther right there, but Meyers stepped casually between us, and Hooks Wiltse materialized at my elbow. Hooks tried to fingerspell something as he led me away. I'd always had trouble with Hooks's lingo because he was a piss-poor speller. He did the signs okay—just couldn't spell English words. He pumped my hand and said, "Good to see you, Dummy," and took me over to where he was sitting with Red Ames.

"What's with the choker?" I asked Ames, whose necktie was frayed and had a thimble-sized vial pinned to it.

"Jinx-breaker," he informed me.

"Red's worn that rag for months," Hooks added.

I grinned at Ames, no doubt the unluckiest flinger I'd ever known. As a rookie he'd had a no-hitter going through five innings. Suddenly the sky got mysteriously black and the game had to be called, though it was only mid-afternoon. Another time, against Brooklyn, he threw a nine-inning no-hitter and was so in control that his outfielders didn't have a single play. Trouble was, the score was still 0–0 after nine innings. In the 10th the Robins got their first hit. In the 13th they beat him.

"Cross-eyed man put the whammy on him," Wiltse explained, looking about as gleeful as he could get. If anything lifted Hooks's customary gloom, it was telling how poor luck had dogged somebody else. "The bird kept laying for him outside the hotel. Red went blocks out around, but he got nailed anyway. Right out in the street."

"You spit in your cap?" I asked, citing common anti-hex practice.

"'Course," Ames said.

"New silk top-hatter." Hooks was almost aglow with good cheer. "Didn't help. Things got so bad the papers started calling Red 'the hoodoo hurler.'"

Ames shifted uncomfortably. "I got this tie from a Broadway star, plus the four-leaf clover." He pointed to the vial. "Wore it ever since. End of jinx."

"What star?" I asked.

"Diamond Lil," he wrote proudly on my pad. "I'm her favorite."

"You're damned ignorant is what you are," I told him, snapping the pencil point in my indignation. No doubt Lillian had pined for me, but she wouldn't stoop *that* low.

Art Devlin joined us and shook my hand. I'd always liked Art, who must be a steadying power on this young club. The four of us talked about old teammates, how Bresnahan was now the Cardinals skipper and others were managing in the bushes or, like me, playing there. I was sad to learn that our old first sacker, Dan McGann, had shot himself to death in Louisville the previous year.

"Three to one Dan died over a woman," Hooks said, which struck me as likely. Baseball Sadies had been the ruin of more than one ballplayer. Chick Stahl, over in the American League, had done himself in a few years back by drinking carbolic acid. The word soon spread that he'd been blackmailed by some floozie threatening to tell Chick's wife about their carrying on.

Not caring for that subject, I was glad when Hooks and Red set to groaning about the new corked ball introduced in the National League last season. The result had been a one-third jump in homers over the previous year. Even Matty had suffered. We agreed it was just one more low ploy by the owners to draw in fans and stuff their own wallets. What was the game coming to? How was an honest slabman to make a living?

"Speaking of Matty?" I asked, "where is he?"

"With McGraw," Ames said. "Lining up tomorrow's pitching."

A good time for me to see him, then. As I approached the compartment door, Matty emerged from it. Brown tweed suit, perfectly knotted tie, wavy dark blond hair parted in the middle. The Arrow Shirt Collar Man come to life. He looked older now and . . . what? . . . a trifle weary? But still with that magnetic power. I used to envy his golden looks and lion-trap brain and especially the way he attracted attention without even trying. But gradually I saw the mask he wore to keep from being eaten up by people. And the reserve he kept from just about everybody—oddly, one of the few he let come close was McGraw, a man about as different from him as humanly possible; for a time the newlywed Mathewsons had even moved into the McGraws'

Manhattan apartment building—and how Matty's aloofness set him further and further apart. The price he paid was too high, even for all the riches he got. One thing he liked about me was the same thing Lillian liked: I wouldn't go off and talk about him.

He saw me and his face lit up. "Heard you were here, Dummy," he signed, fingers fluid and sure as ever. "Good to see you." True to form, Matty hadn't settled for fingerspelling like the rest, but studied a book on Sign and spent hours drilling with me. "Been practicing?"

I knew he didn't mean baseball as he took an ebony case from his leather shoulder bag, and from that a small checkers kit. My competitive urge kicked in.

"I gotta see McGraw."

"Give him a minute; he's having a bite."

We played three matches, with predictable results. I'd seen Matty polish off state champions one after another, sometimes taking on six opponents simultaneously. Once on a dare he'd played blindfolded on three different boards—and won. He was damn near as good at golf and cards.

Matty used to say he liked to play me because he couldn't tell what I'd do next. His claim was that people play games the way they do everything else—the way they think, really. If so, he was a prime example, keeping me off balance while boosting his own position. And making it look easy. No wasted moves. I was a different story. I sized up opponents, too, but where Matty proceeded according to his theories, I went largely on hunch. Take my pitching windup: spinning, herky-jerky, the ball coming out of nowhere, hard for batsmen to pick up, seldom looking the same way twice. Matty's was *always* the same. He was so good, he could spot the ball where batsmen just couldn't do anything with it.

Except for the Athletics yesterday.

"I heard it was you who caught on to the mascot," he signed, as if he'd picked up the thought. "Was it me he was reading?"

"Couldn't be sure," I answered, tactfully.

"Will you watch me in warmups tomorrow?" A frown creased his forehead. "See if you spot something?"

I nodded, flattered. "Think you'll start?"

"Only in a pinch."

We both knew that in the past he could have come back on a day's rest. It wasn't just age. The famous fadeaway, with its unnatural counterclockwise motion, had sapped his arm. Normally he'd use it only half a dozen times in a game, but the Athletics had forced him to it far more.

"Going on stage this winter?" I asked, to change the subject. Last year he'd done a cowboy vaudeville skit in which he rescued the fair maiden from a savage redskin, played, of course, by Meyers. From all accounts it was awful. I'd read somewhere that Matty was mortified when audiences laughed during the climax, but I doubted it. He'd done it for the money, the same reason Ty Cobb was currently touring everywhere, play-acting a gridiron hero, of all things. People were willing to fork out to see their sporting idols in action. Any kind of action, it seemed.

"Might not have time," he answered. "We'll be in Cuba a whole month."

"We . . . ?"

"The team."

I stared at him, a heaviness stealing over me.

Cuba. . . .

In '04 there'd been talk of going to Havana to make up for money we lost when McGraw refused to play Boston in the World Series. In '08 it came up again after the Cubs stole the pennant, but Matty had other commitments, and without him it was no deal. The last couple of years, the Tigers and A's had gone down there and taken lickings from the Cubans. Now the Giants were going, and if I knew McGraw, it wouldn't be to lose. Why the hell did I miss everything? I took a deep breath and stood up.

"Shopping a prospect?" Matty asked. Ex-players could pick up scouting fees by bird-dogging talent in the bushes, but it would have to be a rare prospect to attract McGraw's attention during the Series.

I waggled my fist, telling him "yes," then hooked a thumb at myself. He grinned and said, "Good luck."

The contrast between Mathewson and McGraw struck me again as I entered the latter's compartment. Matty was tall and fair and well-proportioned, moderate in his habits, including speech. McGraw was fat and pugnacious, foul-mouthed, quick to sound off and slow to forgive anything he took as a slight—which covered a lot of territory.

His hair had grayed and thinned since I'd last seen him without a cap. His face was heavier and his skin blotchy. Up close he looked drained, a far cry from the field leader in nonstop motion. His blue-slitted eyes regarded me with no apparent affection as he nudged a yellow tablet forward. On it he'd printed: *"What was the idea of that stunt with Lillian?"*

A typical McGraw tactic: strike first to get the upper hand. I felt my hackles rising, at the same time wishing that she hadn't called him Muggsy.

"Why'd you give me Cohan's seat?" I countered.

"The sonofabitch bet against us—and he's Irish!" McGraw glared at me. He had a reputation for helping ex-players, especially ones down on their luck, but I guess they'd had to come crawling. He beckoned impatiently for me to state my business. This wasn't going the way I'd wanted.

"Good win today," I ventured.

"Doyle missed the fucking plate."

I nodded. "I think Klem saw it."

"Mack saw it too."

"How come didn't he send Lapp back?"

"Because it would have set off a fucking riot!" He glanced at a clock on the wall beside me. So much for chitchat.

"My arm's back, like I told you," I wrote. "All the way back."

His mouth twisted in a skeptical grimace.

"Ask McGinnity, he'll tell you." Twice in the season's final weeks I'd whitewashed my old pal's Newark club.

"I heard about it." McGraw cocked a hip against a writing table. Evidently we weren't going to sit. "As for the Eastern League—" I thought I detected a sneer—"I've got my eye on Tesreau. He's got both size *and* years on you, Dummy."

McGraw's love for big hurlers was no secret. Matty, McGinnity, Marquard, Wiltse, and me—six-footers all. Jeff Tesreau, a big spit-balling cowboy who threw for Toronto, was cut from the same mold.

"I'm here," I told him. "Tesreau's not. Let me show you what I've got."

"A tryout *now?*" McGraw's throat worked with what I guessed was laughter. "During the Series?"

"How about before the game tomorrow?" I persisted.

"You mean, put you in uniform?"

I hadn't thought of that. The notion of wearing that black uniform again brought odd tingles to my spine, but I doubted McGraw would go that far. Well, okay, maybe it would look funny, me on the field pitching in my street clothes. But why not? It would only be for 20 minutes.

"Dummy, you just want that turn you missed in '05, you think I don't know it? You think you're the only one to come around craving one more taste? To do whatever you didn't quite get done before?" He leaned closer, his breath heavy with onions and liquor. "How many of us know when to quit? Hell, I made the same mistake myself. Tried to play beyond when I could."

It didn't come out that neat in his jumble of Sign and fingerspelling, but that was his message. I felt like he'd slipped the casters out from under me, reading me so shrewdly. But I'd come too far to fold up. "I just want my job back," I scrawled on his sheet; then, bolder: "And by God I'll *get* that missing turn next year in the Series!"

He grinned and shook his head at my doggedness. Then something else came into his face, a hint of another McGraw: kind-hearted and loyal—qualities that surfaced when he was away from the diamond and not drinking. "Okay, come see me in Marlin next spring."

Which was better, but still a put-off. How could I be with the Montreal club, which owned me, and simultaneously at the Giants Texas training camp? The only way was for him to buy my contract, as he probably intended to buy Tesreau's.

"Just a quick look-see early tomorrow?"

"You know better. This is business, Dummy, not a sideshow."

I thought it was a game.

"Afterward?"

He shook his head, no longer grinning.

I'd already swallowed my pride; there wasn't much more to lose. "C-U-B-A," I spelled slowly.

He looked at it questioningly.

"Let me come and pitch for you."

"It's for *this* year's team," he said with a frown. "We're taking the wives."

"Everybody's going?" I'd seen in the papers that Marquard had a rich vaudeville contract. "You sure you got enough arms?"

"Dummy, goddamn but you're stubborn! I can't afford anybody else!"

"I'll pay my own way." It came out through my fingers almost before I had the thought.

He looked at me from underneath his eyebrows, and I read his lips as he said, "I gotta admit, the Cubans would get a helluva bang out of you."

What will I say to Della if he agrees?

He shook his head abruptly. "But there's no use boosting your hopes."

When I was nine I'd wanted a wheel of my own instead of sharing Sim's. I'd begged Pa for one for Christmas. Years later I realized the spot it put him in. Money was short. On Christmas morning there had been no new bike. I felt like that boy again. Except this time I didn't sulk, but turned up the pressure.

Wed 7/23/02

That's what I wrote on his tablet. On that day in Brooklyn I'd gotten McGraw his first win as Giants manager. I'd outpitched Jimmy Hughes of the Superbas, a much stronger club. A softness in his face told me that he remembered. He'd been playing then, and the newsboys still called him "Johnny" McGraw. Another memorable thing had happened that day: Jefferies and Fitzsimmons fought their rematch, and rumors had it that McGraw made a pile of dough. Maybe *that's* what he was recalling so fondly.

"I think you owe me this chance."

His face tightened. McGraw didn't care to hear what he owed anybody. On the sheet he drew a large dollar sign, pointed at me, and held up eight fingers, one for each of my years with the team. The meaning was clear: I'd been paid for my efforts.

Then he stepped closer and pointed to a flattened, bulging place on his nose. In the spring of '03 I'd uncorked a heave from the outfield and to my horror saw the ball go straight for McGraw, who was throwing to the hitters. I tried to yell for him to duck, but whatever came out of my mouth made him turn instead—and the ball crashed square into his face. A blood vessel broke in his throat and he bled a scary amount while we carried him to a hospital. He'd suffered sinus and upper respiratory damage. I knew he wasn't fishing for an apology now—I'd given him plenty at the time—but to show that debts between us were two-way. Therefore, cancelled.

That was it. I had no more. I'd thrown my best stuff.

"If anything changes. . . ." he said with a dismissive shrug.

I nodded and left. No bike this year.

Mathewson looked up from a pamphlet titled *Inside Dope on the Wall Street Market*. Earlier that year I'd read about him selling his Reading Railroad stock and pocketing a neat $75,000. His Giants salary topped ten grand. Some people had it all. I plopped down next to him and told him what had transpired.

"Your arm's sound again?"

"Like a gold dollar."

"It'd be good to have you back, Dummy." He gave my shoulder a sympathetic pat. "Tell you what. I'll put in a word for you first chance."

I felt like pointing out that all he had to do was go through McGraw's door to have his chance. But I knew it would just piss McGraw off. And even though Matty had the manager's ear like nobody else, he hadn't seen me pitch in three years. Worst of all, lacking a tryout, he wasn't going to.

———— • ◆ • ————

MY ROOM AT the Majestic was compliments of the Giants, so I figured I might as well stick around for next day's contest. In the lobby I saw a group of the younger players heading out for a show. For an instant I thought of joining them. Then I caught a glimpse of Herzog and decided it wasn't worth the effort. After nursing a nickel beer with Hooks in the hotel bar, I fell asleep in my room over *The Man Who Could Not Lose,* Richard Harding Davis's new book. I hoped it might apply to me, but I didn't get far enough to find out.

Next morning I positioned myself behind the dugout during pregame drills at Shibe. McGraw could hardly miss me there. Somehow he managed to, though, even when I made a big show of watching Mathewson for tipoffs. Which I didn't find.

Early in the game, McGraw had the Giants batsmen taking everything, on the theory that Bender, pitching on just one day's rest, would wear out. I saw the pitcher's lips moving as he stared in at the hitters, and learned later that we were ragging him pretty good. Bender, usually taciturn, was giving it back. A poor idea to rile him, I thought, but things got off to a promising start for us when Doyle doubled and scored in the first.

Red Ames held the A's in check until the fourth, when two hits and three errors—the worst coming on a bunt play when Red nailed the runner in the back of the head and the ball caromed into right—added up to four runs. Hooks took over, but the onslaught continued. Bender, meanwhile, stopped throwing strikes on first pitches as soon as he realized that McGraw had reversed himself and ordered the Giants to swing early. Bender ended up with a four-hitter and a 13–2 victory. A masterful, gutty showing. As for McGraw, he disappeared from the field some innings before it was over.

The perfect finish, I thought sourly.

My pass got me into the A's clubhouse, where champagne flew in airy spumes. Bender sat quietly in the midst of it all, a towel wrapped around his shoulder, looking tired and proud all at once.

I wrote *"Congratulations, Charley"* and handed him my pad. Bender was an interesting mix, his father a Minnesota German Quaker, his mother a Chippewa. Like Meyers he was educated, in his case at the Carlisle School. Before the '05 Series they'd pulled the two of us together for a feature layout ("Pathfinder vs. Lip-Reader") that made us out to be natural-born sign stealers. The truth was, Bender and I *were* damned good at it, but not because of any inborn knack. We paid sharp attention to details and took pains to remember and study them.

"Hell of a game today," I told him. "You deserve it."

He smiled and took my pencil. "Thanks, Luther."

"You gonna retire on all that rich land?" I'd seen in *Sporting News* that Bender's tribe was in line to get a sizable chunk of territory.

"No such thing as rich land in Oklahoma." His neat handwriting put my slouching scrawl to shame. Same as our flinging styles: him smooth as oil, me a jumping jack. He gave me an unreadable look, his chestnut eyes holding a question; then he wrote, "Did they say nice things up there about Johnny?"

It took me a second to make the connection. Bender's younger brother had collapsed and died on the mound the previous month while pitching for Edmonton in the Western Canada League. The word was that he lacked Charley's amazing talent. It was an eerie parallel to Mathewson's younger brother, who'd shot himself to death a few years ago. He also pitched in the minors, and folks said he looked like Matty. Maybe it was just too hard to follow after a star in your own family.

"He got real good writeups," I lied. Mostly they'd retold how John Bender was suspended from ball for a year after chasing his manager with a knife. A good many thought he shouldn't have been let back in at all. "I'm sorry, Charley."

Bender nodded, face impassive.

"Gotta see my pals." I pointed toward the visitors dressing room. "Enjoy your fat Series share."

His lips curled in a smile. "Those New York boys will pocket more losing to us than you did beating us."

The hell of it was, he was probably right.

"Hear they're going to Havana," he added.

I nodded glumly.

"Like to get down again myself," he wrote. "Enjoyed a warm time there last winter."

I stood up to go, then turned back. "Oh yeah, what was it your hunchback was reading off Matty?"

Bender looked startled. "Little Van? Why, nothing, Luther, nothing at all."

A foxy gleam in his eyes told me he was lying. And why should he tell me? I shook his hand again and made my way to the losers' room, where things weren't as gloomy as I'd expected. McGraw's kids had taken a licking from Mack's top-salaried veterans, but they figured to be back. For them the future must look like nothing but peaches.

McGraw and Mathewson weren't around. I said goodbye to Ames, Wiltse and Devlin. They seemed quieter than the others—chances were they *wouldn't* be back for another Series. Devlin looked up sharply while we were talking. I followed his gaze across the room, where Herzog was yelling something and pointing at me. Probably saying I had no business being there. Devlin's jaw tightened and he was about to answer, but I took his arm and signed that it was okay, I was leaving anyway.

Outside, darkness was settling, but people still thronged the streets. Blue pennants with white elephants and WORLD CHAMPIONS 1911 waved everywhere. In a silent world all my own, I passed through the groups of revelers, a mime show on a grand scale, and recalled that McGraw had been responsible for that elephant. Back when the American League was still struggling to get off the ground, he'd made the crack that the Philadelphia club would be its white elephant. Today it had come back to haunt him.

Waiting at North Station for the next westbound train, I couldn't help reflecting that McGraw seemed to be everywhere. He'd controlled my life for years, and now, in a way, he still was. I looked around, thinking that I wouldn't be here again. Across from me, a young couple looked about to quarrel. The man was clutching one of the victory pennants and studying a sporting paper while his wife or sweetheart tried to talk to him. He finally crumpled the paper in exasperation and said, his lips framing the words unmistakably, "Yes, dear, you're right, baseball *is* over!"

Indeed, I thought.

The big leagues, anyway.

For me.

FOUR

Olathe,

1958

The ball on the table was yellowed with age, but staring at it brought back that sweltering, sticky afternoon in Chicago as if it had been only last month. Fourth day of August, 1904. A rare Thursday doubleheader. They'd managed to climb atop the standings for the first time, but their hardbitten rivals, the Cubs, were making a run at them. After dropping the opener they'd had to face Mordecai "Three–Finger" Brown, their nemesis, in the second game. McGraw took him aside and signed that he had to hold them off long enough for them to find a way to win.

A smile played on his lips.

It had been his best day in the bigs.

Holding the Cubs to five scratch hits, he'd let only two runners get as far as second. Brown matched him pitch for pitch until finally the Chicagos' fielding game blew up under late-inning pressure, and the Giants scored. From the mound he speared two liners, one halfway behind his back, and fielded the tough bunts they laid down late, figuring he'd wither in the blast-furnace heat. He went all the way, winning 3–0, and after that they sailed to the pennant, McGraw's first with the Giants.

Squinting his eyes, he wondered if one of those scuffs was from where Donlin had slammed an outshoot against the fence boards that day. Or if any of the discolored spots still held tiny grains of dirt that Bresnahan had ground in, to help him with his hurler's grip?

Dirt. . . .

His thoughts floated from the Cubs ballgrounds to the little piece of Kansas that Della had wanted so bad. That ball represented the whole difference between them: her wanting him at home, tied to their property; him aching to be off in distant cities, breezing a seamed sphere past opponents with cunning and power. . . .

FIVE

DELLA PECKED MY cheek and stepped back to give me a view of her new print dress and shoes that lifted her heels an inch off the floor. Her hair was piled up on her head. Something about her eyes looked different. I stared in astonishment at my wife.

"Well?" she asked.

"You look . . . real nice."

For dessert she served lemon meringue pie but had none herself. By then I'd noticed that she'd dropped some pounds. In fact, she was looking comelier than she had in years, and when we made love that night she seemed agreeably surprised by my enthusiasm.

But my pleasure at her new look was cut sharply the next morning when I spotted the business card resting on our mantel. There was a photograph on it, and I recognized him even before reading the name: Owen Harpenning, an up-and-comer at the local bank. His features were regular, with sandy hair and eyes that I remembered were cornflower blue. The little smile and direct gaze suggested that you could trust him with all your worldly goods.

I wouldn't. Not for a split-second.

"What's this here for?" I demanded.

Della took a breath, then signed, "Owen and I are discussing the property next door."

Owen and I?

"You mean, he's been out here while I was away?"

"You're *always* away, Lu."

Things proceeded to heat up between us as it developed that Mr. Harpenning had driven out in his new tan Studebaker, big as life, and been treated to lunch. More than once. I couldn't pry the exact number out of her.

"Why's he been sniffing around here?"

"He wasn't 'sniffing,'" she replied. "Owen happens to be involved in several real estate dealings. He thinks he knows a way we might be able to finance that land."

"I don't *want* any goddamn land!" The more I thought about her going behind my back and him sitting his fancy-pants banker's butt on my kitchen chair, the madder I got. Double-talking bastards like Harpenning were the ones who'd foreclosed on my folks.

And she'd gotten her hair done!

As if all that wasn't bad enough, I found out from Sim later that Della had gone riding in the Studebaker. Some of Hattie Mae's church group had seen them heading out of town together. That tore it. I left the store early and practically melted the Chalmers's tires racing home.

"It was my idea, not his," she signed calmly, looking not the least bit abashed. "I asked Owen to motor me over to a seminar on crop rotation at the school in Olathe. That's all there was to it, but if you want to think otherwise, go ahead."

"Crop rotation?"

"Yes." She smiled. "It was part of a signed series on new farming methods."

"If you were so damn hot to catch it," I signed, working my fingers practically in her face, "why didn't you ask Sim?"

"I did!" she fired back. "He was busy, and you may remember that Hattie Mae doesn't drive." Unexpressed but hanging between us was, *And you weren't here.*

By then I was so beside myself I could barely see, much less think right. "If he comes out here again," I blustered, "I'll put his nose through to the back of his head."

She gave me a pitying look, which made me even madder.

I caught up with home repairs, spelled Sim at the store, and let Oscar Blake try to talk me into investing in his new self-adjusting shirt. Oscar claimed he was going to revolutionize men's fashions with it, right there from his Baldwin factory.

NO BULGING OUT OR BREAKING WHEN SITTING DOWN, his ads read. ONCE WORN, YOU WILL HAVE NO OTHER. He took my measurements and had a shirt made up. I had to admit that it lived up to what he said. A cloth strap and buckle cinched it close in back, and rubberized stays hooked inside your pants to keep it down when you stood or let it stretch when you sat.

Della's gooseberry pie snagged a blue ribbon at the Vinland Grange Fair. Seeing that her mood was high, I tried to warm the freeze between us by showing off the shirt. It didn't take her much more than a glance to judge the whole rig stiff and unnatural. She sniffed at the buckle in back and thought it doubtful that people would want to hook it every time they got dressed. Nor were they likely to go to the fuss of filling out their "Self-Instruction Measuring Blanks"—if they bothered sending for them in the first place.

So much for Oscar's grand scheme.

At least the two of us were talking again.

I thought I'd settled into home life in decent style, but several times she asked why I was drawn up into myself. I'd explained what happened on the trip, of course, and she sympathized but seemed to regard it as a closed issue. I'd made my pitch to McGraw. He'd turned me down. So move on. Above all, Della was practical. In her view I was able to make a living at what I loved, so what was the trouble? When that was finished there would be the store in Baldwin, or whatever else I wanted to try. She had the good sense not to mention farming.

"I'm good enough to be at the top again," I argued. *That's* what I want."

To Della, for whom the notion of working anywhere busier than Topeka was a nightmare, the distinction just wasn't important. "You're 36, Lu. At most it'd be a year or two. You're taking all this a mite hard."

"I want it, Del."

She tried to look sympathetic, but I knew she didn't really understand. And maybe I didn't either. The real problem seemed to lie deeper, and even with all the words and signs ever invented, I probably couldn't have expressed it.

The thing was, I'd never failed at anything. You'd think, born deaf, that I'd had more than my share of setbacks. Not so. I was raised to go for anything I wanted. Ma used to say that living on the prairie, where horizons stretched to the sky, meant we shouldn't put boundaries on our dreams; us deaf ones were never made to feel more restricted than our hearing brothers and sisters. Everybody made sure I studied hard. I'd taken early to reading—books carried me to places beyond Kansas—and school was always easy. I'd been a star athlete for as long as I could remember, and of course that opened a lot of doors. At every level of competition I'd succeeded.

Hurting my arm had given me a ready excuse for not doing so well. But now that excuse was gone, and for the first time I'd hit a barrier I couldn't get past on my own. If McGraw wouldn't take a chance on me, who in the majors would? Maybe if I burned up the Eastern League next year I'd be bought by somebody. Maybe. But my age was against me.

For the first time I was having to face limits. Not to mention the question of what to do with my life once baseball was over. I didn't have any answers. All I seemed to have was a gnawing pit of fearfulness that I could scarcely admit to myself, much less to Della or anybody else. Just the vague awareness of it made me edgy. I had no idea what to do—except keep busy.

The weather was colder but still clear. Almost every day I'd get the itch to throw, just to prove my arm was still there. At noon I took to stopping by the Baldwin *Bee,* an upstart rival to the *Ledger.* I liked its folksy masthead: *The People's Newspaper—Knows No Clique.* Mort Jenkins, the burly farmboy who caught for the high school team, worked there as a printer's devil. Sim had no trouble persuading him to work with me; Mort's boss counted it an honor. Without fail, Sim came out to kibitz and call balls and strikes on imaginary batsmen. Once I was warmed up and firing, the ball jerked Mort's mitt backward. I knew it made a loud sound because people came over, curious as to the cause. I never failed to signal before delivering breaking balls, but even so, one time I got some real mustard on my drop. It plummeted beneath Mort's glove as if swatted down by an invisible hand, bounced up and caught him in the nuts, knocked him flat, and whooshed the wind out of him. When he could talk again, he said to Sim, "Mr. Taylor, I ain't never seen nothin' like *that!*"

Agreeable praise, even from a raw youth.

It became a daily show. Folks gathered behind the backstop where they could see the ball move, their mouths forming "oohs" and "ahs." I brought out a bat, more balls, and fed straight tosses to Sim and Mort, one catching while the other hit. A squad of eager boys shagged in the

field. I took a few whacks myself. Back in '08 I'd lifted my average over
.200 for the first time as a Giant. I used to calculate that in another twenty
years I'd be right up there with Dutch Wagner and Wildfire Schulte.

The workouts took me back to old times with the family, the Taylor
boys putting on a display. Pa caught for us even when his eyes gave out
and balls left welts on his arms. He never quit. One of my biggest
regrets was that he and Ma hadn't lived long enough to see me pitch in
New York and hear 20,000 people yelling their deaf son's name.

Once Mort got used to me, I was able to work my full stock of
pitches: a blazer that sneaked down and in on righty hitters; an outshoot that broke away from righties at different angles, depending on
my grip; and my bread and butter, a ball that dropped straight down
toward China. I called the last one "Dundon," after Ed Dundon, who
pitched back in the '80s for Columbus of the old Association. Later in
life Dundon used to travel around giving exhibitions, and in Baltimore
he taught his drop pitch to a deaf kid named George Leitner. George
grew up to be my pitching mate on the Giants. Believe it or not, there
were three of us deaf flingers on that team in 1901. The other was Billy
Deegan of New York. They called *all* of us Dummy! We were together
just a few months—the others weren't able to hang on—but the times
we had! Anyway, Dummy Leitner taught the pitch to me, and from the
first I thought it was pure pie. My big hands and over-the-top delivery
made me a natural for it, and I worked hard to perfect it. So my best
pitch had descended, so to speak, from a line of deaf flingers. I took
pride in that.

Mort got pretty snappy at handling them all, and I could tell he was
starting to think he was a budding big leaguer. One day, after whack-
ing my practice tosses around the lot, he took to acting chesty and
yelling, "Throw me some *real* stuff! I'll knock the cover off!"

I looked at Sim, who, after translating, grinned slyly, nodded, adjusted his mask and snugged his wind pad (chest protector) up under his chin. My arm felt loose and good. Sim signaled for Dundon right off. I twirled and let it go. Mort swung so hard that his twisting spikes nearly carved out the beginnings of a new well beside the plate—but he missed the ball by a foot. "Strike!" Sim yelled. Then I treated Mort to a bender that started out at his head and darted down a full yard to cut the plate in half while his knees were buckling and he was ducking sideways. "Strike two!" Sim called. Shaking his head, Mort laid the bat across the plate with a rueful look, his dreams of the big leagues considerably diminished. I felt a tinch guilty, but he'd asked for a taste of the real thing, hadn't he?

———— •◆• ————

MONTE CROMER SHOWED up one day to peer through the backstop's wire mesh as my fastballs poured into Mort's mitt. He kept his mouth sort of pulled down, as if he didn't think too much of the display. Sim turned from his umpire's spot to give him a dirty look, and I knew why: Monte had printed a paragraph about my "pipe dream" of pitching for McGraw again, as if I'd been the one to say it instead of him when he interviewed me. So I guess he couldn't let himself be impressed now. Sim knew, from Hattie Mae, that Monte's wife had been one of those whispering about Della.

I paused for a second to wipe my brow. Thinking I was done in, Monte got a smirky look on his mug. Time, I decided, to make a bigger impression on him. I signed to Sim, who bent over Mort and whispered. I wound up and fired a high one that zipped, as planned, through the space between Mort's upreached hands and over Sim, who ducked. Bowerman and I had pulled it once on an ump giving us nothing but crap for calls. The ball whacked his mask so hard that his false teeth fell out, causing Bowerman to nearly croak from laughing.

This one slammed into the mesh exactly where I intended. A cloud of rust and dust sprayed back in Monte's face, and he disappeared from sight as his knees buckled, his fingers lost their grip on the screen, and he sat down hard in the dirt. Mort said later that he squealed like a shoat. Sim made a production of helping him up, winking at me all the while. The mesh was bent back in a cup shape where the ball hit, and the others there came over to touch it.

Monte didn't wait long to try to strike back. As we were packing up he walked out to the mound with his notebook. "How's Della?" he wrote. "I hear she's doing some heavy banking."

"She was looking to finance something through Owen Harpenning," I wrote back, trying to seem nonchalant, "but that was a while back."

"Sure." Monte smiled. "Owen's out of town just now."

I hadn't known that, and the whole thing was getting under my skin again. "Well, when he gets back, pay him a visit," I wrote. "See, Del and I figured how to wicker him down cheaper than his bank advertises. Owen's a reasonable man. Once we showed him how much extra his bank was raking in, he agreed that it was robbery and decided to come down a whole percentage point and more for local folks."

Monte's face was suspicious and calculating.

"So if you want a good deal on a new car or the like, ask Owen for the "special" rate. He'll know exactly what you mean. Maybe you ought to print a little article on it."

He read what I'd written, read it again, then turned, frowning, and walked away.

———— • ◆ • ————

WE COULD SMELL the season's first snow coming two days before it blanketed Baldwin. Della was excited but I felt trapped. We got into an even bigger fight than our last one, at first over some trivial thing, finally over having kids. Fingers flying, she told me that she'd been willing in recent years, so I couldn't try to use that over her any longer. But even her sign for "willing," hand flat on the chest, then outward with palm up—it can also signify one heart open to another—seemed more of a thrust, a challenge. I denied ever using anything over her. Our hands whirled and brandished, our faces twisted in anger. If I didn't want to be there, Della demanded, then why didn't I just leave?

"So you can see *him*?" I signed. "You got another dress picked out for when *he* gets back?"

Her eyes narrowed and her fingers clenched before furiously signing, "You'll pay to God for that!" It was the closest she ever came to cussing. She stamped off and was back seconds later waving a newspaper cutout in my face: a wire photo of the chorus girl I'd carried on with—the picture that got me found out. Discovering that she'd kept it hidden away like a weapon raised my hackles higher.

"I'm NOT dallying with Owen Harpenning!" she signed furiously. "I would NEVER do such a thing! YOU'RE the one who dallied!"

She started to cry. Women use tears as their biggest weapon. I did something cruel then: just as she started to say something else, I reached over and turned off the gas lamp. The room plunged into darkness and communication ended.

Well, not quite.

Something hit the wall beside my head—the shock of it felt like a baseball slamming a plank—and I was sprayed with liquid and pieces of glass. I hurriedly relit the lamp and realized that she'd tossed a vase. She threw hard, too, which I well knew since I'd taught her. Half of me was shocked; the other half was suddenly sort of tickled. I went over and tried to stroke her hair and pat her shoulder, but she pulled back.

"You thick dolt," she signed, face streaked with tears. "Can't you see anything? It wasn't Owen I was trying to attract, Lu. It was you . . . my own husband!" She buried her face in her hands and wouldn't let me touch her.

It took a moment or two for me to digest it. Then, feeling about as high as a snake, I tried to convince her that home with her was where I wanted to be. She didn't believe me. To tell the truth, I wasn't sure I believed myself. Finally she shut herself in the bedroom, leaving me the davenport to sleep on. From time to time I'd feel her tread on the floor, and think how it didn't seem nearly as heavy as before, and how she'd gone to such trouble to look pretty again.

For me.

Around four in the morning, I stood staring out the window at the falling flakes. Did they make a noise? I tried to imagine what it might be like. To put yourself in my place, try to picture colors you've never seen. Whole new colors different from all others. It was like that for me, except harder, because I'd never experienced *any* sound.

I wasn't much of a churchgoer, except when Ma or Della dragged me, but at that moment I felt so bad that I said a sort of prayer to the snow. I asked for a sign, some direction to follow, something to ease my discontent.

———— • ◆ • ————

NEXT MORNING THE telegram arrived. My snow prayer couldn't have been the cause, since the message was already on its way, but I had no trouble taking it for what I'd wanted.

N.Y. WED NOV 15 1911 - STOP -   WE ARRIVE FLORIDA FRI - STOP -
YOU PITCH MIAMI TUES - STOP -   IF YOU WIN GO HAVANA - STOP -
STAY CUBA THRU DEC 18 - STOP -   I COVER HALF - STOP -   THANK
MATTY - STOP - MCGRAW

I read it again, brain heating up, heart thumping. I'd get my chance after all! I jumped in the air and pumped my fist. It wasn't until after the first rush of pleasure faded that I began to realize just how cut-rate the offer was. "Cover half" meant McGraw wouldn't pay me a salary, and I'd have to fork out for the other half of my travel and lodging. Assuming I won in Miami, that is. What if I didn't? Would he cover nothing? Just tell me to go back home? And thank Matty for what? McGraw made it look like he was reluctantly doing me a big favor. More likely some of his pitchers had dropped out and left him in a tight spot. From every angle the offer bordered on insult, the sort of treatment bushers got.

I wanted it in the worst way.

And McGraw knew that.

I'd need to leave that day, a fact I tried my damndest to break gently to Della. She didn't cry again, though her eyes were swollen. She signed that she understood, that there was no question but that I should grab at this chance. Her right forefinger hooked downward and circled rapidly around her left forefinger. Her hands were trembling and they were saying that I *must* go.

I stared at her, trying to figure out what she meant. Her eyes, green-flecked and hazel, so familiar and so unknown just then, held mine for a long moment. My own feelings had sorted themselves out—I'd lost most of my resentment about Owen—but I couldn't have begun to read hers. Finally she went into the bedroom and returned with a string-tied package. "For Christmas," she signed.

"I'll be back before then," I protested, and handed her the telegram showing a week's travel time before the holiday. The fact was, I hadn't even begun thinking about a Christmas gift for her.

"You can use it on your trip."

I cut the string and the paper fell away; a carton was stamped, CON-LEY STEREO BOX CAMERA.

"I ordered it last July, when you got traded to Montreal," she explained. "So you could take pictures next season and we'd look at them together." Della loved stereopticon views; their depths made her feel she could step into them. Not looking at me, she traced with her fingers the camera's features: a rustproof shutter; a "T" dial for time exposures; a compact case, easier to carry in my valise than the larger bellows models. "Will you take a picture of the moon over the sea?" she signed. "For me?"

I pulled her hard against me and felt her shoulders trembling.

"How about coming?"

She blinked, her eyes wet. "Will Blanche McGraw be there?"

"McGraw said wives, so I'd think yes."

"Jane Mathewson?"

"Sure, to keep Blanche company."

"I like them."

"Then come, Del."

"It'd cost too much."

"We can afford it."

She took a breath, then shook her head resolutely. "I'd feel out of place, Lu," she signed. "Honestly, I'd rather take care of things here."

With Owen Harpenning? Don't think about that.

I told her I understood. Truth was, I felt more relieved than anything else. What I hoped to pull off in the coming month would be hard enough without worrying about her.

"I just hope . . . " she began, hands hovering uncertainly by her cheeks. In that moment I could see the girl she had been, with honey-colored hair and perfect skin and deep brown eyes that looked at me with such love.

"Yes?"

Her eyes lifted and met mine. " . . . that you'll want to come back home again to me."

———— • ◆ • ————

"TAKE THIS." Sim handed me a cloth sack as we stood on the station platform. Inside were pennyroyal leaves, to ward off mosquitos, and a length of red flannel with black tie-cords on each end. "Hattie made it for me in '98," he explained. "Yellow fever's mostly whipped by now, but you never know."

Then I recognized it: a bellyband. When the state raised four regiments to fight Spain, Kansas women had knitted them by the hundreds for their sweethearts and brothers and sons. The color red was supposed to have medicinal power, and the idea was to keep your body warmth in, especially at night when tropical miasmas carried all manner of pestilences and intestine-knotting scourges.

Promising I'd wear it, especially out in the countryside, I searched his face for hints of jealousy. As a boy, Sim had filled scrapbooks with pictures of yachts and sunlit oceans and palm-lined beaches. His chance to see the romantic Caribbean had come thirteen years ago, when he joined the "Fighting" Kansas 20th with visions of going to Cuba to avenge the sinking of the *U.S.S. Maine*. But his outfit was sent to the Philippines instead.

In November '99 they'd returned to a heroes' welcome in Topeka, where thousands turned out. I'd gone and seen the whole grand works: a military parade with dozens of brass bands, the massed blue-clad soldiers swelled by units of National Guard and G.A.R., and led by General Funston himself, a tiny bemedaled man sitting with his wife in a carriage drawn by splendid black horses flanked by Filipinos in native costume. Six of the returnees were Baldwin boys, and the orange hats and sweaters of Baldwin University students made a bold swash in the throng. That night fireworks shot into the sky and cannons shook the ground.

I admired Sim tremendously. I'd known ballplaying heroics, but he'd gone into the world and risked his life for freedom's cause. What I didn't know was that the fighting in the Philippines had been a far cry from his old romantic dreams, or from the Cuban campaigns described so raptly in all the papers.

A year or so after his return, we got drunk one night and he poured it all out. Nightmares had been plaguing him and he needed to talk to somebody. What happened was that Aguinaldo's rebels, opposed to us replacing the Spaniards over them—one tyrant for another, they figured—resorted to increasingly bloody tactics, men and boys calling the Americans *"amigo"* in daylight and murdering them at night. Retaliation was swift and vicious. Both sides used torture, and few prisoners survived. The worst came when the Kansas 20th stormed the shipping center of Caloocan, gunning down Filipinos of all ages and torching the city; few of its 17,000 inhabitants lived to see the next day.

The army put clamps on the press, of course, but a few soldiers wrote home about it, and the Anti-Imperialist League printed their letters. That was about the time Sim told me of the massacre. He never brought it up again, and, except for saying once that it'd be something to see the new canal being dug through Panama, he showed no further interest in foreign travel. Baldwin became his world. Like his dream of becoming a ballplayer, the reality had proved ugly. By now I was the brother who'd seen more of the world. I was the one still playing ball. And I was the one going to Havana.

"I'll write you about everything," I signed, thinking that if he felt any resentment, he was hiding it expertly.

"Just lick the Cubans!" He enfolded me in a hug that nearly lifted me off my feet. "There'll be time to tell me afterward."

We were both assuming I'd get as far as Cuba. First, though, there was the little chore of proving myself in Florida.

———— • ◆ • ————

STORMS HIT ALONG the route, bringing long delays while snow-removing equipment cleared the tracks. I was stranded for two days in Atlanta. Having no idea where the Giants were staying, I sent telegrams to "Miami Ball Grounds" and got no reply. My spirits sank with the realization that I wouldn't make my pitching date. Still, I wasn't about to quit.

The nasty weather stopped at the Florida border as if outlawed beyond. Sparkling sunshine illuminated a landscape the likes of which I'd never seen: mangrove swamps, scrub palmetto, coral outcroppings, dunes covered with sea oats that waved and rippled in every breeze.

Miami was a bustling little town with huge booster dreams, a drummer's paradise. The longest wooden bridge I could imagine was being built to connect the town with Miami Beach, a bug-infested island currently reached by ferries. Tracts of new houses in rainbow colors were springing up everywhere like fields of flowers, and deluxe hotels were racing to open in anticipation of streams of tourists.

"Lavish residential colony," and "winter playground" said promotional puffs thrust at me on the station dock. Walking around, I saw traffic cops in sky-blue uniforms with white belts and helmets, and passed a group of Seminoles selling beadware, several of whom were blonde and resembled no Indians I'd ever seen. The sun seemed more brilliant here than in Kansas. I felt as if I'd stepped into a yellower, stickier world.

Wednesday morning, November 23: the day after I was supposed to pitch. A newsstand had yesterday's late edition, which told me that the Giants had enjoyed several days of hunting and fishing while their wives shopped the town's stores. A big turnout had been expected for the game.

Who the hell had pitched?

I questioned the ticket-seller, who didn't know about the contest, but pointed to a hotel across the street with Moorish domes and green awnings and told me the team had stayed there before leaving earlier this morning.

"For Cuba?"

"Key West," he answered. "Some of our boys went along; they're playing down there next."

"Can I get there today?"

"Rails don't go all the way yet. Tomorrow morning's the best you can do. Want a boat-train ticket?"

An hour later I was on another coal-burner, rumbling along the sunny seacoast and stopping every ten minutes (so it seemed) to take on fuel and water. At Florida City I was directed to the Peninsula & Occidental Steamship Line pier, where I boarded a steam packet. In the waning light of sunset I stared out at the distant keys, low green islands that looked painted on the water, and willed the steamer to move faster. After a few hours of fitful sleep I was on deck again, long before we steamed into port at sunrise.

Key West was a sleepy place: a big coral island with exotic vegetation and salt-streaked sponge and fish docks. A rust-streaked freighter with round tin rat guards clamped on its cables was being loaded by Negro stevedores. During the Spanish war, Key West had swelled to bursting with Cuba-bound boys, but things had long since calmed down. Cigar factories circled the docks and fisheries. Beyond them houses rose above the coral on stilts, a guard against hurricane-whipped waves.

I toted my valise up Duval Street in search of La Concha Hotel, where, according to the steamer captain, I'd find the players if they were still here. Sweating in the morning heat, I approached the desk with a note already written. I didn't need it. On the far side of the lobby I spotted Art Fletcher, the Giants shortstop, slumped beneath a potted palm, studying a copy of *Saucy Stories*. Fletcher didn't look happy about being bothered. He read my note and informed me that they were playing that afternoon and leaving for Cuba that night.

"Where's McGraw?" I wrote.

Fletcher's eyes narrowed suspiciously. He had a big lantern jaw, and he thrust it up at me. "Who the hell *are* you, fella?"

Well, I have to admit, it irked me. I'm hardly your run-of-the-mill specimen, but either Fletcher hadn't noticed me on the train to Philly or I'd made precious little impression on him. No wonder folks think ballplayers are thick.

"Taylor," I wrote. "I'm probably pitching today."

"No kidding?" He gave me an appraising look from under his bushy eyebrows. "McGraw's in the restaurant." He pointed to the far end of the lobby. "Just don't throw me no fast stuff, okay, pal? I can't handle it."

Fletcher was a notorious fastball hitter. How stupid did he think I was? "I'm playing *with* you," I told him. "For the Giants."

Again he sized me up. "Ain't you kinda old?"

I forced back a sigh. "You'll see."

He smirked at me, probably figuring he had another Victory Faust on his hands. I headed for the restaurant and found McGraw and his wife seated over the remains of their breakfast. I tipped my new lid, a lightweight Panama I'd picked up in the Miami station. Blanche McGraw was stout and matronly. Her round face, plain in repose, became warm and alert when she smiled, which she did on seeing me.

"Hello, Luther," she said, making her words easy to follow. "So good to see you here."

"Where the hell you been?" McGraw signed.

"There was snow all the—" I began.

"You look like shit," he interrupted.

"Just need a little shut-eye."

"You're pitching this afternoon, you know that?"

I tried to look nonchalant although I felt like hugging him. He told me to get the key to Wiltse's room—Hooks was out golfing with Devlin and Matty—and grab some sleep. I did as he said. Next thing I knew, Hooks was shaking me and saying it was time to go to the ballpark. He looked more than a little surprised to see me. When I explained McGraw's offer, he nodded and wished me luck, but his eyes were troubled. According to the latest *Sporting Life,* he and Ames were on McGraw's cut list for next year's squad. About the last thing Hooks needed was for me to come and compete for his job. Well, I could feel for him, but I'd been with the Giants before he showed up. And in baseball, even between friends, competition was the law.

A bellboy delivered a black uniform to me. *Snodgrass* was printed inside the collar, so I gathered the big outfielder wasn't making this trip. I remembered him as a rookie; he'd liked his jersey and pants extra baggy, and had a knack for getting on base by letting pitches nick the heavy broadcloth. The togs sagged on me and weren't all that clean either, but it didn't matter. Staring at myself in a mirror, I drew a slow breath. *Back in uniform.* . . . I'd come a hell of a long way to experience this.

———— ◆ ————

THE TINY PARK'S low board fences boosted razor blades, rum, cigars and Coca-Cola. In any kind of wind, normal fly balls would sail right over them. But the sandy infield would slow grounders—an edge for me if Dundon was doing his stuff.

Our opponents were some semipros from Key West and Miami

mixed in with the Jacksonville Tarpons of the Class C South Atlantic (Sally) League. The latter looked more skilled and hungry. Big-league clubs could draft a handful of bushers each year, but they had to be guaranteed jobs, so it was unlikely McGraw would tap anybody this low. Still, it had been known to happen (if not right away, a year or two down the line) and so this was a gold-plated chance for these boys to show their wares. They had nothing to lose and a lot to gain—just the opposite of me. If I breezed through them, it would mean nothing special to McGraw. If I didn't . . . well, I couldn't let myself think about it.

We were using a National League ball. I saw right off that it had changed since my time. The stitching used to be black; now it was red and black, and I'd have sworn the laces were lower, offering my fingers less purchase. The damn owners would do just about anything to give hitters an edge.

Tossing the ball on the sidelines, I got sidelong, suspicious looks from the Florida kids. Maybe they'd wanted to face Matty. Maybe they figured McGraw was insulting them by pitching a has-been. Hell, maybe they considered it beneath them to face a deaf hurler.

We'd see about that.

Although I hadn't thrown in ten days, I quickly worked up a sweat in the hot sun, and my arm felt fine as silk. McGraw studied me, then nodded and whacked me on the butt. *Get 'em, Dummy!*

We batted first, so I took my place on the bench, realizing for the first time how many regulars had elected not to come. Besides Snodgrass, most of the "M's" were missing: Merkle (rumor had him holding out for $4,000 next year), Meyers, Marquard and Red Murray. Plus Ames, who'd backed out at the last minute. No wonder McGraw needed me.

The jittery Florida pitcher walked Devore, our leadoff man, on four pitches. Doyle also walked. Herzog set down a bunt which the kid mis-

played, loading the bases. Devlin, rusty from riding the bench, missed
a squeeze—McGraw was showing no pity for the rattled pitcher—and
Devore was an easy out at the plate. Our next hitter, Beals Becker,
lined to their third sacker, who stepped on the bag for a double play.
The Florida boys had escaped without a run scored. McGraw looked
like he'd swallowed a plate of lemons.

Okay, here it goes!

More butterflies than I'd felt for a long time fluttered in my belly as
I made my first throws from the mound. I saw people in the stands
pointing and making fun of my whirling herky-jerky motion, so I
poured the next one in to Dutch Wilson, Meyers's replacement behind
the plate. Dust exploded from Dutch's mitt and it must have made a
damn good pop, because people looked startled and the funning
abruptly stopped.

Yes, folks, that's a big-league fastball.

Dutch had joined the Giants at the end of '08, when McGraw started
his youth movement. He hadn't played much because we were battling the Cubs to the wire and needed Bresnahan in there, but he'd
warmed me up plenty and knew my stuff. I finished with a couple of
drops, and he nodded approvingly.

Batter up!

I checked my defense: Devlin 1B, Doyle 2B, Fletcher SS, Herzog 3B,
Devore LF, Becker CF, Crandall RF. Becker, extremely fast, had
subbed in the Giants outfield all season and was good enough to start
for most NL clubs. Devlin, normally a third baseman, would do fine at
first. The weakest one was Crandall, a pitcher, in right. In a pinch I'd
work to keep the ball away from him.

McGraw beckoned the infielders to the mound. "Do your fielding
call," he commanded me, and I did. I've been told it's high-pitched,
whatever that might be, and comes out "mmmmaaa" for "mine" and

"yyyyaaa" for "yours." Usually I pointed like crazy too, to avoid mix-ups. Everybody except Fletcher had played with me in the past (Herzog only an inning or two), but McGraw was taking no chances with injuries.

When the parley ended, Herzog stuck around, eyes fixed on mine, long wiener nose lifted as if sniffing dogshit, lips curled in a sneer. I knew he was trying to muck my concentration. Ignoring him, I stared in at Dutch until he finally turned and ambled back to his position.

My first pitch sent the plate-crowding leadoff kid sprawling backward. *Lesson one, son, the inside is mine.* The ump, bless his heart, called it a strike.

I drove the kid back again with a blazer that nipped the inside corner. Strike two. He choked up more on the handle, therefore was primed for a low outshoot, which Dutch signaled, I delivered, and the kid flailed at and missed. Strikeout! The ball traveled around the infield to Herzog, who whipped it back to me with surplus force that stung my hand.

The next two batters fell to the same pattern: blazers in, breaking balls away. Ten pitches. Three whiffs. It was getting harder to ignore Herzog, who burned the ball to me at every chance, but I walked jauntily off the mound, feeing like I owned the grounds. My black-clad teammates swatted me and McGraw gave me a judicious nod. *Not bad,* he seemed to be saying, *against bushers.*

The Florida flinger had a big roundhouse outcurve. Maybe it was dynamite down in these parts, but not against us. I chipped in with a double to right-center as we tallied six times in the second. Like most hurlers, I fancied myself a hitter. In this league I'd probably be one.

We took the field and the ball went around the horn, then Herzog again pegged it my way with bone-bruising force. So I let it sail past and carom off the stands behind first into short right, where Doyle retrieved it. The ump yelled something and I knew he suspected we were scuffing the ball. Teammates would do that for their pitcher: deliberately drop the ball and grind it in the dirt, making it harder for hitters to see, easier for me to put some dipsy-doodle on it.

When I got the first out with another whiff we repeated our charade, Doyle again trotting after the ball. This time the ump pointed a warning finger. I waited till everybody was settled in their crouches, then suddenly wheeled and threw the ball back to Herzog. My wing was at least as strong as his, and I had surprise with me. He barely got his glove up in time to save his skull as the ball ripped the leather off his hand and carried it fifteen feet behind him. Herzog stared at me in slack-jawed surprise. The ump started out, but an irate McGraw beat him to the mound and waved Herzog over.

"What are you two cocksuckers pulling?" He glared at each of us, but not quite so long or menacingly at his young third sacker. If he had to pick between us, there'd be no question as to who would go.

I kicked at pebbles while Herzog studied the clouds.

"Both you shitbirds, knock it off. We're looking like bushers!"

After that, Herzog fed the ball at varying speeds and spots, forcing me to reach and bend—never quite sending it to my glove. Worse than just showing me up, it seemed he was out to sabotage my game. McGraw must have understood what was happening—he'd been a third baseman himself and nothing on a ballfield escaped him—but decided to let it go. The suspicion crossed my mind that he'd told Herzog to try to rattle me. I wouldn't put it past him. No matter, I told myself. There would come a reckoning with Mr. Dick-Nose.

We kept tallying runs and I kept throwing goose eggs. Over six innings I faced just 19 batsmen—their solitary baserunner came on a boot by Fletcher. He and Herzog exchanged cheesy grins, so naturally I suspected it was on purpose. My concentration and control were pinpoint, Herzog and Fletcher notwithstanding, and my pitches jumped and swerved like in the old days.

In the seventh McGraw told me that Crandall would finish up. "Save it." He tapped my pitching arm. "We've got games the next three days." It was his way of saying I was going to Havana. I nodded matter-of-factly, but inside I was as excited as the sappiest rook. "Get out there and coach," he ordered, doffing his cap and wiping his forehead. "Make yourself useful."

It was like old times. In the coacher's box I windmilled runners around, covered my eyes to show the ump's blindness, held my nose for smelly calls, twirled a finger beside my bean to indicate scrambled marbles. The fans loved my antics, the ump took his ribbing good-naturedly, and even some of the Florida kids smiled. Only one incident marred the fun, and naturally it involved Herzog. He was speeding around third. I directed him home with exaggerated arm motions along the lines of a swimmer's crawl. He stopped dead and glared at me. I made a comical bow and waved him on with a flourish, like he was royalty. This made him madder yet, and he took a step toward me. I threw my hands up in the air and crumpled to the turf as if shot, leaving him standing over me with the crowd laughing. The runner behind him came sliding into the base, forcing Herzog to hike for home, where he was out by a gas-house block. I hoped McGraw would fine his ass, but so far as I knew it never happened. Probably he expected us to work it out between ourselves. Okay by me.

In his three innings, Crandall seemed to work lackadaisically, giving up four hits and a run. Which made what I'd done look even better.

We won 22–1.

A grand afternoon.

That evening we dined on turtle steak, gulf shrimp and oysters at a glorified fish shack that called itself Delmonico's Grand Spanish

Restaurant. There, for the first time I saw our whole party: the McGraws; thirteen players; seven wives. Odd there being thirteen of us. The oldest hex of all. Was he really going to Cuba with that number?

McGraw's teams always had to dress for the road. On this trip everybody was fitted to the nines: the women preening in ruffled dresses and hairdos that would have sent Della to her room in a dither; the men strutting in bowlers and striped shirts with wing collars, most sporting diamonds they'd bought with their Series shares. Devore's flashy new shoes with yellow calfskin uppers and tasseled laces drew considerable attention. With Donlin no longer around, Devore and Becker reigned as the club's fashion plates.

As we gathered in the hotel lobby to depart, another ballclub came crowding in. It was the Phillies, just back from Havana. We'd heard they'd been trimmed, a fact which several Giants were quick to throw in their faces. They came back with pointed reminders of the recent Series. Mickey Doolan flipped me the finger for old times sake. Doolan was a dentist in the offseason, which seemed only fitting since he'd loosened more than one runner's molars in rough play around second base. I caught the eye of Sherry Magee, one of the league's top batsmen, and pretended to hit myself in the jaw. Magee looked sheepish. In July he'd disagreed with an ump on a third-strike call and knocked him cold. Suspended for the rest of the season, Magee had somehow talked his way back after only five weeks.

Somebody was pounding my shoulder. I turned and saw Crossfire Moore, stubble-jawed but princely as ever, grinning like a wolf. His nickname came from his side-arm delivery, and he'd thrown the AL's first no-hitter with it. We were roomies in '02, when I jumped to Cleveland. Crossfire was such a pet there that babies and cigars were named for him. I'd probably have stuck there and never played for McGraw if Frank Bowerman hadn't been sent to fetch me back. I was out on the mound one afternoon against the Highlanders when I saw big Bowerman in the stands behind home, flashing dollar amounts at me just like coaches' signs. Once I figured out what he was doing, I shook him off and motioned him to go higher—which confused my own catcher, exasperated the ump, and caused a lot of time-outs. Finally Bowerman reached a figure I couldn't say no to, and that night we were on the train back to New York. My only regret was saying goodbye to Crossfire, a good pal, one of the first big leaguers who'd learned Sign. In '08 Crossfire had come over to the Phils, but even then we scarcely saw each other.

"L-T," he spelled. "Why're you here?"

I told him my arm was healed and I'd just flung a no-hitter. I didn't say against who or for how many innings. "How were the Cubans?"

"Tough," he answered. "Got a nigger kid named Méndez they call their 'Black Matty.' He sure as hell pitched like it against us. Got hitters, too. Big first baseman named Castillo. Catcher called González. Watch out or you'll find yourselves licked, like us." He flashed the wolf grin. "I don't guess McGraw'd care for that."

"No," I agreed, thinking it would be pure hell for any of us who lost to the Cubans. Except Matty, of course, but that wasn't likely.

"I'll make my mark this winter," I bragged, "and then be back up there to lick you in the National League."

"Hope I'm still around for it," he signed. Crossfire's ERA, around 2.50 each of the past two seasons, was good enough for 22 victories in 1910, but this year he'd been the league's losingest pitcher at 15–19. A prime example of how careers went: one year all chesty and on the gravy train, the next hanging over the scrap heap.

As we parted I hammered my right fist on my left hand, forefinger extended, and Crossfire did the same.

Our old way of wishing luck.

———— ◆ ————

OUR STEAMER, the *Miami*, was moored among rusty banana boats and looked like it had seen better days. It also bobbed like a cork. Hooks, who got seasick just thinking about water, already looked pale. Once after a Cubs game he'd spent a three-hour excursion on Lake Michigan puking up his guts. And that water was glassy compared to this. Hooks's wife was coming to Havana, but not for another day or so. It was my wonderful luck to be his roomie in the meantime. We were standing at the rail with the others when a ritzy-looking group came waltzing up the dock. It was led by a humdinger of a peach wearing a form-fitting green silk dress and matching bird-of-paradise hat with a plume waving over her head. Trailed by two men toting her trunks, she marched up the gangplank. On deck she was greeted by the *Miami's* captain, who kissed her hand. A photographer's bulb exploded as she swept grandly toward us, one hand flung out and waving languidly to those on the dock. She passed by in a cloud of perfume, curvy and elegant, and I caught a violet-eyed glance. I waggled my fingers in a friendly hello, and was rewarded with a quick smile.

Hooks nudged me. "Who's that?"

I had no idea but pointed below, where, as if sprouting from the cluster of well-wishers, a sign had risen: *Bon Voyage!* and another: *Miss Soda Cracker!*

We looked at each other. Miss Soda Cracker was the equal of most music-hall queens I'd passed my eyes over, which took in a few. Why was she on this tub? McGraw must have angled for one of the biscuit companies to cover our passage. Whatever the case, I was tickled to see the married players ogling her as much as the bachelors—and trying to hide it. The wives were eyeing her in quite a different way.

Devore stepped brazenly into her path, lifted his derby and with a sweeping bow brought it down over his yellow shoes. Not missing a step, Miss Soda Cracker put a gloved hand on his shoulder and pushed gently, so that he continued to turn farther than he intended and was left facing the line of players as she glided past. We guffawed as Devore turned scarlet.

The *Miami* chugged slowly from the dock. The last of the sun was fading, the water tinted gold and purple. Clumps of hyacinths choked the boat slips and floated in flowering islands alongside us as we headed toward the Atlantic. Gulls swooped in and out. I wished Della were there to see it. In open water we began to move faster. The vague shapes of the Marquesa Keys disappeared in the distance. The air grew chiller, and I shivered involuntarily, partly from cold, partly from anticipation.

Tomorrow I would be in Havana.

PART TWO

THE MOTION

❦

The time was, and not five years ago, when the American
game was nowhere an attractive game beside the brutal
bull fights, but the people are becoming civilized, and
when they do, base ball will supplant the heathenish
sport.

—Henry Chadwick,
Sporting Life, 1889

It's great to be young and a Giant.

—Larry Doyle, 1911

SIX

WHERE THE ROLLING water met the horizon, the dark shape of Cuba gradually emerged. First we saw hills, then the shags of trees topping them, and finally the city of Havana, a crescent of blues and pinks and yellows. Light pouring from the turquoise sky was so bright and clear that everything stood out in almost painfully sharp relief.

Standing beside me, Hooks pulled tinted glasses closer to his eyes. He looked dead, having spent the night doubled over a bucket in our cabin. Once I'd tried to rouse his spirits by tossing a pail of seawater over the transom and acting as if we were about to capsize, but Hooks was too far gone to care if we went down. I poked his arm and pointed toward El Morro, the ancient castle fortress marking the entrance to Havana Harbor. I recognized it from the guidebook I'd bought in Key West and spent the night studying while Hooks was emptying himself. The pitted gray walls of the fortress looked grim and unwelcoming. I felt a trifle let down. I guess I'd wanted white sands, hammocks beneath swaying palms, waterfalls plunging down the sides of bluffs.

"Don't touch me." Hooks released his grip on the railing and lurched off in the direction of our cabin. As we entered the busy port, we were met by a tug nearly as big as the *Miami,* its deck crowded with hat-waving, brown-skinned Cubans whose mouths moved rhythmically in some kind of chant. A banner billowed at the rail: ¡BIENVENIDOS GIGANTES! ¡EL JEFE MCGRAW! ¡MATTY LANZADOR SUPREMO! I checked the tiny dictionary I'd brought with me. "Welcome Giants!" "Boss McGraw!" "Matty Thrower Supreme!" I liked it that a pitcher was a "lanzador." The word looked fierce.

I moved over to where Matty stood with his wife, Jane, who greeted me with a friendly smile and a wink of her gray eyes. She wasn't beautiful like the showgirls who threw themselves at the star pitcher, but attentive and kindly. He'd made a good pick.

"What are they yelling?" I knew that he'd been studying Spanish for this trip.

"'¡El Mono Amarillo está aquí!'" He laughed. "'The Yellow Monkey is here.' They remember McGraw from 20 years ago."

"Yellow monkey?"

"Seems he played shortstop on a barnstorming team that wore bright yellow uniforms."

The tug was beside us now, and the Cubans attention focused to my right. I turned and saw Miss Soda Cracker preening in a red dress trimmed with white ermine. Her trademark plume—this one crimson to match the dress—waved in the salt breeze. Her heavy-lashed violet eyes flashed at Matty, took in Jane, winked coquettishly at me.

"Stay away from her," Matty signed.

After a minute or so of appreciating Miss Cracker, the Cubans suddenly grew even more excited as McGraw appeared on the upper deck, his jaw thrust out like an emperor surveying his subjects. If this had been a moving picture, the title card would have read: *Triumphant Return of the Yellow Monkey*

"How often has he been here?" I asked.

"Just once," Matty answered.

"You're joshing me. Twenty years ago?"

"I guess the way he jumped around in the field caught their fancy. And later, of course, he became famous. Cubans are real strong for the game. Some claim that they're the biggest ball nuts anywhere."

I could believe it. They seemed to worship McGraw. Recognizing that she'd been upstaged, Miss Soda Cracker curtseyed in his direction, but McGraw was oblivious.

A band greeted us on the dock, the brass instruments bobbing and glinting in the sun. I caught the *thump* of the bass drum. Massed onlookers gyrated to the music with hip-thrusting motions that would've landed them in the calaboose back in Baldwin.

Miss Soda Cracker swept down the gangplank and into a hansom drawn by matched white horses. A few men with big box Graflexes and heavy tripods practically maimed those around them in their haste to photograph her, but most paid her only passing attention.

It was *los Gigantes* they wanted.

White-belted cops kept them off us while we climbed into open carriages and set off along a broad, paved palm-lined avenue crammed with vehicles of all kinds. Fruit vendors and lottery-ticket drummers snaked their way through it all to pitch their wares at us.

Those of us without wives—Devore, Wiltse, Herzog, Wilson, Becker and me—all rode in one carriage. Herzog and I gave each other the freeze as we rolled along, rubbernecking and waving. Devore pointed up to a balcony bursting with flowers and tropical plants. From their leaves an olive-skinned girl gazed down at us, her jet hair cinched with jeweled combs. She looked like somebody I'd seen in one of the Spanish paintings at the Metropolitan. Realizing that we'd spotted her, she drew a shawl over the lower part of her face—but not before a tiny smile played on her lips. We whooped and waved. An older woman materialized on the balcony and whisked her inside and slammed the heavy shutters.

"Shoot," said Devore. "They *are* chaperoned, like I heard."

"Wouldn't help you if they weren't," Becker told him, "since you're homelier than a mud wall."

I studied the few women visible on the street, noticing that they walked in pairs or small groups, not alone, and wore considerably more face paint—it seemed to have a queer whitish cast to it—than most U.S. women. They seemed to appreciate our looking at them. Were they flirting behind those black lace fans?

Sweating in my dark suit, I envied Cuban men, looking cool and comfortable in pleated white shirts worn outside their pants— guayaberas, my guidebook called them—and light linen jackets.

We turned on to the Malecón, a broad curving shoreline drive completed during U.S. occupation. Waves broke against the seawall and misted us with salt spray. Residences were adorned with balconies and verandas, scrolled facades, tiled roofs, and fancy wrought iron. Angels and gargoyles looked down from upper stories. Narrow streets running up off the Malécon were dark with mystery. I wanted to jump down and set off exploring them.

Our destination was the Plaza Hotel in Vedado, Havana's modern section. Things there didn't look nearly so interesting. In the square outside the hotel, another band played while we were photographed hoisting glasses of champagne with the mayor and his cronies, most of whom made speeches welcoming us famous Gigantes. Representatives from the local sporting papers had their say, too. McGraw soaked it all up like an official ambassador.

I got a kick out of the others not savvying anything. For once I was no more ignorant of events than anybody else. The highlight of the ceremonies came when a handful of older Cubans stepped up to shake McGraw's hand. It turned out that they'd played against him in '91. He hugged them like long-lost brothers. I had the disturbing realization that some of them weren't that much older than me.

It was announced that each time Mathewson pitched, a national holiday would be declared. Matty looked down modestly as everybody applauded. A canny move. Sunday was the big ballgame day in Cuba, but since Matty refused to pitch on the Sabbath, the holidays would boost the gate back up. Reporters surrounded him the instant the ceremonies ended, and he had them feeding out of his hand when he answered a few questions in Spanish.

"Are you confident of beating José Méndez?" they wanted to know.

"I like to face the best," he answered, giving them precious little—and of course they loved him for it.

Our luggage arrived in the lobby along with a new teammate. He was a husky 20-year-old utility player named Gene Polson, with fair features and a shock of hair so blond it was nearly white. He showed his teeth and flounced his hair a lot, and it didn't take me long to decide that Mr. Polson was stuck on himself. He'd arrived a few days ago. He was sporting one of those Cuban shirts, and I saw him telling Devore the best places to find whores. Polson seemed to know everybody; last June he'd come up from the bushes to fill in for a week or so. Nobody bothered to introduce me, and when I saw him carrying on like long-lost brothers with Herzog and Fletcher—kissing their butts, to say it plainly—I didn't bother to approach him.

At least we no longer numbered thirteen.

We soon set off on a tour of Old Havana, through twisting streets jammed with pushcarts and humanity. The heat and glare were fierce, and I envied Hooks his shaded glasses. Our tour guide's accounts of the buildings we saw in the Plaza de Armas went right by me, but I appreciated the royal palms growing there; in their shade, pigeons strutted on the cobblestones and old men played dominoes and sold lottery tickets.

In one corner stood an ancient ceiba tree. Red scarves were tied around the gigantic trunk, and at the base were piles of pennies, fruits, and rum-soaked cakes. The guide explained that they were offerings to various gods, and that many more were buried between the protruding roots. Several chicken heads and a scary-looking black doll hung from the branches.

"Gods?" said one of the Catholic players. "You mean saints?"

"*Sí*," the guide said. *"Santos."*

"It's voodoo, you bonehead," McGraw said. "Brought in from Africa by the slaves. Those things are blessings and hexes."

We exchanged uneasy glances. Nobody seemed sorry when we moved on. On the street I became aware of a shoeshine man staring at me. As our eyes met, he crossed himself and pointed to his ear. He seemed to know I was deaf, but how could that be? He rubbed his fingers together, the universal sign for money. I pointed to my shoes, polished and shiny. He shook his head and repeated the gesture.

"What's he want?" I asked our guide.

He smiled. "He has a prediction."

"About me?"

"*Sí*. He wants a dollar."

"Don't do it," Hooks advised. "May be a hex."

I thought about it. Why had he singled me out? How had he known I was deaf? Turning him down might be worse than playing along. I handed over a Cuban dollar. The old man broke into a missing-toothed grin.

"He claims to be a *brujo*," the guide wrote, "and so he knows special things."

"What's a *brujo*?"

"A witch."

"See?" Hooks demanded, reading over my shoulder. "Damn it all, Dummy, let's go!" Without looking back he strode along the sidewalk.

The guide listened to the old man's words, asked him to repeat them, then said with a trace of a smile, "He says you will give birth while you are here."

"What? He thinks I'm a woman?" I stared at the old man, half amused, half irked. "I gave a dollar for *that?*"

"He says that your *muerto*, your protective spirit, confided this to him," reported the guide. "If you don't like it, you must talk to the spirit."

"Swell, I'll do that." Irritation was winning out.

"Give birth to *what?*"

"He says it will be a boy."

"Tell him I want my money!"

The guide laughed.

In the Plaza de la Catedral I wanted to see the site of Columbus's remains, which my book said was in the ancient twin-spired cathedral. But we learned that everything had been returned to Spain twelve years ago—and maybe had been the wrong man anyway. By then, Hooks's appetite had finally come back. I was hungry myself, and so for pennies we bought sesame-seed candies and a delicacy called *turrón*, concocted of almond paste and nuts.

Sellers offered every fruit drink imaginable. We consumed a number as we sweated through the afternoon. In Florida, where it was still plenty hot in late November, dark winter hues were already in fashion. Not so in Havana. Light-colored finery would prevail here until just before Christmas, the end of our trip, when temperatures on a bitter cold day might plummet to the 70s.

We were on our way to a cigar factory when McGraw abruptly called a halt and insisted that we visit a clothier instead. At the "Departamento de Ropa" in Don Orlando's *Bazar Inglés*, we were fitted for white linen suits, either at the Giants' expense or that of our

Cuban hosts, we never knew which, though McGraw carried on like it came straight out of his pocket. Meanwhile, Don Orlando himself scurried around us, double-checking everything his clerks did.

"White is the color of royalty," he exclaimed, according to the guide, and McGraw nodded sagely. But I noticed that we were being fitted for the low end of royalty; our suits cost eight Cuban dollars each instead of the deluxe model for fourteen.

Outside, McGraw punched my arm playfully. "Well, Dummy, what do you think of Havana?"

"Damn quiet here," I told him. It was our old joke. I'd said it in Marlin during our first spring in Texas, and McGraw nearly collapsed in a laughing fit. Ever since, he'd repeated the question wherever we went. I have to say this about the man: he loved a good laugh. It didn't necessarily have to be at somebody's expense—but usually was.

While the wives prowled Obispo Street's exclusive stores that were stocked with the latest European goods, we went back to the Plaza for our uniforms and gear. McGraw wanted to get a feel for the ballpark and shake off our rustiness before tomorrow's game. No workout was scheduled, but that didn't stop reporters and photographers from dogging us.

The city boasted two pro clubs: the Havana Reds and Almendares Blues. We would play a 12-game series against them, facing one and then the other, at the new Almendares Park Stadium in the Cerro district, a hilly section sprinkled with the summer homes of plantation owners. The ballpark was a pleasant surprise. I'd expected a barren, sun-baked field like in Key West, but this one rivaled Montreal's Atwater Park. The grass was thick and the soil loamy, not hard-packed sand. Gray clouds were gathering overhead. We were told that it rained here nearly every afternoon and the field's drainage was excellent. There were two single-tier stands flanking home, and bleachers behind a low outfield fence painted dark blue. Too good a backdrop for hitters, I judged, and made a mental note to wear my old undershirt with its big flapping sleeve, to promote some visual confusion.

McGraw worked us surprisingly hard. At first I thought he was just making a show for the Cuban press, but then I decided it went beyond that. Big-league teams had come down here, like us, at less than full strength, and gone away losers. It wasn't going to happen to Little Napoleon if he could help it.

Spectators crowded in until there must have been nearly a thousand. Some were drinking, and things got rambunctious when a couple of them tried to take a turn at batting. Herzog, meanwhile, drew a crowd by plucking liners out of the air and snapping up everything on the ground near him. Whatever his faults, I had to admit he was a hell of a third sacker. Somebody started calling him *el mono joven*—the young monkey—which didn't noticeably please Herzog, but he was quick to pick up the bills and coins they threw his way after flashy plays. It was the custom here, we were told. Trying to get in on the act, Polson pulled some tricks too, most of which involved catching the ball behind his back, but he flubbed too many and McGraw told him to knock it off.

The flingers took turns tossing to the hitters. I considered grandstanding a little for the crowd myself, especially while I served up straight balls for Herzog to wallop around the field. But I decided against it. Showing him up wouldn't serve anybody. If things went right, next season we'd be teammates.

———— • ◆ • ————

THAT NIGHT AT the Plaza we sat down to a lavish welcoming banquet. White-jacketed waiters served sea turtles stewed in the shells, pineapple-stuffed ducks slathered with mango sauce, and chickens gorged with red bananas. Heaping bowls of eggs fried with rice accompanied vegetables I couldn't begin to name. Then came carts spilling over with desserts; my favorite was *boniatillo,* a sweet potato pudding simmered in cream and covered with shredded coconut.

We got more speeches from local bigwigs, who gave the impression that our arrival was second only to having kicked Spain off the island. I looked to Hooks to tell me what was said, but most of the time he didn't know. Devore and Becker got goofy on champagne-and-guava punch; their heads were bobbing over the dessert plates by the time McGraw went to the podium to announce two late arrivals.

The first was umpire Cy Rigler, who would work all of our games. They called him the "fighting ump" because Rigler was big and husky and backed down to nobody. I liked that he called low strikes, which suited Dundon. When he was working the bushes down in Evansville, Rigler had revolutionized his trade by raising his arm to indicate strikes so that fans in the bleachers could distinguish his calls. The practice spread quickly, something I'd been wanting for years. Before that time, I had to get ball-strike calls from my catcher because I couldn't see through the ump's mask well enough to decipher what he'd said. Up at the podium, Rigler got a laugh by saying he'd been fishing in Jacksonville and caught some baby gators—but threw 'em back because they looked too much like McGraw.

Next up was Sid Mercer, sports scribe for the *New York Globe,* dapper, dark-haired, young and sophisticated. He'd come on the big-league scene in 1907, so I'd seen him work two seasons. Mercer had treated me better than most, calling me Luther instead of "Dummy" or "the mute hurler Taylor" or what have you. Still, my stomach tightened at the sight of him. I hadn't considered that my performance in Cuba might be splashed across a New York sporting page. Well, I told myself, be glad he's here. Prove your arm's back, and Mercer will be quick to publicize it.

McGraw intercepted me on the way out. Hooks's wife had arrived and they would take another room. I'd be getting a new roommate.

"Who?" I prayed he wouldn't say Polson.

His eyes glinted with humor. "You'll be surprised." As understatements go, it was a whopper.

SEVEN

I WAS DREAMING that Della threatened to paddle me if I didn't come home and grow up and stop being a boy. Her hands were flying in my face—deaf folks dream in Sign, which shouldn't surprise you—and I couldn't get a word in. All at once something thumped the bed. I opened my eyes and found myself staring into the smiling features of none other than Turkey Mike Donlin, so named, it was said, because he could strut even while sitting down.

"Wake up, laddie," he said, a tell-tale odor of hooch accompanying the words. "'Tis old times renewed!" He signed as he spoke, elegantly, poetically even, if such a thing can be. I used to claim that if anybody could sign with a brogue, it was Donlin when he was crocked. Which was kind of funny, considering he was American as cherry pie.

Old times indeed, I thought, shoving aside the bottle he thrust at me. The gray light coming in the window told me it was still very early. We'd roomed together from '04, Donlin's first year with New York, to '06, when the goddamn batboy left some bats crossed in front of our bench (violating one of the game's biggest hoodoos), and sure enough, within minutes Mike broke his leg sliding and was done for the season.

"Mabel here?" I asked.

"Home," he answered, without explaining. Which figured. If she were, he wouldn't likely be boiled as an owl.

"McGraw sent for you?" I signed.

Donlin flashed a toothsome grin. "He loves his Turkey Mike."

It was true. McGraw admired Donlin's fiery spirit while despairing of his habits. It was hard not to like Donlin—except when you couldn't stand him.

"How much you getting paid?"

"Same as everybody," he said. "Five hundred."

Damn! I was getting nothing and paying half my expenses. I vowed to talk to McGraw right after I showed my stuff against the Cubans.

"I needed dough and I was told . . ." Donlin winked broadly ". . . that a man can wager in grand style down here."

I'd been told the same thing. My thoughts began to take a new direction, hardly unusual around Turkey Mike. The man was a born conniver. Life through his eyes was like a vast pool table, full of tricky angles and best savored in the company of cronies.

"Get rid of that poison," I told him, pointing at the bottle. "We got a game today."

"And you can be sure I'll be ready." He plugged the bottle and stowed it in the closet. "But young Devore . . . perhaps not. I rescued him from the bushes."

I looked at him, perplexed. "The minors?"

"No, the *bushes*—" he spelled it out—"behind the hotel. The lad was asleep in the green leaves. I helped him to his room—carried him, mostly." Donlin laughed. "Maybe McGraw'll pay me a bonus for nursemaiding his babes."

"And who'll nursemaid you?"

Grinning, he pointed at me. A faint scar ran from his left cheek to his jaw, the work of a knife in some long-past barroom scrap. Rather than disfiguring Donlin, it seemed to make him even more of a wonder to women.

Wagging a finger in refusal, I climbed out of bed. The notion of watching over Turkey Mike in Havana was enough to bring on hives.

"I'll be up in time for lunch." He set about peeling off his clothes, and the instant I stood up he dived beneath the covers. His hand emerged and signed, "Get another bed in here for tonight, okay?"

On the road with Donlin . . . it was all coming back.

———— • ◆ • ————

THE CROWD OVERFLOWING Almendares Stadium must have cleaned the city out of red fabric. Many of the fans were better turned out than the Havana Reds themselves, whose uniforms were worn and patched. They cast covetous glances at our new-model gloves and equipment bags bulging with bats and balls. They warmed up with speed and snap, though, and I could tell they knew their business.

The day was perfect: hot enough to work up a sweat, breezy enough to keep the bugs off. Aside from Miss Soda Cracker, whose plume waved from a box seat, almost no women were visible. During the pregame speeches and introductions, I saw bottles tilting up to mouths, and I began to understand why cops on horses were stationed every 50 feet inside the fence. The beauty of Mathewson's pitching kept things under control, though. *"El Caruso del beisbol,"* the morning *El Mundo* had called him, and he lived up to it. After a month's rest he looked like the Matty of old, mixing speeds and brushing the corners and rarely needing his fadeaway.

We took the lead in the first, not much fooled by the curveballs of the Reds starter, one Juan de Dios Pareda. We rapped out 13 hits, but the Reds were fine fielders and knew every cranny of their ballpark, so we only turned them into four runs.

It was enough for Matty, who struck out nine and scattered the hits he gave up. One came on a flyball that Devore should have caught but lost in the sun. The hapless left fielder also went 0–for–5 at the plate. McGraw gave him withering stares and finally replaced him with Polson. The rookie's posturing on easy flies drew some hot comments from Donlin who, amazingly, looked like the Turkey Mike of old, playing flawlessly and covering center with his distinctive swagger. "Donlin was born on Flag Day," McGraw liked to say, "and has paraded around ever since!" On one play Donlin raced back deep to snatch a sure extra-base clout by leaping high against the fence. In his four times at the plate he lashed a single, drew a walk, and stole a base. All of it despite his late-night carousing. How did the man do it?

The Reds scored their only run because of a horse. Devore, looking as sick as Hooks had on our sea voyage, and far worse than his outfield mates, Becker and Donlin, neither of whom was exactly daisy-fresh, chased a long hit that bounded straight at one of the mounted cops. The horse sidestepped nervously as Devore tried to plunge beneath it for the ball. A kick sent him sprawling and the Cuban hitter sped all the way around the bases. Most of us thought it was pretty funny, but not McGraw, who appealed to Rigler. Then both he and Rigler appealed to the Havana manager, who appealed in turn to a stadium official.

Seeing fans standing and pursing their lips, I asked Hooks what was going on.

"They're whistling," he told me.

"Whistling?"

"Yeah, they do that to boo here."

The horsecops stayed where they were.

In the ninth the Reds brought in a fuzz-faced pitcher named Adolfo Luque, who looked like the real article as he sent us down in order, finishing by striking out Dutch Wilson on a wicked inshoot.

The final score was 4–1, and other than Herzog, who got a finger spiked—he packed the wound with tobacco and later poured in whiskey to keep out infection—everybody seemed content with the start of the series. Even the Reds. True, they'd lost, but it was to Matty, and they hadn't been routed. They figured to do better against our lesser hurlers. Which included me.

"Wait for Méndez!" the crowd chanted.

It wouldn't be a long wait. Tomorrow we played the Almendares club, and he was their star. Like everybody else, I wanted to see how good he was.

We'd all chipped in to bet on ourselves. The Cubans wagered on anything: whether a batsman would get a base knock, strike out—whatever you wanted to pick on any play. The trouble was, with Matty working, the only action we could get was whether we'd win by at least a 3–1 margin. We'd covered it—barely—but our take amounted to only a few dollars each.

I noticed Fletcher and Herzog frowning at Donlin as they pocketed their paltry winnings. Donlin was collecting bills from a Cuban with a diamond stickpin and gold teeth. "Fifty bucks to the good," he bragged when I went over to him. "A grand afternoon's work."

"What'd you do? Put a thousand on us?"

"Nope, just ten—against us, sort of."

I stared at him until he guffawed and confessed that he'd bet Devore wouldn't hit a ball out of the infield. In five trips the little outfielder had popped up or grounded out every time.

"Cinch bet," Donlin crowed, "knowing the shape he was in."

"You bet against your teammate?"

He shook his head. "No, they'd've figured Devore and me were in cahoots." He pointed at the grinning, gold-toothed Cuban. "I paid *him* to bet for me."

———— •◆• ————

THAT NIGHT, AT another banquet, Donlin mystified the waiters by asking for his favorite dish, corned beef and cabbage. We were then treated to moving pictures of the recent World Series. The Giants watched themselves in action, a first for most. Herzog didn't share in the fascination, but bent Doyle's ear with complaints. It seemed that the National Commission had sold filming rights to the Series for $3,500—then backed down when the players asked for a share. Now it was clear that somebody had gone ahead anyway, and Herzog wanted his cut.

"Why's he always so hungry for cash?" I asked Donlin.

"I came here for dough myself," he answered.

"Yeah, but you didn't just get a Series share."

"Well, I heard that some of the boys blew off their Series money in a big craps game right after they got it. Nobody'll tell me who lost, but. . . ." He left it hanging, and I knew who he figured one of the losers had been.

Watching the movie wasn't McGraw's idea of swell entertainment, either, but our hosts insisted that he tell them all about each play. It seemed to make no difference that we'd *lost;* it was the glory of being in the thing that mattered. Donlin and I had no stake in it, and nobody really cared if we left, which we did as soon as our desserts were gone. Havana nightlife didn't heat up till later, so we decided to kill some time in our room.

"Buck don't seem to care much for you either," I signed as we headed up the tiled stairs. "He still pissed about his rookie year?"

"It's more recent than that." He grinned. "Last June, when I needed to play ball again, McGraw took me on long enough to get in shape. I didn't do much, mostly subbed for Snodgrass, then got sold to Boston. But before I left they threw a day for me at the Polo Grounds."

I nodded, picturing it. Donlin was always the fans' darling.

"They gave me this big flower arrangement and the photogs asked everybody to line up behind me. Herzog and Fletcher got red-assed, and McGraw had to order 'em back in line." He gave me a wink. "So those two birds probably think I'm horning in on their action here, too."

"Maybe you are," I offered.

"Well, I'm fed up with their long mugs already," he signed. "And that yellow-haired grandstanding yannigan better stay clear of me too."

"Don't do something stupid," I cautioned. "I need you here to talk to me."

"Why, Dummy, I didn't know you cared." He fluttered his eyes. "Here, I'll play you the latest."

Donlin had replaced his cylinder-type gramophone with a Harvard disc player. He pulled out a stack of the new flat grooved recordings and showed me "My Melancholy Baby" and "When I Was Twenty-One and You Were Sweet Sixteen." The last made me think of Della and I felt sad. When we were those ages, things between us had been sweet indeed.

Donlin set down the needle on "Oh, You Beautiful Doll" and turned the volume up so I could feel the vibrations. It was an old pastime for us. I liked knowing what went on in the world, even if I couldn't fully experience it. Donlin knew I was partial to tunes from shows, so he next put on "Everybody's Doin' It" which he said was popularizing the Turkey Trot, a dance invented by Vernon and Irene Castle. He signed the lyrics for me, his feet tapping all the while. Giants teammates used to practice fingerspelling by doing billboards we passed on the way to the ballpark. Not Donlin. He'd always done song lyrics.

When the tune finished I asked him to play "Stealing Home," the song he and Mabel did on stage together. I'd been best man at their wedding.

He shook his head.

"Why not?"

He put up his hands to show he didn't want to discuss it.

Jesus, I thought, *they've split up.*

"Let's have a slug instead." He pulled the Irish whiskey from the closet and extended it to me. I let some roll down my throat, then couldn't help coughing.

"Dummy, you been dry too long!"

He was right. Most of my life, really. Kansas was the second dry state (after Maine) to come into the Union, and had already voted for the Prohibition Amendment currently going around. I used to booze it up pretty good during my oats-sowing days; sometimes it still irked me to go home to no legal liquor. Donlin's whiskey gave me a glow, but it was weighted by the awareness that my roomie was ready for a full night. I could manage Donlin up to a point. I could manage booze up to a point. But not the two together. Still, when he headed out for Old Havana, I went along.

Somebody had to take care of him.

The darkness was soft and balmy, velvet-warm, as if still charged with the day's sunlight. The streets pulsed with the energy of the *Habaneros* thronging them. At the corners were lamplighters called *serenos* wielding long poles to set the gas globes aglow. We stopped at smoky cafes in narrow streets. Donlin downed rum while I sampled juice concoctions—pineapple, grapefruit, orange, tamarind, watermelon—at a bargain nickel each.

We walked along the fashionable Paseo del Prado, where the shops were still open. Donlin eyed elegant women stepping from *volantes*— these were low-slung curtained cabs rigged with long shafts from the back of a horse, where the driver also sat—who swept by us on their way into the stores. Donlin's face got a look I'd seen before.

"Mike," I cautioned, "you don't talk to unescorted women here."

"Who says?" He followed a pair of beauties into a glove shop. "Good evening, ladies."

They didn't turn.

"Michael Donlin, lately of Broadway theater." With a flourish he produced a calling card. "Currently appearing with the New York Baseball Club."

Apparently deciding that he wouldn't leave on his own, one of the women looked around. Donlin flashed a smile meant to dazzle her. She lifted a hand and waved him away with a casual motion, as if shooing an insect, her lips pursing in what I imagined was a "ftt." Her face was coated with white powder (later I learned it was pulverized egg shell) which gave her a slightly ghostly look and set off her black hair.

Donlin said something and, cat-quick, she slapped his face. Seeing his body tense, I grabbed him before he could make things worse. After a long moment he relaxed, and I let go. He bowed with mock courtliness and said, "'Tis your loss, ladies," then turned and walked out the door with erect grace, as if he'd rebuffed *them*.

"What the hell did you say?" I asked.

"That I'd like to share a piece of papaya with her. McGraw told me it worked every time. I shoulda known that bastard would set me up!" He straightened his shoulders. "The night's not done, old pal."

I pulled him around so he faced me. "We can't afford to mess up over women here, neither one of us." I prodded his chest. "But especially you."

Ten years ago, Donlin, dead drunk, had attacked a showgirl and her boyfriend. It cost him $250 and six months in jail. A few years later police had yanked him off a train in Albany. At the time he was waving a pistol. Again he was drunk; again over some floozy.

"I'm married now, Dummy," he protested.

Mabel had gotten him on the wagon, but she wasn't here. My concern must have been plain, for he clapped a reassuring arm around my shoulder. "I just want to socialize should the chance come."

For him, I thought, it usually did.

We strolled down the Paseo toward the harbor, where a club called Centro Asturiano sat beside the ritzy Hotel Miramar. From its doors poured tobacco smoke. I began to pick up vibrations of drums.

"Music," said Donlin, doing a nifty little slide-step. "Let's go."

Inside, it was steamy and reeked of sweat and cigars and perfume. Donlin made a beeline for the bar, then we moved into a dimly lit room where Negro musicians were playing and dancers of various skin colors swayed to the surging beat. It was too packed for sitting. The number ended. It seemed that I still felt a distant rhythmic pulsation. Donlin must have caught it up too, for he grabbed my arm and pointed to the rear. I followed him through a door marked EMPLEOS, and we were out in the night air once more.

"There's what we want." He pointed to an adjacent terrace where elegantly dressed people sat at small tables. A tuxedo-clad band was playing, and couples twirled on the tiled floor. "Come on."

He vaulted over the low wall that separated the establishments. I hesitated, then followed. People were decked out in dark evening clothes. Donlin's navy blazer and light slacks were a bit more suitable than my wrinkled white suit—but not by a whole lot. We'd never have gotten in the front door. That didn't stop Donlin from grabbing an empty table as if he was a regular here. I'm no shrinking violet, but his chestiness amazed me.

The waiter gave us the fish-eye as Donlin gulped down the drink he still carried and ordered two more. When he laid a $100 Cuban bill on the table the fishiness vanished. Donlin asked something about the dancing couples, and learned that they were doing the *danzón*. Donlin spelled it for me, and added, "He says it's all the rage here."

I wished I'd brought my camera. Here was the view for Della: a three-quarter moon reflecting on the water in a lane of gold-white framed by two palms. The air smelled of the sea and of the flowers on trellises behind us. Candles in tin lanterns cast cones of light around the patio. Finding that my rum drink went down too easy, I pushed the glass aside and studied the nearest dancing couple, who parted and stood alone, facing each other, eyes not quite meeting, then moved close again. The man's right hand pressed to the woman's back, arm encircling her, fingers of his left hand gently clasping her right, which held a handkerchief, so that their skin did not actually touch except through the diaphanous fabric. They stepped and turned and bent together as if they were one.

I'd assumed that Donlin too was caught up in the spell of it all until I realized it wasn't the dancing couples he was gazing at, but a pair of young women seated across from us. Their escorts stood up abruptly, and I guessed from the men's sullen faces there'd been some kind of quarrel.

A new number was beginning, couples taking the floor.

Donlin stood and beckoned for me to follow as he headed for the women. *No, Mike!* I grabbed for him, too late. Even if I'd had a notion to dance, I wouldn't have tried it there. Della and I used to pull off a mean waltz, beating out the time ourselves. Sometimes we were embarrassed when we strayed from what the hearing folks were doing, but what the hell, we had fun. This music, though, in my rumpled whites, with one of those showy women . . . you couldn't have paid me.

Donlin bent over the prettier one. She wasn't wearing the white powder and didn't look Cuban—more European or American. She smiled up at him, took his hand, and rose to dance. Then I recognized her. No plumed hat now, and her hair was down instead of gathered up, but there was no mistake: Miss Soda Cracker.

Well, well, things were getting interesting.

Donlin carried off the *danzón* in fine style. Not exactly like the others, of course, but grandly. The man was so graceful that he seldom looked bad in any situation, and his vaudeville work allowed him to shine here. He bent Miss Soda Cracker back and twirled her, hips twisting as they reversed direction together, Donlin with flashing teeth and slicked-down black hair, she with bright eyes, flushed cheeks and silk-stockinged ankles.

He threw in steps I'd seen in New York ragtime clubs, and Miss Cracker pulled off some eye-popping swivels, all the while looking at Donlin in a way that would melt marble. People at tables were staring at them, even some of the other dancers. When it ended, everybody applauding, Donlin bowed and held her hand while she dipped in a curtsey. Whoever Miss Cracker was, it was a sure bet she'd had some training.

"Thank you, sir." She smiled sweetly and turned toward her table.

Donlin did not let go of her hand.

I saw then that the two Cuban men had returned. They were young and muscular and didn't look pleased. The darker-skinned of the two seemed to be Miss Soda Cracker's escort. He looked vaguely familiar. It occurred to me that he resembled a matador I'd seen once on a poster near the Mexico border: the same lithe grace and alertness. Both men ignored the other woman, who was talking urgently to them.

Let her go, Mike!

He didn't, being Donlin, although Miss Cracker, aware that her escort had returned, was glancing anxiously at him and tugging to pull free while trying not to let it show. The Cubans said something to each other and started onto the floor.

Oh, shit. I got up fast.

The darker one—Matador—headed straight for Donlin. The other moved in at an angle. Donlin gave no sign that he saw them. In an elaborate show of courtesy, he guided Miss Soda Cracker several steps toward her table, bowed, and swept his arm toward her table with a flourish worthy of a duke. She stepped away with some alacrity. The two men closed on Donlin. Only then did he appear to notice them.

Scowling, Matador said something.

Donlin shrugged and smiled, hands spread, no doubt saying he didn't speak the language. He looked amiable but I wasn't fooled. I knew the signs. Donlin *always* looked like that before he went off. Once at the Polo Grounds in a big game against the Pirates, he muffed a ball and some steel-lunged moron called him a motherless mick bastard. Donlin, wearing that same friendly grin, charged into the overflow crowd and laid the boob out with a poke to his chops, then piled into his chums. It took a squad of cops to haul him out.

"No! No! No!" I yelled, desperate to distract them. God knows what actually came out of my mouth, but at least it got their attention. Matador shot me a warning look, as if to say, "Don't mix in this." The other said something that was probably uncomplimentary.

Pointing to my ears, I put on my dopiest grin. Maybe it wasn't the best thing to do, but nothing better occurred to me. I'd have stood on my head if I thought it would rein Donlin in.

With a burst of rapid-fire Spanish, Matador prodded Donlin in the chest with an accusing forefinger. Donlin knocked it aside, then, in the blink of an eye, spun and cracked the other Cuban in the jaw with his elbow as the man was about to launch a sucker punch. He staggered backward. Donlin turned to face Matador, who was letting go with a roundhouse right.

I've been blessed with fast mitts. Over the years I've won any number of bets snatching flies (the buzzing kind) out of the air. Now, stepping in front of Donlin, I relied on that quickness to deflect Matador's punch. I even had the good sense to use my left hand. I managed to intercept his fist, but not squarely. The heel of my hand hit the edge of his, knocking his little finger inward against itself. He clutched it to his chest and doubled up as if he'd been shot, all sign of fight gone.

Couldn't have hurt THAT much, I thought.

Donlin grabbed me and pointed to the wall where we'd come in. He wasn't smiling any longer. We vaulted off the patio of the Hotel Miramar, pushed our way back through the Centro Asturiano, and flagged down a passing hack out in front. I began to breathe normally again when I saw nobody chasing us. My relief was short-lived.

"Well, we came here partly to lick Méndez." His eyes shone with excitement.

"What do you mean?"

"The one whose hand got hurt," he explained. "That was their big cheese, Méndez, the one everybody talks about."

My heart seemed to stop. It suddenly made sense that Donlin had shown the rare good judgment to flee. Now I knew where I'd seen Matador: staring out from all the sporting pages. If the Havana cops caught us, they'd throw away the key to our cell.

"How'd you know it was him?"

"Alma told me."

"Who?"

"Alma . . . Miss Soda Cracker. A sweet kid from Jersey. Known her for years. She's fronting for a biscuit company over here. They told her to stay close to the baseball action to get publicity." He grinned. "I guess being close to Méndez is one way."

I tried to take it all in. "And the other guy?"

Donlin shrugged. "Some cousin of his."

My brain seemed encased in Jello. I recalled the impact of Méndez's fist hitting my hand, the unmistakable feel of his finger giving way. Christ, I'd injured the very guy we'd come to beat: Cuba's Black Matty, his blazers faster than Walter Johnson's, his benders more baffling than Nap Rucker's, the guy who'd pitched his Almendares team to victories over every big-league visitor.

And we were to face him tomorrow.

EIGHT

NEXT MORNING WE coached along the Malecón and out to the end of
one of the wharves jutting into Havana Harbor. There we stood in a
somber line and gazed at the hulk of the *U.S.S. Maine*, a few hundred
yards offshore. Until recently only its mast and a section of superstruc-
ture had been above water, but now engineers were finishing the huge
job of building a cofferdam around the site, then draining it to reveal
the entire battleship. Patched up enough to float, it was undergoing a
"dry autopsy." Bodies trapped below decks for the last dozen years had
been recovered, taken to New York and paraded up Broadway in flag-
draped coffins before moving on to Arlington for burial.

It was a melancholy sight: the rust-stained, barnacle-clad hulk with
the Stars and Stripes floating above it. We could see the gaping hole
and tilted stacks and twisted steel that marked the blast itself. I thought
of Sim and how much he used to want to come here. When the engineers' studies were completed, the once-proud *Maine* would be towed
into the open sea and allowed to sink for good. Few Americans had
seen it since 1898. Soon nobody would ever see it again.

McGraw gave a talk about the strides Cuba had made under U.S.
supervision. He saw progress everywhere in Havana since his first visit
two decades ago. Sewers had been unclogged, shanties torn down,

parks weeded and replanted, thousands of houses and streets scrubbed free of mosquito larvae. No doubt he was right, but it seemed that not everybody was happy with us. YANQUIS GO AWAY! was scrawled in paint on one of the wharf's pilings.

In the project office, photographs showed the *Maine* in happier days. A panoramic shot of the crew assembled on deck included several colored sailors, and I saw Polson call Fletcher's attention to the same men in a picture of the *Maine's* baseball team. Blacks weren't allowed on white teams in the States, but things must have been different on the *Maine.* Polson mocked the Negroes by hanging his arms apelike, rolling his eyes and putting on a stupid grin. It irked me. Ma and Pa had raised us Taylor kids to respect everybody—otherwise we didn't deserve it ourselves. I didn't care much for Polson anyhow, and it was getting harder to respect him. I wondered what impressions he did of *me* behind my back.

Before Fletcher or anybody else could react to the blond rookie's antics, McGraw cut him dead. "You gonna make fun of niggers, you better be able to beat 'em on the field!" he barked. Polson would be playing at first today, Devlin taking third, as Herzog's swollen finger didn't allow him to grip a bat. "You'll have one throwing at you this afternoon."

McGraw meant Méndez.

Donlin and I exchanged an uneasy glance. That morning I'd checked the English-language Havana *Post;* to my relief there was no mention of the Cuban star being injured. Maybe we were going to get away with it. At least until Méndez saw us at the ballpark.

———— • ◆ • ————

ELEVEN THOUSAND FANS showed up to see us take on the Blues. There were three classes of tickets: *sol,* which meant standing in the sun around the outfield; *gradas,* or uncovered bleachers; and *glorieta,* or shaded grandstand. Almost all were sold out. It was more than the Phillies had ever drawn, and McGraw looked delighted.

True to his Sunday tradition, Matty wasn't even at the ballpark. Nor, to my considerable relief, was Méndez. The Blues announced that if our ace wouldn't appear, neither would theirs. Donlin knew one of the Blues, third baseman Rafael Almeida, who'd played for Cincinnati the past season. Almeida told him in broken English that Méndez had sprained his pinky. He might have been able to pitch that day, but was waiting to face Mathewson.

They'd put a good face on things. The afternoon brightened considerably for me. And for Donlin even more so when Miss Soda Cracker took a seat behind our bench and waved her plume flirtingly at him.

Without Méndez throwing, we didn't figure we'd have a lot of trouble with the Blues. Things went true to form when Devore's leadoff pop fly was carried over their shortstop by a sudden gust, good for a double. He scored on two infield outs, and we were up 1–0 without a true hit.

The Blues didn't roll over. Their hurler, one Eustáquio "Bombín" Pedroso, mystified us with sweeping outshoots that brushed the corners, and misfortune struck us when Crandall walked off the mound rubbing his shoulder. I leaned forward, hoping to catch McGraw's eye, but he sent Hooks in. Which was fair. A manager should go with his regulars first.

I was getting damned itchy, though.

All along we'd been told that the Cubans were dead-on fastball hitters but couldn't handle breaking stuff. Hooks found out different. Choking up, the Blues repeatedly stroked his benders behind the baserunner. Their first five knocks went to right. Looking rattled, Hooks failed to hold runners close, and they turned our own stolen-base weapon against us. After six innings we trailed 5–3 and couldn't seem to decipher Pedroso. In his coacher's box, McGraw stood with hands on hips, pug face reddening.

His pent-up aggravation tore loose in the seventh, along with a few other things. We'd loaded the bases with nobody out; it looked like we'd finally gotten going. Wiping sweat from his face, Pedrozo threw a high blazer to Becker, who popped up to shortstop and slammed his bat down in disgust. Fletcher, a .319 hitter, took his place. Pedroso nibbled at the corners for two strikes, then came in with a nasty dropper. Fletcher was ready and golfed a sinking liner down the right-field line. A sure triple. Except that somehow the Blues right fielder, a jackrabbit by the name of Cabanas, raced over in time to pluck it off the tips of the grass—one of the best catches I'd seen. Still, we'd get a tally, since Doyle, one of our leading speedsters, had played it safe and retreated to third. Now he broke for the plate.

Then, to my amazement, Cabanas banged in a white ribbon that came in over the cutoff directly to catcher González, a husky six-footer who blocked the plate and laid a tag on Doyle as he crashed into the catcher and sent him toppling. A nice try, but it looked like Doyle was out. Then we saw the ball rolling loose beside González.

Rigler spread his arms wide. "Safe!"

McGraw, jubilant, thrust his fist into the air. Now we trailed just 5–4, with men on second and third. But something seemed wrong. Almeida was yelling and waving at González, who threw him the ball. Almeida stepped on third and looked to Rigler for judgment.

This time the ump's right hand shot up, thumb extended.

Doyle was out for leaving the bag too soon.

McGraw charged from his coacher's spot like an enraged boar. I caught some of what was came out of his mouth, and figured it was just as well that Mrs. McGraw and the others were occupied with church affairs this Sunday. I sneaked a glance at Miss Soda Cracker—Alma, the nice kid from Jersey—and wasn't overly surprised to see her grinning.

Rigler was a big man, over six feet. As a rookie in '07, he ejected a record 37 players and was the only ump to tussle with all eight NL clubs. Word had it that he was studying to be a lawyer, and already carried himself like a judge. He showed no fear of McGraw as he observed the shorter man's mouth-foaming tirade. Finally McGraw sprinted back up the third-base line and pantomimed catching a fly ball. An instant after his hands closed, he catapulted himself forward off the bag to show how Doyle had been within the rules.

"No, Meester McGraw," piped up Almeida from his spot nearby. "He leave early."

McGraw whirled on the Cuban, his face going even redder. "You want trouble with me?" he bellowed, thrusting his face into Almeida's.

Having played in the NL, the young Cuban presumably knew McGraw's ways. Why he'd spoken I couldn't imagine. Almeida's dark-skinned face closed down as he turned to talk things over with his shortstop. No doubt he figured nothing good would come from taking on McGraw. Besides, the umpire had ruled for his team. It *looked*, though, like he'd been intimidated by McGraw. I glanced at the stands, where men were yelling and shaking their fists and waving bottles and goatskins.

Catcher González strode up the baseline, mask pulled back over his head. He stared grimly at the Giants manager. I couldn't see what McGraw said, but I saw him point imperiously for González to get back where he belonged. Doyle later told reporters that McGraw said nothing offensive—but as team captain Doyle would naturally stick up for his boss, who, according to Donlin, was yelling, "Who IS this sonofabitch?"

Things got uglier as González demanded to know what McGraw had called him. Almeida tried to get between them, but he was scarcely taller than McGraw and had trouble holding off the big catcher. "It's nothing," Almeida said, demonstrating moves worthy of a *danzón* master. *"Nada, Miguel, nada."*

"What did he call me?" González insisted.

"A joking name," said Almeida.

"I called you a sonfabitch!" McGraw said over Almeida's shoulder, displaying a working understanding of street Spanish. "And I'll say it again all you want, you cocksucker: You're a *son of a bitch!"*

"What?" González grabbed Almeida by the shoulders. "What is he saying?"

"Hijo de perra," Almeida said. *"Es nada."*

"HIJO DE PERRA?"

González bellowed it so loud that it must have carried to the stands, where fans exchanged dark, incredulous looks. The catcher lifted Almeida as if he were a doll and set him aside. Holding his ground, snarling and spitting venom, McGraw cocked his fists. Rigler, moving with impressive speed for a man of his bulk, wrapped himself around McGraw while several Blues restrained González. By then we were all out on the field, two knots facing each other, the red-faced antagonists still yelling insults.

Bottles and fruit were landing around us. Fans swarmed over the restraining rope in center and were cut off by billy-wielding cops. González broke free, still mouthing, *"Hijo de perra!"* and made another lunge at McGraw. It took five teammates to stop him.

"That does it!" McGraw yelled. "We don't play till that asshole's gone!"

Which of course started a new rhubarb. We milled about, rocks and more bottles pelting the turf around us. It was starting to look like we were going to have an all-out riot. At the Polo Grounds I'd seen just about every kind of fracas—one opening day we'd even been pelted by snowballs—and scenes like this scared the dickens out of me.

Spurred by fright, my brain went into top gear.

Once in a tight late-season game we were ahead when it started raining buckets. The victory was ours if only Hank O'Day, the ump who cost us the '08 pennant, would just call the damn thing. But he refused. So we played on, soaked to the skin. The crowd got ugly. O'Day threatened to call a forfeit if we didn't restore order. McGraw's main answer was an attempted punch, which didn't help.

Struck by an inspiration, I had borrowed the crew chief's hip-waders and a lantern and trotted out to my coacher's spot, cutting a ridiculous figure as I waved my arms trying to clear away enough raindrops to see our batter. It didn't exactly boost O'Day's mood—he threw me out—but it made the crowd laugh and eased a dangerous situation.

Maybe now. . . .

I spied a short-handled groundkeeper's rake set against a corner of the grandstand. I went over and got it, then moved cautiously along the box seats, dodging missiles and trying to ignore fists, until I came to Miss Soda Cracker. She looked frightened—and also lovelier than ever. On my pad I scrawled, *"Borrow your hat?"*

She instinctively touched her headpiece, which was yellow with a matching feather. Her lips moved too fast for me to follow, so I pointed to an ear. She looked confused. I took the pad back and added, *"To help Mike?"*

Her eyes went to the field and found Donlin. He looked amused by the scene around him, having seen it a hundred times before: ballplayers stalking around trying to look fierce. To Miss Cracker it must have seemed terribly menacing (and maybe it was—but only because of the agitated, drink-fueled crowd) and she unpinned her hat and handed it down, shooting me a glance through fluttering lashes.

I'd seen some of the Cuban players get ornamental ribbons, called *monas,* from women in the stands. Like knights carrying ladies favors. After a fashion, I now sported one.

There wasn't time to waste. Polson was scuffling with one of the Blues, both of them swinging wildly. González jumped in too, and everybody started surging about with renewed force. I crammed the yellow hat on my head, grasped the business end of the rake, and set off brandishing the wooden handle like D'Artagnan of *The Three Musketeers,* one of my favorite tales. Chest puffed out, I pranced stiff-legged back and forth between the groups with fancy thrusts and parries, the yellow plume swooping above.

The crowd gradually worked itself out of its agitation as folks began to laugh and clap. I learned later I was playing a familiar role: the bull-fight clown who burlesques the deadly sport while distracting the beast.

The dispute finally required the intervention of a Hero of the Revolution, a mustachioed general whose chest was studded with medals. Addressing the crowd through a megaphone, he told them to settle down and enjoy the glorious victory to come. When it was translated, McGraw bristled but kept quiet. The general announced that Rigler's decision would stand: Doyle was out. Polson and González were banished from the game for ignoring warnings not to fight.

This last was not received happily by the Cubans. The big catcher threw his mitt on the grass and spat in McGraw's direction as he stalked off the diamond. To the crowd it looked as if McGraw, finding himself on the losing end, had tricked the Blues out of a star player—a loss hardly matched by Polson.

Pedroso warmed up with a new catcher, and finally Dutch Wilson stepped in to hit. He whiffed on three pitches. The inning was over and we'd failed to score. McGraw looked like he'd eaten gunpowder and washed it down with kerosene.

In the seventh the Blues added a run to their total. Donlin scored on a double and some heady baserunning in the eighth, but that was all we could do. It ended with us on the low end, 6–4. We trooped off the field, a somber bunch. We'd been outhit, outpitched, outfielded, outrun and outscored.

———— • ◆ • ————

AT THE LOUVRE HOTEL we sat on a terrace overlooking the Almendares River, drinking Planter's Punches. A tasty mix of rum, lime juice, grenadine and soda, it had been invented hereabouts by the sugar bosses. McGraw limited us to one each. When Donlin started ribbing Devore, who'd had another wretched game, the manager silenced them both. The wives arrived in a throng, then came the Blues manager with a dozen Cuban dignitaries—there seemed no end of officials wanting to meet us. We moved inside for yet another banquet: crabs steamed in coconut milk; beef soaked in Spanish sherry; the usual fried plantains and beans and rice. If we didn't cut this out, in three weeks they'd have to roll us onto the boat.

McGraw was asked to make a speech, which he carried off pretty well, given how pissed he was at losing. When he'd come here in '91 with Al Lawson's barnstormers, he related, "crowds" numbered only several hundred, and the Cuban players' enthusiasm had exceeded their skills. He described pitchers launching themselves forward like cricket bowlers to deliver the ball on the dead run, not knowing or caring that the rules called for one foot on the slab. The Americans had nearly laughed themselves out of several games.

He wasn't laughing now, I noticed.

That night we saw *The Seller of Cadavers* at Teatro Tacón. The melodrama was in Spanish, so none of us could follow it—and I didn't care for what I did follow. Given the rich food and drink and the theater's close atmosphere, a number of us dozed off. Donlin kept nudging me. He loved any kind of theater, and actually had tears in his eyes at the end when the heroine stood alone weeping.

Back at the Plaza, McGraw called us together. "Practice at ten," he announced, glaring around. "And until you start playing like men, there's a midnight curfew!"

We shuffled our feet and stared at the tiled floor. Havana nightlife didn't get cooking until around twelve—just when he wanted us in our rooms. To my surprise it was Devore who spoke up. "I ain't got a contract here," he declared.

McGraw impaled him with an icy stare. "You'll follow my rules or get on the goddamn boat! Ever since we got here, you've been a sorry excuse for a ballplayer!"

It was harsh but basically true. Devore was 1–for–10 at the plate and looked half asleep in the field. Staying out nights was killing his game. He took a deep breath and kept his mouth shut. Nobody else had anything to say.

Back in our room, Donlin put another new song on his phonograph: *I want a girl just like the girl that married dear old Dad. . . .* Della didn't exactly fit that bill, but it made me think of her, and so I began a letter in which I told her about the game and the theater visit. I didn't mention that they'd taken place on Sunday. She'd have concluded I was in a Babylon of corruption.

Which, from her standpoint, was highly accurate.

Donlin, of course, hadn't the slightest intention of heeding the curfew. He heaped bedding under his blanket to make a human form, then primped in front of the mirror. When he saw me looking, he winked.

"Can't disappoint Alma," he signed. "We're meeting at Casino Español. Wanna come?"

Thinking mournfully that when he got caught I'd lose my only true chum here, I was tempted to go along to prevent it. But if Crandall couldn't pitch tomorrow, it might be me. Maybe Turkey Mike could dally all night and play up to his old form, but I knew I couldn't. Besides, he was already under contract to Pittsburgh next year. He didn't need McGraw like I did.

"Don't sign any baseballs," I advised.

Donlin laughed. It was an old trick, and McGraw had used it to snag his share of unsuspecting violators. How it worked was simple: at the time curfew commenced, a ball was given to a night clerk or elevator operator. He would then ask any incoming players to sign it for his kid—and the ball thus became evidence. A slick feature of the scheme was that a coach didn't have to stay up all hours to catch curfew-breakers. Donlin was far too canny for such snares.

"I'll not go out as baggage either," he signed, grinning. One spring in Marlin, McGraw had herded us all into the elevators to our floor to make sure nobody escaped. Donlin foiled him by sprinting to a freight lift and going down again before the passengers had emptied. McGraw nearly popped an artery trying to find his star outfielder.

"See you." Opening the shutters, he looked down at the garden patio. Typical for Havana, the window had no glass. Shutters kept out rain (and bugs during the few evening hours when prevailing sea breezes died); otherwise, conditions were so mild that glass wasn't needed. He stepped through the window, eased himself down a flower-covered trellis, and vanished into the shadows at the bottom.

Next thing I knew, Donlin was getting into the next bed—don't ask me why it woke me up; I can't explain it, but I often *feel* movement near me—and the grainy light told me dawn was approaching. I dressed and went down to the lobby to check the early editions. The *Post* wasn't out yet, but the banner headline of *El Mundo* was easy to translate: *¡DERROTA DE LOS NEOYORQUINOS!* Defeat of the New Yorkers. Stale news.

Farther down, another bold caption was more interesting: CON-FLICTO INTERNACIONAL. A subhead spoke of McGraw and González, *"haber hablado de sus respectivas madres en tono despectivo."* Insulted each other's mothers. Sure enough, in the text that followed, I found the words *"hijo de perra."* Son of a female dog. Amazing they'd print that.

Three photographs were splashed across the page: Rigler trying to separate the two teams; McGraw and González going at it jaw to jaw; and me prancing with my plume and rake. *"Un Sordo Cómico y Pacífico"* captioned my picture. My dictionary told me it meant "Deaf Comic Peacemaker." Not bad. An accompanying box held a capsule of my Giants career, the information provided by Sid Mercer. Three times in the text I was tagged *"un lanzador sordo."*

Deaf players must have been rare in those parts.

I leaned back and tried to take stock. Would this hurt me with McGraw? In the past he'd enjoyed my antics and been quick to put them to his own ends. But this time I'd lampooned him too. I searched for our itinerary, which was printed each day. This morning we were scheduled to visit a botanical garden. Scratch that, I told myself. We'd be working out.

———— •◆• ————

WHILE WE DID our stretching and easy ball tossing, Hooks and Devlin razzed me pretty good about the spread in the papers. Doyle and Becker crossed bats to make a show of mock fencing. Herzog and Fletcher gave me hard looks, and Polson mouthed the word "showboat." Which was pretty good, considering I suspected him of grandstanding that scrap just to get on McGraw's good side. The busher must think playing ten games in the bigs made him a veteran.

McGraw ran a two-hour practice that ended with laps around the ballpark like in spring training. Even Matty wasn't excused. It was clear he had punishment in mind. I'd been studying Crandall, trying to guess how his shoulder was, and I finally asked.

"A little stiff," he admitted. "I could probably go."

Something told me he couldn't. I tried to see it from McGraw's viewpoint. Using Matty again would probably bring a victory, but at the cost of taxing his arm and also making it look like McGraw could win only with his ace. Yesterday Hooks had thrown eight rugged innings. Which left Crandall and me. Would McGraw risk hurting Crandall? Or take his chances with me?

I found out after practice.

"You put on a show yesterday," McGraw signed as we left the field.

"Thanks." I was tempted to say, *So did you.*

"Looks like you got quite a following here already." There was a gleam in his eye, but I couldn't tell if it was friendly. "How's the wing?" he demanded. "Strong?"

"Yessir."

"Good," he said, "because this afternoon you're on the mound."

NINE

WITH DEVORE SLUMPING and Herzog still not ready, we weren't at our strongest. On the other hand, I'd seen the Havana Reds but they hadn't seen me. The sun was out full force and I worked up a sweat, arm all oiled up, pitches working like nobody's business. Becoming aware of a commotion in the stands, I glanced over and saw a bunch of kids waving at me. When they saw me looking they unfurled a banner. I stared at its message: ¡VIVA EL SORDO!

A fan party all my own! I stood there marveling for a few seconds. Then I had a new surprise: they were *signing* to me. A lot of it I didn't get, but there was no mistaking the hands raised from hearts to form fists. They were rooting for me to beat the Reds. Rooting against their countrymen! It touched my heart. I was used to deaf rooters coming out wherever I pitched in the States, but I hadn't expected it here.

El Sordo. I liked it.

Thinking that the pictures in *El Mundo* had brought these kids out from a deaf school, I wondered if this was what McGraw meant by my following. I walked toward them and tipped my cap, which set them jumping wildly and waving their hands, and I got a good idea from their eyes what I was to them. More than a big leaguer. *Their* player.

They reached for me and I shook their hands. At the far end of the banner, which was bumping up and down riotously, stood a brown-robed priest. A thin man with an aquiline nose and alert eyes, he nodded as he caught my glance. The kids' teacher, I supposed. He touched his chin with his open palm and again with three fingers. Then he crossed himself. Graceful movements. He was wishing me good fortune and God's blessing.

Thanks, Padre, I'll take all the help I can get.

Rigler signaled for the game to begin, and Devore stepped up to the plate. Pitching for the Reds was Luque, the stocky kid who'd thrown a strong inning against us two days ago. Out in the field the Reds looked confident. Their rivals had shown we could be licked—and today they weren't facing Matty.

Devore failed to get on, but Doyle singled, took second on a passed ball, third on a long fly, and scored on a balk. Not exactly a booming display, but I walked out to the mound, up by a run. I felt jittery anyway. My warmups exploded into Wilson's mitt, and he motioned for me to calm down. I tried, but everything had too much on it and swooped beyond my control. I walked the first Red, who promptly stole second.

Mad at myself, I got a fly out, then fanned the next hitter on balls that nipped the corners—and sneaked a glance to make sure McGraw had noticed. On a 3–2 count their clean-up hitter chased an outshoot and sent a nice four-hopper to Doyle.

It went through his legs!

The runner was off with the pitch, of course, and just like us the Reds scored without a hit. After Donlin hauled in a skyball, I walked quickly to our bench. Anger had chased the jitters away. If my damn infielders didn't play big-league defense, how the hell was I supposed to do my job?

Donlin tripled and tallied in the third, and through five innings the score stood at 2–1. So far in Havana we'd failed to notch more than one run in any inning, and I knew McGraw was bemoaning the absence of four of his regular batsmen: Meyers, Snodgrass, Merkle, and Murray. If Donlin hadn't showed up, we'd be even more anemic. Just as if I hadn't come, our pitching would be threadbare.

The one-run edge looked bigger as I backed the Reds off the plate, caught the corners with nasty shoots, and brought Dundon in for the kill. Matty had scarcely looked any better. I felt happier than I had in months. Years, maybe.

It all changed in the sixth.

Luque finished the top of that inning by striking out Wilson. As he stepped from the mound he swept his arm in a gesture that took in not only Dutch but our bench, as if brushing us all away. That's how we saw it, and so did the fans. They jumped up and clapped and stomped and yelled and threw money at Luque as he came off the field. Naturally, it pissed us off, from McGraw on down. Who did the fresh kid think he was?

Just as naturally, I dumped their leadoff man on his butt. Any right-thinking flinger—one of McGraw's, anyway—would do the same. If the Red had acted chesty as he stepped back in, I'd have low-bridged him again. But he didn't. I dished up a spinner that came down the middle like a fat fish, then darted in on his hands. Swinging at it and trying to pull back at the same time, he got his feet tangled and ended up in the dirt again. Wilson grinned and fired the ball back.

It made sense that I'd go outside after coming in on him twice. He shifted his stance. I fired a smoker down the middle. Leaning over the plate, he pulled back fast, but since he didn't want to watch a hittable strike go by, he swung—so late that the ball was in Wilson's mitt by the time he got around. Once again he'd looked like a rusty gate, and his face tightened.

With the count 1–2, I teased him outside. He squared as if to bunt and watched it go by. Was he bluffing? Would he lay one down with two strikes? McGraw thought so, for he motioned Polson and Devlin in at the corners. On 2–2 he squared again. I came off the mound in a hurry, ready to pounce.

He didn't bunt but poked the ball, which skittered past me and to the right of Polson, who should have gone to the bag and let Doyle take it. Instead he lunged sideways and made a flashy dive. Polson wasn't much with the stick, but he was a decent glove man—in his own view no doubt another Hal Chase—and he came up with the ball in front of Doyle. Nobody was covering first. My spikes slipped as I sprinted for the bag, which just put me farther behind the runner. There was no chance to get him. Nonetheless, Polson made the underhand feed as if I were there, the ball arcing over the base and dropping in foul ground. If Wilson hadn't been on his job and backed up, the runner would have taken second. Polson had done it to show me up. Enraged, I went for him. Dutch blocked me, meanwhile telling Polson what he thought of his stunt. Fletcher came over from short, probably to stick up for the busher, but decided to keep his peace when he saw how steamed Wilson was. Still, he gave me a level stare that said, *Where were you?*

Which made me sorer yet.

That's when I decided, like a fathead, to take things into my own hands. If we were playing for ourselves, so be it. I held up three fingers, telling the hitter and everybody else that I'd whiff him. Not only that, but I turned and pointed to the deaf kids sitting behind their banner. I'd do it for them. They jumped up and waved their hands to let me know they'd gotten the message.

I wound up with exaggerated determination. The batsman expected a blazer, but got a lazy roundhouse shoot that had him leaning forward. He watched it sail past for a strike. I gave him the same pitch. Again he was fooled. He had every reason to expect the hummer now, for it looked like I'd set it up. And sure enough, the ball came in hard and high.

Now, placed right, a high fast one would have been damn near impossible to hit. But I wanted more. I wanted to show him up. I gave him Dundon as hard as I could deliver it. The trouble was, it's easier to get a break—any kind of break—on a ball thrown low rather than high. I'd learned to throw Dundon straight overhand with a sharp snap of the wrist, bringing my fingers down over the face of the ball just before releasing. It strained my arm, just as Matty's fadeaway did his, and it took even more to make it work if I came in high with it.

Dundon careened in. Figuring to crush it out of the park, the Red swung from his heels—and went over it by a foot. Exactly what I'd wanted. But somewhere deep in the bundled cords just below my shoulder I felt a tiny "pop," and knew right away I'd hurt something. A panicky feeling started to build in my chest. *Breathe,* I commanded myself.

I couldn't rub the place and give it away. Not with every eye in the place on me as the disgruntled Red batter trudged off and the next one stepped in. The deaf kids were bouncing like bugs. McGraw and the benchwarmers were grinning. The infielders were snapping the ball around with cocky assurance. It should have been a sweet moment.

It was awful.

Flexing my arm beneath my shirt, taking care to hide the movement, I couldn't feel anything. But when I went into my windup, arms rising over my head, there was a needle of pain.

Goddamn!

I followed through after releasing the ball, but there wasn't much on it. The hitter's eyes lit up as he smashed it over Fletcher. Off with the impact, Donlin cut over and held the Reds at first and second. But the next hitter clubbed one in almost the same place, scoring their lead runner and tying the game. Wilson came out to the mound. He didn't talk Sign, but his face said that he knew something was wrong. I waved him back, but after I served up three straight wides to the next batsman, McGraw himself paid a visit.

"You look like you're favoring something," he signed. "You wearing out?"

I shook my head. It wouldn't do to plead tiredness. I hadn't even finished six innings, and at age 36 I couldn't afford to be weary this soon.

He stared at me for a long moment before leaving.

I spotted my next pitches, working the hitter to 3–2. Wilson signaled for the drop. I shook my head. He called for it again and I shook him off. We settled on an outshoot. Throwing it, I felt a tongue of pain lick down from my shoulder nearly to my elbow. The batsman sent a scorcher down the line but too near Devlin, who speared it backhanded. I'd been lucky, and I knew it. Two outs now. If I could get one more and rest on the bench for a few minutes, maybe. . . .

The next delivery brought the sharpest sensation yet. The ball sailed over everybody. By the time Wilson retrieved it, runners were on second and third. Worse, I'd involuntarily reached for my shoulder. McGraw was off the bench like a shot.

"You're hurt, ain't you?" he demanded.

I held finger and thumb close, saying it was nothing.

He didn't buy it. "You're coming out."

"But you don't have anybody."

He turned and waved to right field. "Becker's pitched some."

Maybe in the bushes, I thought.

McGraw took the ball from my hand and shoved me toward the bench. "I'm not gonna be responsible," he signed, "for ending your pitching days."

Who could argue with that? Feeling sick to the depths of my soul, I trudged to the bench. On a day to prove myself, all I'd shown was that I could showboat and get hurt. I wanted to punch somebody. Lucky for the two likeliest targets, McGraw was already berating Polson, and Herzog was warming up to go in at third; if either had so much as smirked, he'd gave gotten a pasting.

McGraw's trainer rubbed my arm with wintergreen and wrapped it in a towel. I didn't feel anything while he did it. Sitting there, the sharp odor of the liniment in my nose, I began to think maybe McGraw had been hasty. Then I lifted my arm above chest level and felt a warning twinge. My spirits plunged again.

Becker warmed up with medium-speed tosses that the Cubans eyed with interest. Despite his dandified ways, Becker was a Kansan like me, raised down around Wichita. From fooling around with him in practice, I knew he had a trick pitch—an emery ball he'd learned from Russ Ford, the Canuck hurler now with the Highlanders. Becker had played with him in Atlanta when Ford happened to scuff a ball and discover that the rough surface provided more traction. Since then a rule had been passed against defacing balls, so Ford, like others, had taken to deception, hiding his emery cloth in the heel of his glove; last season he'd won 26 games with it. Ford was known to be something of a dude with the ladies, too, so maybe Beals had also copied that from him.

I watched him scrape the ball on his belt buckle and deepen the scratch with his fingernails. *Good,* I thought. His first throw showed excellent movement, but because I'd left him with a 3–0 count, he delivered it right down the pipe. The batsman walloped it through the middle, and both runners scored.

Now we trailed 4–2. The next hitter slammed a scorcher toward the gap, but Donlin ran it down for the third out. All the runs were tallied to me. I'd be the loser unless we came back, in which case Becker would get the victory.

I sat there morosely.

Luque got himself tossed for spitting when Rigler didn't give him a strike call. We couldn't touch his replacement, though, a control artist named Carlos Mederos. Where did the Cubans come up with all these young arms? We had five measly hits for the day, Donlin's triple our only extra-base knock. Becker was terrible, walking five, hitting a batsman, and balking twice, but despite it all somehow kept them from scoring again.

It ended 4–2.

The Reds danced on the field like they'd taken the World Series. My arm throbbed as I walked off the diamond. Passing near the stand, I felt a tug at my sleeve and looked up to find the brown-robed priest leaning over the railing. He signed something that I couldn't decipher. Just then I was in no mood to try, either, and probably would've just waved goodbye if my attention hadn't been caught by a tall, lean boy standing at his shoulder. Seven or eight years older than the kids, he looked to be between eighteen and twenty. His dark eyes were fixed on me. When I didn't respond to the priest's second try (which he finger-spelled, saying something about being sorry to bother me), the boy's face slowly hardened.

Almost like he was challenging me.

The priest spread his hands in a supplicating gesture. "Please," his lips said, and I could tell by the way his throat moved that he was not mute. He made a circle in the air to include the three of us. He wanted us to talk. Normally I'd drop everything—this wasn't just a figure of speech in my case—to converse with a deaf kid who wanted to see me, priest or no priest. But I was in no mood and McGraw was herding us off the field. I averted my eyes and walked on. All I can say for myself is that I was heartsick and scared. Even so, I didn't feel good about it.

At the Payret Theater that night we watched a group of mimes stage what was supposed to be a humorous skit. One, a figure on stilts and stuffed with pillows, wore a version of our black uniform and was baited by another dressed as a Havana Red. When the Giant held up a sign that said "Mathewson," the Red swooned. Other mimes portrayed McGraw, Rigler and González in their big set-to, the funniest part coming when they donned wigs and went on scrapping as their mothers. Finally the Giant tottered and crashed to the stage, which grated on us, though we tried to be good sports. McGraw, I noticed, was grinning jauntily like he'd never had so much fun.

When we got back to our hotel he didn't bother threatening us. No more curfew. He just said we'd practice every morning till our next game, four days off. We knew he meant to work our asses off. Most of the married players stuck around the hotel bar with their wives. Most of the single ones set off to visit a gambling club.

Donlin followed me up to our room and watched me apply arnica. "Your wing hurt bad?"

"Naw." I lifted it gingerly. Was the pain less? I wasn't sure. "Sore is all."

He nodded matter-of-factly. For ballplayers, aches and pains were normal.

I capped the jar and pulled on my coat.

"Going out?"

I nodded.

"Want company?"

"No, I'm gonna get some air, walk around town, think over some things."

"Be out long?"

"Maybe all night, the way I feel now."

We'd avoided the subject of my pitching that day. Donlin knew me too well to bring it up now. "Keep out of trouble," he signed.

From him, that was good.

Pushed by restlessness and worry, I walked the busy streets for a long time before finally settling in a terraced cafe off the Malecón. There I decided the hell with it and drank Planter's Punches and stared out at the white-foamed breakers smashing against the seawall. The drinks dulled the throbbing in my arm, which I kept flexing. The best thing for it would be rest . . . the absolute last thing I'd come here for. I drank more rum. It got to be very late. I left a pile of money on the table and set off unsteadily for the Plaza. Habaneros moved around me as if music was built into their bodies. I envied them. *Their* arms worked.

Something was different in the room. My first inkling of it came when I caught a trace of perfume and figured Donlin had used a new shave soap. Then I saw the bedclothes humped high in his bed. Had McGraw gone back to a curfew? If so, why hadn't Donlin fixed my bed too?

Then the hump moved, rhythmically.

I couldn't believe it. Could Donlin . . . or somebody . . . ? I slipped the covers back far enough to see that it was Turkey Mike. Below his shoulder were the pale, straining features of Miss Soda Cracker, her mouth open in what must have been a pleasurable cry. Donlin was oblivious, but she sensed something and opened her eyes and her mouth contorted into a scream as she snatched the covers back over their heads. The hump moved more urgently than before, no longer rhythmical.

It wasn't the first time Donlin had pulled something like this, and in the old days I probably would have laughed. But we were no longer a couple of wild kids loose in Big Town. I was drunk, dispirited, fed up with today, and wanted to sleep. I snapped on the chandelier—the Plaza lacked hot-water plumbing and individual baths, but boasted electric lighting and fans— and slammed the door behind me. I didn't feel like waiting in the hallway and facing Miss Soda Cracker, so I went out through the lobby and paced the streets for another twenty minutes.

When I returned she was gone. Donlin sat in green silk pajamas patterned with shamrocks. He looked contrite. "You said you'd be out all night."

"What the hell's wrong with you?"

His chest rose and fell. "Remember that cousin of Méndez? Well, turns out he's got pull with the government and fixed it so poor Alma's getting deported. Leaving first thing tomorrow. She lost her swell job over it, and I felt pretty bad." He waved at the bed. "We had a few drinks and things sort of. . . ."

"What about Mabel?"

He looked stricken. "What about her?"

"It don't matter to you that you're married?"

"Let's not talk about it."

"Let's do," I persisted. "What is it, Mike? You down here running from Mabel?"

"I'm here for the dough. Period." His hands chopped out the curt answer.

"Okay, but you always crow about how much more you make on stage—with Mabel."

"You don't get it." He stood up. "She's sick and can't work. I've been nursing her for weeks." He took a breath. "I'll be nursing her again when this is over."

"What's the matter with her?"

"I told you, I don't want to discuss it. Look, my coming here was her idea. Mabel knows how I love the game, the sunshine, hell, even McGraw." His fingers were moving very fast. "She wanted it for both of us, see? One last time, she said."

I had the disturbing thought that maybe Della had sent me out one last time.

"So you do *this* for her?"

Donlin's eyes flashed. "She knows who I am, Dummy," he signed. "Even better than you do. It happens that Alma and I are old chums and this isn't the first . . . let's just say I've known her a long time. Alma's had her own troubles. She needed to talk. Then, like I said, things got away from us. I'm sorry it happened like this—but I ain't gonna crawl because *you* say so!"

He went over to the wash bowl and splashed water on his face. I could appreciate that he was dealing with some struggle of his own. I should have forgiven him, but I couldn't do it.

As I climbed into bed I half expected to see him get dressed again and go off carousing. Instead, not looking at me, he turned off the light and got back into his bed. I lay there in the soft tropical night, thinking of Mabel, of Della, of my hurt arm.

TEN

Olathe,
1958

Starting out, he could barely feed himself on what he made hurling in places like Mattoon and Lincoln, but Della had made up her mind that as a professional he needed the best. So she'd tricked him into letting her outline his feet and then sent the paper with her money to the factory back East. On his eighteenth birthday she presented him with a pair of Claflin's "Professional" spikes, the finest made. The uppers were tough, flexible kangaroo skin; the spikes were unbendable and clog-resistant. The shoes were feather-light on his feet and fit better than any he'd known.

"These make my glove look awful," he'd joked.

"You'll get that next," she'd promised.

Was it that day they'd gone up to Coal Creek Valley? The day of their first lovemaking? No. His birthday came in February. The day he was thinking of had been balmy, "cotton" from the trees falling on them. Must have been in June.

Driving Pa's hard-springed buggy, they had stopped at old Schinkle's store (the gas pump hadn't even been put in yet) for sodas, then bumped along Devil's Backbone, a rollercoaster of swales and ruts and ridges; they climbed past the Kelleys' farm, called "Bittersweet," and finally up to Simmons Hill, where the Signal Oak stood at the peak overlooking three valleys. Lanterns had hung on its branches during the Civil War to warn of approaching Rebs. On its trunk he carved their initials inside a heart, then he led her down to one of the creekside narrows.

They spread their blanket in dappled sunlight beneath a canopy of cotton-woods and hickories and walnuts. Soon their kisses took all their breath. Beautiful beyond measure, she looked into his eyes as he unbuttoned her shirt-waist, smiling when he fumbled at the job. Her breasts seemed white as ice-cream mounds to him, their nipples cotton-candy pink. Freed of cotton under-garments, she was a marvelous complexity of swellings and hollows. Then he was naked, too, and charged with urgency.

Her lips framed silent words as he entered her, her fingers whispering against his chest, his neck, his face. She shuddered once and then he felt her respond, her hips rolling. At the last instant he tried to pull back, too late. They worried about it afterward, but nothing ever. . . .

Never mind that.

His gnarled fingers were bent from arthritis now, but he looked down and saw that they were stretched out nearly straight. In his mind they had touched Della again. By God, he wouldn't mind living that day over.

The shoes on the table were split and cracked, one of the spiked triangles long missing. More than once he'd been on the verge of throwing them away, but couldn't quite do it. Those old shoes of his had dug into so many distant diamonds. . . .

ELEVEN

EL MUNDO'S CARTOONS showed Doyle with his fingers in a butter churn; Becker with a mop and bucket (signifying his mop-up pitching role); bifocal spectacles (top half labeled *"plancha"* or windup, bottom half "hit") to enable us to see Méndez's fastballs; and McGraw simultaneously oiling our spikes to boost our speed and drinking a valerian-root potion to calm his nerves. One column gloated that since the Reds and Blues had licked Mr. Mack's A's after they'd trimmed the Cubs in the Series last year, and since they'd now taken two of three from the current National League titlist, shouldn't they be Co-Champions of the World?

It wore a little thin. Especially galling were the Habaneros lining the streets each morning, winking and smirking as we piled into autos that took us to practice. We grinned our way through it, but a resolve was growing among us. Even Matty, usually unflappable, looked a bit tight-jawed.

The next three days we worked out in the cool morning hours. McGraw ran us till our tongues hung out and gave slackers extra laps. Polson picked up a lot of them. If winning depended on our legs, we'd be ready. I didn't throw at all, not even easy tosses, and tried to keep my arm low. A strained cord was all, the trainer said. I hoped so. Seeing my long mug, McGraw assured me that injuries were part of the game. I'd shown well against the Reds, he said, and there would be more chances for me. Meanwhile, with Crandall recovered and Matty and Hooks rested, I'd be held out of this weekend's games.

Trying to be of some use, I ran bases in McGraw's endless drills. Standing at the plate, he'd yell "one down" and give me a sign. I'd take off as he fungoed the ball, running and sliding hard, never going half-speed like the others. Once I dumped Fletcher at second, and he bounced up and came at me. Protecting my arm, I slapped the side of his head twice with my open left hand before he scarcely realized it. He telegraphed a roundhouse right that I ducked under easily. I poked my knuckles into his belly, then as he gasped for air I gave him my clown's grin.

While Fletcher didn't have much quit in him, he must have recognized he was out of his depth. Herzog came running over with Polson close behind, but Doyle and others headed them off. I noticed McGraw trying to hide a grin. He liked his players in fighting spirits. I shook Fletcher's hand later to show no hard feelings. But not Herzog's or Polson's.

As for Turkey Mike, things between us stayed cool. We didn't see each other that much except at workouts. He came in late and slept until just before practice. We took pains not to wake each other. I read in the *Post* that Miss Soda Cracker had finished her publicity tour and returned to Florida. Star pitcher Méndez, "the most popular man in Cuba," according to the reporter, "might bring her back soon for personal reasons."

Not likely, I thought. Donlin had fixed that.

———— •◆• ————

ONE AFTERNOON THE deskman handed me a calling card:

PADRE CIPRIANO

ORDENA DE SAN FRANCISCO

LA ESCUELA DEL OREJAS

SAN PEDRO APOSTOL

MATANZAS

It had been left that morning. With my dictionary I translated: "Father Cipriano, Franciscan Order, School of the Ears." On a wall map the deskman showed me Matanzas, a port city a half day's journey away. He didn't know anything about the cleric other than that he'd seemed eager to see me.

School of the Ears. . . .

Had the Padre brought those kids all that way to see me? With a sense of shame I remembered brushing him off after the game. He'd written nothing on the back of the card. How was I supposed to contact him?

———— • ◆ • ————

NOVEMBER 30 WAS the month's fourth Thursday, which made it Thanksgiving, as decreed by President Lincoln four decades back. More important to us, it was the day Matty and Méndez would finally square off. McGraw called a meeting after breakfast. I sat practically at his feet, just like in the old days, so as not to miss anything. Looking around, he announced, "I didn't come here to get whipped by a bunch of coffee-colored Cubans!" His eyes drilled into ours. "Anybody got anything to say?" Nobody did. "Okay, ante up." He sent the trainer around to collect cash. "Twenty-five bucks each. Enough so you'll play your guts out. Put in more if you want a bigger take."

I thought about ducking it. I wasn't drawing a salary and I couldn't play anyway. Then I decided what the hell, I could use the winnings. It was hard to imagine Matty losing today.

———— •◆•————

THE PAPERS HAD boosted this match all week, so it was no surprise that the crowd was big and rambunctious. Railroad workers had even threatened to strike if they weren't given time to attend. I looked around in vain for the brown-robed priest and the deaf kids, especially the tall boy whose eyes had stared so belligerently into mine. There was no reason to expect them, but I felt a twinge of regret.

A banner draped from the right-field bleachers bore a picture of Méndez and the words, *¡LA PERLA NEGRA!* The Black Pearl. That section was jammed with dark-skinned fans. Did Jim Crow exist here? Black Cubans made up at least a third of the population, and from what I'd seen so far in Havana, everybody mixed pretty freely. No separate water fountains or toilets for colored, like I'd seen in Florida. Yet it was clear that the poorest folks here were Negroes. All the people we hob-nobbed with at banquets were lighter-skinned and made a big thing of their Spanish background. In baseball things seemed more blurred. Blacks played for both Havana teams, and some, like Méndez, were stars. A far cry from the States, where Organized Ball had shut them out ever since Reconstruction.

What if the same thing had happened to deaf men?

Finished stretching, I ventured one tiny lob toss, and to my joy there was no sting. McGraw glared a warning, but I had no intention of try-ing another.

The Blues had warmed up somewhere else. Now they marched in through the players gate, bringing the crowd to its feet. McGraw scowled, hating to be upstaged, as they took their positions. The solid bulk of Mike González squatted behind the plate, while Méndez, a lean figure, stalked to the mound. In uniform he looked older than he had in the nightclub. I judged him to be a shade taller but slighter than Luque, the other young hurler who'd shown so well against us. But where Luque was rough and showed his youth, Méndez was smooth, his windup compact and easy, the ball exploding into González's mitt. There was a catlike energy to him, fierce and controlled. And an arrogance that went beyond surface chestiness. I'd seen it in Mathewson, too, even before he was an ace. No matter the situation, those guys acted like they *knew* they could handle it.

Not content with spanking dirt from González's mitt with his blazers, Méndez took to breaking off an eye-popping assortment of shoots and curves. My teammates, if not exactly awed, were highly curious. McGraw picked that time to send Sid Mercer out to bet the money he'd collected from us—no doubt thinking that right now, with Méndez showing off, odds were as good for us as they'd get.

Matty came to the bench, face beaded with sweat. The temperature had climbed to 85 and humidity was at least that high; the heavy clouds were starting to break up without unloading the rain they'd promised. Down here it took scarcely a handful of throws to be ready, but Méndez went on with his show. Maybe he hoped to intimidate us.

McGraw began to counterattack. "WHO IS THIS GUY?" he yelled from the first-base line. "WHO DOES HE THINK HE IS? WHO EVER HEARD OF THIS GUY?" Hooks told me that it carried through the whole ballpark. Méndez ignored him, but González and some other Blues began shooting McGraw hard looks.

"You know what to do," McGraw told me, pointing toward third.

I did indeed. I jogged out to the coacher's box and set to work. Each time Méndez went into his windup I yelled "MAMA!" It was something I could reliably get out, and I'd learned that a single word can get under an opponent's skin, on account of him wondering why anybody said *that*. At the first "mama!" Méndez halted his windup and turned to stare. His eyes narrowed as he recognized me. Shoulders lifting and neck bowing, he fixed me with a flat, deadly stare. He ignored González, gesturing behind the plate. Seeing how I had his total attention, I made a quick decision. What the hell. There was probably going to be a fracas before the day was out anyway. Twirling and dipping, I mimed doing the *danzón* with an imaginary partner. Méndez slammed his glove on his thigh and kicked at the dirt like an agitated bull. González ran out to calm him down. I tucked my hands in my armpits and flapped my arms like a chicken, giving him a few more "mama"s. There was, Hooks said, a scary hush in the stands.

Rigler summoned McGraw and me. A recent rule back home barred coaches from talking to opposing pitchers. No such thing existed here, but Rigler called on us to observe it anyway. Which, predictably, set off McGraw, who maintained that his "Who is this guy?" had been addressed to the ballpark at large, not at any of the Blues. And since I couldn't engage in what was properly "speech," how could I be talking to Méndez? Meanwhile, on the mound, the Blues manager had joined Gonález in pacifying Méndez. Rigler gave up and bellowed "PLAY BALL!"

Devore stepped to the plate. As Méndez went into his windup I gave him a full-throated "MAMA!" while waving my sweater in a circle to distract him. His first pitch went straight at Devore, who fell away barely in time to avoid being skulled. The next one nailed him in the back, the force of it sending him sprawling.

While our bench howled threats I saw McGraw's lips saying, "About time the little bastard got on."

"MAMA!" I yelled as Méndez threw to Doyle. The ball sailed high and González had to leap for it. Méndez gave me a venomous glare.

About to blow, I thought. The next pitch was also high. Then, as if the young hurler didn't have enough to think about, McGraw added something new.

"His foot!" he yelled to Rigler, pointing at Méndez and kicking his spikes to indicate something amiss with his stance on the rubber. The next offering skidded in the dirt beneath González's mitt, Devore taking second.

McGraw was on it again. "Watch his foot!"

Rigler gave him a cynical look. He'd seen it all before, but had little choice but to go out and dust off the rubber so he could observe Méndez's placement. The pitcher glowered at him, muscles along his jaw working.

"MAMA!" I yelled.

"*¡Come mierda!* he retorted, saying it enough times that I got the Spanish. I had no idea what it meant, but a pitcher talking back was usually a sign that you'd gotten to him.

"MAMA!" I blasted. I knew it meant the same thing in Spanish. What I didn't know was that Cubans made such a big thing of it. I wasn't trying to insult his mother, at least not the way McGraw had insulted González's. But Méndez took it as the same thing. He came off the mound and headed for me. I watched him come, my pulse speeding pleasurably—I *love* to spar, especially when the other guy means business—and fretting over my arm had made me feel mean.

Luckily, González hauled him in before he got to me. The crowd looked ugly; things were starting to hit the turf around us. Rigler threatened to toss both McGraw and me if we made another peep.

Méndez tried to pull himself together, a hard thing after the work we'd done. He worked carefully, but Doyle made it to first on a dribbler, which didn't help him. Herzog's fly sent Devore to third.

One out, runners at the corners.

Turkey Mike stepped in, grinning.

It was too much for Méndez. He turned and stared for a long moment at the center field fence, his shoulders rising and falling, and I had no doubt what would come next. Neither did Donlin, who low-bridged in a hurry beneath a head-seeking smoker. McGraw protested to Rigler, who merely looked at him as if to say, *You brought this on yourself.*

Méndez gathered himself to throw again. Donlin called time and rubbed his eye with a thumb, his middle finger pointing at Méndez. He held the pose long enough to make sure the pitcher got it.

No doubt the next pitch was supposed to shear Donlin off at the knees, but it was so poorly thrown that it went behind him and clear under the grandstand. Rigler applied the ground rules and waved Devore home and Doyle to third. Méndez tried a curve. Donlin slapped it to the right of their slick-fielding shortstop, who gloved it backhand. With scant chance of getting Donlin at first, he elected to try for Doyle at the plate and uncorked an amazing, off-balance throw that might have had him. But González, either surprised at finding the ball in his mitt or at seeing Doyle stop on a dime and dash back toward third, had trouble plucking it loose, and fired late to Almeida. Everybody was safe.

Becker, another lefty, less vulnerable to Méndez's shoots, stepped in. Along with Donlin he'd been our hottest hitter. Swinging smoothly, he golfed the ball over the second baseman on a sinking line. The right fielder tried for a shoetop catch but the ball got under him and all the way to the fence. Both runners scored, and we led 3–0.

Which pretty much decided it.

Mathewson gave up three singles, walked none, and no Blue got as far as second. Méndez, too, settled down and showed us what everybody was excited about: pinpoint mastery of his blazers and outshoots.

We scored again in the seventh on Fletcher's leadoff double, but that was all we got. It ended 4–0 in a crisp hour and 40 minutes. I'd never seen Matty more in command, not even in the '05 Series. There was no longer much question who was the top pitcher.

Or maybe the top agitators.

Méndez had shown a lot of grit, though, in pulling himself together after that disastrous first inning. If his right fielder had caught Becker's liner or at least stopped it, or if his wild pitch hadn't gone under the stands, the score would have been 1–0.

Only Donlin and I knew *all* the pressure we'd put on him.

Our Cuban clubhouse man told Donlin that Méndez had come looking for us after the game, but his manager pulled him away. "Keep your eyes open," he told us. "Señor Méndez has many friends."

Swell, I thought.

"I think I'd be willing to pay $50,000 for that kid," McGraw said, standing us all drinks back at the Plaza, expansive after the victory. "Damn shame he's a nigger."

"Officially?" Matty said.

"Yup," McGraw said. "Of course, González was one too—till he got an affidavit swearing his blood's full Castilian. I just found out Boston's gonna sign him."

Matty smiled knowingly. "Wish you'd gotten him?"

"Maybe." McGraw was notorious for later signing players he'd tangled with, Herzog being a prime example. How, I wondered, could an affidavit change somebody's color? Almeida, a rookie for Cincinnati last season, was darker-skinned than some of the Blues. When he'd been called a nigger by fans in the States, Donlin said, he'd produced the document that made him "white."

McGraw's race standards were notoriously flexible. Ten years ago he'd tried to sign Charlie Grant, an infielder with the colored Columbia

Giants of Chicago. Calling him "Tokahoma" after a creek near Cincinnati where Grant grew up, McGraw tried to pass him off as a Cherokee. It might have worked, except that Charlie Comiskey of the White Sox had seen Grant play and nixed the deal. According to rumors, part of McGraw's intent in coming to Havana was to scout unsigned talent. Other clubs were snapping up Cuban prospects, and he wanted his own.

After more drinks we sat down to a Thanksgiving turkey feast with trimmings, though there was no cranberry sauce and the stuffing was so loaded with onions and garlic that we could have set our collective breath afire.

With dessert came our winnings—800 bucks. The Cubans had bet to the hilt on Méndez. My $25 had nearly doubled.

The boozing that night didn't end at the hotel. Around midnight McGraw and Rigler—for all their on-field hassles they were drinking pals—talked Devore into taking them to a huge new structure called La Politeama, to see an exhibition of jujitsu. Devore knew the place well, having spent most of his nights there gambling on jai alai. Donlin wanted in on it, and asked me to go. It was his way of trying to patch things up. I couldn't refuse. Before too long, though, I wished I had.

After a few matches we began to get the drift. Jujitsu combatants got points for various maneuvers, the winner getting the most. I marveled at the balance and reflexes of those quick fellows. We especially liked the bone-crunching slams to the mat, but wanted knockouts like in boxing, so we stamped our feet and made a fuss. Calling attention to ourselves was a mistake. McGraw and Rigler suddenly felt heavy hands on their shoulders and turned to find a cluster of Cubans leaning over them. One was talking; the others looked pissed. It was clear they hadn't come to pay tribute.

"What do these boneheads want?" McGraw demanded.

Rigler, who spoke the most Spanish, said, "They're *amigos* of Méndez. They don't like the way you rode him today. Or the fact that I let you do it."

"Tell 'em to get lost."

Rigler listened some more. "They also didn't care for González getting kicked out of the first Blues game. Claim we're rigging things, to win bets."

McGraw looked up and snapped, "Fuck you!"

Even if they didn't know the words, the import was clear. They crowded closer, nearly encircling us. Donlin caught my eye and moved his thumb, indicating which one he'd go for. I gave a tiny nod and picked my own target, a glowering, wide-shouldered Cuban who loomed big as an ice wagon. He stood nearest the corner. I'd do my fighting there, able to see who was coming. In a brawl, deafness could be a sizable disadvantage.

McGraw stood up, his face inches away from the group's leader, and said he didn't give a royal shit about past games. He was here to celebrate kicking the Blues' behinds today.

The Cuban brought up the *hijo de perra* business.

McGraw caught the phrase and didn't wait for Rigler's translation. He thrust a finger into the Cuban's chest and barked, "I'll *ee-ho* YOUR *pair-ah,* cocksucker!"

That did it. The man started to swing and Rigler clamped a bear hug on him. Devore snatched a chair and brandished it like a lion-tamer. The guy Donlin had designated as his made a move for Rigler, and Donlin clipped him neatly on the jaw. Yelling for everybody to settle down, Rigler let loose of the main Cuban, who promptly socked McGraw. Another gave Rigler a blow to the side of his head. No sense hanging back. It was time. I jumped at my guy, who was about to sucker-punch Donlin, and things got blurry as fists flew and bodies flailed. While not a boxer, Donlin had hair-trigger reactions and a right hand with the kick of a mule. Devore was tricky and quick. Since most of the Cubans were intent on McGraw and Rigler, we held our own at first. But soon we were backed up, and the only plus was that they were thick as fleas on a yellow dog and got in each other's way. It looked bad for us as McGraw toppled backward and Rigler fell over him. But instead of piling on, the Cubans began to disappear, replaced by cops in blue uniforms with brass buttons.

The squad captain motioned for us to extend our wrists. Breathing hard, we looked at each other. Devore and McGraw had bleeding noses; Rigler's scalp was cut and he showed the beginnings of a shiner; Donlin's shirt was nearly torn off and his chest wore a trail of scratches; I felt a lump bulging out my forehead. I flexed my shoulder; it seemed okay. Risking it had been stupid.

As we rattled and bumped to police headquarters in a two-horse paddy wagon, McGraw suddenly broke into guffaws and clapped Donlin on the back. "Just like the old Oriole days!" he chortled. "We had some fun tonight, boys!"

Rigler didn't appear to share his glee.

In the station McGraw looked around with a proprietary air. "Don't worry, they'll just keep us a little while for show." He seemed familiar with Havana police procedures. "They can't look like they're soft on us."

It took a lot longer than he thought. We slumped on a bench until four in the morning, when the handcuffs were taken off and we were ordered to return at nine A.M. I had to shake Donlin's brains nearly loose to wake him in time. Once there, we were dealt with by a soup-strainer-mustached official. He peered sourly into our red eyes and spent an eternity trying to make typed sheets match our identities. My failure to speak insulted his authority, and for a second or two it looked like I was going to a cell.

Finally he got it. *"El Sordo!"* His face broke into a startling grin. *El Cómico!"*

I nodded modestly. Things looked brighter, at least for me. The official scowled at McGraw and said he must sign a formal apology to the Cubans he'd assaulted, to the police, and in fact to all Havana for the trouble caused by his *beisboleros.* We were fined $25 U.S. each. So much for yesterday's winnings.

"Bullshit!" said McGraw. "They started it!"

Rigler elbowed him.

"Yeah, okay, *sí,"* McGraw said finally. "Where do I sign?"

T W E L V E

DRAWN BY LURID press accounts of our late-night brawl, a good-sized crowd watched us take on the Havana Reds beneath overcast skies. Temperatures were in the mid-70s, practically a cold snap for these parts. Maybe it was the comfortable weather, maybe the law of averages. Whatever the cause, things finally came together for us. Devore sprang to life, knocking out hits and stealing bases, sparking the rest of the lineup. He was equally bright in the field as he sprinted back to the fence to make a leaping grab of a deep drive. The fans showered him with cash, as they did Herzog for his flashy fielding at third. Hooks notched ten strikeouts and nabbed the victory, 5–2. We'd taken three of the first five games.

The only shadow for us came in the ninth, when Donlin pulled up lame after running to first. Polson, the logical replacement, had been complaining of a charley horse, so McGraw sent me in to run. A sign promptly appeared in the bleachers: *¡VIVA EL SORDO!* On the first pitch I lit out for second and went in safely with a big showy hook that kicked dirt on their second baseman, who didn't look happy about it. Nor did Polson, moments later, when I came home on a base hit and received a shower of coins and old Spanish bills. Seeing his peeved look—this was money he might have gotten—I flipped him one of the bills, which he tore up.

Next morning's headline in *El Mundo*, roughly translated: COLD AIR CAUSES REDS LOSS.

It gave us a laugh at breakfast.

The Almendares Blues didn't need any excuses that afternoon. They led in the eighth, 2–1, behind Pedroso, who was as baffling as the first time he'd licked us. Donlin robbed them of a third score on a dazzler of a play, weak leg and all. Going back on a blast to deep center, he used his bare hand to vault high off the rump of a mounted cop's horse and glove the ball just before it dropped over the fence. Only Donlin would have had the brass to try it.

The leg was bothering him, so Polson hit for him next time up. The rookie, slumping so far, decided to borrow a bat from Devlin, who'd been hot. Sure enough, he bounced a single through the infield. A lot of players believe there are only so many hits in a bat. When Devlin found what Polson had done, he blistered his ears. Polson kicked his spikes at the bat and Devlin had to be held back from flattening him. McGraw chewed Polson out, too, which put the blond rook in a worse funk.

In the eighth Devore doubled home the tying run and scored on an infield hit with daredevil running. We led, 3–2. In the bottom of the frame Crandall walked the first Blue. McGraw looked down the bench. I pointed to my pitching arm and gave him a thumbs-up. He'd said no work this weekend, but after giving me a long look, nodded finally. I dashed out to the mound.

It felt good to be throwing. Mixing shoots and medium-speed hummers, not trying for strikeouts—I wasn't about to haul out Dundon—I put the last six Blues away and nailed down the victory. Leaving the field, I found myself in a circle of leaping boys—the deaf ones, my special fans. I couldn't figure out how they'd gotten past the police line until I saw the brown-robed priest, Father Cipriano, coming behind them.

Swarming like monkeys, the kids pinched the black fabric of my uniform as if it had religious properties, and tried to shinny up my legs. Several hand-signed their names. I fingerspelled L-U-T-H-E-R, and although they looked puzzled, the effort sparked giggles and excited gestures. A photographer from *El Mundo* snapped a picture that appeared the next morning under the caption EL SORDO Y LOS SORDITOS. When Father Cipriano moved his mouth to speak to the photographer, it confirmed for me that he wasn't deaf.

The Padre's hand felt small and smooth in mine as we shook. I noted the cowl behind his head and the rough rope belting his waist. Something to do with a vow of poverty, I seemed to recall, knowing that Franciscans cared for the poor. These boys qualified; they were practically in rags. His eyes moved fondly over them. "Bless you for letting them come near," he signed, his hands elegant and fluid, a mix of Sign not wholly familiar and fingerspelled English.

One of the kids thrust a stub pencil at me. I signed scraps of paper, ragged school notebooks, even a shirttail. One who'd been holding back offered up his treasure: a ragged trade card showing me as a Buffalo Bison. Wondering how it found its way to this barefoot kid on a tropical island, I signed the back, writing my name over *"Piedmont: the Cigarette of Quality."*

"They have a gift for you," the priest signed.

One of the smallest boys handed it over: a piece of heavy paper about two feet square, tied with a ribbon. It was a drawing of me sliding into second, grinning like a lunatic as I slid around the baseman's tag. A good likeness, it caught the dirt-spilling turmoil of the instant. *El Sordo Taylor, Jugador Mayor* was printed at the bottom.

The Deaf Taylor, Best Player.

They'd all signed their names.

Over the years I'd gotten a lot of gifts, but none touched me more.

"Who drew it?" I asked.

The priest pointed to the grandstand where the older boy sat alone above us. As before, his eyes were fastened on me. Father Cipriano beckoned for him to come, but he made no sign that he'd understood. He looked defiant and vulnerable at the same time. Was he afraid?

"What's your name?" I signed.

The dark eyes wavered but there was no other movement.

"L-U-I-S." The priest spelled it carefully. I had to ask him to repeat the "U," which he fashioned like a "V," and the "S," which he formed with fingers loosely curled instead of clenched.

"He is shy in your presence," Father Cipriano added, "but I insisted that he meet you."

I wondered why on both counts. "Luis is in your school?"

"He used to be. He helps me with the boys when he's not working."

"And you're all here from . . . ?" I tried to recall the place.

"Matanzas." He smiled. "We left at dawn and I'm afraid it will be midnight before we're home again."

We seemed to be out of things to say. I thanked him again for the gift and watched as Luis helped some of the kids back up into the bleachers. Twice their size, he was gentle with them, like a kindly big brother. His eyes found mine again. Why did he stare like that?

"Does he know Sign?" I asked the priest.

"Oh yes," he answered. "Luis is extremely intelligent."

I held up a pencil and mimed signing an autograph for him. He didn't respond. I shrugged. I sure as hell wasn't going to beg the kid.

"I will try to correct his manners." Father Cipriano looked disappointed. I sensed that Luis was his favorite. "I apologize for him."

"No need."

The boy began to herd the others toward the gate. He was whip-cord lean and moved like an athlete.

"Does he play ball?"

Father Cipriano nodded, then signed rapidly, "Would you come to Matanzas?" His eyes probed mine. "Please?" It surprised me. Surely he knew I couldn't leave the team. Nobody had said we'd play outside Havana. I spread my hands in a gesture of helplessness.

He signed that he understood. *"Adios."* Saying it also with his lips, he made the sign for a journey and accompanied it with a heavenward glance. Blessing me.

"Adios," I repeated.

He strode away, robe swaying. The kids' excitement reminded me of the first time I'd seen a deaf ballplayer. Soon after I'd started at Olathe, a bunch of us were taken to see a barnstorming team play one of the local clubs. The visitors' star was Jumbo Lynch, a deaf hurler. Word was that he'd once played for Anson's Chicagos. We reacted to Jumbo like the Matanzas kids had to me, wanting to touch him, hoping some of his ability would rub off on us. I didn't recall how Jumbo fared on that long-distant day, but I knew he'd planted the profound idea that one of *us* could succeed against the best hearing players.

———— • ◆ • ————

"HELL, I'VE MADE better catches than that," Donlin was saying, his arm hooked over my shoulder. Sports scribes flanked us at the Plaza's bar. "One time we were out in California—it was after the 'oɪ season—playing winter ball for San Diego. Dummy'd split a nail on his pitching hand, but had this one-hitter going against San Berdoo. Score was zero-zero in the twelfth. Best-pitched game ever seen in those parts. Somebody nailed a long one that I had to practically climb over the fence to catch. Saved ol' Dummy's game for him. When we won, 1–0, I thought he was gonna kiss me right there on the field." He pulled at his drink and grinned. "But I was shy. We didn't know each other good enough for that."

"What's he saying?" I wrote on my pad. "Mike caught something?"

It got a laugh.

"Show 'em your trophy," Donlin urged.

I pulled my watch from my trousers, gold and gleaming. I'd gotten it at the end of that California winter, after I took us to the championship. Donlin's name was inscribed on it, with the rest of that team. It ran a little fast, but I'd carried it everywhere.

The reporters separated to make room for McGraw. One asked if maybe he'd been too hasty last season in peddling Donlin. "Maybe so," McGraw said, looking thoughtful. Turkey Mike had always been a pet of his (a .333 career average didn't hurt), and they'd even played together in St. Louis before McGraw took him along to Baltimore and then New York. Donlin got away with murder before the booze finally caught up with him. In '08 McGraw took him back from the vaudeville circuit, even restored him as team captain—with a no-alcohol clause in his $4,000 contract. Donlin stayed on the wagon and nearly took us to the pennant. But by next spring he'd fallen off again. Back to the stage. It looked like McGraw and him were finally done with their long dance. Seeing the empty hooch glasses in front of Donlin could hardly please McGraw, but there wasn't much to say so long as his center fielder played like he did today.

The manager's flinty eyes shifted to me. "Need to talk," he signed.

I followed him up to his second-floor suite, where enormous windows opened out over lawns and flower gardens. Mrs. McGraw emerged from another room in a house dress with bows and ruffles. I gave her my courtliest bow, and of course she melted and hugged me.

The McGraws had no children. She treated players like sons, always showing a soft spot for me. I went back to McGraw's beginnings in New York. Not to mention that I'd stuck with him in that brawl.

McGraw rolled his eyes as I kissed the air near her fingertips, imitating the Spanish grand duke we'd seen on stage. It made her smile, and so it probably pleased McGraw, too, though he wouldn't show it. He shooshed her away and offered me a cigar. When I declined he nodded approvingly—he'd never smoked or chewed—and poured tumblers of rum over shaved ice and lemon wedges.

"To winners!" he offered, and we raised our glasses.

Spread out on a table was a sheet with gate totals.

McGraw saw my glance and beckoned me to go ahead and look. The six games so far had drawn over 40,000 people and collected nearly $20,000, which seemed like a lot until I remembered that the same number of World Series games drew 180,000 paid admissions and gross receipts of a third of a million dollars. Still, somebody around here was piling up dough. I wondered how much of it was going to McGraw.

He tapped my shoulder and handed me a fresh-written check in the amount of $250 U.S. I stared at it. Was he sending me home?

"Blanche found out you weren't getting the same as the others," he signed. "I told her you haven't been worth a dime, but she raised hell anyway."

So he was giving me half-pay.

"Here, take it."

Nice of you to make me feel so darned good. He might have mentioned how well I'd thrown before my arm acted up. Or how I'd closed out today's game. Trouble with McGraw was that he didn't appreciate spot pitchers nearly so much as starters went all the way. Excepting Crandall, that is. Anyway, wiring home a chunk of money was bound to improve my standing with Della.

"Something else," he signed. "That priest with the deaf school came to see me. Said you told him you couldn't visit his school without my permission."

Not exactly the case, but I let it go.

"He came up here like I was the Cardinal or something, wanting you to go to Matanzas. You willing?"

"When?"

"We got some days off. How about tomorrow?"

I shook my head. A fishing trip in the Gulf was scheduled.

"Wednesday?"

"I guess so." Why was he pushing? Had the Padre appealed to his Irish Catholic roots? So far as I knew, McGraw was no more a church-goer than I was. "What's it about?"

"Claims he has a kid who can outpitch Méndez." His eyes narrowed as he signed. "A deaf kid."

So *that* was the reason. It must be Luis. Why hadn't Father Cipriano told me?

"He said I'll be glad to give any amount of money once I see the kid throw."

"That's what he wants? Money?"

"Looked like it to me," he answered. "I figured his school was in trouble. But he said no, he wants nothing. Just to help the kid—who's got some kind of problem."

"What kind?"

"He wouldn't say," McGraw signed. "Wouldn't let the kid throw for me, either. Said there was only one person with a chance of making it happen."

"Me?"

He nodded.

So far I'd gotten nothing from Luis beyond a pencil sketch. What would I accomplish by going to his hometown?

"Tell you what," McGraw offered. "If the kid's what he's touted to be, and I land him before Bancroft and those Cincinnati bastards, I'll get you another $250."

"When?" I pressed, wondering if Mrs. McGraw had already ordered him to pay me in full.

"The minute he's signed," McGraw said. "Cash on the barrel head. You make the first judgment. Then I'll want to see him for myself."

I made him wait while I pretended to consider it. Now there was no doubt that he wanted a hotshot young Cuban pitcher all his own.

"Okay," he said grudgingly. "I'll throw in what you've been kicking about—a chance to make the club next spring." He held up a cautioning hand. "But only if the kid's the real goods."

I pointed to the pad. "Put that in ink?"

He wrote it out and added his signature.

I scrawled "DONE" in big letters. If Luis was my ticket back to the bigs, I'd go all the way to hell to land him.

And fix whatever problems he had along the way.

PART THREE

THE TARGET

To find you, son,
I cross the seas.
The kindly waves
Take me to you.

José Martí, *Ismaelillo*

THIRTEEN

THE MOTION OF the boat grew rockier with the rising wind as we chugged back toward West Havana. I sat with Donlin looking out between the rails at the swelling sea. First thing that morning, we'd both seen a *médico* and gotten the same verdict: muscle strain from *esfuerzo violento o excesivo*. The doc noted that mine was about cleared up, but gave Donlin a foul-smelling liniment and told him to rest. Which was fine with Donlin. Fishing, which I'd loved all my life, didn't interest him at all. Turkey Mike was a citified boy.

Herzog had landed a marlin, and up on the foredeck he and the others were still celebrating with bottles of rum. Rare for Donlin not to be in the thick of it. I sensed that like me he felt a big distance from the younger guys. Earlier Herzog had come by with Polson in tow like a duckling, as usual, and cautioned us about spraining our fingers from talking so much. It pissed Donlin off.

"One day soon," he signed, "I'm gonna fix that prick-nosed, jug-eared bastard."

"Calm down," I told him. "We just got through with one fight."

"Who asked for your help?" he said. "*I'm* the one who's gonna mix with that bird."

I wasn't so sure he could handle Herzog, a rough customer by any scale, and reportedly with some training in pugilism. I was sort of itching to try him myself. But not here, today, on a boat.

Donlin stared reflectively at the horizon for a while. "I figure I got a year of playing left," he signed. "After that I'll be damned if I'll go down to the bushes." He caught himself. "Sorry, Dummy, no offense."

I waved it off. Sometimes I felt the same way myself. The difference between us was that there was nothing in my life I loved as much as baseball. Sad, maybe, but I'd probably go on playing as long as I could. At whatever level.

"What you got in mind to do?" I asked.

"Head out to California," he replied. "Where I did most of my growing up. Make moving pictures."

I considered it. Donlin's handsome dark looks and fine teeth should work on the screen. "I see you as one of them drugstore cowboys," I told him. "Wearing your ten-gallon hat, shooting off your pistols."

"I didn't say be *in* pictures." He laughed. "I'm gonna make 'em!"

Donlin could probably sell block ice to Eskimos if he aimed to. No reason he couldn't be a flickers magnate. Unless Pacific Coast women and booze proved too much for him, of course, but that would be true wherever he went.

"Mabel would go along?"

"Sure." He got a guarded look on his face. "She's all for it."

He was lying.

"Still carry your stub?"

He gave me a glance, knowing I was testing him, and took out his billfold. He showed me the tattered ticket to the opening of his first Broadway show with Mabel Hite. I'd been there that night, three years ago. Donlin had done some singing and hoofing; with Mabel's help he wasn't bad. She loved to tell how Donlin first sparked her curiosity after he'd been put been out sliding home and she read in the paper that he "suicided at the plate" and so she visited the ballpark to see his act. Nature had taken its course. Polo Grounds rooters loved her and took to greeting Donlin with, "Oh you, Mabel's Mike!"

"It was in my uniform pocket yesterday, like always," he said. "It helped me make that catch. You satisfied?"

I shrugged, still suspicious.

"Why don't you come too?" he signed. "Hell, you're funnier than Arbuckle and them others. We'd team up, see? I'd handle the business end, you'd be the star."

I tried to imagine it.

"Remember how I wanted you to come into stagework with me?" he pressed. "Well, moving pictures will pulverize vaudeville, wait and see. And you don't need a voice. Don't miss out again, pal."

I grinned and shook my head. No matter what the pay, I just couldn't see myself play-acting for cameras. It didn't seem like much of an honest calling. Of course, looked at that way, ballplaying probably wasn't either.

"Once we was established, you'd bring Della out," he went on. "Make a new life out in L.A., where the weather's always like this. That winter we played in San Diego, Dummy, remember? That was *living.*"

I tried to picture Della giving up her beloved prairies for a stretch of coast tucked between the Pacific and the mountain cliffs. I couldn't see it.

"No, Mike," I told him.

He nodded as if it was expected.

It was like Donlin to think of heading off full-bore across the country, to plunge into something he had no experience with. Maybe he could do it because he had no roots to speak of. As a boy he'd been passed among relatives after being plucked from his dead mother's arms at the age of six months. It happened during the collapse of the Ashtabula railroad bridge in northeast Ohio. Their train crashed into the ravine below and two-thirds of the 150 passengers were killed. It was one of the century's worst disasters, and papers still printed stories about it. I'd read in one that it happened on December 29, 1876.

Which posed a puzzler: Donlin gave his birthdate as May 30, 1878.

Either he'd made it all up, or he'd been found in his dead mother's arms a year and a half before his own birth, or he'd deducted some from his age.

I leaned toward the last choice. Which made him almost as old as me—but not in the eyes of ballclub owners. I wished I'd had the sense to do likewise. I'd be 34 instead of 36. Dwelling on it was useless, though, so I shifted my thoughts. McGraw had made it clear how I could boost my chances to get back to the big show. If it turned out there was a deaf kid anywhere near as good as Méndez (or Pedroso or Mederos or Luque, for that matter), he'd face a two-barreled lingo predicament trying to pitch in the States. He'd need a very special coach.

Who better than a veteran deaf flinger?

———— • ◆ • ————

THE RAILROADS WERE Cuba's pride. Every few days there seemed to be a new ceremony for the completion of a line to some distant part of the island. We attended one that also marked the anniversary of the first aeroplane flight from Florida to Cuba. Along with scores of rail-workers and a handful of *hombres pájaros* (birdmen) we'd watched the arrival of the same flyer, a crazy Irishman named McCurdy, who made the original flight. When he touched down safely, Donlin immediately set about trying to wheedle his way into being taken aloft.

Give me the good old train any day.

I didn't realize until after leaving the Villa Nueva station what it meant *not* to be on one of the new lines. Traffic to Matanzas was handled by United Railways of Havana, built decades ago by the Spaniards. Damaged during the war, the system had been more or less patched together. Now, laboring up the slightest grade, the ancient locomotive belched smoke and cinders. There was no glass in the windows, of course, and coal dust settled over everything.

I'd had two choices: a two-hour route for $4 Cuban or a four-hour route for $2. Wanting to see more countryside, I'd picked the second. Three ticket classes were offered and since I had no wish to sit with tourists and rich Cubans in the first-class cars (though they were farthest from the cinder-belching locomotive and offered cane seats), and since third class seemed to attract as much livestock as people, I picked a second-class car, where, if I translated right, luggage per *viajero* was limited to one suitcase, one hat and one gamecock.

The growing morning heat didn't help, but once we got into open country, my spirits began to lift. I'd thought the light was remarkably clear in Havana. Out here it positively shimmered. Bathed in luminous rays, the fields of tobacco, cane and pineapples made patterns of brilliant greens. Whenever we built up enough speed so that the smoke passed over us, the air was honeyed with the fragrance of blossoms and lush vegetation, and I sucked in great lungfuls.

The ticket-seller had written *lechero* on my pad. By now I'd gotten his meaning: a milk-run that stopped at every crossroads. Negroes and mulattos, most of them rural peasants called *guajiros,* thronged the platforms of the country stations and piled into the second- and third-class cars, their white sombreros jamming the window spaces and their scrawny horses and mules left in the hands of relatives. The men wore hand-stitched *guayaberas* cruder than the ones in Havana, the women wore dresses of red and yellow and orange. There seemed an idleness out here as palpable and thick as the heat itself. I felt myself calming down, spreading out, becoming comfortable.

Some boys crowded onto my seat, so naturally I pulled coins from their ears. They begged me to do it again and again. I'd seen that Cuban parents indulged their sons while keeping a tight rein on their daughters. I let the boys keep their coins and handed another to a shy girl who clung to her mother and hid behind the palmetto fan she'd been waving. The father smiled and said something. I pointed to my ears and then to my pad, where I printed, *"Escribe Inglés?"*, a phrase from my dictionary.

He looked at me closely, reached for the pad, and printed, *"Beisbolero?"*

I nodded.

"Los Gigantes?"

I nodded again. Then he amazed me by printing, "You name Señor Talor? *El Sordo?"*

When I admitted I was, he announced the fact to the rest of the car. At least one other passenger seemed to know who *El Sordo* was, and the rest looked excited to be riding with a celebrity. At the next stop, the first man insisted on buying me a cold guava punch.

I learned that he was a regular in the bleachers, *"un fanático del sol,"* who followed both Havana teams. He'd seen most of our games, including the one where I'd clowned for the crowd.

"Where are you going?" he asked.

I showed him Father Cipriano's card. On seeing it he promptly crossed himself and announced this new information. My stock rose even higher. Not only a famous *beisbolero*, but one traveling on religious business!

I asked if he knew of any deaf ballplayers.

No, he didn't. But the regional teams were getting ready for the all-island championship tournament, and perhaps a *sordito* played for one. Not, he added smugly, that any of the provincial squads could score a single run against the mighty Reds or Blues. With a sly look he added that perhaps my real mission in Matanzas was to scout Nico Santellan, a slugging outfielder whose fame was growing. Was I trying to get him before a Havana club did?

"No," I answered, making a mental note to ask Father Cipriano about Santellan.

The heat was intense by then, the car sweltering. The air was taking on a thick, charged quality, scented less with flowers than with a pungent, earthy odor that my new friend told me came from *guarapo*, the juice of sugarcane. Harvesting was in full swing. We passed gangs of straw-hatted *macheteros* hacking at the tall stalks, smoke billowing from fields being burnt off for easier access.

At Sabana de Robles a rail spur branched off to Madruga. My friend touted it as Cuba's Saratoga, and suggested we stop off for a healing mineral bath. "I and my family will escort you," he said solemnly.

"Won't this delay you?" We were still several hours from Matanzas.

He said there was no hurry and nothing would please him more than to show me the spa. Anyway, it lay in the direction he was taking his family. He quoted a proverb: "A dog has four feet but chooses only one path."

Maybe it lost something in translation.

Madrugas proved to be considerably less than advertised. A decrepit hotel housed the baths. There were sagging walls, cracked floor tiles, dirty towels—and flies, lots of flies. It sat on a hillside and the air was cool, which would have been grand except that the baths were also on the cold side—maybe I'd gotten so used to the climate that I now considered anything below 80 degrees chilly—and the water stank of sulfur.

Back at the station with 45 minutes to wait, I walked to a rise and looked out over what my guidebook called the *Loma de Gloria*, or "Valley of Glory," where tobacco hung from rafters to dry and cane waved in thick fields. Mills spewed smoke that rose in black columns. Lines of royal palms wandered over the green savanna, taller and slimmer than any trees I'd ever seen. I took out my camera and snapped a picture for Della. In the hazy distance I thought I could make out the sea, but maybe it was just more hills.

Bound for Matanzas again, I watched thunderheads build and the sky turn black. Rain suddenly came down in a solid sheet, draining the heaviness from the air and slanting in through the windows. Passengers laughed at the drenching, their white teeth flashing. I tried to picture Kansans on the Union Pacific reacting likewise.

Maybe Baldwin could stand some *guajiros*.

We pulled into a domed station at the south end of Matanzas, a poor section called Pueblo Nuevo, as the afternoon light was beginning to thin and go golden. Droplets of rain clung to foliage, and the ground was damp and musty-smelling.

The city was two centuries old but had remained fairly small. Sitting between the Yumurí and San Juan rivers and fronted by a deepwater bay, it was originally an outlet for cattle and hogs—*matanzas* means "slaughter." The surrounding fertile plains were first planted with tobacco but by mid-century Matanzas had become Cuba's sugar export center. It was sugar money that enabled the town to become known as the "Athens of Cuba."

Following a tip from the trainmaster, I wrote *"Versalles"* on my pad and showed it to a hack driver. We set out at a canter along the shore-front and I gazed at the bay's turquoise surface. No trace of the recent squall was visible now. Kids were playing ball on a pebbly beach, barefoot runners racing around bases of heaped-up shells, the ball hurtling against an iridescent sky. I had a flicker of homesick memory: throwing with Sim in the fading light.

We crossed the San Juan River on a modern steel bridge. On the far bank stood narrow pastel-colored houses with hanging flowerpots, shuttered windows, striped awnings, worked-iron balconies, and heavy wooden doors. Moored before them were flat-bottomed boats that resembled a cross between everglade skiffs and gondolas. It looked like a picture-book scene of Venice.

We came to the Plaza de la Vigía, the city's historic heart, where the Palace of Justice was still under restoration. In 1898 it had been shelled by the *U.S.S. New York* during a barrage on Matanzas Bay. Across the square stood the ornate Teatro Sauto, where Sarah Bernhardt had performed last year—scraps of posters for it were still in place. The nightly promenade had begun in the Plaza, men strolling one way around the *paseo,* women passing the other. I was struck again by the seemingly free mix of dark- and light-skinned people, smiles on their lips, faces aglow in the slanting light.

I like this place, I told myself.

We crossed the other river, the Yumurí, over an ancient stone bridge and entered the old, elegant section of Versalles. I liked the idea of the deaf school being here, not in some squalid slum. The driver looked at me, his mouth framing the question "hotel?"

I nodded and gestured for him to pick one for me. He lifted a questioning thumb to indicate top price range. Again I nodded. Yes, luxury. Why not? McGraw was increasing my worldly wealth.

He let me off at the *Hotel Leon de Oro,* halfway up a terraced hill. The Golden Lion's nightly charge was $8.50 Cuban, rum included. I was shown to a high-ceilinged room with windows opening on a balcony overlooking the sea. Mosquito netting hung over the linen-decked bed, and pillows were piled against its ornate brass bedstead. The ocean looked almost purple now, and twilight blanketed the slope. Odors of garlic and cooking meat wafted up to me, and I felt the first pangs of hunger.

"Un guiá?" wrote the desk man on my pad as I registered. I understood he was offering me a guide.

"If he writes English," I answered, in fractured Spanish.

He showed up within minutes, a student at the local five-year high school. His name was Bernardo. In the waning light we walked back over the stone bridge to Parque Libertad, where even more people were out walking than at Plaza de la Vígia. At its center stood a new bronze statue of José Martí, the revolutionary leader. Bernardo seemed indignant that I didn't know anything about him. As we circled back along the bay, he pointed to the small castle and fort of San Severino, and launched into a passionate speech about corpses tossed in a "shark hole" to be devoured in the sea outside the fort. Bernardo made it clear that he was a four-button all-wool patriot and that he had no great love for Americans. Which puzzled me a bit. After all, it wasn't us who'd tossed Cubans to the sharks. Hadn't we fought and died for their freedom?

At the foot of the hill where the Golden Lion perched, Bernardo called my attention to a twin-spired church and wrote *"San Pedro Apóstol"* on my pad. Recalling the name from Father Cipriano's card, I asked if a deaf school was there. He pointed to a stone structure behind the church and told me it was the parish school and did indeed have deaf students.

"I have business with the priest."

"Shall I tell him you're here?"

I'd thought to wait until tomorrow, but since the Padre and I were such close neighbors, why not? Bernardo returned to say he'd been told by a secretary that the good father would visit me after this evening's Mass. Looking a bit perplexed that I rated that sort of attention, he said goodbye and wished me well.

In the hotel's small dining room, I chose *biftec* over codfish. The

steak was tough, but all else—bread soup, fried plátanos, sweet pota-
toes, a dessert of *flan*—was excellent. Afterward, I sat on my balcony
and enjoyed the spectacle of lamps blinking on along the curved strand
of the city. It felt good to be alone. Ever since hooking up with the
team in Florida, I'd been surrounded by others.

Now there was some time to think.

I swatted a mosquito half the size of Vermont on my neck and
rubbed on some of the rosemary Sim had given me. After strapping on
the bellyband fashioned by Hattie Mae—I doubted it would do any
good, but it made me feel close to them—I was pouring a glass of my
complimentary rum when I felt a draft of air behind me. I turned and
there stood Father Cipriano in his brown robe. I noticed that the rope
belt held three knots. What did that mean?

"Hello," he signed. "May I join you?"

I poured another glass.

"*Salud,*" he wrote on my pad. The sight of a churchman sipping spirits was one more reminder that I was not in Kansas.

"Thank you for coming," he wrote. "As I told Señor McGraw, I
think you are the only one with a chance to help Luis."

"Help him with what?"

"The boy is headed for bad things if someone can't straighten him
out. I've known him all his life. He respects me, but I can't seem to help
him now. Since his genius is for baseball—"he wrote it *el beisbol*—"perhaps you can do something."

"What exactly is his problem?"

"'Exactly?'" He smiled and shrugged. "That is hard to put into
words. Luis is nineteen. He has no brothers. His father was killed in the
war for independence. His mother . . . well, perhaps you will meet
Señora Natalia. Luis is having trouble finding his way to being a man."

"How much of it is his deafness?"

"A great deal, of course, but there are other things." He paused. "I don't wish to be negative. Luis has a great athletic gift. You are deaf, Mr. Taylor, but you've done something with *your* gift." He straightened from the pad to look at me, and signed, "What I'm hoping for will become clearer after you see him throw a baseball. If he's willing, that is."

"He might not be?"

"Luis trusts nobody outside his family. When I told him that you had agreed to come, I think he didn't believe me."

"So I'll see him throw, maybe, and . . . ?"

"If you think he's as good as I do, you'll want to help him."

"The boy doesn't have to be a great athlete for me to do that," I protested.

"Then you are a better man than most." He looked around. "I had a monastery room readied for you, Señor Taylor, but I think you've done better here. But if you wish to stay another night, you will be welcome."

"Thanks. . . ." I hesitated. "How should I refer to you?"

"The boys call me Father C."

"Father C. it is."

"I'll come for you after breakfast."

"You're convinced I'll like his throwing?"

"If not," he signed, his eyes holding mine, "I'll be greatly surprised."

———— • ◆ • ————

AT DAWN I STOOD on my balcony watching the sun emerge from the eastern sea. White mist hovered between the ridgebacks like ghostly plow disks, the tips of the tallest palms seeming to float in the vapor. The air warmed quickly and the mist began to burn away, revealing tiled roofs and stone houses. Father C. suddenly appeared beside me.

"Beautiful here," I told him.

"Come," he said. "I'll show you a fine vista."

"Are we meeting Luis?"

"Yes. He'll meet us during his break from work." He gestured toward the hillside. "Come with me now."

I followed him up a steep path from the Golden Lion to the crest of the hill. There we stood gazing out on the whole of the Yumurí Valley, a broad, green plain through which a river sparkled like a ribbon of jewels. Except for scattered sugar mill stacks belching smoke into the sky, it might have been Eden. I shared the thought with Father C., who smiled.

"Too many problems here for Eden," he signed. "But yes, it's beautiful, even more than in the past, when there were many more mills."

"Where they'd go?"

"Destroyed in the war."

"Not rebuilt?"

He shook his head and did not elaborate.

"Luis works at one of the ones left?"

"He works at our parish bakery. Luis believes that working for a mill is merely a new form of slavery." The priest smiled ruefully. "Such ideas have not made things easier for him." He gave me a sidelong glance. "This was the center of slave trading here, you know. It was abolished only forty years ago."

No wonder so many Negroes here, I thought.

"Can you guess the one event," he asked abruptly, "where you'll find all people—the purest African to the purest Castilian—rubbing shoulders with no distinction?"

I shook my head.

"At a cockfight. No *sombra* or *sol*. No better or worse seats, unlike at even our most common music clubs." He smiled, but there was a hardness in his eyes. "Only at a fighting ring where creatures try to kill one another in frenzies of bloodletting."

I was at a loss for a response.

"There is a great anger here," Father C. went on. "Luis resents those who have shut him out, and that feeling is shared by many others, for different causes. There are those organizing even now to do something about it. A powerful movement. For all its peaceful appearance, Matanzas may soon be a powder keg."

"Where is this movement?" A guarded look passed over his face as he waved vaguely toward the eastern mountains. "Around." Abruptly he changed tack. "Like every Cuban boy, Luis loves baseball—that American game. I saw the way he looked when he watched you pitch. There was something in his face I haven't seen for years. Seeing you out there, a deaf man pitching for the famed *Neoyorquinos*—I think he experienced hope."

Which could turn out to be a cruel thing, I reflected.

"Does Luis think I've come to scout him for the Giants?"

"How could he not?" the priest answered. "It's the truth, no? But Luis isn't stupid. I don't think he expects you to sweep him away and make him a star."

"What *does* he expect?"

"That is hard to say. Maybe nothing. Maybe he's only cooperating to satisfy me." He took a slow breath. "All I know is that the children look to you simply as a hero, but with Luis it's more complicated." With a smile he asked, "Would you like to see the *sorditos* in school?"

"If Luis is as good as you say," I asked when we were halfway down the hill, "why isn't he playing for somebody? Luque can't be much older than him, and he's already a pro."

"Without something extraordinary happening, I'm afraid Luis won't get that chance," Father C. replied. "Not in Matanzas."

I looked at him curiously. "Aren't the provinces forming teams for the big tournament?"

"Yes, and that is happening here too. Tryouts and selections will take place this weekend. The best players from a half-dozen local teams will then begin practicing for the tournament." His mouth tightened as he added, "Luis deserves to be one of them."

"But he won't?"

He shook his head. "He is hated by the most popular player here. They have been enemies since childhood."

"Is that player named Santellan?"

He looked at me in surprise.

"You're hoping I can do something about *that*, too?"

"I suppose I am." He signed nothing for a moment. "What I am truly interested in is Luis's *soul*. Once he was a loving boy, a bright spirit. Now he is on the way to . . . I don't know what. I fear for him."

"Santellan caused this?"

"No, but Nico symbolizes what stands against Luis. All his life the hearing boys have persecuted him. They've beaten him, torn his hair, once even slashed him with a knife. Luis would become so infuriated that he'd throw fits, rolling on the ground and making ugly sounds. And so the others said it proved what they'd believed, that he was possessed by demons."

I nearly tripped over my feet as I stared at him. Deaf kids were commonly seen as retarded or even crazy, but possessed by demons? Not in these times. Not in the U.S., anyway. But who knew about Cuba?

"You're still close to Luis?" I prompted.

"I've tried to guide him. For a long time it seemed to work. But in the last few years . . . I know I'm losing him."

I tried to picture where and what I'd be without my loving family, the patient teachers at Olathe, my baseball career. I didn't like the picture I got. "I'll do what I can," I promised. "Luis *is* willing to pitch?"

Father C. grinned. "Did you bring a well-padded mitt?"

I'd brought one of Dutch's. "It's in my room."

"After that we'll go to the grounds." He glanced at the sun. "It's almost time."

FOURTEEN

THE INFIELD AT Palmar de Junco ("Junco's Palm Grove") was pebbly and rutted, and the rain-washed outfield grass was ankle-high in places. A cow grazed peacefully in right field. Since there were no palms in the vicinity, I questioned Father C. about the name, but he did not know.

"I can tell you that the first formal baseball match in Cuba was played here on this field," he offered. "A team from Havana came down one Sunday in 1874. It was in December, this time of year. After the contest they banqueted together. I understand that in those days they played with ten men to a side, another shortstop between first and second."

December 1874. That game took place two months before my birth. Baseball itself began only 30 years before that. A wonder it got to Cuba so early.

"There was no *glorieta* back then," the priest continued, pointing to a small covered stand behind home. "Everyone sat together in the sun, rich and poor. Much more democratic. Maybe that was why the Spanish disliked the American game so much, but there was no containing it. Soon every sugar mill had a team. Every man and boy, no matter his place—even if he'd recently been a slave—could play. If he was good enough, that is."

"You know a lot about it," I signed. "Did you teach Luis to play?"

"I tried to help." Father C. laughed. "But as he grew older I could hardly see the balls he threw, much less catch them. No, it was his grandfather who taught him. He was one of the great early players. In fact, he played many years here on this ground."

"Was he killed in the war too, like Luis's father?"

"Here he comes." Father C. pointed to a gap in the outfield fence where the tall, lean boy was stepping through. "No, the *viejo* is still alive."

"Does he live here?"

"I don't really know where." He looked into my eyes. "Please don't mention it. Luis's *abuelo* is wanted by the authorities. One more of the boy's difficulties. All right?"

I nodded. It occurred to me that Luis was carrying more than his share of burdens. He approached to within a few yards, face expressionless, dark eyes fixed on me.

"Buenos días," I mouthed.

He returned the wariest hint of a nod. His cotton shirt was soiled and he wore no shoes.

"Where's his glove?" I asked Father C.

"He borrows from others when he is able to play."

I pulled my Spalding model from my bag and tossed it to Luis. The leather was well-oiled, the pocket molded just right. He looked like I'd tossed him a cask of jewels. I brought forth Dutch's round mitt and a new white baseball. Moving back a few feet, I lobbed the ball to Luis. He caught it deftly and scrutinized it as he had my glove. I doubted that he'd ever handled a new ball.

We threw and caught, gradually stepping apart until some 50 feet separated us. I took care not to tax my arm, and Luis matched my slow velocity, which puzzled me. At his age I'd have been quick to pull out

all the stops to impress a visiting big leaguer. Not this boy. He simply
returned what I gave him, throwing easily with a natural follow-
through. Once when he thought I wasn't looking, he shot Father C. a
quizzical look, as if to say, *What is this?*

Okay, youngster, time to find out a few things. I motioned him to the
pitching slab, wishing I'd thought to bring spikes. Without them he
wouldn't get as much purchase on the mound.

I settled behind the plate in a squat, groin muscles protesting, and
nodded for him to throw. He didn't move. What did he want? A sign?
Then I realized that he was waiting for me to spot the mitt for a target.
Who was being tested here? With embarrassed alacrity I set up low on
the right-hand corner of the plate. Luis lifted his left leg, spun, dipped
and suddenly the ball slammed into the leather. I hung on to it, mostly
because he hit the center of the pocket, but the impact sent me back on
my butt. I glanced at Father C., whose thin face wore a knowing grin.
I reset myself on my haunches and spotted high on the left. Again the
ball hit the mitt's center. This time I was ready, but not completely, for
his velocity was, if anything, even faster. I gave him another target. He
threw another bull's eye—the fastest ball yet—and my hand felt like it
was on fire.

Damnation!

Hiding my excitement, I gave him a casual thumbs-up, then flip-
flopped my hand, indicating I wanted to see a breaking ball. Luis signed
something to Father C. with a frown. Too bad, I thought. Hell of a
smoke thrower, but the smoker's all he's got.

"Luis wonders," Father C. signed, "if you want to see his different
fastest pitch."

Different fastest?

"Tell him to shoot it in here, however fast he wants."

He shot it, all right, not nearly so fast as the others—but it damn near finished me. I spotted the mitt on the center of the plate. The ball came rocketing in, seemingly from his shoulder socket. I didn't actually see it leave his fingers. There was plenty of spin, but I couldn't dope it out fast enough; my brain registered a warning *uh oh!* and I shifted the mitt backhand as the ball came in high on the outside, half a foot above the target I'd set. Then it sank—my god, did it!—and dipped back in toward the plate. I was still leaning right but it came exactly where I originally set up. It glanced off my glove, nearly tearing my thumb off, then rolled to the foot of the grandstand. Seeing Father C.'s amused glance, I sprang to my feet, grabbed my pad and wrote furiously, "Is he trying to kill somebody? I didn't say an inshoot!"

Father C's amusement vanished. He relayed the message to Luis. Looking surprised, the boy signed back rapidly, and for the first time I was able to get snatches of it. "He says he doesn't know 'inshoot,' just his 'other fastest ball.'"

I had him show me how he held it: fingertips on the curve of the stitching and touching no other seams. I'd have sworn he couldn't get that kind of movement with that grip. Hurlers work for years trying to develop a workable inshoot, that is, a ball that moves in on a same-handed hitter. Some think it's impossible. Luis seemed to have a natural one.

"Again," I signed, and took my stance. This time, though strongly tempted otherwise, I held the mitt still. The ball slammed against my hand with jarring force, and again I barely saw it. The news scribes liked to write of "blinding speed." This kid actually had it. He threw a "heavy" ball, too, the kind that would send shock waves up hitters' arms—or shear their bats off if they didn't connect square.

God hadn't made many arms like this one.

I wrote "curve" on my pad. Luis looked at it, took my pencil, changed the *e* to an *a,* so that it read *curva,* and nodded solemnly.

Father C. smiled proudly. *Fine, son,* I thought, *we'll call it your way. Just so long as you can throw it.*

Again he surprised me. Using a different windup, almost side-wheeling (which we'd need to work on eventually, to avoid telegraphing), he delivered his *curva*. It swept in toward an imaginary righty's hip, then flashed downward and into my mitt. Wanting to jump up and dance, I motioned for him to do it again. He broke off another, maybe even sharper. I nodded as if what he'd shown was routine. But it wasn't. Not for me. Or Hooks. Or Crandall. This kid was moving and placing the ball like a young Matty.

"Where'd he learn all this?" I asked Father C.

"It began with his grandfather, like I told you. Later I did what I could. My first desire, you see, was to be a *beisbolero*. Only when I knew that I lacked the talent did I follow my mother's wishes and join the Franciscans." He smiled. "So, although I cannot do it at top form myself, I teach my boys the game. And I believe Luis *can* do it."

I think I believe it too.

The boy signed something, a lot of it not quite matching up with the Sign I understood, so Father C. relayed, "Luis would like to see your drop pitch."

I showed him how I gripped and released it, but that wasn't enough. Luis took my mitt, ran behind the plate, and motioned for me to throw. I faced a dilemma. To work properly, Dundon had to be thrown hard. *Okay, I can do just one.*

I warmed up with medium-speed tosses, Luis snapping the ball back from his catching position, showing me again that he was an athlete. Once he got his full growth, he'd be the tip-top goods.

I signaled that the drop was coming. The ball plummeted so swiftly that it would have gone beneath Luis if his reflexes hadn't enabled him to trap it in the dirt. He squatted there for a moment, then looked up at me with an expression that suggested a new level of interest. Maybe even respect.

I felt a twinge in my shoulder and knew better than to press my luck. Luis insisted on trying the drop himself, without much success. Not surprising. I'd spent years perfecting the elusive combination of grip, wrist snap and release. Sometimes I still couldn't get it all right.

He kept trying, though, and managed a slight downward break. I liked his determination but told Father C. to call an end. It wasn't good for the youngster's arm, and I didn't want to take chances. Luis didn't need another pitch anyway. With his blazers and benders, he'd be a handful for anybody. Thank God he hadn't been scouted. All I needed was to see him in a game situation. If he handled that, we were in business.

It was close to noon. My throat was parched. I spotted a soft drink vendor in the street and led the others toward him. Some boys who'd been watching on the diamond pointed at Luis, yelled, and ran away. Luis's face darkened in anger.

"What was that about?" I asked.

"The mill workers will be coming out for siesta," Father C. said. "Those boys are going to tell Nico Santellan about Luis being here." He looked worried. "There's bad blood. It might be better if we left now."

"Okay, soon as I pay."

Three soft drinks cost 18 cents. A picture of Hughie Jennings holding a Coke and doing his "Ee-yah" yell in his Detroit uniform decorated the vendor's cart.

"Tell Luis I faced Jennings a couple times," I signed. "Suckered him on high blazers."

After getting definitions for "suckered" and "blazers," Father C. relayed the information. "Luis remembers Señor Jennings managing the Tigers when they came to Havana; it was when the great Méndez struck out Señor Ty Cobb."

"Luis may have the stuff to be like the great Méndez," I informed them.

Eyebrows lifting, Father C. was about to respond when something behind us took his attention. I turned and saw a knot of young men heading our way. They moved purposefully and I didn't like the look of it. Their leader was about Luis's age, compact and very muscular. Where Luis's presence was hawklike and watchful, this boy was like a mastiff with raised ruff. It didn't take a brain trust to dope out that he was ordering Luis off the field. Or that he was Nico Santellan.

I couldn't follow all the rapid-fire Spanish as Father C. stepped between the two, and wouldn't have understood it anyway. From his gestures I gathered he was saying that the diamond was for everybody. At length he pointed to me, and an incredulous look came over Santellan's face. I stepped closer and he introduced us. *"Nico . . . Señor Taylor, lanzador de los Gigantes."* He signed for Luis and me as he spoke. "He's here to see Luis pitch."

"The freak"—Father C. told me later he used the word *mutación*— "can't play here."

"He isn't a freak," the priest corrected, still signing as he spoke. "Just a deaf boy. Señor Taylor is deaf as well. *El Sordo.* Perhaps you've heard of him?"

Nico fixed me with a suspicious glance. Luis was coiled as tight as a cornered snake, eyes fastened on his antagonist. I didn't see how either boy could back down. Then I had an idea. I signed to Father C. what I had in mind. Luis wasn't able to follow it, or surely he'd have reacted.

The priest considered. Looking reluctant, he nodded. "Señor Taylor is here to scout certain young players," he told Nico. "Can you find a bat and swing at a few pitches?"

"That *he*"—Nico hooked a thumb at me—"will throw?"

I nodded.

When the others understood that a Giant pitcher was going to throw to Nico, several ran off to find a bat, and others to spread the news at the mill. It took Luis a minute or two to figure out what was happening. When he did, he slammed Dutch's mitt in the dust and started to leave. But then he halted, teeth bared and body trembling with frustration, as he saw Nico laughing at him. My heart went out to the boy. He must have thought I'd switched the spotlight to his enemy. I grabbed Father C.'s shoulder and signed urgently. If Luis could just be patient for a few minutes. . . .

How Father C. mollified him I had no idea, but after some kicking at the ground with his bare feet Luis allowed himself to be led to the grandstand. Nico immediately objected, but we were ready. Father C. told him that unless Luis stayed there'd be no chance to display his hitting. And so both boys silently agreed to our compromise, each looking resentful.

A banged-up bat showed up, accompanied by a crowd of mill workers. Some of them looked pretty rough, and I saw a jug passing among them. They looked me over with stony eyes. Maybe I didn't fit their idea of a big leaguer.

Well, I didn't intend to pitch like one, either. In the hitter's box Nico brandished his bat weapon-like, challenging me. I liked his spunk. He was already bigger than Donlin, and nearly as chesty. But I didn't bite. My purpose wasn't to show anybody up. I threw straight balls at medium speed, splitting the plate. Lord knows, I'd had enough practice. Excepting the rare occasions when McGraw handled the chore himself, all of us hurlers had to toss batting practice.

Nico fouled one off, then began knocking line drives. I'd brought extra balls, and as fast as his friends could shag them, he sprayed shots around the field, a lot of them banging off the fences. The kid had a good swing and natural power. After ten minutes I called a halt. I'd planned to call Luis down to hit a few and see how Nico looked in the field.

It didn't quite work out that way.

Disgusted that I'd thrown nothing but easy balls, Luis refused to come on the field. Which was fine with Nico, who mimed that he was afraid of my baby pitches. Outraged, Luis ran to the mound and demanded the balls from me. He intended to show his enemy some real pitching. Nico stood at the plate laughing.

Well, I thought, here was my chance to see Luis in a pinch. Not a game, certainly, but a highly charged situation. How would each of them handle it?

I signed to Luis that I'd stand behind the backstop and call balls and strikes. Eyes fiery, he shot back that there would be no balls. I took my place, Nico regarding me distrustfully, probably thinking I intended to help Luis, the two *sordos* conspiring.

I'd seen tense pitcher-batter faceoffs, including some that decided pennants. Matty against Dutch Wagner. Three–Finger Brown against Donlin. Me against Frank Chance.

None were any tenser than this.

Luis started with a blazer so hard that Nico, though he'd obviously expected it, swung late and nearly went flying off his feet, which were shod in heavy working brogans. He backed out of the box and kicked them off.

The problem's more than your footwear, I thought, and realized how hard I was rooting for Luis. He was the underdog here. I remembered a hulking hearing boy who'd loved to torment me thirty years ago. One day I mustered my courage and fought back. He was licking me pretty good, but I kept going at him till a passing adult broke it up. Soon after that, I took my first boxing lesson.

Luis's next pitch, his *curva*, came in tight. Nico's front foot slid a tiny bit into the water pail, but his knees didn't buckle as many hitters' would have, and as the ball broke over the plate he pulled it hard down the line foul—a good showing on a tough pitch.

In that situation, seeing Nico's hands down at the end of the handle, I would have wasted one, tempted him with something unhittable. Luis wasn't going that route. Glaring in, he held up two fingers to indicate the number of strikes on Nico. Then he held up three to indicate that the whiff was coming. *Then* he thrust his hand toward the plate to signify he was coming with a fastball. Nico's jaw tightened and the muscles of his forearms bunched.

Well, kid, you better make good on it.

Maybe, on second thought, it wasn't a bad idea. Maybe Nico was so tight that he wouldn't get around in time. Or maybe Luis was trying to trick him and had no intention of throwing a fastball—but I doubted it.

The blazer came in dead center and Nico timed it perfectly, shoulders swelling as he swept the bat in a powerful arc. At the last instant the ball swerved up over it and slammed into the screen, spraying me with dirt and rust. I thought I'd seen the ball brush the wood and alter its trajectory ever so slightly. But I wasn't sure. And of course I'd heard nothing. Nor had Luis. I caught Father C.'s eye and cupped a hand to one ear. He knew what I meant, but he shrugged and spread his hands. It was up to me. I raised both hands to signify a foul tip.

Nico eyed me with surprised satisfaction while Luis spat and stalked around in a circle. They took their stances again, every eye on the slender pitcher. Luis wound up and delivered straight overhand. I saw from his release that he was trying to throw Dundon.

No, I thought, *mistake!*

The ball came in chest high. Instead of dropping, it hung. Nico didn't miss this one. He whipped the bat and sent the ball soaring high into the sky and far beyond the fence. It would have been out of any ball grounds I knew.

Nico grinned up at his pals, who were on their feet, their mouths open in cheers and taunts. I felt sorry for Luis, standing angrily on the rubber. I tossed him another ball, made placating gestures, and signed to Father C. to tell them that this wasn't the World Series but simply a tryout, and that I wished to see ten more pitches.

Luis waited grimly for Nico to step back in. The instant he did, he unleashed a jaw-shaver. Nico hit the dirt and bounced back to his feet, mouth working. A snap of his powerful wrists sent the bat spinning at Luis, who ducked as it came at him, Nico following it at top speed. Wild-eyed, Luis hurled my glove at him and plunged forward with fists raised.

Oh hell oh hell oh hell! I dashed around the screen. They were rolling in the dirt, flailing with fists and knees. I wasn't the only one heading for them; the mill workers surged around me, and I was alarmed to see Father C. bumped aside. More alarmed yet to see the bat snatched up from where it lay behind the mound.

The sight of them piling on Luis set me off. Even though he'd provoked the whole damned thing, the boy had more than he could handle in just facing Nico. The others had no business jumping in. I started peeling them away, not bothering to be gentle about it. I'd gotten rid of a couple when one of the drunks clipped me on the neck with a long-necked bottle. I probably shouldn't have hit him as hard as I did, but there wasn't much time to reflect on it. I felt hands on me and swung around to confront new attackers.

My head seemed to explode.

Everything became brilliant white.

FIFTEEN

WE USED TO have a horse on our farm who rhythmically kicked the door of his stall. I'd press my hands against the boards to "hear" the jarring reverberations. Now I seemed to be experiencing it again, except that I felt the pounding at the base of my skull, where waves of pain radiated.

I opened my eyes and saw that I lay beneath some sort of thatched roof. Shafts of light slanted down through it. My face was bathed in sweat. Making the effort to wipe it seemed impossible. I drifted off into darkness again on steamy currents, dreaming of my forehead being stroked by something cool. After a while it seemed too real to be a dream.

Forcing my eyes open again, I saw a human shape that slowly sharpened into that of a girl. She was dabbing absently at my head with a damp cloth. While she dipped the rag in a pail and wrung it out, I saw that she was about fifteen, amber-skinned and slender. Her cheekbones and nose and narrow jaw could have been Luis's. Must be his sister. I tried moving my head. Bad mistake.

The girl turned, her face concerned. Her lips moved in speech, then she caught herself and held up the rag. Did I want her to continue? Oh, yes. I closed my eyes and she went gently back to work. I think I dozed again. She was in the same position but the light seemed different, the thudding less insistent. I lay on a lumpy mattress and she sat beside me, her hip pressed against mine. Seeing my glance drop, she frowned and stood, her breasts and hips outlined beneath her cotton shift. I tried to raise a hand to pacify her, but she walked swiftly out of the hut.

There was more stirring as an older woman came bustling in. She was tall and thin, her face creased and sun-darkened, her hair covered by a bead-ornamented shawl. A long thin cigar stuck out from her mouth, acrid smoke curling between us. She plumped herself down on what looked like a milking stool and fanned me with banana leaves. The kindness of it was not matched by the expression on her eyes, which regarded me suspiciously. She jerked her head in the direction the girl had taken, then astonished me by glancing significantly at my crotch. The meaning seemed clear: she was checking to see if I'd gotten hard. She must be the girl's mother. Which would make her Señora Natalia, whom Father C. had mentioned. Luckily, my pecker had behaved. If not, it surely would have withered under that stare of hers. The whole thing was too strange for me. I drifted back to sleep.

I woke to discover it was dark outside and much cooler. The thudding had lessened to a throb. A candle burned on a crude dresser at the far end of the hut. By its light I saw Natalia combing her hair, which was long and streaked with gray. When her eyes met mine in the cracked glass of a small mirror, she wrapped a scarf around her head, like Aunt Jemima on the new pancake mix boxes. Nodding curtly to me, she looked no happier than before. Maybe it was because I was occupying her bed. She moved to the doorway and waved, and seconds later Father C. entered.

I managed to sit up, but the effort left me dizzy. He loosened a bandage on my head and examined my skull. Holding up two fingers, he asked how many I saw.

"Twelve," I answered, which made him smile. He told me he'd been worried; my humor was a good sign.

"What day is it?" I asked.

"Same day, close to midnight."

It seemed that a hundred years had passed. I waved at the hut's walls. "Luis's house?"

"His mother's *bohío*."

"What happened after . . . ?" I pointed to my bandage.

"Everybody was so surprised that they stopped fighting. The man who hit you was drunk, but even he seemed shocked by what he'd done. The others took him away, fearing I would call for the police."

"Did you?"

He shook his head. "I took a chance. Luis suggested bringing you here. We carried you in a wagon from the bakery. Your breathing was strong and I knew that a *médico* would simply say to watch over you, which we have done."

"Has word of it gotten out?"

"Some of the workers talked, of course. The rumors are wild, and a reporter already came to the rectory. I don't know how long I can stall him and all the others who will follow."

I saw his point. Word of a Giant injured by a ballground mob would bring an invasion of reporters.

"Shall I say that you took ill and will answer questions tomorrow?"

I tried to think. Letting the rumors grow wouldn't be good, but publicizing the kids' fight and my injury was the last thing we wanted. Anyway, I didn't feel up to being questioned. "The day after?"

He nodded agreement. "Are you hungry?"

I smelled food cooking and realized that I was ravenous. With his help I managed to get outside into the night, where Luis was stooping with an armful of wood for a cooking fire tended by the tall, thin woman. Seeing me, he straightened and gave me a smile, the first I'd seen from him. It made him look younger, like the boy he was despite his athlete's body. I put out my hand and he took it.

"You've met Luis's mother?" Father C. wrote on my pad, *Señora Natalia Serros Avelar.*

I stared at the long, strange name. Nodding to her produced a wave of dizziness. "Please say I'm grateful for Señora Avelar's care." To my surprise, she responded herself, signing back that I was welcome. Her expression didn't *look* welcoming, I thought, mindful of her probing stare at my privates.

"Luis's sister," the priest went on, writing, *Señorita Teresa Luna Serros Avelar.* "She is called Luna."

The girl was ladling out yellow rice and beans. Natalia said something to her and she lifted her eyes, then looked down again before I could sign to her. Did the Avelar women think I was a lunatic rapist or something?

My dented skull didn't keep me from emptying my plate. While I ate, Natalia flattened a tobacco leaf on her thigh, crushed others into bits which she spread evenly, rolled the leaf, licked its length to seal it, snipped off one end with a knife, and lit it. As she puffed away, she offered us fermented *guarapo.* I declined. My head was woozy enough.

Moving to the rectory seemed like a good idea, but things got blurry fast when I walked a few steps. Luna was standing closest to me. As I teetered I hooked my arm over her shoulders to keep from going to the ground. She bent with my weight, then straightened and braced an arm around my waist, and for a moment I felt her warmth and softness. Glaring at the girl, Natalia looked ready to burst into flame. I was amazed to see Luna return the look with equal heat. What the hell was going on? Natalia pointed imperiously at me. I thought she was ordering me off the premises. "He is in no shape to leave," she told Father C. "I will tend to him."

I asked whose bed I was taking, and learned that Luis spent his nights either at the bakery or in a nearby lean-to of palm boughs. Luna was going off to sleep at a friend's. Natalia had begun to make a pallet for herself behind a cloth partition which I gathered was normally occupied by the girl.

Left alone, I plunged back into sleep. Sometime in the night I awoke to the feel of hands on my head and the sight of Natalia silhouetted over me. Behind her, on the dresser, candles burned again, flanked now by black statues and coins shining in the flickering light. Something birdlike hung from the ceiling, and with an uneasy feeling I remembered the chicken heads in the tree in Havana. A pungent odor rose from a brass bowl behind the candles and mixed in my nostrils with the reek of Natalia's cigar. I tried to raise my head but her hands held me down with surprising strength as her fingers probed my temples. She washed my face and hair with herb-scented water. Then, after chewing on something that smelled like coconut, she spit the resulting paste into her palms and began rubbing it into my scalp. Finally she wrapped my head in a white kerchief and signed for me not to remove it.

Time seemed to melt away. I entered a floating space where I hovered effortlessly. At some point I became aware of her touching the exact source of pain in my arm. *No*, I wanted to tell her. *Leave that alone!*

She probed away but I felt no pain, just a soothing warmth. I tried to look up and see her face. Her scarf was off, her hair a halo of snakes backlit by the candles like a Medusa statue I'd once seen. Hardly a comforting vision, yet I felt oddly safe and protected.

In the morning, ignoring the questions I signed, she removed the kerchief from my head and scraped the paste residue into the brass bowl. She gestured for me to get up. I did so and felt surprisingly clear-headed. My balance was better. I traced the wound with my fingers and scarcely felt any swelling. I flexed my pitching arm: it was strong, the twinges of pain gone.

We shared a breakfast of *cafe con leche* and bread. Then she beckoned for me to follow her up to a wooded ridge. With a questioning expression she pointed to a cluster of tall palms, then to my chest, then back to the palms. Asking me to pick one. I walked over to the tallest, which made her smile. She buried the paste at its foot.

"Why?" I asked.

After making some signs I couldn't follow, she took my pad, wrote the word *orisha,*, and made flapping and fluttering motions.

Spirit? I wrote back, guessing.

She looked at it blankly. Then I remembered the shoeshine man's word. *"Muerto?"*

Her eyes rose to mine with depths of surprise in them. I made a linking motion, suggesting she was connected to the words I'd written. She nodded and wrote *"casa en santo"* and pointed down at the *bohio*. Then she pointed at herself. *"Una santera."*

Which about finished what we had to say on the subject. I gathered that she fancied herself some kind of spirit worker. Out in the light I could see her clearly. Natalia had once been a beauty, I decided; probably looked a lot like Luna. She wasn't any older than me, but life had taken its toll. Not to mention the cigars.

I slept most of that day, Natalia checking on me often. At noon she brought up a bucket of river water and scooped some out into a shell decorated with bits of yellow glass. She rinsed my head, her touch tender. Once, I thought, she even almost smiled.

In midafternoon I stumbled out to pee behind a thatched canopy that covered a woodpile. Luminescent blue dragonflies circled me. The heat intensified my drowsiness. I was tucking myself back into my pants when something moved beside my head. I looked up and froze. Inches from my face was a snake, its head seemingly as large as mine as its tongue darted at me. Wrapped around a roof pole, it hung down in languid coils. It must have been ten feet long.

AAAAAAAAAAAAAAAAAAOOOOOOOOOOWWWWWWWWWW!

I don't know how it sounded, but that's how it *felt* as I threw myself sideways, hit the ground rolling, sprang up and sprinted madly, my arms waving like I was thrashing through 12-foot corn, my mouth open the whole time. Whatever came out must have been godawful, because Natalia came running pell-mell. When I pointed to the snake she burst out laughing.

"His name is Eleuterio," she signed. "He lives here. He is our pet."

"Your *pet?*" Breathing hard, I repeated the hand-stroking sign incredulously.

"A *maja,* one of the few snakes found in Cuba. He's very tame. He wanted to know you, that's all."

A shudder passed over me, which made her laugh again.

In late afternoon she gave me the strangest treatment of all. After lighting the candles and setting out the bowls around us, one of which held nothing but smooth stones, she took a chicken egg and began rubbing it slowly over me. Some places she stroked were far too familiar for comfort, but when I squirmed she pushed me down with her strong hands. I felt an odd tingling sensation while it was happening.

When she finished, we walked back up to the ridge. She handed me the egg and gestured for me to throw it. I tossed it some hundred feet away, where it splattered against a rock. Looking pleased, she led me there. To my surprise what had splattered was hard and dark, almost fibrous. I was at a loss. The sun couldn't have done that already. The egg she'd used must have been old and rotten.

"You." She pointed at me, then made a face to indicate that the dark stuff had come from me. Poisonous stuff. Bad parts of me. Of my nature. But now I was cleansed.

I didn't feel any different, but what the hell. I signed my thanks, feeling almost fond of this leathery woman. After another nap and a light supper, we sat companionably together and watched the stars come out. Pale lunar moths fluttered around us. I tried a sip or two of her jacked-up *guarapo* and felt it fire my whole system.

Luna came home and had a bite to eat, after which Natalia suggested pointedly that she leave. The girl looked ready to argue, but didn't when Natalia glared. Something was definitely on between those two.

Before I went to her bed again, Natalia thanked me for helping Luis. She put her hand on my arm and I put mine over hers. What I had, I realized, was the closest thing to a family feeling I'd had since leaving Baldwin. Here I was, sitting beside Natalia Avelar, a very odd woman indeed, outside her *bohio* in the Cuban countryside. And I felt thoroughly at peace.

———— • ◆ • ————

LUIS WOKE ME with a gentle shake and offered to help me to my feet, but there was no need. I felt better than I had in weeks. Outside, wood fires scented the morning air. Natalia and Luna weren't in view. Luis scooped cold rice and beans on to a plate, added a piece of coarse bread, and handed me a small cup of syrup-thick coffee. He had a note from Father C. The interview would be this morning at nine.

As we walked down the hill I looked back at the small hut, firewood piled beside it, chickens and pigs prowling in front for food. I hadn't had a chance to properly say thanks. If things worked out the way I wanted, though, they'd all be thanked beyond their dreams.

Luis was nearly my height, and he took long strides. I had to ask him

to slow down as I felt a trace of dizziness. At the rectory Father C. ush-
ered us into a white-walled room with a carved desk and low benches.
Over an altar a crucified Jesus hung on the wall.

"You look better," he signed.

"How'd she fix me up so fast?"

"Natalia is well known as a healer." He smiled. "Since you
befriended her son, I'm sure you received her very best treatments."
He glanced at the far door. "The reporter is here. He will ask about
rumors that you were injured. I think for everybody's sake, it might be
better. . . ."

"Not to deal with rumors?"

He nodded, almost imperceptibly. "The *borracho*, the drunk who
struck you, has been punished."

"Oh? What happened?"

"He himself was beaten by others at the mill, friends of Nico, who
were ashamed that you, a famed ballplayer, were so treated." He
rubbed his hands together. "Neither boy will admit being responsible,
but I think they're both sorry."

"Maybe some good will come of it."

"Maybe," he agreed. "But there are divisions"—he signed it by using
groups and *divided*—"here that are very old."

"Divisions?"

"Going back to the war for independence and even before. There
are ignorant people, too, who say harmful things."

"Such as?"

"Do you really want an example?"

"Sure, why not?"

"Very well. They say that Luis is a monster and that he was deaf at
birth because Natalia mated with demons who dwell in the trees on
her property." His face was unreadable. "See what I mean?"

In my mind's eye I saw the palm that I'd picked out and beneath which she'd buried the paste. "Did they say which tree?"

"*What?*" He looked at me sharply.

"Never mind," I signed. "Luis knows that people say those things?"

"And worse, too. I've tried to shelter him here, you understand? The boy *looks* like he is ready to be a man, but in fact he is not ready to deal with the hearing world. If he could start by playing baseball with the others, then. . . ."

I nodded. *I understand that better than you.*

A small balding man with a prominent nose was shown in. Notepad poised, he bounced on the balls of his feet while Father C. introduced us. He was from the *Matanzas Libertador,* the leading local daily. His name was Gómez and he was a distant relative of the nation's current president, which maybe explained his self-importance. At once he asked why I was there and why my presence had been kept secret from city officials, who, of course, were embarrassed at not welcoming such a prominent visitor. While he spoke he stared at my head for signs of damage.

I felt like I'd been ambushed.

"I'm traveling for pleasure," I signed.

"And perhaps finding young players for Señor McGraw?" he inquired slyly after Father C. translated.

"Mr. McGraw's players are *always* on the lookout for good young players," I countered.

"Is it because of the regional tournament?" he pressed. "Is Señor McGraw sending his men to scout the best youths in the competing areas?"

I tried to look mysterious.

"You don't deny it?" With a smirk he made a note on his pad. I could see it in print: *Taylor did not deny* . . . . Gómez was creating the story himself. All I had to do was sit tight and let him have his head, like a horse going home to the feedstall. McGraw might not like to be pictured as talent-hungry, but big-league clubs, especially the Cincinnati Reds, had already been combing the island. Anyway, I could always claim I'd misunderstood the questions. Being deaf has its advantages.

"The Cubans are fine players," I signed.

Father C. awarded my vagueness an approving glance.

"You came to look at Nico Santellan?" the reporter pressed.

"Is he good?"

Gómez studied me sourly, then tried a new tack. "Was there a racial fight at the grounds?" he said, and watched my face for a reaction.

Racial? Did he think the fight was over me? "What are you talking about?"

"You deny you were injured in a racial fight?" he said, trying the same trick.

"Of course I deny it."

Stroking his chin, playing Sherlock Holmes or somebody, he said, "Who besides Santellan was involved?"

Didn't he know? "Look," I signed, "if Santellan is the kind who gets into racial fights, maybe we won't be interested. What else should Mr. McGraw know about him?"

Gómez stared at me, lips pursed. I'd called his bluff and made it seem like he'd tarnished the reputation of the local favorite. He shook his head and complained to Father C. that nobody would tell him who the parties were or who had struck me. "So you *are* interested in Nico," he said, trying to recover.

I smiled. "Is he good?"

"Okay, señor." He puffed his cheeks. "Why are you here?"

I looked around as if he meant the rectory. "I'm interested in deaf children. I try to visit schools like this at every chance." I turned to

Father C. for confirmation, and he nodded gravely.

End of interview.

Looking a deal less important than when he'd come in, Señor Gómez departed.

"You were very skillful," Father C. signed.

"New York training," I told him.

"*Are* the Giants players scouting Cuban boys?"

"Not yet," I answered. "But if McGraw goes for my plan they might be."

"And what is your plan?"

As I described it his eyes widened. "When should Luis be told?"

"For now, just urge him to keep his arm in shape."

He smiled. "No need for that—he throws for hours every day."

I looked at my watch. Almost time to leave. "By the way, what did Gómez mean by a 'racial' fight?"

"Remember how I told you that Matanzas was a center of slavery, and that there are divisions here? Well, for many of the *gente de color,* the black Cubans, the promises of independence have not come true. They're as bad off under the U.S.—" he smiled wanly—"I mean *our* new government, as they were before. Maybe worse. There is much ill feeling."

I waited for him to go on. "So?"

"So perhaps Señor Gómez thought that the dispute was due to those feelings."

"But he was wrong. It was just baseball and a deaf kid being picked on, wasn't it?"

"Yes." He looked evasive. "Probably."

"What are you telling me?"

"Do you know about the *reconcentrados*?

I shook my head.

He took a book from a shelf and spread it open before me. "The *reconcentrado* program was the work of the Spanish General Weyler, called "The Butcher" and for good reason. To prevent the *guajiros* from helping insurgents in the mid-'90s, he ordered the entire rural population—peasants all over Cuba—herded into fortified zones. Eight days' notification was given. No foodstuffs were allowed. Livestock had to be driven into the camps. Nothing was to be left for the revolutionaries. Anybody disobeying was shot." He pointed to the book. "The Butcher's promise to feed and shelter the *reconcentrados* was a terrible lie, and most of their houses and fields were burned after they left."

I stared in shock at photos of children with swollen stomachs and running sores.

"Nobody knows exactly how many died of starvation and sickness, but it was between 200,000 and 450,000. A third of all the rural people simply vanished. In Matanzas alone, in two months time, 10,000 died, and twice that number altogether during the *reconcentrado*."

"And the Avelars . . . ?"

"They had to go with the rest. When Luis's father and grandfather stood up to the *reconcentrado* agents, Luis saw his father shot dead. He was five years old."

My heart seemed to have stopped beating.

"They were among the fortunate," he went on. "Natalia's father—Luis's *abuelo*—managed to save the *bohío* from being destroyed, but they lost all the surrounding acres."

"Who got them?"

"The rich," he answered curtly. "After the war, sugar was our only hope to end the hardship. But the mills, increasingly owned by foreigners—" I could tell from his face which foreigners he meant—"were consolidated and run with new mechanical equipment. Which meant more of the land could be planted in cane, so naturally the *ricos* acquired it. The poor people still living here had little choice but to work for the mills at starvation wages."

That's why Luis thinks of it as slavery, I reflected.

"So Gómez thought *those* things had surfaced at the ball diamond? Involving the boys families and what happened before?"

"Who can say? But, yes, it's possible." He brushed his hands as if to shoo away the topic. "You will return soon?"

More questions came to mind, but I could see he didn't want to go further. "Depends on McGraw," I signed. "I'll wire you as soon as I get his answer."

Before leaving I had a brief catch with Luis during his lunch. We drew a crowd of bakery workers, most of them Negroes; they watched appreciatively as Luis unlimbered his arm and smoked the ball to me. I had him toss a few benders, then called an end. The display blew any lingering doubts from my mind. Luis Avelar was the genuine goods.

I wrote *"adios"* on my pad and told Luis in Sign that I hoped to be back soon. I think he got the idea. Even so, it was hard to walk away feeling his eyes on my back. At the top of a rise I turned and waved. He waved back.

A sphere of silence linked us.

———— • ◆ • ————

I TOOK THE shorter route this time. The train huffed along the coastal foothills in a fairly direct line, and I stepped out into Havana's Regla Station shortly after dark. Being on the city streets lowered my spirits. My brain clung to green visions of the Matanzas countryside.

I ferried across to Havana proper and hailed a *guagua* (wah-wah), one of the small buses named for the constant din of their klaxons, which Donlin claimed I was lucky not to hear. I'd departed on

Wednesday, December sixth. Now it was Saturday the ninth. Only some 80 hours had passed. It seemed like far more.

The lobby of the Plaza Hotel was filled, as usual, with rich Cubans, Europeans and Americans. A timeless place, seemingly disconnected from everything around it. At least I wasn't likely to be clubbed with a bat here.

Instead of the usual three weekend games, we'd been scheduled for four straight, Saturday through Tuesday. I'd missed that day's game, in which Matty had coasted to a 7–4 win—Father C. had simply wired McGraw that I was spending extra time with Luis—and only two games were left for the following weekend, our last in Cuba. Which meant two things: first, I could expect to be called for mound duty soon; and second, I'd better get started right away on my big plan.

At that moment McGraw came through the saloon's half-doors with Pepe Conte, Havana's leading baseball scribe. They shook hands and Conte turned and departed. McGraw spotted me at once and his face brightened (thank God) which probably meant he didn't know about my head injury. He motioned me to a table, ordered drinks, and gave me a quizzical look. "Well?"

"I think he's the real article," I signed, and took out my pad. In the minutes that followed, it slid rapidly between us as I laid out my idea. McGraw's eyes narrowed like they did just before he raised at the poker table. He banged a fist on the table and clapped me on the back. "Goddamnit, Dummy!" he exclaimed. "We got us a sure-fire winner!"

Already it was "we." Soon the plan would be his. I didn't care. I just wanted it to happen.

"I'll chew on Pepe's ear tonight. We've got to get this rolling. Seems to me that empty date next weekend would be perfect!"

I'd already suggested it, but what the hell.

"Another drink?"

I said no, I needed to sleep.

To my surprise, Donlin was sitting at our writing desk laboring over a letter. A telegram and a half-empty bottle shared the table. He grabbed me in a bear hug, his breath heavy with liquor.

"Missed you, chum," he signed. "Glad you're back."

There was a slump to his shoulders and a vague heaviness about him. Rare for Turkey Mike.

"You in the dumps?"

He looked at me, then reached for the pad. "Things ain't working so good for me here, Dummy."

"Only ten days till we sail."

He took a slug from his bottle, wiped the mouth on his sleeve, held it out. I shook my head. "Mabel's real sick," he wrote. "I want to go home, but I gotta make some dough. Bills are piling up."

"Medical?"

"And other things."

Knowing Donlin, that meant liquor and gambling.

"How much medical?"

"Twelve hundred."

Jesus. And Mabel's illness ruled out the stage. Suddenly I added a couple of things together. Maybe Mabel wasn't going to get better. Maybe she knew it and she'd sent Donlin here to do what he loved best. Maybe the telegram confirmed it. Had he known? It would explain some of his actions. I hoped I was wrong, but I felt stunned. How could I help my old pal?

"I've got a scheme cooking," I wrote on my pad. "If McGraw okays it, I'm thinking there might be a place for you."

"Involving cash?"

"Maybe."

He studied me, knowing I wasn't devious by nature or given to schemes. I'd gone to see a kid pitcher. Chances were I'd draw a bonus from McGraw if the kid signed. But how would that help Donlin?

"Come on, Dummy, fill me in!"

"You'll be first to know."

———— •◆• ————

NEXT MORNING'S HEADLINES were taken up with the McNamara brothers, convicted of dynamiting the Los Angeles *Times* building last year. They'd kept mum about accomplices and now were on their way to San Quentin Prison. One of the brothers was quoted as saying he looked forward to a better future. Which was interpreted to mean that he expected pardons for them once California elected a labor governor in 1912.

It sparked a lively conversation at breakfast. Most of the players and wives were outraged by the very notion of bomb-throwing radicals; several favored the McNamaras' immediate execution. To my amazement, Josh Devore, of all people, spoke up for the convicted men, not to forgive them but to suggest that maybe they'd been driven by desperate circumstances. What, he wondered, was the *Times'* position on workingmen? Well, you'd've thought he'd tossed a bomb of his own. Several of the wives refused to look at him, and one ordered her husband to take her away.

I thought Devore made a good point. He was only saying that some folks were having hard times, and things should be looked at before making easy condemnations. Twenty years ago my family had felt the iron screws of a business panic. While corn and wheat prices dropped through the floor in unmanaged markets, high tariffs kept eastern manufacturers cozy and sent costs of equipment to the sky. I remembered my father's anger as faceless bankers foreclosed on our land. He didn't throw any bombs, but he might have sympathized with some who did.

McGraw came in and listened, then snapped, "Quit jawing about that stuff! We face Méndez today!" Pepe Conte walked into the dining room and made a beeline for him. They talked with heads close together, then the manager motioned for me to come over with my pad. A genial, broad-faced man, Conte knew English well.

"In Matanzas you scouted two players," he wrote. "One was named Santellan?" He waited for my nod. "And the other?"

"I'd rather not say yet," I wrote back, aware of McGraw's startled expression. "It will be a surprise, believe me. Does this mean the game's going to happen?"

They exchanged a glance, then Conte grinned happily. "A week from Sunday," McGraw signed. "If Pepe and his boys do their job, it'll draw one hell of a crowd."

"Don't we already have a game that day?"

"We're moving it to Monday. This could be bigger, right Pepe?"

"Very likely," Conte agreed, excitement in his eyes. "But who will coach the youngsters? Should we ask the Reds and Blues to do it?"

McGraw's mouth formed a "no" at the same time I was shaking my head. "It's *our* show," he said emphatically. "Just the Giants' and the sporting writers'."

Neat how'd they'd divvied it up between themselves.

I knocked on the table to get their attention and pointed to my pad: *I'm going to coach them.* McGraw's small blue eyes appraised me. I hadn't asked but told him. He didn't like that. But the plain fact was that nobody else could do the job—not when it came to Luis Avelar.

"If it won't leave you short of pitchers," I added, trying for a diplomatic touch.

"Shit," McGraw said scornfully. "I could pitch against them myself. Anyway, Becker's been pestering me to throw again. So, no, you won't be missed." He held my eyes for a long moment then looked at Conte.

"What do you say, Pepe? Dummy's coaching would keep it our show."

"One of your Giants handling the boys—I like it." He looked at me. "But Señor Taylor, how . . . ?"

I pointed to my ear and smiled, knowing what he was thinking. "I'd want Donlin to help me out," I wrote, and added that Father C. could translate for us. "Maybe Señor Conte would also lend a hand." I saw from Conte's pleased look that I'd played the right card. Baseball writers always think they know what to do on the field.

McGraw was eyeing me shrewdly. "You got a notion to play us tough, don't you?"

"I guess so." I looked straight into his flinty eyes. "Don't you want that?"

He put back his head and laughed. "You've always been a little touched, Dummy. Sure, you can have Donlin, so long as you don't try to play him against us." He said something to Conte, who nodded eagerly. "Pepe likes the idea of being involved with the kids. He'll help out all he can."

We shook hands, my heart racing.

It was on!

"Want to make a prediction right now?" McGraw demanded. "How much we boot your asses by? Ten runs? Twenty?"

"Can I see what I've got first?"

"So you can back down?"

"Maybe," I told him. "Or maybe to judge how much we'll beat *you* by."

They both had a big laugh over that.

SIXTEEN

Olathe,

1958

On the trophy table, beneath his championship pin, lay a 1905 World Series program bearing the players signatures—McGraw later called it his strongest club—as well as those of all the deaf folks who'd flocked to visit him. Coming from hundreds of miles around, they had been thrilled to put their names down beside those of the Giants and to pay respects to one of their own, a deaf man who'd made it to the top. Demand for tickets had been fierce, but he made sure they got as many as he could arrange, often paying for them himself.

Always in those days his hotel room door stood open (partly for safety, of course, since he couldn't hear emergency knocks), and deaf visitors were welcome at all hours. He knew that he was an inspiration to them. What they hadn't known was that they inspired him, too, infusing him with the feeling that he was playing for more than himself.

It had made him stronger.

His teammates had played jokes: reaching in to turn off the lights in the middle of a lively conversation; telling a bellhop to get up to his room because he'd had a stroke and lost his voice and needed to be rushed off to a hospital. Donlin, naturally, was the worst; he could be counted on to wager that this Taylor fella was the snootiest high-hat a desk operator had ever seen. Turkey

Mike would win when the deskman tried to hail him crossing the lobby—and of course get no response.

One spring in Texas he'd gotten revenge. Following his malicious instructions on how to mount a horse, Donlin, hopelessly citified, swung up into the saddle facing rearward. The horse, duly annoyed, took off—Donlin's eyes were big as plates, his mouth open in mortal terror—on a wild gallop before dumping him in a tumbleweed patch.

He grinned as he recalled McGraw informing Donlin that he'd have to pay for the horse. Which put him in mind of the time when they'd spiked Hooks's steak with chile peppers and, after the fireworks, tried to convince him the meat had come from a Mexican jumping cow. Then there was the classic that Doyle had pulled: tossing firecrackers under the chairs of dozing sportswriters while the players yelled "War's broken out!"

More than anything else after leaving the game, he had missed the endless pranks and plots and friendships—hell, even the quarrels—that went into the camaraderie of being part of a team.

Of being in it all together.

SEVENTEEN

THE IDEA SPREAD like a wind-blown cane fire. San Antonio, Cárdenas and Pinar del Río, all fairly near Havana, fell in line first. Cienfuegos and Santa Clara were right behind. Then came outlying Camaguey, Manzanillo and Santiago. All were committing their top two or three players. Pepe Conte made sure all positions were covered, and we said we'd try to play each boy at least an inning. Except pitchers; I insisted that they come with the understanding that they might be strictly backups. This would be Luis's show for as long as he could handle it. I'd convinced McGraw that pregame attention would hurt the boy, and Conte, quick to spot a publicity angle, agreed to hold back on announcing our starter. I also insisted that while the boys' home managers could attend the practices and the game, the all-star team would be handled strictly by us.

Coaches Taylor and Donlin.

This thrown-together squad of youngsters would face the National League champs on a Sunday, the nation's huge baseball day. Our game against the Blues had been pushed back to Monday. The kids' national tournament would begin the day after that. It was all coming together in Havana.

I thought maybe Conte would have to do some tall convincing to get the regional teams to accept us as the kids' managers. But they saw

it as a good thing, an honor, in fact, for the boys to be coached by
Donlin and me, and everybody seemed excited. The regional teams
would get to test their best youngsters against the pros—at the same
time scouting their opponents' stars. Some of the coaches were concerned about their boys being humiliated by the great Christy
Mathewson. McGraw promised that it wouldn't happen. Matty confirmed this by announcing that he would be departing for home after
his next mound appearance on Thursday.

With all the regions committed, McGraw and Conte capped things
by announcing that proceeds from the contest would go to promote
baseball throughout Cuba. Conte had Victor Ortíz of *El Mundo* and all
the other sporting scribes working hard to drum up interest. The exhibition was shaping up as a red-letter event. If the kids could give a good
account of themselves, it'd be gravy all around.

One question kept popping up: Since I'd already picked the young
all-stars' starter, why wouldn't I identify him? Already Ortíz referred to
him in print as *"El Misterioso."* I promised to announce him once the
team was assembled. It didn't offer much satisfaction to hungry
reporters, who continued to pester me about it.

I was pretty good at playing dumb.

———— • ◆ • ————

WE BEAT MÉNDEZ 6–3. Herzog's round-tripper was the big blow, but
before that, Donlin and Méndez got into a war. Plunked hard in the
back his first time up, Donlin laid down a dribbler in the hope that
Méndez would cover first. Wisely he didn't. Next time up Donlin got
drilled again. Instantly I was up and running to head him off. "NO!" I
signed urgently, "WE GOT BIGGER FISH TO FRY!"

While Donlin slowly simmered down, I caught McGraw's steely
look from the coacher's box. He'd seen what I signed and recognized

what it meant: to me the boys'game counted more than this contest.

I knew he wouldn't forget it.

———•◆•———

NEXT DAY I started against the Reds. Before the game the all-star kids from San Antonio, the first to arrive, gawked at us in our black uniforms like we were gods. My toughest job might be to convince them that the Giants were just ballplayers, like themselves.

Rusty from lack of work and maybe still not 100 percent after the whack to my head, I never did settle into a comfortable pattern. The Reds kept knocking out hits, but I managed to set them down without scoring. Donlin's triple sparked a five-run second inning for us, which you'd think would've made things easier for me. It didn't. I tried to bear down, but couldn't find the strike zone on a regular basis. In the sixth the Reds loaded the bases with one out, and only a snappy double play by Fletcher and Doyle bailed me out. But by then our lead was 8–0.

"That's it," McGraw told me when we came in. "Hooks needs some time."

"But this is my day," I protested.

"Don't you sass me," he retorted. "You're gone!"

You're gone. . . .

I sat on the bench and sulked as we went on to win 10–2, our easiest victory so far. Eating at the pit of my stomach was the fear that I'd failed my test with McGraw. He'd already made up his mind. I was gone.

———•◆•———

I SPENT THE TRIP hatching plans for every problem that might come up with the boys. Suddenly I was looking down at the broad green plain broken by the two rivers, and then at Matanzas itself, a sun-washed grid. I hoped Father C. had gotten the boys to practice together. In Havana the all-star game had taken shape like a dream, but if things were wrong here my plan was in trouble. One reason for holding back Luis's identity was my fear of not being able to produce him.

At twilight I sat in the rectory with Father C. I wanted to go and find Luis, but he said that if I did so at this hour Natalia would surely insist on giving up her bed again, and to refuse would be an insult.

"The four boys are ready to leave tomorrow," he assured me. "Matanzas will be well represented. Nico and his friends are full of boasts that they will be the best of the young players."

"And Luis?"

"He shows nothing, but he is throwing the ball faster than ever."

"The others accept him?"

Father C. raised his eyebrows. "To be truthful, they ignore him. But at least they don't attack him. They can't help but be aware of how he's throwing. And that without him this wouldn't be happening."

I felt a crimp of frustration. "But Luis shows nothing?"

"He protects himself."

"What would it take to make them all friends?"

Father C. shook his head. "You can't expect these boys to sort out a knot that has been years in the tying." He paused, then went on. "Luis hides his feelings, but he knows that this is the chance of his life. Perhaps we shouldn't expect more just now. It is hard for people to change."

"You're a priest. Can't you just give orders to their families?"

He shrugged. "The Church is not so powerful in Cuba as in many places."

"Why not?"

"Well, it didn't help that José Martí was excommunicated. Or that the *reconcentrado* tragedy went unopposed. During the struggle for independence a great deal of our land was lost, and then U.S. occupa-

tion brought separation of church and state. Civil marriage is now per-
mitted, so people needn't come to us for that sacrament any longer."
He smiled faintly. "And of course there is *santeria*."

"Which is?"

He looked at me for a moment. "It is what Natalia practices." He
reached for a bottle of wine and poured for us. "You didn't come here
to talk of such things." He lifted his glass. "To the adventure that
begins tomorrow."

———— • ◆ • ————

ACCOMPANYING THE BOYS were Father C. and a stocky man named José
Rincón, coach of the local team on which all but Luis played. Besides Nico,
whose skin was about the same caramel tone as Luis's, there were two
boys of darker complexion: Antonio "Tony" Paguey, a catcher built like a
fireplug (I paid him close attention since he'd likely be handling Luis) and
Isidore "Izzy" Beltrán, a second sacker. Tony was quiet and solid; he kept
to himself. Izzy was exactly the opposite, a monkey-like jokester, con-
stantly moving and talking. All the boys had slicked their hair and were
turned out in their best clothes: guayaberas, cotton pants, sandals. The
others looked more prosperous than Luis, but not by a hell of a lot.

Most conspicuous about each was the new glove he carried. Father
C. and Rincón had launched a quick campaign, and some of the town's
merchants had chipped in for gloves and a dozen new balls. The boys'
overseers at the sugar mill were giving them the time off. Hundreds
planned to journey to Havana on Sunday.

"In this country," Father C. said, "baseball works miracles." He
signed "miracles" by combining "wonderful" with "work" and then
crossing himself. I thought I detected a hint of envy.

On the trip, Nico and the others talked among themselves, and
while they didn't include Luis, which would have taken Father C.'s

help, they didn't exactly *exclude* him. I followed the Padre's lead and didn't try to force things.

Halfway to Havana, Luis fingerspelled something with lightning speed—and of course I couldn't follow. With encouragement he tried again, using broad signs: "How did you learn to throw?"

"Tossing rocks," I signed back.

Something glinted in his dark eyes. "Me, too."

I saw Father C. looking on. "Ask the others," I signed. "Please?"

He did so. Nico and Tony looked blank. Izzy grinned and said he'd thrown at things too, enraging his father by knocking unripe bananas off trees. When it was relayed to Luis, he glanced at Izzy, and the two boys exchanged a quick smile. A start, I hoped. If things worked out the way I wanted, they'd all be damned proud to bask in Luis's friendship—especially when he signed a big-league contract.

We checked the boys into a modest hotel just inside the walls of Old Havana. I got a kick out of seeing them try to act nonchalant. The first time I'd stayed overnight with a team, it had been in a boarding house in a tiny Kansas town. Nothing on the order of this, certainly, but I'd behaved the same way: trying to look savvy while hoping nothing would tip me for the rube I was.

We'd scheduled our first workout that afternoon, and Donlin was waiting at Almendares Park. Cavorting over the field were twenty boys from around the country, most of them in their late teens. Baseballs flew everywhere.

"They ain't world-beaters," Donlin reported glumly.

"What does that mean?" I demanded.

"They're damn green."

"That's why *we're* here. What'd you expect—the Cubs? Hell, Mike, you think you and I looked any different at their age? Let's see what they can do in a workout."

McGraw and Conte had made preparations like those of Father C. and José Rincón in Matanzas, but on a grander scale. There were new spiked shoes, workout knickers with sliding pads sewn into them—a source of marvel to the boys—and sleeveless shirts with "ALL STARS" emblazoned in English across the chest. If they hadn't known the term before, they grasped it now, and looked proud as kings.

We sent them to their positions and put them through drills. Donlin was soon ordering the outfielders around like McGraw himself. Rincón knocked out infield grounders that would have challenged the Giants' sackmen. With Father C.'s help I managed the pitchers and catchers. I made Luis promise to throw nothing but straight balls. Despite his obvious reluctance he kept his word. The idea was not only to prevent him from throwing his arm out before Sunday's game, but to keep McGraw from finding out exactly what he had.

Already a small crowd in the stands was studying everything. The managers of the Havana and Almendares teams were there, plus some of their players and writers from the leading papers. And fans, of course. This country was baseball loco. I wanted to get rid of them so the kids could concentrate on their jobs, but Donlin reminded me that on Sunday they'd be playing before a colossal crowd. Better they got a taste of it now. Besides, Cuba's best diamond was being made available to us. How could we order its usual occupants away?

Anyway, my main concern was McGraw, who I knew would try to steal the show. Sure enough, halfway through our workout he strode onto the field in his black uniform, causing a sensation among our youngsters—the famous *Mono Amarillo* himself—and we had no choice but to halt everything while he paraded among them and signed their gloves and charmed them with his Spanish. He even worked briefly with infielders at third base, his old position.

May your tips work against you, I thought, grinning and pretending I was glad he was there.

"So what's your deaf kid got?" he demanded.

"Take a look," I signed, as Luis zinged a fastball into the mitt of Tony Paguey with impressive pop. Luis delivered again. McGraw studied his motion with a practiced, expert eye.

"What else does he throw?"

"You're seeing it," I lied.

"Maybe he'll shape into something." His mouth pulled down in a veiled sneer. "Someday."

"Good control, huh?"

"Hell, you know our guys'll time those balls and hit 'em all over the park after an inning or so. It'll be a long afternoon for your kids. The crowd, too. You've let the fact that he's deaf warp your good sense. How about we start one of the others?"

"Now hold on, you promised I'd have control over—"

"Okay, Dummy, okay." He held up his hands. "Do it your way. We'll draw a hell of a crowd anyway. Now, about this lad Santellan. . . ." McGraw had practically drooled as he watched Nico drill shot after shot in batting practice.

"He's the goods," I signed. "Better grab him before Cincinnati does."

"We'll see," he signed, "come Sunday."

———— • ◆ • ————

"SHIT, WE AIN'T got a snowflake's chance." Donlin shook his head dolefully. "Nico and a couple others can hit okay, and most of 'em field their positions. But we need more than that to cash in."

"We've *got* more." I tried to look confident. "If things break our way, we might only need a couple of runs."

"How we gonna get 'em?"

"That's what we gotta dope out. One thing these boys got is young legs. They're faster'n hell. Let's work 'em in the sliding pit. Maybe come the pinch we can steal a run." I punched his arm. "Wouldn't it be something to lick McGraw at his own speed game?"

"Got to get on base first."

"That's your job, Mike—yours and Rincón's. I'll be working on how to stop their hitters."

———— •◆•————

MATTY HELPED US in two ways. The first was unwitting. With all our boys watching from prize *sombra* seats, he lost to the Blues, 7–4, who waited him out, made him come in over the plate, and smacked the ball. The Blues airtight defense included a circus catch of a deep drive hit by Becker, who kicked the dirt in frustration.

Maybe Matty had spent too much time lately on the golf course and dealing cards with McGraw at the American Club. Maybe his mind was set on going home. Whatever the cause, his loss encouraged our kids—they'd rooted hard for the Blues—beyond anything Donlin or I could've said. They saw for themselves that even with Matty pitching, the Giants could be trimmed.

That particular cake got frosted when Matty went out for a pinch hitter and I got to throw the last inning. McGraw sent me in against the Blues' toughest batsmen, maybe hoping I'd get dumped on my ass in front of the kids. Since I only had to go one inning, I used Dundon to whiff the first two Blues, then got the third when I fielded a dribbler and ran the ball over to first myself, to the disgust of Polson, playing there. As for Donlin, he rapped out two hits and played his usual expert defense.

The all-star coaches had put on a tip-top show.

No game was scheduled Friday, so we had use of the diamond. After

lengthy fielding drills, Rincón pitched batting practice and we finished
with "work-up," six against the field. By then we'd pretty much settled
on our starters and our hitting order.

Toward the end we worked on signs. Donlin and I considered this
extremely important. McGraw was a master sign thief and during the
game we wouldn't have Father C. as our go-between. Donlin knew
only one word the boys understood—"no"—and I had fun watching
him struggle to get his ideas across.

"Not easy being a dummy?" I asked.

"Damn hard," he replied. "You'd probably get some respect from
me, if I didn't see how much this tickles you."

He found ways to reach the boys, however, and all of us shared the
language of baseball. Working with Luis and the others, it dawned on
me that I was more content coaching on that diamond, surrounded by
the boys, than I'd been pitching on it the day before.

Matty's other contribution was a personal visit. Accompanied by
Conte, he dropped by at the end of our practice. He had to get back to
New York, he said, to meet a deadline for *Pitching in a Pinch,* a book he
was writing with one of the scribes. The boys' eyes were big as he
shook their hands. Yesterday's loss had not dimmed the renown of *Don
Cristobal,* as the papers now called him.

Father C. translated as Matty told the boys that the Cubans were
great *beisboleros* and that he'd been lucky each time he'd won here. He
called Donlin one of the best players ever, and said that with him as
their coach they would be strong against the Giants. Then he put his
arm around me and said, *"Un lanzador magnífico!"* and everybody
cheered.

Matty asked about our starting pitcher. I decided it was time to
unveil Luis. As they shook hands Matty took note, I was sure, that
Luis's fingers were nearly as long as his own.

"So this is the next Méndez?" he said aloud as he signed the question to me.

Pepe Conte's head spun around. *Oh, no,* I thought. It would be all over tomorrow's papers. The other players eyed Luis curiously; his ability was unknown to all of them but Nico. Luis blushed violently. But it seemed to me that he also straightened himself a tiny bit. My thoughts took a new direction. Nobody but Father C. had believed in Luis's ability before now. Maybe praise was just the ticket. What was to be gained by holding back?

"It's possible he could be *better* than Méndez," I signed.

"*Mejor que Méndez!*" Conte blurted. Luis blushed again and looked down at the floor. Matty bent and lifted the boy's chin. "Do everything Señor Taylor tells you," he said, "and you'll be fine on Sunday."

Thank you, Matty.

"Do you actually have hopes of winning?" Conte asked Donlin. Excited by his unexpected scoop, he was eager to broaden it.

Donlin started to answer, then glanced at me.

"Any chance of you beating the Giants?" Conte said in English to me, mouthing it slowly.

I shrugged and finally nodded. Sure, a chance.

"*Muchas gracias!*"

———— • ◆ • ————

SATURDAY'S SPORTING HEADLINES referred to Luis as "*Sordito*" and "*Protegido del Dummy*" and "*Arma Secreta.*" Little Deaf One. Dummy's Protégé. Secret Weapon. "TAYLOR CLAIMS YOUTHS CAN WIN!" screamed the English-language *Post*. Things had taken a dramatic turn. What had seemed merely spectacle was now touted as a genuine contest. COULD the New Yorkers, lacking Matty, Donlin and me, be defeated by the thrown-together young Cubans? That Donlin and I gave them the barest chance was electrifying in itself.

Interest in the contest, high from the beginning, now soared. Lodging in the vicinity of Almendares Park vanished and was running short elsewhere. At the Plaza Hotel anybody who might have a newsworthy opinion was accosted by the scribes. The Giants took it good-naturedly, except for Herzog and Fletcher. Accompanied as usual by Polson, they stopped me in a hallway and demanded—it was the first time Herzog had bothered to write on my pad—whether I had the guts to back up my boast with a wager.

I hadn't boasted about anything and told them so.

"You're plenty chesty for the goddamn papers," Herzog said, his long beak inches from my face. "But yellow now?"

I felt myself heating up. "What kind of bet?"

They exchanged a look. Herzog answered: "We outscore you at least two to one."

I rolled my eyes in disbelief.

"Three to one," Fletcher offered, as if tossing caution to the winds. A sucker deal. You could get those odds taking the Havana Reds against us. Did they think I was that stupid?

"That's tops," Herzog wrote, his manner implying that only a yellow skunk would turn it down. "You said you could beat us!"

"We've still got one more practice," I answered. "See me after that." I walked away, feeling their unfriendly eyes and knowing they'd be back with another offer.

———— • ◆ • ————

McGraw MADE A point of keeping Donlin and me on the bench that afternoon. He wanted to show he could win without us. Using the inside game he'd perfected, McGraw did everything possible to erase the memory of the Blues victory. Hooks pitched smoothly and kept the Reds off balance while Herzog, looking as formidable as I'd ever seen him, got a hit every time up.

"Bring on your babies," he sneered at me.

It ended with us on top, 4–1, by a wider margin than Herzog and Fletcher and Polson had offered. As if the kids were on a par with the local pros.

What daring sports, those three dinks.

Things were shaping up pretty good from our standpoint. McGraw announced grandly that he would man third base himself against us; Herzog would move out to right and Polson to center; Becker would pitch. Anticipating the last, I'd started throwing the boys my version of Becker's emery ball. McGraw had Crandall ready to come in whenever he wanted, and my hope was to get to Becker before that happened.

That evening I had a secret catch with Luis. His control was flawless as he hammered my mitt. How he placed the ball was almost uncanny. Had Natalia worked a spell on him?

"Will your family be here?" I asked.

Father C. had arranged for them to come, he answered, then surprised me by writing in Spanish on my pad. I beckoned to Rincón, who had a bit of English. José got across to me that Luis was hoping his grandfather would show up.

"Is that possible?" I wrote.

"I doubt it," Rincón asserted.

"Why?"

He gave me a strange look. "The sonuvabitch is a goddamn *bandido*."

Which ended that conversation.

———•◆•———

THAT EVENING AT the boys hotel, Donlin and I paid for a feast of *paella*, a dish I could eat every day. Pepe Conte almost had to use his fists to keep the other sports scribes outside. He promised they could enter the hall after we'd finished our meal.

While they waited we went over our signs once more. Then we announced that Nico would be the team's captain. He was the superior athlete, respected by everybody. All of the Matanzas boys would start—Nico in center, Luis pitching, Tony catching, Izzy at second— which greatly pleased Rincón and Father C.

A graceful, silver-haired man in his sixties approached me when the writers spilled in. Father C. introduced him: Señor Esteban Bellán, one of the pioneers of Cuban baseball. Born in Matanzas, Bellán had played in the U.S. for the old Troy Haymakers clear back in the 1860s.

Small wonder the Matanzas kids played so well, with a tradition like that. After a courteous exchange, Bellán said that he'd enjoyed the dispute-marked game in which I'd clowned while McGraw fumed. He'd also read of our pugilistic exploits in the Havana nightclub, and said he appreciated a man who knew how to defend himself.

"Do you happen to know an old-time player named Fowler?" he asked.

"No, why?"

"A man of that name played with the old Red Stockings. Big man about your height, a little heavier, looked a bit like you, except your hair's redder." Bellán smiled. "He used his fists pretty well, too."

We stood for a moment gazing at the youngsters, who were doing their best to act experienced as they talked with the reporters. I noticed that Rincón stayed close to Luis and shielded him from the press men.

"If the *chicos* play even half decently," Bellán said, "it will be celebrated all over the nation."

"We're going for a lot more than that," I told him.

"I'm sure you are." He smiled indulgently. *"Hasta mañana,"* he said, moving away.

Yes, I thought. *Mañana.*

PART FOUR

THE DELIVERY

⚜

The enumerators who took the census under our military
occupation acknowledged the difficulty of distinguishing
among a people whose prevailing physical characteristics
are dark skin and black hair. . . .

Forbes Lindsay,
Cuba and Her People of To-Day, 1911

EIGHTEEN

EARLY SUNDAY MORNING, game day, Father C. conducted a Mass attended by Donlin, Rincón and the boys. After breakfast we held our last pregame meeting. The youngsters looked tense and drawn, and I suspected they hadn't slept much. Neither had I. We went over signals again; in the heat of the contest they could be crucial.

Donlin and I both gave little pep talks. We told them that only by giving McGraw the fight of his life could they hope to earn his respect.

"Why do you wish to defeat your teammates?" one of them asked.

Mike explained that with the exception of Devlin we hadn't spent much time with the Giants who would be on the field today. No particular bond of loyalty existed. We wanted to lick them just as the Havana and Almendares players would want to humble *them* when they reached their primes—just to demonstrate that they could.

We told them their opponents had been no better than them at their age, and in some cases not nearly as good. The Giants had experience, of course, but they were still young themselves and they were on foreign turf. They'd never seen us in action, but we knew them thoroughly.

"Most important, they don't know Luis," I stressed. "If we back him up and use our heads at the plate, we'll hold our own—and maybe have a chance to win. *That's* what we're after!" Logical or just hopeful, it produced cheers.

Finally we played our trump card. Father C. signaled to Rincón, who wheeled in a hotel cart. On it hung uniforms of brilliant white, with "CUBA" emblazoned in bold black letters on the jerseys and each snowy cap bearing a black "C." The opposite, by design, of McGraw's colors.

It wasn't until Rincón displayed their names stitched inside the jerseys that they realized the uniforms had been made for them. Even then they scarcely believed it. With vaudevillian gusto, Donlin then delivered a few lines in Spanish that he'd practiced with Rincón. The gist of it was: *"El Sordo* says that if we win today, the uniforms are yours to keep forever!"

I'd said nothing of the sort. Win or lose, the boys would keep their uniforms. But it was a hell of a moment.

Donlin must have given it just the right touch. Their mouths opened in yells as they sprang up and pulled the uniforms off the rack and began putting them on, looking at each other in wonder, fingers tracing the name CUBA. Jersey shirttails flapping around his hips, his eyes suspiciously moist, Luis signed something to me.

"He regrets that his father is not alive for this day," Father C. translated. "But he thinks that perhaps his spirit is in you."

"Wait a second," I protested, "I'm not *that* old. . . ." I stopped abruptly. If Della and I had started when we first got married, a child of ours would be about Luis's age.

I *was* old enough.

"He wishes to express his family's gratitude," the Padre signed formally, "along with his own."

I nodded gravely, overcome by feeling.

"I don't think you can imagine," he went on, glancing at the boys donning their uniforms, "what this means to them."

Maybe not. But I saw how clever we'd been in the choice of "CUBA." Donlin had argued for "ALL-STARS"; I'd preferred the names of the regions; Father C. and Rincón had insisted on "CUBA." Now we saw its impact: Luis and Nico and the rest represented the future; they carried the hopes of the *nation* in a far deeper way than did the Havana pros. Today they would challenge, in friendly competition, the country that had helped liberate them and now showed signs of becoming a new dominator. Their coaches' colors were more ragtag: Donlin and I in our black Giants togs; Rincón in his green-trimmed Matanzas uniform; Father C. in his customary brown Franciscan habit.

We marched out to the street, the boys moving with self-conscious pride, gloves dangling from their wrists, all but Father C. carrying spikes.

Another surprise waited: two motor sedans to carry us to the ballpark just as the Giants were transported in Havana. Onlookers crowded the sidewalks, heads turning to track us and mouths open in cheers. The boys waved back, shyly at first. Donlin had said it would be too much, would turn their heads, cost us whatever focus on playing remained after the excitement of the uniforms. I countered that we were only copying what McGraw had done with outstanding success. A lot of ballplayers were drunks and roughs, and most high-class establishments barred them. McGraw insisted that his players be treated as gentlemen, booking us into Pullmans, putting us in $5-a-night hotels, treating us like the champions we became. No reason it wouldn't work here, I reasoned; if nothing else, the motor caravan would boost their memories of this singular day.

———— • ◆ • ————

TICKET BUYERS STOOD for a half mile outside the grounds. Mounted police kept watch over the turbulent column. A banner proclaimed, *"¡VIVAN LOS JÓVENES! ¡VIVAN EL SORDO Y EL SORDITO!"* Laughing, the boys pointed at it. By now they seemed to accept Luis's being singled out, probably reasoning that if he was regarded as an ace, he must *be* one.

The day was mild. At first we had the park to ourselves, and I set Luis to work fielding bunts near the plate. Sooner or later McGraw would try to bunt the boy out of the game. Here was a chance to practice without tipping him. Luis came off the mound with agile grace, his pickups cat-quick, his throws sure. As he worked up a sweat some of his nervousness began to disappear. A good sign. For us to have any real chance, he'd have to survive all the crap McGraw would throw.

Doyle and Herzog led the Giants onto the field. Next to the kids they looked big and invincible. I watched McGraw halt dead in his tracks and scowl at our new uniforms. He'd made a splash by supplying warm-up gear and gloves, but now he realized that he'd been outdone. Conte and Father C. had talked the American Embassy into footing the bill—an act of good will that would be duly publicized. By now McGraw had probably also heard about our auto caravan. He yelled something at Donlin.

"What'd he say?" I asked.

"He wants to know why you and I aren't wearing the new whites, seeing as we've gone over to the Cubans."

"Tell him he can have one for himself if he's so jealous."

Donlin chose not to pass it on.

"Those guys must look slick to the kids," he signed worriedly, moments later, eyeing the Giants infield play, where bullet throws from Doyle, Fletcher, even McGraw, zipped with casual accuracy into Devlin's long trapper's glove. I watched them too and it gave me a bad moment. Who did we think we were, trying to face down the Giants?

"You get our money placed?" I asked, almost hoping he hadn't. We'd thrown in a hundred each. The Giants were runaway favorites, of course; the latest betting line seemed to be whether or not they'd beat us by at least ten runs.

José's taking care of it," he answered.

I went to the bullpen and watched Luis throw. Single overhead pump. High upswinging leg. Torso twisting. Back leg thrusting. Arm whipping in a swift arc. Feet aligned and body crouched for defense after the release. Resembling Méndez in his lean frame, he generated the same astonishing speed. If he could keep his concentration he'd give the Giants a few things to think about.

For a while anyway.

I'd worked out private signs between us. As we reviewed them he glanced anxiously at the crowd that overflowed the grandstand and bleachers. Harried groundsmen were stretching ropes 15 feet in front of the low outfield fence to accommodate the surplus fans. Balls hit in among them would be a nightmare for outfielders; luckily, ours were speedier than McGraw's with Donlin out, and capable, I hoped, of cutting off drives.

I put a hand on Luis's shoulder and felt a tremor. The boy must be scared. I had a terrible moment. What if he took an awful soaking today? What the hell was I doing? With big deliberate movements I signed directly before his face, trying to focus his attention. Just throw fastballs, I told him. Nothing else.

He swallowed and nodded.

Rigler dusted home plate and summoned the captains. Doyle sauntered out for the Giants. Nico went for us, flanked by Rincón and Donlin. It was agreed that balls hit into the on-field throng would be doubles. Rigler cautioned against inflaming the crowd, which drew a laugh from Doyle, who remarked that the pups were the fans' darlings and anybody crossing them would be massacred. But in practically the same breath he reported McGraw's objection to us being the home team. After all, the Giants had played eleven games there to none for the kids.

"That's prime grade horseshit!" Donlin exclaimed.

Rigler said sarcastically that the Cubans would indeed be the home team, since it happened to be their country. We all knew McGraw's tactics: make outrageous demands at the start, get turned down, hope for an edge later.

Doyle gave Donlin a whispered message as he turned away: "I think the Old Man wants to run up the score."

Swell, I thought, when Donlin told me. Just what we need. Still, what did I expect? McGraw probably had bets down too, and with cash on the line we could expect little in the way of mercy. Making the kids look bad would also drive down what he'd have to pay to sign any of them.

As if conjured by my thinking of money, Herzog and Polson showed up. "You robbers still trying to hold us up?" Donlin said contemptuously.

"We'll go with what the papers say," Polson told him. "Six runs." He was lying. The early editions had set the margin between eight and ten. "You got this secret pitcher and all," he smirked.

"Twelve runs," Donlin said. We'd already agreed on our position.

"Seven."

"Ten."

Eight," Herzog said. "And that's final."

"Okay," Donlin told him. "You're on for a hundred, even though we know you're trying to clip us. But we want a kicker, just in case we beat you."

"You beat US?"

"Yeah. We want that same eight. You pay us $800 if we trim you."

"To hell with you!" Herzog snapped.

"Fine," Donlin said calmly. "I guess it shows you ain't got the guts to back your sure thing."

They huddled for a long moment. "Sure, we'll do it—but for $500," Polson said. "Which you ain't never gonna see anyway."

"We damn sure will if we lick you," Donlin told him.

"If," Polson sneered.

"Who's holding stakes?"

They looked at each other.

Donlin grinned. "Ain't got that much cash, huh?"

"We figured this'd be a gentlemen's deal," Polson said.

"That'd be fine," said Donlin, "if I saw any gents on your side."

"We'll get the dough," Herzog told him. "Trainer good enough for you?"

"He'll have *our* cash straight away." Donlin turned away with a look of mock alarm. "Now don't whip us too bad, hear?"

Our bench was on the third-base side. I stood behind it tensely as Rigler called for play to begin. Luis looked hair-trigger tight. Who could blame him?

Devore stepped in on the left side, fidgeted with his bat, and stepped out again as Luis started into his windup. Playing tricks already.

Stay put, you half-pint dink!

Luis's first pitch was a blur that soared over Tony Paguey's mitt and thudded off the foot of the grandstand. Devore studied it, bat on shoulder, head swiveling to follow its passage. Grinning, he took his stance again.

You didn't show your damn teeth at Méndez!

The second pitch was so far outside that Tony had to lunge for it. The ball glanced off his mitt and rolled to the stand again. Devore raised his hands as if to say, *What can I do?* In the coacher's box McGraw was making noodle-armed motions and goofy fingerspellings, trying his best to rattle Luis.

The next pitch rocketed at Devore, who flung himself backward, bat flying across the plate. "He's gonna kill somebody!" McGraw yelled at Rigler. "Get him the hell out of there!" Rigler waved for him to shut up, whereupon McGraw hooked a thumb in the air to let everybody know he thought Luis should be thrown out. Did he really think Rigler would eject Luis before he faced a second hitter? Some of the Giants, Polson and Fletcher in particular, were shaking their fists. In the stands people were standing and yelling down at McGraw.

Three pitches and already everybody was steamed.

I took advantage of the commotion to go out to the mound, where Luis rubbed his fist in a circle over his heart. Telling me he was sorry. He looked young and alone. I stood close to him and signed with my hands held low; with our eyes cast down we could feel apart from everybody.

"You're making it too hard," I told him. "Do what you did warming up—throw to Tony's mitt, nothing more." I saw his eyes flicker toward the stands. "What is it, Luis?"

He peered at a section of bleachers. I looked too: pulsating masses of people, dark spots in the brilliant sun.

"What's wrong?"

He signed something I didn't get. I asked him to repeat, and caught the sign for family.

"They aren't here?"

"*No mi abuelo.*" He fingerspelled it.

I felt a sting of irritation as I recognized the word for grandfather. Of all the damn things to be thinking about. And how the hell could he be so sure, in all the teeming humanity, that one person was missing?

"Well, when he *does* show up," I told him, "do you want him to see you already beaten?"

He looked at the ground.

I took hold of his shoulder and waited till his eyes met mine. Each time he glanced away I squeezed harder. Finally our eyes stayed locked.

"The way you're looking at me now—that's how I want you to look at Tony's mitt. As long as it takes, no matter what the batters do, no matter what McGraw does, you stand there and look at that mitt until it's just you and it. *Then* you pitch. If they hit the ball, they hit it. Understand?"

He breathed deeply. *"Sí."*

I went back to the bench thinking of all the scrapes I'd been in over the years. Coaches and teammates offered what they could, but in the end it was up to me. Now was Luis's time to show what he was made of. Simple as that. Maybe I'd gotten him in over his head, but it was too late for second-guessing.

The next ball came in hard but without much movement. Luis was aiming it a little, dart-throwing, trying to throw a sure strike. But that was okay. Everybody in the ballpark knew Devore wouldn't be swinging. Rigler's right hand shot up.

With the count 3–1, I had a hunch what Devore would do. Donlin nodded quick agreement and flashed signs that went back to when we'd played together in San Diego—anything to stymie McGraw. *Watch the bunt!* It would have been easier with Father C. on hand to help us, but McGraw had thrown a fit at the notion of the Church opposing him.

Luis came down the middle again. Devore dropped the barrel of the bat on the ball and sent it rolling along the third-base line, legs already churning toward first. We'd partly determined the bunt's direction by keeping our third baseman back and sending our first sacker in. It was up to Tony and Luis to cover the right side. The ball was too far up the line for Tony to have a chance. It was Luis's play and he sprang forward.

Things looked good for Devore, already halfway up the line. Luis had to field the ball with his back to first base. What happened next electrified the ballpark. Luis snatched the ball barehanded, body twisting and arm whipping beneath him as he shot it to first without seeming to look. Rudy Ordoñez, our rangy first baseman, did the splits along the baseline and extended his long arm. The ball smacked into his glove a split-second before Devore's foot thudded on the bag. Rigler, in good position to see the play, gave the thumbs-up. *Out!*

The crowd went loco, of course, and showered money on the field, which set off McGraw, who bitterly argued the call. Instead of his having a speedy runner on and our young hurler shaken, we'd gotten the important first out and Luis's play had jacked our spirits to the sky. And maybe, just maybe, planted the first tiny doubts in our opponents.

Luis kicked fretfully at the rubber while our batboy went around picking up his money. If his confidence was boosted, he gave no sign. He'd pulled off a play in a thousand, the fans were in a frenzy, and he seemed oblivious.

You had to be deaf for that.

Doyle, another lefty, got the count to 3–1, then fouled off a smoker that shattered his bat. Boosted by nerves, Luis was looking even faster than Méndez. I glanced at the Giants bench and saw all eyes fixed on him. In his coacher's box McGraw stood with crossed arms, scowling. He knew he'd been sandbagged, that I'd reined Luis in while he was watching. Did he wonder what else the kid could do? Once Luis got his control, it would be a treat to show him.

"Ball four!" Rigler signaled when Doyle took a close one on the outside corner. Donlin jumped up to argue and I had to grab his shirt to pull him back down. Rigler gave us a look that said, *What the hell's going on? It's an exhibition!* Herzog stepped in on the right side, of late the most dangerous Giant hitter. McGraw flashed a rapid set of signals. I didn't see steal or hit and run (surely he'd changed signs today), but my gut told me one or the other was coming. Doyle was quick and they'd waste little time in testing Tony.

Suddenly Luis whirled and ripped the ball to Ordoñez. Doyle didn't have that much of a lead and he'd been watching Luis. Nonetheless, Ordoñez slapped the ball on his wrist as his fingers touched the bag. Rigler called him safe, but Doyle and everybody else knew it had been by an eyelash.

A little bit more for McGraw to chew on.

Doyle broke with the next pitch and it looked like his speed would carry him in safely. Lucky for us, the hit-and-run was on and Herzog had to protect him. Woe be to any of McGraw's players who disobeyed his signs. Red Murray once ignored a bunt order and socked a home run and McGraw still fined the bejeesus out of him. Now Luis's rising blazer took Herzog by surprise and the ball ticked foul. Doyle was sent back to first. Staring at Luis, twitching the bat like a cat's tail, Herzog had to be wondering how the skinny kid mustered all that power.

McGraw was tricky to dope out, but right then it made sense for him to bulldog us, keep the pressure on till shown he couldn't have his way. Following my sign, Luis threw to the outside, making it easier for Herzog to hit behind the runner. Which was exactly what he did, rapping the ball smartly between first and second as Doyle broke again with the pitch. A perfect hit and run—except that we hadn't sent Izzy to cover the bag (standard with a righty at the plate) but sent our short-stop instead. Even so, the ball was hit hard, and Izzy had to quick-crab to his left.

To first! Take the sure out!

But Izzy spun counterclockwise, much as Luis had on the bunt, and snapped the ball to second as the runner arrived. Another tight call for

Rigler, who signaled the out. Doyle's hard slide prevented a throw to first. Doyle, always the gent, helped our shortstop to his feet. Not one for sportsmanship unless it profited him, McGraw charged up to Rigler and argued with him chest to chest. When the big umpire ordered him away, McGraw turned and glared out at Izzy, who promptly bent and smoothed the infield dirt, providing McGraw a view of his butt.

Herzog, the new runner, spat a stream of tobacco as he stared at our shortstop. I didn't like the look of it. Just as it was McGraw's natural bent to pour kerosene on every competitive situation, it was Herzog's to spark a flame.

Hitting in Donlin's cleanup spot was Art Devlin, reliable at the plate with some power, but hardly in Donlin's class. On a 2–2 blazer that Rigler ruled a ball, Herzog sprinted for second. Tony rifled the ball there as Herzog went in with one leg straining for the bag, the other bent and lifted. Izzy deftly avoided the spikes and slapped the ball, too late, against Herzog's neck. The Giant got up slowly, mouth working, as he glared at the boy. Donlin and I tensed, ready to jump, but Izzy trotted back to his position without so much as a glance back at Herzog.

Becker stepped in. During the long season he'd backed up McGraw's outfielders but in Havana he'd made the most of his chances and proven himself one of the few Giants to hit the Cubans consistently. McGraw had him batting fifth, perfect for driving in runners.

Against Devore and Doyle, the earlier lefties, it was hard to tell whether Luis had been using his pitch that swerved away from them; his control was so shaky that it hardly mattered. Now it looked like he was getting a better feel of things. His first pitch started inside and swerved over for a strike. Looking thoughtful, Becker backed out and rubbed dirt on his hands. When he was ready, Luis threw it again and he swung, too late.

Go to the curve now? No, I decided. Not yet. Luis's next pitch was spotted inside like the others. Expecting it to swerve over the plate, Becker swung. But the ball rose and he cut under it for a clean miss.

Strike three! Side out!

The boys streamed off the field like puppies. Izzy twisted Luis's cap and mussed his hair. Luis's somber expression lightened as the others pounded his back. They were accepting him. And why the hell not? Hadn't he just stopped the mighty *Neoyorquinos?* I headed for the first-base coacher's box with a glow spreading through my chest.

"You were lucky as shit," McGraw mouthed, straightening up ponderously after bending for a ground ball.

"Right," I agreed with a cheesy grin.

Izzy went down on three pitches, our second batsman on four. I'd tried to ready them for Becker's lazy drops and shoots, but the overeager Cuban youngsters lunged at everything in reach. I thought about bunting at McGraw but he was playing in too close.

Most of what Becker threw to Nico was unhittable. Still, he slammed a ball inches over McGraw that carried all the way to the fence (Donlin joked that it hit the boards four times trying to get through) after hooking foul. McGraw threw up his hands as if surrendering and made a show of retreating behind the bag. A wise choice. That shot could have killed him.

I nudged Donlin. "Let's show bunt."

He made the sign to Nico, who squared around but took a low pitch. McGraw was hopelessly out of the play if the ball had been laid down. He knew it and the fans knew it. Donlin told me that they were starting to ride him. Grinning, McGraw spread his hands to the crowd and shrugged. But his eyes found mine and they belied the grin. We were playing cat and mouse with him—and he wasn't used to being the mouse. He called something to Becker.

"Low bridge coming," Donlin predicted.

Becker's next pitch—what he considered his fastball—caused Nico to hit the dirt. Looking determined, the muscular Cuban lined the next ball back up the middle, and if Becker hadn't ducked he would have been brained. It should have dropped in for a hit, but Doyle had shaded that way and made a leaping grab for the third out.

It seemed we'd been up to bat only a matter of seconds. McGraw's cold blue eyes were slitted as we passed again. "Now you get yours."

"Right," I signed again, amiably.

Swinging for the fence, Fletcher popped up and slammed his bat down in disgust. McGraw came up to bat. Three times he stepped out of the box as Luis began his windup, all the while talking to Rigler and pointing at Luis's feet. The same ploy he'd used against Méndez. Luis looked confused.

"Plunk the sonofabitch," Donlin urged.

I shook my head. Throwing at him would inflame things and bring retaliation. I signed to Luis to ignore him, but his concentration was spoiled and he walked both McGraw and Wilson. Polson stepped in, a weak hitter. We pulled our corners in. Sure enough, Polson dumped the ball up the third base line. Luis tried to duplicate his sensational play, but this time he was too late.

Bases loaded. Only one out.

Devore drove a 2–1 blazer deep to right center with nothing but grass beneath it. I clutched my hands to my head. Donlin slammed a fist on the bench. The runners had gone with the pitch and it looked like they'd all score. Nico was sprinting over from center, desperately chasing the ball though it looked far beyond him. At the last second his body flattened out and seemed to hang parallel to the grass, his glove twisting in a backhand reach. The ball struck the leather hinge and stuck there even as he hit the ground and bounced like his stomach was rubberized. He scrambled up and launched a chain-lightning peg. Two of the runners had alertly reversed themselves, but Polson was tearing around second on his way to third. Our relay to first put him out by a hundred feet. Double killing! Without Polson's blunder the runner on third would have scored.

We'd gotten out of the inning.

McGraw gave me a bug-eyed look as we crossed paths, then set about skinning Polson for his bonehead play.

I'd spotted a tipoff in Becker's windup: On fastballs he brought his hands up even with the bill of his cap, on curves and shoots no higher than his throat. Veteran batsmen could have used it to give him a pasting, but our kids were too green. Nico alone seemed untroubled by Becker's dipsy-doodling emery balls, knocking solid hits his next two times up.

He was our only baserunner.

McGraw's men were beginning to time Luis's smokers and drive them. Lucky for us, almost all their drives went straight at somebody. In the fourth with two out, the score still 0–0, McGraw came to the plate with the bases loaded. No pointing at Luis's feet now; he was all business. In his playing days he'd averaged .330 and been especially nasty in the pinch. He might be old and fat now, but his will to dominate was fierce as ever, and over the years he'd never stopped taking hitting practice.

Luis's first pitch backed him off the plate. Ball one. Tony spotted his mitt low and outside and Luis hit it with a blazer. Rigler called a strike, which drew a homicidal glare from the Giants leader. Luis threw again in the same spot. McGraw checked his swing. Another strike. McGraw looked ready to brain the ump. Crowding the plate, forced to protect the outside, he backed off in a hurry from an insider burner and looked anxiously at Rigler, who signaled a ball.

Damn! Three and two. McGraw fudged toward the plate again, expecting Luis to go back outside. Okay, I thought, time for the *curva*. It wasn't the best breaker I'd seen from Luis. It probably wasn't even a strike. The ball came in hard toward McGraw's belly, which hung over his belt as well as over the plate, and he froze in surprise. Then it broke, maybe too low, maybe not. McGraw's reflexes were still good enough that he recovered, but his flailing swing missed. Strikeout! Donlin pounded on my head in his excitement.

Once again we'd escaped.

Little Napoleon's expression told me that I'd better cut a wide path as we passed. I kept my face straight, my eyes lowered.

Inside I was howling.

Adding salt to his wounds, Donlin had our leadoff man bunt. McGraw lumbered in too late to make the play. When our second hitter fouled off another bunt in his direction, he called time and with bitter gestures waved Herzog in to take third and Crandall off the bench and out to right. "You had your fun with an old man," he signed as he stalked by me to his bench. He was taking himself out of the game.

Go ahead and snivel, I thought. If he'd busted the game open last time up, he'd be crowing like a damn rooster. As for that "old man" applesauce, hell, he was only two years older than me.

It felt good to drive McGraw out, but maybe it wasn't too smart. Herzog was a hell of a third sacker, which cut down our bunting chances—and apart from Nico that was the only threat we'd shown.

"Odds are dropping," Rincón reported after talking to a man sporting a large diamond. "They're only favored by five runs now."

"Anybody think we'll win?" Donlin asked.

Rincón relayed the question. "Not many."

"What odds?"

"Six to one against."

Donlin grinned at me. "Want in on that, Dummy?"

Might as well, I thought. I was in up to my neck already. "Fifty bucks," I told him. "If we lose I'll have to borrow from McGraw."

"Me too," he said. "Let's lick him instead."

Doyle singled with one out in the Giants' fifth. "Can you believe it?" Donlin suddenly exclaimed. "Mac flashed the old Oriole steal sign: pulled his bill down over his eyes. You think he forgot I played on that team?"

"McGraw never forgot anything."

To our surprise Doyle did break for second and Tony's throw arrived late.

"The boob *is* using the old signs!" Donlin exploded. "He does it again, we'll nail him out by a block!"

Two pitches later, McGraw pulled his brim low. Donlin countered with our pitchout sign, and Luis and Tony executed it perfectly. But Doyle didn't move.

"He crossed us," Donlin signed glumly. Instead of stealing McGraw's sign, we'd handed him a chance to get one of ours. He gave us a nasty grin.

An instant later we jumped to our feet as Herzog slammed a liner that our third baseman leaped to catch, then alertly whipped the ball to Izzy at second in time to double off Doyle. The third twin-killer we'd pulled off. McGraw shook his head and lifted his hands and looked upward as if for divine help.

"Pinch me, Dummy," Donlin signed. "I don't believe it!"

I didn't either.

McGraw soon gave us something new to think about by kneeling in the first-base coacher's box and setting his cheek down almost on the chalked line each time Luis wound up, meanwhile gesturing with one hand, as if to the hitter. It was an act, we decided; just one more stunt to distract Luis.

Still, we told Tony to wait till the last instant to set his mitt so McGraw wouldn't have time to tip the location. Luis's *curva* was doing good work now mixed in with his blazers. With luck we might be able to hold them off another inning or two.

I had no idea how we could score.

Donlin did, though. He pointed out that two Giant infielders were out of position. If our kids laid the ball down and ran like hell, maybe something would happen.

The first squibber rolled between Becker and Devlin. Both went for it. Both hesitated. By the time Devlin picked it up and fired to first, it was too late. The second one went to Becker's right. He came off the mound fast and slipped trying to make the pickup. For the first time we had two baserunners. The crowd was carrying on like a house of lunatics. With Luis up and nobody out, it was a cinch we'd bunt again. McGraw brought Devlin and Herzog in so far they were practically on top of the plate.

Swing, Donlin signed.

Luis managed to make contact—not much, but enough that the ball rolled past Devlin. Now we had the bases loaded. The grandstand rivaled the Polo Grounds at its craziest, and the boys were looking around with wide eyes.

McGraw huddled with his infielders. Walking off again, he roared at us, "Cheap bushers!" I thought those were his words, anyway, and judging from the veins standing out in his neck, I was sure he roared them.

Izzy, our next hitter, also squared around but Becker delivered a doodler so high that it almost got past Dutch Wilson. That was the last straw. McGraw stomped onto the diamond and ordered Crandall to the mound. Polson took first and Becker took his usual outfield post. It was their best defensive lineup. And in Crandall we faced the ace pinch hurler in the game.

McGraw was using all his weapons.

Bases loaded. No outs. 1–0 count. Infield in to choke off the run. Izzy tried his hardest, but Crandall's drops were too much and he struck out on three straight. Bearing down as if a World Series paycheck was at stake, Crandall whiffed our next man on three more. Nico brought us to our feet by clouting one to deep left—but not quite deep enough. Devore hauled it down against the rope for the third out. The crowd's spirit dropped like a punctured airship.

"Next time I'll get it done against him," Nico vowed grimly to Rincón.

Not likely, I thought. Whatever it was Nico had hit, Crandall wouldn't serve it to him again.

The Giants wasted no time in coming right back at us. Luis alternated walks and whiffs until once again the sacks were loaded. Devore pranced off third. Herzog took a wide lead at second. Becker edged away from first. At the plate stood Fletcher, cool and menacing. I told Luis to throw strikes and be alert for the squeeze. Even with two out I wouldn't put it past McGraw.

"What the hell's he up to now?" Donlin signed.

The stocky manager was crossing from his first-base coacher's box to the third-base side. Why? For a better sighting angle on Tony? But that made no sense. With the right-handed Fletcher in the batter's box, McGraw's view was blocked from third. Then I saw that he wasn't looking toward the plate. Instead he was studying Luis as he talked to Devore.

"Look out for the steal!" Donlin yelled to Rincón, suspecting they'd try to exploit Luis's deliberate windup and high kick.

Luis toed the slab and looked in. Devore broke for home. It was only a feint, but an excellent one. Luis did not balk but stepped back with his right foot and made a quick off-balance toss to third. Devore barely got back under the tag. I was proud of how Luis had handled it.

Then McGraw pulled the rottenest stunt of all.

"Here, let me see that ball!" he said, taking a step toward our third baseman. His Spanish was flawless, Rincón informed me later, and the command carried the full weight of McGraw's personality.

"No!" Donlin screeched. But it was too late. Our young infielder dutifully tossed him the ball. The instant it was in the air, Devore again broke for the plate—this time not faking. McGraw stepped aside, of course, and the ball dropped to the turf and rolled behind him. Our youngster stood dumbfounded for a second before he scrambled around McGraw, who made no effort to get out of his way. He retrieved the ball and drilled it to Tony, blocking the plate. But before it reached him the sliding Devore hooked a foot around and touched the plate.

Then everything went to hell. The runners were moving. Herzog found the baseline blocked by our shortstop and knocked him aside on his way to third. He had the right of way, and it wasn't viciously done. The boy stayed cool. But not Donlin, who jumped up with mayhem in mind. I clutched his jersey and slowed him down until until Rincón, a big strong customer, could take over. Donlin was bellowing that he would fix Herzog, who was urging him to come.

I yanked out my pad and scrawled, *"Don't let Mac steal this game!"* I added, *"Please!"* and took it to Rigler.

Technically McGraw was within the rules: time hadn't been called and the ball was in play. But he'd stooped to a damned low trick against kids.

Rigler looked troubled. His glance went from my note to the stands, where people were waving their fists and stomping their feet and brandishing bottles. Some of the Giants also glanced around uneasily, surrounded as they were by 12,000 pissed-off folks, all of them backing the boys. Rigler had to decide for or against us. Finally he waved his arms in a crossing motion to signify that the run had not counted, and pointed for Devore and the others to return to their bases.

McGraw was on him like a small bear, feet kicking in an angry dance, cascading dirt with his spikes and shouting in Rigler's face. All of which further aggravated the crowd, from which missiles rained. Rigler retreated toward second base, McGraw dogging him. Finally he wheeled and I saw his lips clearly: "John, I'm not gonna let you take this game on a goddamn trick!"

"No timeout was called!" McGraw persisted.

"I called it!" Rigler thundered. "Get back to your spot or I'm throwing you out!"

"You and who else?" McGraw demanded, standing on his toes and bellying up to the big umpire like a bantam cock.

"The whole Cuban army, if it takes 'em! Now get the fuck out of here!"

McGraw spun around in frustration. Our eyes met. He hooked a thumb at my note still in Rigler's hand, and snarled, "Screw you, Dummy!"

In that case, Mr. McGraw, screw you too.

It took some effort to get everybody back in place. Donlin was still agitated. Devlin was trying to pacify Herzog, which I appreciated, but the brawny third sacker didn't seem to be paying much attention. Polson was strutting around striking poses. Fans in the bleachers were trying to jump down on the field. I caught a glimpse of Father C. in his first-row grandstand seat, arms raised in what looked like both a benediction and a plea for calm.

Just as Rigler was finally snugging his chest protector and about to call play again, some new commotion broke out. Heads turned toward the right field bleachers, where dark-skinned men pressed through the crowd like a tidal surge. A banner appeared over them: ¡ARRIBA CUBANOS MORENOS! The crowd around them was strangely still, faces watchful and expectant, the police beginning to exchange wary glances. On the diamond, most of Luis's teammates were looking at him. His face brightened as he made a small wave to the newcomers in the stands, one of whom, an elderly man, came down to the railing. Despite his years he was powerfully built. His woolly hair was gray-white, but the proud African features seemed chiseled from mahogany. His eyes held a burning quality, and even two hundred feet away I could feel the proud force of the man's presence. Gravely, he returned Luis's wave.

What the hell was going on?

I felt a nudge at my arm. Rincón beckoned for my pad and wrote something I couldn't decipher. "*Abuelo.*" I shrugged and shook my head. He wrote, "*papa + papa*" and pointed to Luis. I stared at it for what seemed like a century before I got what he was trying to tell me.

The old man was Luis's grandfather.

But that couldn't be. He was black as coal.

Rincón nudged me again. "*Elias Serros,*" he'd written. "*Come from montañas.*"

Shouldn't his name be Avelar? Then I remembered that "Serros" was part of Natalia's long handle. Her maiden name, I supposed. This man must be her father, Luis's maternal grandpa. Then it all came together: Father C. employing blacks (and Luis) in his bakery; telling me of the black opposition and of Luis's grandfather being wanted by the law—which would explain the cops' tension; Gómez calling it a racial fight. Luis and his sister Luna must have gotten Natalia's lighter coloring. Maybe in Cuba skin color was no big affair where baseball was concerned, but in the States it was the kiss of death.

Until then I hadn't fully realized how much I'd put into the dream that had seemed to be coming true that afternoon, or how much hope I'd taken from it until, with a sinking heart, I felt it shredding.

The Giants would never sign Luis.

Nor would any other big-league club.

NINETEEN

"A NIGGER!" MCGRAW yelled, storming over to us after a quick conference with Pepe Conte. "YOUR KID'S A NIGGER!"

Donlin was looking at me for an explanation. My mind refused to work. In the bleachers more banners were popping up, the words MORENO and NEGRO prominent. The police looked increasingly jittery, and later we learned why: hundreds of Elias Serros's supporters were massed outside the ballpark to make sure he would get out safely; thousands more were rumored to be on the ready throughout the city.

"WHY DIDN'T YOU TELL ME?" McGraw demanded.

"I just found out myself."

"YOU STUPID BASTARD!"

He shouldn't have said that. As much as he'd cast me in the role of buffoon—and I played along—I'd always thought that beneath it lay a core of respect. I did something then that I never thought I'd do: I deliberately turned my back on John J. McGraw.

Rigler came over and threatened to call the game if we didn't start playing.

"Fine." Donlin grinned at McGraw. "We'll take the forfeit and go collect our winnings."

"WHAT!" McGraw's face turned even redder, which I hadn't thought possible. "YOU BET AGAINST US?"

Donlin, bless his crazy soul, had the brass to laugh in his face. I grinned my clown's grin. "Something wrong?" I signed. "I'm just a stupid bastard."

Rigler told us we had thirty seconds. McGraw retreated grudgingly. My brain was still addled. I had to ask Donlin what the count on Fletcher was. No count. Luis hadn't yet thrown a pitch to him.

The battle began again. During the rhubarb Luis had tried to keep warm by throwing to Izzy, but his first pitch showed that he'd lost something. Fletcher was a tough nut, good at getting grazed by pitches where it didn't hurt much. Now he crowded the plate as if daring Luis to hit him, which would send home the first run. The ball came so far outside that Tony had to lunge to block it. Grinning mockingly, Fletcher practically stood on the plate.

"Put him on his goddamn can!" Donlin signed.

He was right. I'd do it myself without thinking twice. Send Fletcher's cap one way, his bat another, his ass a third: whoops goodbye Dolly Gray. If a pitcher couldn't control the space over the plate, the hitter would. So when Luis looked at me for the sign, I pointed to my chin. He wiped his brow with his glove and brushed it over the letters on his jersey. Asking me to repeat it, wanting to be sure.

A white streak went straight at Fletcher's eyes. Unless paralyzed by the sight, no sane man could hold his ground. Certainly not the savvy Fletcher, whose alert reflexes shot his legs from beneath him and sent him sprawling backward. McGraw came screaming out of the coacher's box as Fletcher dusted himself off and glared daggers at Luis. But when he stepped back in I saw that he wasn't nearly so close to the plate. Nor were his spikes dug in like before. Fletcher would never admit it, but Luis had put some fear in him.

Now, with a 2–0 count, we had to get him out.

Luis went into his windup. McGraw and the runners taunted and did everything they could think of to get under his skin. About the only thing working for the youngster was that he couldn't hear them.

The pitch was high. Fletcher watched it go by. It looked like Luis was aiming again. I signaled to Rigler for time and strode out to remind Luis to just rear back and *throw* the damn thing.

When I got there he looked stricken. I asked what was wrong. He stared at the ground, then glanced in his grandfather's direction. I realized that he was afraid of shaming himself. The count was 3–0 and the Giants looked about to break the game open. The old man had come, at some risk to himself, only to see his grandson lose. Well, the hell with it. There were worse things than getting beat on a ballfield. He'd shut out the National League champs for five innings. How could that be failure? I put my arm around his shoulders and turned us away from the infield. With my left hand I signed, *No matter what, son, this day belongs to you.*

Luis glanced up at me at the word "son." I'd spelled it out in Spanish, *h-i-j-o,* and meant it in a general sense. I realized that he'd taken it more literally. And suddenly I found myself wishing he was my son. I'd have given anything for a boy like him. Right then I felt as close to Luis Serros Avelar as if he were my flesh and blood.

The moment didn't last. Luis's eyes widened as he glanced at the right field stands. I turned and saw Elias Serros standing again, a dark, commanding figure, and I felt a thorn of resentment. Why'd he have to show up here today? Where had he been when his grandson was just a deaf boy needing help at home?

Serros slowly raised a hand and closed it into a fist. He brought his other hand up, fingers open, and enveloped the fist. What did it mean? I didn't exactly know. Courage, strength, unity. All of those—the old man's force was considerable—but something more, too, as if by an act of will he was trying to impart some granite quality.

Too late, pal. Nice play to the crowd, though.

"See?" I told Luis, masking my thoughts. "He doesn't care whether you win or lose. He's sharing the power of this moment." Recalling a phrase from the newspapers, I fingerspelled it. "He's saying, *Viva la fuerza!* Trust your pitches and throw to Tony."

Luis took a ragged breath and squared his shoulders. He nodded and I turned away. It was up to him.

Dark-suited runners dancing off all the bases. Fletcher waiting with a 3–0 count. Two outs. Beside me, Donlin was yelling something. Fletcher abruptly stepped out of the box and glared at us. Then, reading Donlin's lips, I realized that my old pal wasn't yelling but singing. He was warbling "Goodnight Ladies," one of his favorites.

Fletcher took it as a slur on his manhood, naturally. Not only that, but music during a game happened to be one of his biggest hoodoos. If anybody on the bench so much as hummed, he'd yell, "Kill that shit, Caruso, you're robbing me of hits!"

Donlin met Fletcher's drop-dead glare by crossing his eyes and waggling his head like a lunatic. It might have been comical, except that everybody knew the potency of cross-eyed jinxes. Short of bodily harm, Donlin was doing about the worst he could to a teammate. Seeing Fletcher's face contort, I felt a glimmer of hope. If he could hit the ball in his present state—hell, if he could hit an airship with a shotgun—more power to him. I signaled for the blazer.

It's questionable whether Fletcher even saw it he was so wrought up. He swung with all his might, but the smoker, one of the hardest Luis had thrown all afternoon, was by him. It was on the high side, too, maybe not a strike, and he had no business chasing it. McGraw yelled something at him and Fletcher's mouth worked angrily.

The count was 3–1 now and Donlin kept on singing. Fletcher made vicious cuts with his club and took his stance. I signed for a curve. Luis threw it perfectly, a big rainbow arc. Fletcher nearly blasted the ball's stuffings out, but he'd been so anxious that it was foul by 50 feet. With two strikes Luis finally had an advantage, since Fletcher had to go for anything close. I decided on a blazer away and prayed he'd bite. If he swung as hard as he had the last two, the likely result would be an infield grounder.

Those were my theories, anyway.

Luis put it exactly where Tony set his mitt. Fletcher flicked his bat and deliberately fouled it off, a nice bit of work. Which left me in a quandary. The smoker again? Back to the outshoot? No, I decided. I'd seen Luis practicing Dundon and getting a decent drop almost every time. Nobody knew he had such a pitch. Even if not thrown perfectly, the surprise of it might be enough. I flashed the sign and followed it with the question. This time I was the one wanting confirmation.

As Luis gave it I thought I saw a hint of a smile.

It came in like a two-inch artillery shell, seemingly the same smoker that Fletcher had nearly fractured himself trying to hit. This time he was looking for it. With a level swing—no torquing for power now— he swept the bat through the zone. The ball should have shot outward on a swift line but as it reached the plate it dipped like a barnswallow and bounced on the plate, where Tony's quick hands trapped it. He tagged Fletcher, who stood staring at his bat.

I'd witnessed it but I could scarcely believe it. We were out of the inning and still hadn't been scored on. Luis's teammates swarmed over him and I caught glimpses of him grinning as he returned Izzy's hug and slapped Tony's mitt. The grin broadened as Nico patted him on the shoulder.

Well, how about that.

Bottom of the sixth. The crowd now seemed a wild, relentless thing, *willing* us to win. I wondered what the sound of it was like. Whatever terrific noise had assaulted McGraw's ears over the years in Chicago and Pittsburgh and Brooklyn couldn't have been greater than here.

The kids looked almost chesty, their awe of the big leaguers gone. Since we'd promised everybody a chance to play, Donlin tried to make some substitutions—but the bench wanted us to stick with our best. They were all caught up in it now; they thought we had a chance to win.

Donlin and I wanted to think it, too, but we still couldn't figure how to get a run. With Herzog and Polson at the corners and Crandall on the mound, our bunting game was shut off. In the sixth Crandall allowed a bloop single but nothing more. Neither team scored in the seventh. Luis seemed to be getting stronger as he and Crandall dueled through the eighth.

The ninth.

The tenth.

Mixing an occasional Dundon with his fastballs and the big hooking outshoot, Luis was looking as tough as anybody I'd ever seen. Including Matty.

At the end of the tenth I waved for our other hurlers to warm up. Donlin grabbed my arm and shook his head. "He's still strong!" he signed. "We gotta win this damn thing."

I decided he was right. At Luis's age I could pitch all week. What exactly was I saving his arm *for?* Our other young flingers wouldn't be able to handle McGraw's tactics; using them would amount to giving the game away. The kids deserved better. Luis went out for the eleventh.

It looked to me like the Giants were starting to press. What should have been a one-sided exhibition had become a grim, prolonged struggle. They'd gotten no breaks and the kids were playing them like hard-bitten equals. The crowd was on their backs. McGraw was riding them hard. None of which helped at the plate, where their first two batsmen overswung and went down on weak grounders.

Polson stepped in. Despite his swagger he'd shown little the whole time in Havana. He tossed his blond locks and waggled his butt and whipped his bat as he dug into the box. On the first offering he was fooled by a drop, which up to then Luis had used only as a putaway pitch. Polson stared down at his shoes, then showed a cheesy sort of smirk, as if he had something up his sleeve.

On the next pitch he bunted wide of first. Our first baseman, Ordoñez, moved to his right and fielded it. His toss to Luis, racing to the bag, was high. As Luis reached up to take it, Polson lowered his head and shoulder and crashed into his ribs. Luis hit the ground and lay there writhing, the ball clutched in his glove. Rigler made the out call, which Polson didn't question; in fact he looked pretty satisfied as he picked up his glove behind first.

Donlin got to him at the same time I reached Luis. The boy seemed to have nothing worse than the wind knocked out of him. I saw Mike jawing hard at Polson when without warning the big rookie uncorked a punch that caught him on the cheek and sent him down to one knee.

A red haze spread behind my eyes. I tried to hold it off, not wanting the kids' day to end in a brawl. Polson was standing over Donlin, back toward me, yellow hair hanging down below his cap. I reached for it, thinking to pull him away—but was yanked sideways myself before I could do it and, spinning, found myself face to face with Herzog, whose fists were balled.

Finally! my brain exulted. *Let's GO!* Another part responded, *Don't do this to Luis!* I started to raise my hands in a peaceful gesture, then sensed something coming at my face. Later Donlin told me that he yelled at that instant, so maybe I got his warning somehow, who knows? I twisted away in time for Polson's punch to graze my jaw instead of cold-cocking me. Stepping sideways, I set my feet and lashed out with a jab that snapped his head back so smartly that his cap flew off and his blond locks whipped around his face.

I spun back toward Herzog, but he had backed off, his mouth twisted in contempt. "Go ahead," he mouthed distinctly, pointing at Polson, "he's yours."

Polson's eyes showed fear and I felt the fight draining out of me. I'd had enough of him. Not true for Donlin, though, who charged Polson and went right through his guard to land a punch that bloodied his nose. Before Mike could sock him again I wrapped my arms around him.

Fletcher came running and Devlin stepped into his path. Becker and Devore appeared beside Herzog. Then Hooks, bless his heart, never a threat to anybody, aligned himself with Donlin, Devlin and me.

And there we were: the old Giants facing the new.

Suddenly McGraw was between us—"you fucking bushers" was all I caught from his lips—trailed by Wilson and Doyle. No doubt he imagined tomorrow's papers with pictures of his players battling each other. Doyle spoke urgently to Donlin—the captains, past and present—who finally nodded reluctantly.

Rigler wanted to eject Polson, but McGraw pointed out that Hooks was the only bench player he had left and promised that Polson would be on a boat that night. The rookie was finished.

I walked Luis around behind our bench until I was convinced he was okay.

Finally the game resumed.

We managed two base knocks in the bottom of the eleventh. Either Crandall was losing his stuff or we were getting used to his nasty shoots.

But we didn't score.

On to the twelfth.

McGraw had his hitters stepping out after every pitch, rubbing dirt on their hands, dusting themselves off, tapping their spikes—anything to stall and upset Luis. By then Rigler, no doubt mortally sick of McGraw's shenanigans, was giving us a wide strike zone, and Luis took advantage of it, working in and out. He had trouble only with Crandall, who stubbornly fouled off six straight pitches before chopping air on a Dundon that looked damn near as good as one of mine.

Or maybe I just wanted to think so. I realized that I was pitching this game through Luis. Nothing matched being on the mound, of course, but this was starting to come close.

Conte showed up with the stats so far. For Luis: no runs, seven hits, seven walks, twelve strikeouts. We'd made just one error behind him. A great showing for the kids. Forty-nine times out of fifty the Giants would lick us. Maybe this would be the 50th game.

I studied the stocky Crandall as he warmed up: short compact windup, explosive arm whip. He was dropping his shoulder now and not getting his back into the motion, a sign of weariness, and his fastballs, normally heavy and active, had lost some of their movement. McGraw must be seeing it, too. How long would he stay in?

We decided to wait everything out, make him throw more. Our first hitter worked the count to 3–2 before lining out to Doyle. The second walked, again on 3–2. Crandall bounced that pitch in front of the plate. Donlin and I exchanged a look. If we could get our runner to second, a hit would win it.

Izzy, our fastest man, was coming to the plate; they had to be worried he'd bunt. Sure enough, McGraw pulled his corner men in. We signed for a hit and run, but the instant Izzy stepped in, Crandall quick-pitched him. It was an old tactic, one I'd pulled myself on occasion—sometimes even before my fielders were ready—and I was always tickled when I snuck one in for a strike. Last June the American League had outlawed the practice, but that cut no ice down here.

This time it backfired. Izzy looked up as the ball was on him. Crandall had thrown it inside and it cut in further. Izzy twisted away just enough so that it grazed his shoulder, then laid the bat across the plate and started for first. It set off a whole new rhubarb, McGraw claiming that time was still out—as if the quick pitch hadn't been his own idea—and thereby putting himself in the rare position of showing up his own hurler.

Tony Paguey, stepping up to the plate, had line-drive power but was slow afoot. Nico stood on deck. What should we do? Crandall was death on bunts, possessing an uncanny ability to nail runners at third though he was right-handed. We ordered Tony not to swing. Fake the bunt, do whatever—but take every pitch. Better a whiff than a rally-ending double play. The winning run waited on second. We had to get Nico to the plate.

At that point McGraw sent Hooks to the bullpen to get warm. Just what the kids needed, I thought glumly: to face another savvy big-league pitcher for the first time.

On a 1–2 count the ball seemed to nick Tony's hands. Donlin and I leaped up, thinking it would load the bases for Nico, but Rigler cut our delirium by ruling that the ball had struck the bat. Crandall then mustered everything he had to blaze one past Tony, who followed orders and kept his bat on his shoulder. Rigler's right hand shot up. Strikeout.

Two down.

Nico strode to the plate. Despite his earlier vow he'd shown nothing against Crandall, who worked him more cautiously than ever and missed the plate twice. Disgusted, McGraw slammed a bat down on the grass. Crandall got a strike on an off-speed bender, then fired a third ball far outside. That was too much for McGraw. He called for Hooks as Crandall went back to right, Devlin took first and Polson headed for the clubhouse.

"They're gonna walk him!" Donlin exclaimed.

We watched as McGraw strode toward Wilson and motioned for him to extend his mitt wide of the plate. It made sense. Hooks was a southpaw and his chances would be better against our next hitter, Ordoñez, a lefty.

But something about it bothered me. Why was McGraw telegraphing it so broadly, even going so far as to mime a lob outside? I'd seen him order dozens of walks. Never had he stood out there flagging it to the whole world. I had a sudden dark hunch.

"Tell him to swing!" I signed urgently.

"Swing?" Donlin echoed, astonished.

"At anything over the plate! Hurry!"

Donlin's eyes narrowed as he caught my idea. He signaled Rincón, who called to Nico and flashed our hit-away sign.

If it was a fake, McGraw's men play-acted it nice as pie, the infielders looking relaxed as Wilson stood with his right arm out to his side as a target. Hooks moved nonchalantly—*too nonchalantly?*—into his stretch, held it for a second as he checked the runners, then twisted leisurely into his motion. At the plate, Nico looked just as casual.

Get ready! my brain screamed. *He's gonna smoke you!*

By the time Hooks released the ball, Nico was crouched in his coiled-snake stance. The ball burned in, nothing on it but pure surprise, belt-high over the heart of the plate.

Nico met it there with all his strength.

Donlin said later it was the loudest thing he'd ever heard. I'd like to think I felt the shock of it, but that's just wishful. The ball leaped off the bat. We all watched it climb the sky and soar high above the left field fence.

And drop from sight far beyond.

For an instant everything seemed suspended. Then Nico leaped high and broke into a wild dance as he started toward first. Then it was bedlam. People running over the field chased by cops. Beer and rum and wine and Coke and *aguardiente* spraying everywhere. Coins and bills showering down on us. Nico mobbed by the team between second and third. Luis pressing his hand to his heart and extending it to Nico, who took it in both of his, the two youngsters dancing in a circle. Then all the boys piling on them and toppling to the ground, mouths open, faces lit with exultation.

I'm not sure Nico ever made it around the bases. But no umpire in the world, not even O'Day, would have dared make a Merkle call in that situation. Anyway, Nico *did* touch first.

Fletcher stayed at his position, spitting tobacco. Herzog gave third a vicious kick. McGraw stood with hands on hips staring at the boys, maybe reminded of the jubilant Athletics after they'd won the Series. Except that this was wilder. With the fans churning around him he made a show of grinning and lifting his arms as if he'd helped produce this marvel. In fact, he had—but not the way he was letting on. Devlin and Doyle alone had the good grace to come over and congratulate us. None of the others did.

Nico and Luis got hoisted up by the crowd, and Donlin and I soon followed. When they finally put us down and we escaped to our dressing room, Luis came up to me. He clasped his hands over his heart and then over mine. He hugged me hard and I hugged back. It was one of the best feelings, the best times, I'd ever had. Luis's eyes were wet and

I'm pretty sure mine were, too. The boy's heart had opened, and no spoken words could have added to what passed between us.

Donlin appeared suddenly. "He's gone!"

"Who?"

"That sonofabitch Polson!"

"Hell, let him go, Mike," I told him. "He's a back number now. Go get our money before it vanishes too."

Father C. came in, eyes aglow as if tiny candles were lit behind them. He got into our hugging act, then crossed himself and proclaimed it all a miracle. Nobody argued. When I got the chance, I drew him away from Luis.

"Padre, why didn't you tell me about Serros?"

Some of the glow faded from his face. "I meant to," he signed, "until I realized what a grand thing you intended for Luis. I couldn't bring myself to risk spoiling it. I feared that if Señor McGraw found out. . . ." He looked at me with a hint of pleading. "Luis's father is long dead; nobody in the States would have known his color. Believe me, I didn't dream that the *abuelo* would show up today."

So he'd thought he might get away with it. It made sense. And who could blame him?

"At least Nico can play in your country," he signed, "perhaps with your Giants, yes?"

I nodded, thinking it likely that already McGraw was scheming ways to sign Nico. "What about Luis?" I asked. "Will it hurt his spirit to see Nico go on where he can't?"

"Luis is a hero in Havana today," Father C. replied. "Tonight he will be one in Matanzas and soon all over Cuba. Tomorrow's papers will rave about *El Sordito,* the new pitching sensation, and thereafter Luis's circumstances will be vastly different. Would you not have given him that?"

Just then Luis beckoned us to the door, where Elias Serros stood against the background dusk. Up close he cut an even more impressive figure: barrel chest, powerful jaw, piercing black eyes, cordovan skin sagging but muscles corded beneath it.

"My family belongs to you," he said in halting Sign—it was clear he hadn't spent a lot of time talking to Luis—and then he spoke to Father C., who translated: "After your game tomorrow you must come to our *bohio* for a celebration festival."

I acknowledged the invitation with a nod. "Will you be there?" I signed.

A wary look came into his eyes. "Perhaps," he replied. "In any case you must come and help the family honor Luis's becoming a man, now that you are one of us."

How could I refuse? And yet . . . Della expected me for Christmas. If I left Havana a day or two later, I might not get home in time.

"Furthermore," Father C. translated, "you must visit them each time you are in Cuba, for they are forever in your debt."

I doubted I'd be back. Which pretty much cinched it.

"Tell him I'll come."

THE BOYS AND their families and coaches framed their farewells with lavish praise and blessings. For Donlin and me it got pretty embarrassing. One old man informed us through Father C. that they were all going back to their homes in glory.

In glory. . . . I liked that.

At the Plaza later, Donlin and I bought rounds for all Giants who wanted them. It helped soothe ruffled feelings. Herzog and Fletcher accepted our drinks, though they must have been smarting over their lost cash. We wondered if Polson had stiffed them on the bet, but since they didn't bring up the subject, we didn't either.

Doyle said some of the kids reminded him of himself at that age; they'd showed a lot of grit and deserved the victory. Becker and Devore praised their tight outfield work. Hooks told me he hadn't liked the idea of throwing the sneak pitch; he'd even thought about tipping us to it, but was afraid McGraw would catch him.

As for McGraw, he blustered his way through as usual. Nobody but his "old boys" (Mike and me) could have "whipped them green Cuban piss-ant boys into shape." Even so, we'd only won on a trick (as if it hadn't been *his* trick) and the Giants had "let down a mite" since it was only a "circus game."

I nearly choked on that last one.

"You're not a bad coacher, Dummy," he informed me—faint praise, seeing how I'd outmanaged him all afternoon—"but as a scout you're a godawful flop."

I felt like saying I'd scouted good enough to field a squad that skunked him—something Mack's high-priced pros and the two Havana clubs had failed to do.

"Look, I didn't know Luis was any part Negro," I told him. "All I knew was that his grandpa was some kind of outlaw." It pained me to think about that part of the afternoon, and some bitterness seeped through as I signed, "Nico's white enough, right?"

"Probably," McGraw agreed. "But see, we already knew about him."

I got the message. He was saying I wouldn't get a bonus when Nico signed with him.

"Since you used up all my arms today," he signed, "you're pitching tomorrow." The gimlet eyes held a malicious glint. "Give it all you got."

I will, I thought. But inside I had the heavy feeling that even a no-hitter might not be good enough.

———— • ◆ • ————

THE PAPERS TOUTED it as a sign of things to come for Cuban ball. The 12,000–plus attendance had outdone even the turnouts for Detroit in '09, the island's first big-league visitors. The Giants paid admissions were now pushing 70,000—you can bet McGraw counted the kids' exhibition—which eclipsed the Tigers series total of 65,000.

That it wouldn't have happened without our game became obvious when only 2,000 diehards showed up for our finale. This despite the morning papers trumpeting the match-up of *El Sordo*, the all-stars' *Maestro Magnífico*, versus José Méndez, *La Perla Negra*.

In the clubhouse McGraw drummed it home that he didn't intend to leave Havana on a losing note. Donlin overheard him tell the trainer that he needed to get the taste of being whipped by those goddamn punk kids out of his mouth.

It made us feel chesty all over again.

I didn't pitch tip-top, but I pitched lucky. Blues got on base in every frame but only scored twice. Every time I used Dundon I felt things straining in my arm, so I discarded him early. Feeling scary tweaks on my other pitches, too, I tried to pace myself. Lucky for me, a good many of the Blues' knocks went straight to our fielders.

We managed only six hits off Méndez, but one was a homer by Fletcher. Donlin went 0-for-2 with two walks and didn't score, but he made some fine plays in center. Like me, he realized that this was almost certainly his last game for McGraw. Maybe we should have felt sad. We didn't. Our thoughts kept going back to yesterday—when we hadn't played at all.

In the eighth I couldn't pretend any longer. The tweaks were shooting pains. I told McGraw I needed to come out. Instead of praising me for getting by on guts, he said he had wondered how long I'd keep crawling out there.

Thanks, Mr. Little Napoleon.

Hooks came in to get the last six outs, and we won it, 4–2, which meant we'd taken the Cuban series 9–3—or 9–4 if you counted the kids' contest, which of course McGraw did not in this case. Conte came around with our final stats, already calculated through that day. Donlin topped the batting at .343. Among the hurlers, my 2.13 ERA was second only to Mathewson. True, I'd thrown fewer innings than the rest, but still I'd come out better than Hooks or Crandall.

McGraw pocketed the sheet without examining it.

No matter, I consoled myself. The figures would be printed in the sporting weeklies. Baseball people back home would see what I'd done. Maybe I could still hook on with a big-league team.

But I was fooling myself and I knew it. Deep in my bones I sensed that my arm would never again be up to major league form. I'd had a chance to learn that down here, and maybe it was best that McGraw was being hard-assed. Made it easier to wrap things up.

He wasn't quite finished with me. Back at the hotel, damned if he didn't pull one of his trademark turnabouts. He called me up to his room, and when I entered handed me a draft for $250.

"You don't need this, Dummy," he wrote, "considering all the bets you won yesterday, but fair's fair. You helped us down here. And we just signed Santellan, hell of a prospect." His face softened. "Sorry it didn't work out with the deaf boy Avelar. I saw for myself why you were so high on him."

Then he handed me a parcel. Inside was a black uniform. At first I thought I'd damaged Snodgrass's and he wanted some of his money back, but inside the jersey was sewn *Taylor*. It was my 1905 World Series uniform.

"Had it shipped," he wrote. "I'd have brought it from the get-go, except that I didn't know you'd be here till after we'd already packed. Keep it for a souvenir." A tight smile played on his lips. "You earned it."

It was a sendoff, his way of saying our business together was done. As we shook hands I thought about how hard it was to sum up McGraw. And how pleased he'd be to know that I thought it.

———— • ◆ • ————

THE CORRIDORS SWARMED with players and wives and hotel porters moving their luggage. They would steam from Havana tonight, and tomorrow in Key West split into two groups, bound for connections in New Orleans or New York. Much as I wanted to see Luis again, I also wanted to be going home.

Packing his gramophone with care, Donlin seemed to wish just the opposite. With an odd burst of feeling he hugged me, then scrawled in my pad, *"Don't forget about me,"* and signed, *"Your chum, Turkey Mike."* My throat felt tight when I read it.

Why did it seem *everything* was ending?

Instead of going down to the harbor I said my goodbyes in front of the hotel. Blanche McGraw planted a kiss on my cheek. Hooks and Devlin said they'd meet me here next winter, which we all knew wouldn't likely happen. Doyle was cordial as always. Devore pumped my hand. Crandall said politely that he hoped we'd work together again. McGraw clapped me on the back. Donlin gave me another hug.

They boarded their autos and were gone.

In my room I wrote a long letter to Della. I told her about the money I'd made, and said I was planning to buy her a special Christmas present: the latest deluxe-model Easy Washer. After promising to be home for all the yuletides to come, I set out to explain why I might not make it in time for this one. I tried to find words to tell her about Luis, but discovered that I couldn't. How was I to say I'd found a boy who felt like a son?

One we wouldn't have together.

I ended up sitting alone looking out into the night, remembering how Donlin had gone out that window, missing him. Hell, I missed them all. As I packed my things, folding the black uniform with care, it occurred to me that I'd spent a big part of the last 20 years living out of a grip. When I was young, things like that had never mattered. The game was pure fun and I'd have played for nothing, but lately it seemed a lot more like work. I flexed my arm and felt tendrils of pain. It was hard to contemplate but . . . maybe my playing time was about up.

———— • ◆ • ————

THEY STOOD IN a mass on the station dock: Luis, Nico, Izzy, Tony, Rincón, Father C. and what looked like his entire school. As I stepped off the train the deaf kids tugged at me and leaped in excitement. With the players I climbed into a flower-decorated carriage and we rolled through the streets like conquering heroes. In the Plaza a bandstand was draped with banners bearing our names. People surrounded us: we sat beneath a sunshade on the stand and looked down on a lake of faces every hue from creamed coffee to ebony.

Politicians made speeches that bored Father C.'s kids beyond endurance—though they came alive each time Luis and I were called on to stand. Sunlight fell through the trees in dusty shafts. The air was mild and perfumed.

When it was over, Luis, Father C. and I took a *volante* out along the Yumurí River. I marveled at the red earth and the lush green vegetation bursting from it. Gangs of cane-cutters were everywhere, dark faces glistening with sweat, grinning and lifting the wide cutting knives, called *calabozos,* high in salute as we passed by. Like everybody else, they seemed boosted by what we'd done.

I asked Luis about his plans. He signed that he would play baseball. Would he go on in school? He shrugged. What about when he was through with ball? Either I didn't sign it right or he wasn't used to thinking in terms of choices. All he knew was that he'd never work in the fields or mills. Better to stay in the bakery forever.

José Rincón tells me the Havana teams are asking about you," I signed. "Will Father C. negotiate for you?"

He nodded.

"If you take care of yourself, baseball can be a fine life."

He grinned. "Like for you?"

"Like for me."

People thronged the *bohío* and the surrounding clearing. Father C.

explained that the nearby mills employed many in the local *cabildo*. They'd given workers time for this festival even though the sugar harvest was at its peak. What was a *cabildo*, I asked. A society formed by the Church generations ago, he explained, to promote religion among the poor blacks, both slave and free.

"And these still exist?"

He hesitated. "They exist again."

A pig was roasting in a pit and three goats were being stewed in a blend of rum and other delicacies. Natalia and Luna worked at cookstoves with other women, bending over platters of rice and beans and chicken, boiling yucca to serve with a garlic-laced oil called *mojo*. Men were drinking *aguardiente* and beer, laughing and wrestling. Every one of them shook my hand. They smelled of sweat and the cane fields. A ballgame had been in progress—I spotted a crudely carved bat and lopsided ball—but now the feast was nearly ready, and everyone looked hungry.

Flanked by Luis and Father C., I was seated at the head of a long bench and served choice portions. We ate and drank as the sun lowered and dusk came on. The women brought courses of fish and chicken and pork and goat. Except for the toasts to Luis, I tried to hold back on the *aguardiente* flowing so freely.

"Will Señor Serros be here?" I asked.

"Too dangerous," Father C. replied. "He risked a great deal by going to Havana."

"He really is a bandit?"

"He is more than that. Elias Serros spent years earning enough to buy his freedom from slavery. With that same determination he managed to educate himself. Nobody here has his stature or power. He leads the forces of black men who talk of taking their rights by force if there is no other way." The Padre spread his hands. "So to the government, yes, he is an outlaw."

"How does Luis feel about him?"

"Respects him—practically worships him. But there are too many times, like today, when he is absent." The priest touched my shoulder. "To tell the truth, right now I think he is closer to you. You have been like a father to him."

There it was again.

When we finished eating, he took me into the *bohio* and sat me before an altar on which rested some of the things from Natalia's healing ceremony: bowls filled with shells and dried plants; black dolls in human shape. The candles were lighted, the air heavy with fumes of burning herbs. The largest statue was of a woman draped in a fiery red mantle. Father C. signed that she was Saint Barbara, whose father had been struck by lightning before he could slay her for being a Christian. Among other things she was the patroness of those who made and used fireworks; her festival, a spectacular event, had taken place only a few weeks ago, early in December.

"An odd thing was prophesied then," he signed, "namely, that a David would arrive—as in the story of Goliath—and be silent in his triumph."

"Who made that prophecy?" I asked, reminded again of the shoeshine man who'd said I would have a son.

"A local *santero* or *babalao* . . . I don't know which one . . . It might even have been Natalia."

"And you think it was about Luis?"

"Possibly," he signed. "Or you."

It gave me the willies to think much about it.

"In honor of our victory," he signed as he started to rearrange the altar, "I'm going to say a Mass for the Dead, including those from the *reconcentrado* time—among them Luis's father."

A damn queer way to celebrate, I thought.

People crowded into the *bohio* until there was scarcely room to breathe. A door behind the altar swung open, and three men sat there behind large drums. Father C. began the Mass, none of which I could follow. Given the close-packed bodies and flickering candles and thick aroma of the herbs, I had to fight off drowsiness. I gazed into the bejeweled eyes of St. Barbara and imagined that the statue was staring back at me. *What was she thinking?* When Father C. finally came to the naming of the dead, I saw people's lips moving—but they didn't seem to match the priest's. Afterward, he told me they were saying the names of their own departed ones. That way all vexing spirits would float away and leave them in peace.

"I'm afraid I must float away too," he signed, smiling. "The next part is not for me."

"Why not?"

He motioned toward St. Barbara, then wrote *"en santo"* on my pad. I looked at him questioningly but he did not explain. Signing that he would see me off in the morning, he stepped out into the darkness.

Natalia entered, smoking her customary cigar. Luna and another girl placed bowls of okra, corn meal and oranges before the altar. A wooden basin spilled over with strands of red and white beads. People tied the strands around their necks and prostrated themselves before the altar. I felt the drums beginning to throb, the pulsations growing in intensity and interweaving with the smoke curling from herbs and candles and cigars.

Some of the women began to move rhythmically: a sort of shuffling, jerking dance, not in pairs, their bare feet thumping the packed earth. They wore varying shades of red trimmed with white lace, their hair bound with crimson scarves, bracelets on their wrists matching their necklaces. Red and white. Dressed up for Saint Barbara. Unlike the rest, Natalia and Luna wore beads of yellow and white. What did that signify?

Somebody put a bottle into my hand. I was parched and it seemed rude to refuse. A river of fire ran down my throat and teared my eyes. When vision and breath returned, I saw that things were picking up fast. Now men were dancing too, some of them with almost dainty steps, and the dancers' eyes were looking a bit glazed and unfocused. A powerfully-built *machetero* stripped off his shirt and began leaping high and landing with pulverizing stomps, his head bending nearly to his knees and thrusting up again. Once I'd gone to a revival with Della, and when some of those folks starting speaking in tongues they'd looked a bit like this fellow. I hadn't heard the "tongues," of course, but the writhing and drooling and rolling eyes had been plenty for me. I'd cleared out in a hurry. Now I wanted to do the same. But whatever I'd drunk seemed to have stolen my willpower and rusted my joints.

One of the women—Natalia, maybe, but with all the smoke it was hard to tell—thrust a pair of cutting blades into the man's hands. I noticed that the handles were painted red. As he swung them the *machetero* seemed to grow taller, his torso swelling. His eyes were dilated and his teeth bared in what looked like a gathering rage. Yet all the while he was talking to the others, darting from one to another in an almost teasing way, and they seemed to be bantering back. I tensed as he spun the knives faster, a deadly whirl of steel. People backed off but didn't look particularly worried.

After a minute or two the big man began to tremble. A woman squatting beside me tapped my arm and confided, her lips moving so slowly that I could not mistake it, *"Changó está aquí!"* As she spoke she lifted herself slightly off her haunches, as did those around her.

Puzzled, I looked around for this Changó fellow. The woman shook her head and pointed to the big dancer. *He* was Changó. Sweat spun off him as he whirled and beat the air. I don't know how long it went on, but I began to grow dizzy, my mouth dry as wool and my stomach uneasy. I was trying to will myself to climb to my feet and head for the door when the *machetero* abruptly broke off his dance and strode straight for me. I tensed until I saw that his face wore a sort of dreamy smile. He placed the blades on the earthen floor. Cradling my head tenderly in his huge hands, he kissed the spot where the bandage had been. I hadn't been aware of any sensation there for days, but now I felt a throbbing. He rubbed my face with his fingers.

I should have been mortified, I guess, but I don't recall it if I was. Nor do I remember leaving the *bohio,* but the two of us were suddenly outside beneath a blazing canopy of stars that seemed to blur and spin. I felt drunker than ever in my life. The fingers on my temples sent a warm current through my brain, at once comforting and frightening. I tried to shake free, or maybe just *thought* of it, and found that I couldn't. Staring into the glittering eyes so near my own, I realized that the man's face was not in the least threatening. It was serene and even joyful. He threw his head back and opened his mouth wide.

And I heard laughter.

Heard it!

Nothing I'd experienced could compare to it. Which might not be saying a lot, since I'd never heard *anything.* So *this* is sound, I thought, and had my first inkling of what words like "deep" and "rumbling" might mean. Even while it was happening, I told myself that it must be my imagination. And yet I'd never imagined anything like *that.* Whatever caused it did not originate inside me. If it wasn't sound, it was as close as I'm ever likely to come.

Something else happened too. As the laughter faded, the man's heavy African features softened and changed and became those of Elias Serros. He smiled as if we shared a joke. *We two are players,* the wise eyes seemed to be saying, *no matter how serious the game.*

I tried to match his smile, to show I understood.

But by then the *machetero's* face was back.

His hands released me. My temples felt cold where they had been. Now people were moving all around us, their bodies bending and twisting. The big man took sweets from a plate offered to him by a shapely *mulatta*. His arm circled her waist and pulled her against him. The drums beat faster. People were moving wildly, brushing against me. Disconcerted, my legs unsteady, I became aware of a throbbing in my groin and discovered a perplexing new reality: my pecker was stiff, a condition my thin cotton pants failed to hide.

I bolted through the dancers and didn't stop until I reached the darkness of a clump of palms—the same trees where Natalia had buried the egg. I grabbed the trunk of one and held on while the planet teetered and spun. The sweltering air was charged with electricity. Everything went white and I felt a sickening, heartstopping impact as a bolt struck nearby. It smelled like the air itself was on fire. When I could see again, a dense black cloud was blotting out the stars. Where had it come from? Rain spattered down, cool and soothing, first a shower, then a torrent pouring through the trees. I felt a heavy-headedness, a comfortable drowsiness, stealing over me.

———— • ◆ • ————

THE SKY WAS DIFFERENT. The stars had come back. I lay on my back in the wet leaves. Something was touching me. My head jerked up and I saw a dark figure silhouetted over me. In the dim starlight I thought I recognized Natalia. I started to rise but she pushed on my chest and raised a finger to her lips. Did she think I could talk?

I wondered if I was dreaming. Things certainly *seemed* dreamlike as I watched her untie the red shawl draped over her shoulders. In the darkness it was the color of old blood. As it fell to the ground I saw that she wore nothing beneath. The flesh there was paler and smoother.

Rain matted her hair and flowed down over her shoulders and through the shadowy slope between her breasts, droplets ornamenting the dark nipples. My groin was beginning to throb almost painfully. Her skirt fell away and she lowered herself on to me, back arching and hips rocking. There was nothing gentle about what she was doing. I tried to slow her. She scowled down at me, her mouth forming words. I heard nothing, but her eyes and body told me she wanted—demanded—my seed. I felt an internal tide rising, growing burstingly close. Then Natalia's face was Luna's, her smooth, unlined face a match for the supple body working atop mine.

A girl the age my daughter might be.

I recoiled and tried to yank away. Instantly Natalia returned and reached to claw at my chest, hips thrusting fiercely with quick, urgent strokes, the points of her buttocks grinding my hip joints, the warm wetness of her enveloping me. And then the stars all seemed to rush together and I felt myself slip over the edge of somewhere I'd never been.

———————•◆•———————

SUNLIGHT SLANTING DOWN through the trees burned my face. I sat up and brushed at bugs circling my nose. My brain was fogged. In the brightness of day, the night's events seemed remote and unlikely. I'd gotten mortally drunk and had crazy visions, I told myself. But when I clambered to my feet I found that my pants weren't buttoned; the pubic hair was damp in places and there were streaks of dried semen. Christ, what had I done?

It took all of my willpower to walk into the *bohio*. Natalia looked up as casually as if my being there was normal. She sat me down and handed me a small cup of black Cuban coffee. One swallow and the fogs in my head started to roll back. Luna appeared and served papayas. I couldn't look at her. Both of them acted as if nothing unusual had happened.

Maybe nothing did, I tried to tell myself.

"Where is Luis?" I asked.

"At work," Natalia signed. "He left with Father C. after the Mass."

Did I see a spark of humor? I started to raise my hands to ask . . . what, exactly? If she'd given herself and her daughter to me?

It was too ludicrous, too embarrassing.

I was in the middle of thanking her for her hospitality when she said something to Luna, who went off for a stub pencil. Natalia dictated and the girl printed laboriously in Spanish on a scrap of paper. She handed it to me.

"What does it say?"

Natalia shook her head and gave the paper a dismissive wave. It would speak for itself. I tucked it in my pocket and signed, "I must go."

"Yes."

We stood and faced each other uncertainly. She reached out and shook my hand gravely, man-like. Again I thought I caught a glint of humor. I risked the barest of smiles and she returned it. For an instant I saw Luis and Luna in her face, and knew for certain how beautiful she had once been. I started to sign something, but she pointed down the hillside, where I saw a mule-rigged cart and a *guajiro* squatting beside it in the rutted road, waiting for me.

———— • ◆ • ————

"IT IS CALLED A *TAMBOR,*" Father C. signed as we waited for Luis in the rectory. "A ceremony to thank the spirits—they are known as *orishas*—for favors."

"And in this case you think I was the favor?" I'd told him of the blade-wielding *machetero,* the Changó business, and the storm. I wasn't about to relate what happened with Natalia.

"Yes, definitely."

"Why did you leave early?"

"I cannot condone *Santería* with my presence. You see, the African slaves learned our teachings by adapting the saints to their old gods. At midnight during festivals they often change from one to the other. La Caridad, for example, becomes Ochún, a peaceful, loving god. It is Ochún whom Natalia serves. Santa Barbara, whose feast was this month, becomes Changó, the warrior god of fire and thunder. You see? Each god has its corresponding saint, with its particular emblems and colors and—"

"For Changó red?" I interrupted.

"Yes, red for fire and for wrath—which must be rightfully directed or it will consume a soul."

"And Ochún?"

"Yellow and white. Ochún is a soothing presence whose medium is water—the opposite of Changó, you see? Cooling and healing. Quenching the fire."

I remembered the rage in the dancing man's face and the rumbling laughter as he seemed to become Elias Serros.

And Natalia in the rain. Quenching the fire.

I handed him her note.

"Your seed will attract other sons," he translated.

I asked him to repeat it; then, "Attract? Not produce?"

He nodded slowly. "A curious way to put it."

Remembering the shoeshiner's prophecy, I tried to make some sense of it. *Other* sons?

"I suppose she is saying that you will repeat your experience with Luis, that this won't be the last time for you."

Your seed will attract other sons.

I felt movement behind me and turned to see Luis. His face was lit by a sly smile. I couldn't help but notice how much more confidently he walked. One hand was hidden behind his back. He brought it around to reveal a carved human figure. It had the size and dark hue of the dolls on Natalia's altar, and at first I assumed that it was a saint. Then I saw that it was a baseball player, carved from mahogany. A pitcher. Finally I realized that it was me. The grinning face even had a scarred lip and flattened nose. He'd caught my peculiar motion, too, leg lifted high and arm drawn back like pulling a bow string, ready to come over the top.

"Luis began working on it," Father C. signed, "when he first saw you in Havana."

"You mean, before . . . ?"

He nodded. "Now you know why I came for you."

The angles and proportions made the figure appear to have been frozen in motion. The sculpting was rough, but somehow that made it more lifelike. The boy had so much talent. With training he might make an artist. Could I take Luis home with me? I tried without much success to picture him in Baldwin.

He waited anxiously for me to react. I put the figure to my heart and told him it would stay with me forever. He swallowed hard. I put my arms around him, and we stood holding each other.

"Can you stay longer?" Father C. asked.

I shook my head.

———— • ◆ • ————

AS THE TRAIN slowly picked up speed I leaned out the window. Father C. lifted his hand. Luis stood motionless beside him. Then he thrust his right arm high, a triumphant gesture. In his hand was a baseball signed by the all-star team and coaches. I had one like it in my valise. Mirroring his gesture, I raised the wooden statue. The distance between us widened. We held out the tokens to each other as if they would continue to link us.

The train curved around a bend.

EPILOGUE

Olathe, Kansas
April 1958

He lifted the figure from the table while wheeling himself to the speaker's lectern, where he managed to pull himself upright and to stand unsteadily behind the microphone. Not that he had any use for it, but the politician had held forth there and he didn't feel like being outshone at his own event. A pinched feeling in his chest told him that the effort had come at a cost. Another reminder that his time was short. Well, he'd always put on a show; no reason to stop. His thumb stroked the dark wood as he looked out at the expectant faces.

He prided himself on looking clearly at things, not making up lies about some golden past. Unlike some old-timers he could name, he wasn't given to complaining that the game had gone to hell in modern days. Baseball had changed, that was all, like everything else. Why shouldn't it? He'd intended to sign his thanks and let it go at that. But as he gripped the figure, aware of the boy shadowed at the side of the room, he felt reluctant to have this moment end. He'd loved it all so much. The play. The work. All the sons he'd known. Luis had been the first of hundreds he'd coached over the long decades. Once even made it to the majors. So many sons. He'd given his best to all of them, even the ones who'd reminded him of Herzog or Polson. He'd especially prized the ones with touches of Donlin or Hooks. But of them all, it was Luis his mind kept calling up.

So little was left from back then. . . .

He glanced down the table and his eyes met those of his wife, who smiled encouragingly. A wonderful woman. His third spouse, deaf like the others, childless like the others. He'd almost expected to see Della sitting there.

When she died, back in 1931, only in her forties, he'd been devastated. His grief led him to remarry before very long, to a woman too old to bear children, and by then he'd stopped thinking about it. His playing days behind him, he was content teaching and coaching at the Illinois Deaf School. Years later, when that wife took ill and passed on, his loneliness wasn't so great as before. But he was pleased that he'd met the woman who was now his wife. She was companionable, took care of him, understood that there had been just one Della. Together with Sim, she would make sure he was buried beside Della in their Baldwin plot, not far from the giant oak where he'd carved their initials almost 70 years ago.

Della. . . .

When he finally got home in that winter of '11, their marriage nearly ended right then. The extra cash and the Easy Washer didn't begin to mollify her hurt spirits, nor did the newfangled overhead shower he and Sim put in. Nor the fancy cream separator he'd rush-ordered from Sears in Topeka to surprise her with on New Year's Day. Sleeping on the davenport for what seemed weeks, he'd tried to explain what the Cuba trip had done for him: offered hope where there had been none. Della weighed it all, but he suspected she took it as some new criticism of her, namely, that he had to go looking for sons because she hadn't provided them.

Things were barely patched up between them by the time he left again for spring training. It wasn't until later, when he began teaching, that she came to understand the change he'd undergone. Long before then, they'd bought the land she wanted, and Della poured all her energy into it. The crops she put in soon brought a cash return, and thereafter she took delight in hiring deaf farmhands to help her work it.

Playing ball, he'd hung on in the Eastern League, getting by mostly on savvy before throwing his arm out for good in '13. Still, he had enough left to star for a topnotch semipro team out of Akron for awhile. But teaching and coaching deaf kids increasingly took over from his playing, until finally it was down to an occasional old-timers game.

For years he'd tried to keep in touch with his old Giants teammates. But Donlin and McGraw passed away a quarter-century ago, and Matty, a gas victim in the Great War, even before that. After Mabel Hite died in '12 of intestinal cancer, Donlin had quit ball for good and gone to Hollywood. He used to see Mike in movies occasionally, usually playing the part of a ballplayer; nothing on the screen rivaled his real-life antics. Gradually he'd lost contact with Hooks and the others.

He wasn't sure how many were left.

With Father C.'s help, Luis had sent several notes in the months following his visit, telling of how he and Nico led the Matanzas nine to the tournament championship. Father C. added that it was a sure thing Luis would be picked up by one of the Havana teams.

It seemed not to have happened.

Early in 1912 the end of the sugar harvest brought what came to be known as the "Black Uprising." Starting with demonstrations for equal rights of black Cubans, it quickly built to strikes, and turned violent when the Cuban army, aided by U.S. Marines, was sent to crush the movement. By the time the shooting ended, thousands were dead and the movement's leaders captured and executed. Elias Serros had been among them.

Word of it didn't arrive until months afterward, when Father C. finally wrote. Not only had the Avelars lost their abuelo but their property as well. The priest didn't say where Natalia and Luna had gone, only that Luis was taking it very hard and thinking of leaving Matanzas. There was no mention of baseball. Typhoid fever had been ravaging the parish, and Father C. himself was sick.

He'd wired money several times.

No more letters came.

When the Giants journeyed to Havana in following winters, he wrote Mathewson to ask if he would check with Pepe Conte about Luis's whereabouts. Conte sent his regards to Señor Taylor but said that Luis had disappeared some time ago and he had no information. In Matanzas later for an exhibition game, Matty made some inquiries on his own; he found no leads and had nothing to report, except that a new priest resided at Father C.'s parish. Luis's victory over the Giants had grown into a legendary feat by then, and Matty said he was sorry he'd missed seeing the boy pitch that day. Those who did, McGraw included, agreed that it had been possible only because of his, Dummy's, coaching.

Flattering, he thought, but only half true at best. Luis's arm was the best he'd seen in a lifetime of watching ballplayers. He prayed that somehow, in spite of the century's ravages, Luis had survived and married and raised children of his own. Wherever the Avelars might be now, he hoped that they were safe in the new struggle, that they and the other guajiros would not have to suffer again.

With the bent, arthritic fingers of his pitching hand he stroked the familiar contours of the little wooden hurler. Natalia had said that he would attract many sons. He looked out at all the faces, and then, his hands finally speaking with signs from his heart, he tried to tell them how happy he felt and how lucky he'd been to spend his life with people like them. When he finished, they stood up for him, their hands fluttering in applause.

He held the statue aloft like a championship trophy, which in a way it was. The chill of the place was still upon him, but in a portion of his mind the tropical sun was suspended in full glory over a Caribbean ballfield, where frenzied rooters opened their mouths in silent roars while his Cuban boys stood with arms raised in salute. Luis's fingers spoke to him and he answered back, their combined excitations so powerful it seemed that they must reach across the years and even to heaven.